The SWEETEST Oblivion

THE MADE SERIES

DANIELLE LORI

For AJ
My only inspiration for falling in love.

Playlist

World Gone Mad—Bastille

Rocket Man—Elton John

Human—Aquilo

Waterfalls—Eurielle

Her Life—Two Feet

Like I'm Gonna Lose You—Jasmine Thompson

Madness—Ruelle

Fireworks—First Aid Kit

Seven Nation Army—The White Stripes

Dirty Diana—Shaman's Harvest

Holocene—Bon Iver

Hurt For Me—SYML

Soldier—Fleurie

CHAPTER
One

"There's no such thing as good money or bad money.
There's just money."
—Lucky Luciano

Long Island, New York
Elena

MY HOME WAS PICTURESQUE. A RED FRONT DOOR WITH A GOLDEN KNOCKER. Black and white checkered flooring. A wooden staircase with a lacquer shine and a sparkling chandelier. However, I'd always wondered, If I pulled back a corner of the wallpaper . . . would it bleed red? If this world was as transparent as glass, soft *splats* would drip a pool to the marble floors.

I stared at the TV in the corner of the kitchen, hardly processing the newscaster's voice, but when *murder* passed her ruby red lips, the word resounded in my mind. My throat tightened as I twisted the ring on my middle finger.

While my home, my *life*, was built on piles of dirty money, I'd always been able to say I hadn't contributed to the balance. Not until earlier this year, that is. Now, blood was on my hands and guilt watched me while I slept.

Voices from the foyer drifted to my ears every time the swinging door opened as our servants came in and out, preparing for lunch.

A feminine trill of a laugh, my cousin Benito's lively timbre, and a voice I'd vaguely recognized as I left the church this morning. It was low, smooth, and indifferent. The hair on the back of my neck rose. I knew it belonged to my future brother-in-law.

And it was partly—*wholly*—the reason I was hiding in the kitchen, though I would never admit it.

"You are too beautiful for that frown, Sweet Abelli," my mamma said, as she entered the room with the cacophony of our guests' conversations following her.

I shifted under the weight of her words. For obvious reasons, I hadn't heard that nickname in a while. I'd grown out of the name some, especially when I realized I was the girl adored for all the wrong reasons: I wasn't hard to look at, I was quiet when I should be and polite when I wasn't. Like a childhood dress that didn't fit anymore, I was stuck in the world's expectations for me. It took years of feeling like a pretty bird in a cage until it all became too much . . . and I escaped.

"I don't know why you watch this, Elena," Mamma said, stirring the sauce on the stove. "All that nonsense is depressing."

Mamma was married to Salvatore Abelli—a high-profile boss of one of the biggest organized crime syndicates in the United States. Sometimes I wondered if the naivety was denial, or if she would truly rather watch *Days of Our Lives* than worry about my papà's affairs.

"I'm not sure who to vote for in the election," I answered absently.

She shook her head in disbelief, and I guessed it *was* odd for the daughter of a mob boss to care about the legalities of the government.

"Your papà isn't happy with you," she said, looking at me under her dark eyelashes with that pursed-lips-you're-in-trouble expression.

"When *isn't* Papà unhappy with me lately?"

"What do you expect after what you did?"

Six months had passed, and I swore she brought it up every day. She was like a dog with a bone, and I honestly thought she enjoyed the mistake I'd made because she finally had something to chastise me about.

"Why didn't you come meet the Russo after church today?" She pointed her spoon at me. "I'm not buying the act that you forgot and were waiting innocently in the car."

I crossed my arms. "I just didn't want to. He's . . . rude."

"*Elena*," she scolded. "You don't even know him."

"You don't need to meet someone with his reputation to know his character, Mamma."

"*Oh, Madonna, salvami,*" she muttered.

"And he won't understand Adriana," I added tersely.

She snorted. "Not many will understand your sister, *figlia mia.*"

The gardener did . . . but I wasn't going to share that with Mamma, or by the end of the day he'd be at the bottom of the Hudson.

Earlier this week, Papà had announced that Adriana would be marrying Nicolas Russo, the don of one of the five families in New York. My past transgressions were still tender wounds, but with this news added to the list it was like they'd been cut back open.

I was the eldest sister; therefore, it was my responsibility to marry first. But because of my mistake, my sister had been thrown under the bus—and to a man with a reputation. Everyone knew that when someone had a reputation in this world it meant one thing: stay the hell away from them.

"Besides, Nico is a perfect gentleman. If you would've met him this morning after church like you were supposed to, you would know that."

I'd strode right out of the church doors and to the car before I could be corralled to meet my future brother-in-law. I was practically a pariah to my papà, so I was surprised he'd even noticed my absence. Besides, I was sure Nicolas Russo's gentleman act was nothing but smoke and mirrors.

Since Nicolas's papà had died five years ago, the twenty-nine-year-old and youngest sitting don had become well-known in the underworld. Following his father's footsteps, he was a cheat, had more blood on his hands than the entirety of the New York State Penitentiary, and was unremorseful about it all. At least I imagined he was unapologetic. The newscaster wouldn't have reported a new victim with the name "Zanetti" every morning for a year—the family Nicolas had once feuded with for killing his papà—if he felt at all guilty. He was going straight to Hell with that attitude if you asked me.

"I did meet him, Mamma."

She raised a brow. "You did?"

"Well, no."

Her expression darkened.

"But I shared a look with him," I insisted. "And that was all I need-ed to see to know he wouldn't be good for Adriana."

She rolled her eyes. *"Ridicolo."*

A glare and a look were the same things . . . right? It was an ac-cident, really. It was as I was walking down the church steps that my gaze caught on the meeting I was supposed to be attending. Papà and Mamma stood on either side of Adriana and across from Nicolas Russo—and that was usually how a bride and groom met in this life. Arranged marriages were par for the course in the *Cosa Nostra.*

In annoyance at the entire situation, my eyes had narrowed slight-ly before glancing at my future brother-in-law, only to find he was al-ready looking at me. That was how the glaring occurred—an accident, you see. But I could hardly convey that to the man, and if I had smiled it would've come off condescending, so I just . . . went with the glare and hoped it wouldn't get me killed.

Nicolas's gaze had hardened a flicker to show he didn't like it, but after a second of heavy eye contact, he returned his attention to my papà like I was nothing but a leaf blowing by. I'd let out the breath I was holding and went to hide in the car. There was no way I was meet-ing him after that exchange. I'd just avoid him until the end of my days.

"Stop worrying and trust your papà."

I made a *hmm* noise because I'd overheard from my cousin Benito that the alliance was for collaboration on some weapons deal, nothing more. My sister was a pawn in some large-scale trafficking agreement. How romantic. Even so, we knew this day would come. I held no ex-pectations for a marriage of love, and neither did Adriana.

The problem was, my sister believed she was already in love.

With the *gardener.*

"Elena, go see if Adriana is ready for lunch."

"She told me last night she wasn't coming."

"She's coming!" Mamma snapped, followed by muttering in Italian.

With reluctance, I pushed off the counter and headed out of the kitchen. The newscaster's voice trailed me out the swinging door, and, like a warning, that word *murder* spilled from red lips once more.

On an Evening in Roma played from the antique record player as I headed toward the staircase and took in the guests in the foyer. My papà's sister and husband, a few male cousins, and my brother Tony, who was shooting an intense glare in Nicolas's direction. Tony leaned against the wall with his hands in his black suit pockets, alone. His girl-friend wasn't Italian and was rarely invited over. My mamma disliked her just because she was dating her son.

I loved my brother, but he was reckless, impulsive, and lived by the code, "If I don't like it then I'll fucking shoot it." And it looked like he wanted to shoot Nicolas Russo. There was some history between the two, and it wasn't the good kind.

My gaze caught on a striking woman with . . . interesting style. She stood next to a man who I assumed to be her grandfather, but then he slid a hand onto her ass. She only pursed her lips like it was an annoyance.

She wore a mink shawl in *July*, over a thin olive-green dress, and thigh-high boots. Long dark hair fell in smooth waves, and with her fake eyelashes and large hoop earrings she was like an ad to the seventies era. And, as if she wasn't doing her job well enough, she blew a pink bubble and popped it, her eyes narrowing on me like I was the one whose style was four decades too late. If polar opposites were ever in the same room, it was her and me, undoubtedly.

Almost home free with one hand on the banister, my father's voice sounded behind me. "Elena, come here."

My stomach dipped and I closed my eyes in defeat, but I only hesitated for a second because that voice was non-negotiable.

My hands grew clammy as I made my way to where my papà stood next to Nicolas. When I reached my father's side, he took my arm and gave me a smile, but it didn't reach his eyes. Papà looked ten years younger than his fifty-five, with small streaks of silver through his black hair. He was always in a suit, and you'd never find a wrinkle in it, but that gentleman look was just a façade. I'd first seen how he'd gotten his reputation when I was seven, through a crack in his office door.

"Elena, this is Nicolas Russo. Nico, this is Elena, my eldest daughter."

I'd done this dance a hundred times, just a different day, a different man. However, this time my breath was cut short, as though I was about to be pushed off a plank and into shark-infested water if I looked up at him. *He's just a man*, I reminded myself. A man with the worst reputation in New York State, easily.

Why did I glare?

Inhaling for courage, I tipped my head, not being able to see him under the brim of my hat. A warm rush of recognition ran down my spine as I met his heavy gaze. Light brown eyes, the color of whiskey on ice, and thick, dark lashes. It gave him a brooding expression, almost as if he was looking into the sun, yet he was looking at me as though he was being introduced to one of the servants and not someone he would call "sister-in-law."

I stood a few inches taller than Adriana, and even in my heels the top of my head wouldn't hit his chin. I had the strong urge to avert my gaze and focus it eye-level on his black tie, but it felt like he'd be winning something if I looked away, so I held his stare. My tone was as polite as it always was in company. "It's a pleasure—"

"We've already met."

We what?

His indifferent voice ran down my spine, with a strange thrill following in its wake. He'd hardly said anything, but it now felt like I was standing on Russo turf instead of Abelli. As if a six-foot diameter around him was claimed as Russo no matter where he stood.

Papà frowned. "When did you two have the chance to meet?"

I swallowed.

Something amused and dangerous played in Nicolas's gaze. "Earlier at church. Remember, *Elena?*"

My heartbeats collided with a crash. Why had my name rolled off his tongue like he was more than familiar with it?

My papà stiffened beside me, and I knew why he did: he thought I'd done something inappropriate with this man, like his tone had suggested. Heat rushed to my cheeks. All because of one mistake I'd made six months ago, my papà thought I'd come on to my sister's fiancé?

I blinked through my apprehension. This was due to a really short, not even that hostile glare? This man had found out my weakness and was now playing with me.

Frustration clawed at my chest. I couldn't very well go and make this situation worse by disagreeing with a don my father would most likely believe over me now. And so, I forced my voice into the lightest tone I could muster. "Yes, we've met, Papà. I forgot my jacket in the church and ran into him inside."

I realized my mistake too late. It was July; I hadn't worn a jacket. And Nicolas knew that.

He pulled a hand out of his pocket and ran a thumb across his bottom lip, giving his head a small shake. He looked impressed I had played along but almost disappointed at what a poor job I'd done.

I did not like this man—not at all.

A cold whisper ran through my blood as my father looked between us like he was unsure.

"Well, all right," Papà finally responded, patting my arm. "That's good, then. I'm sure Nico might have some questions for you about Adriana. You know her best."

My lungs expanded, and I took in a breath. "Yes, of course, Papà."

I would rather eat a handful of dirt.

The front door opened and my mamma's brother and Papà's consigliere, Marco, entered with his wife. My father said a parting word and went to greet them, and just left me with this man, whose presence was beginning to burn.

He stared down at me.

I stared up at him.

As a corner of his lips lifted, I realized I was amusing him. My cheeks heated with annoyance. Before, I would have murmured something sweet and made my leave, but that was *before*. Now, I couldn't keep my expression polite as I met Nicolas's—Nico's, whatever his name was—gaze.

"We have *not* met," I said firmly.

He cocked a brow in a cavalier way. "You sure? Here I was under the impression you had me all figured out."

My heart fluttered so fast it couldn't be healthy. I had no idea what to say because he was right. This interaction wasn't doing anything to prove he wasn't who I thought he was all along, however.

He smoothed an absent hand down his tie. "Do you know what assuming gets you?"

"Killed?" I breathed.

His eyes fell to my lips. "Smart girl." The words were deep and soft, and a strange part of me felt like I'd done something good.

My breaths turned shallow when he moved to walk past me but stopped by my side. His arm touched mine and it burned like the lightest licks of a flame. His voice brushed the side of my neck. "It's nice to meet you, Elena." He said my name like he should have earlier: without any insinuation. Like I was something he could check off his list before he walked away.

I stood there, staring ahead, while absently returning a couple smiles to family members.

So that was my future brother-in-law. The man my sister would marry.

Maybe I was a horrible person, but some guilt drifted away and out the door another person just entered.

Because I was suddenly glad it was her and not me.

CHAPTER
Two

"Nothing personal, it's just business."
—Otto Berman

Elena

IT WAS WORSE THAN I'D EXPECTED.

Adriana was primly folding a blouse and placing it into a suitcase on her bed. She wore an oversized Tweety Bird t-shirt and Christmas socks, and wads of toilet paper lay scattered about the room.

A few years ago, Adriana went through a rebellious stage and chopped her hair off into a pixie cut. I'd never seen my mother more horrified. Adriana had lost her credit card, her acting classes at our all-girls school, and got glowered at every day for a month. It'd grown into a sleek bob now, but it was then I'd learned that cutting your hair in this house was worse than murder.

With dark blue walls, white crown molding and golden accents, Adriana's room would appear fit for a home staging . . . if it didn't look like a costume designer had thrown up in it. Posters from famous plays like *The Great Gatsby* hung on the walls. Weird stage props sat on the vanity: feathers, hats, and masquerade masks. Things that made your head hurt while trying to figure out their purpose—like the giant rabbit's head on the bed.

I didn't believe Papà knew he was paying for every penny of

Adriana's dramatic art school's stage props. But my father didn't concern himself with my sister too much. As long as she was where she was supposed to be, he was happy. He just didn't understand her, nor she him.

With a sigh, I grabbed the blouse from her suitcase and went to the walk-in closet to hang it back up. She ignored my presence, brushing shoulders with me as she passed with a pair of jeans.

"What's with all of the toilet paper?" I asked, sliding the shirt onto a hanger.

She sniffled but didn't respond.

The last time I'd seen her cry was at our nonno's funeral when she was thirteen. My little sister was one of the most unemotional people I'd ever met. In fact, I thought the idea of emotion repelled her. My stomach twisted with concern, but I knew Adriana appreciated pity as much as she loved chick flicks. She hated them.

I grabbed the jeans from the suitcase and headed to the closet. "So, where are you going?"

She passed me with a yellow polka-dot bikini. "Cuba. Saudi Arabia. North Korea. Pick one."

We continued this dance of packing and unpacking like a human conveyor belt.

My brows knitted. "Well, you didn't exactly give me a good list. But Saudi Arabia is out if you're planning on wearing this bathing suit." I folded it and put it away.

"Have you met him?" she asked, walking past me with a zebra-printed robe.

I knew she meant her future husband.

I hesitated. "Yes. He's, uh . . . real nice."

"Where am I going to fit all my props?" She threw her hands on her hips and stared into her small suitcase like she'd just realized it wasn't a Mary Poppins bag.

"I think they're going to have to stay here."

Her face scrunched up like she was about to cry. "But I love my costumes." Tears were running now. "And what about Mr. Rabbit?" She grabbed the giant rabbit's head off the bed and held it next to her own.

"Well . . . I'm not sure about North Korea's shipping policies, but I'm betting Mr. Rabbit won't pass."

She threw herself on the bed and whined, "What about Cuba?"

"It's probably a better possibility."

She nodded like that was good. "I have an *Alice in Wonderland* production coming up." She wiped her cheeks, already finished crying.

"Who are you playing?" I knew it wasn't Alice. My sister didn't like anything mainstream or blonde.

"The Cheshire Cat." She smiled.

"Yeah, that sounds like you." I went into the closet and found a thin-strapped black dress she could wear to lunch. It took a moment to find it because it was squeezed between a Legend of Zelda and Peter Pan costume.

I set the dress on her bed. "You better get ready. Almost everyone is here."

"Ryan broke up with me," she deadpanned.

My expression softened. "I'm so sorry, Adriana."

"He doesn't understand why I'm getting married and doesn't want to see me anymore. So, he must not love me very much, right, Elena?" She looked at me with big brown eyes.

I paused.

Explain rationality to my sister and ease her heartbreak a bit, or rip the Band-Aid off?

"Right."

She nodded. "I'll be down soon."

I was downstairs, turning a corner in the hall near the library when I collided with something warm and solid. A breath escaped me as I was forced a step back. I knew who I'd run into before I had to look.

Russo.

Unease drifted through my body like a kindled flame. We were no longer in a foyer filled with people, but completely alone. It was so quiet I could hear my heart beating in my chest.

I took another step back as if to get some footing, but it was mostly just to put myself out of his reach, some kind of survival instinct kicking in.

He stood there in a gray suit and a smooth black tie. He was larger than life in this hallway. Or maybe this hall was just small? No, it looked like a normal-sized hallway. *Ugh, get a grip, Elena.*

He regarded me like someone would watch *Animal Planet*—like I was another species and possibly dull entertainment. He had a cell phone in one hand at his side, so I assumed he must have been making a private call.

This hallway was more of an alcove made of arches behind the staircase. Some large potted plants blocked our view from the main hall, and a green glass lamp on a side table cast the area in dim light. However, it was bright enough to see the flicker of impatience behind his gaze.

"You going to stand here and stare at me all day, or are you going to move?"

I blinked.

"And if I say stand here and stare at you?" It was out of my mouth before I could stop it, and I instantly wished I could reach out and take my words back. I'd never spoken to someone like that—let alone a boss—in my *life*. My stomach dipped like a tilt-a-whirl.

With the phone in his hand, a thumb came up to run across his jaw. I imagined he did that while thinking of how he was going to kill a man.

He took a small step forward.

As if we were the same poles of a magnet, I took one back.

He dropped his hand to his side, the slightest bit of amusement coming to life in his eyes as if I'd just done a trick that entertained him. I suddenly had the distinct feeling I didn't want to be his entertainment. And an even stronger feeling that I already was.

"Thought the Sweet Abelli was sweet."

How did he know my nickname?

I didn't know what came over me, but I suddenly felt free of that name—maybe because he'd never met that girl before. I wanted to be someone different. Especially to him, for some inexplicable reason.

"Well, I guess we were both fooled then. Here I was thinking a gentleman apologized when running into a woman."

"Sounds like someone's been making assumptions again," he drawled.

An odd thumping began in my chest, and I shook my head. "It wasn't an assumption."

He took a step forward, and once again I took one back.

He slipped his hands into his pockets as his gaze fell down my body. It was hardly leering and more observant, like I was in fact another species and he was wondering if I was edible.

His eyes narrowed on my pink heels. "You think you've got some proof, huh?"

I nodded, feeling strangely breathless under his scrutiny. "My mamma said you acted the perfect gentleman at church."

"I did *act* the perfect gentleman."

"So, it's a matter of *if* you want to be one?"

He didn't say a word, but his neutral expression confirmed it as his stare traveled back up from my heels.

"And I'm guessing you don't want to be one right now?" I realized I shouldn't have said it as I was saying it.

His heavy gaze reached mine, burning me.

He gave his head a slow shake.

Okay.

I'd stood my ground long enough, much longer than the Sweet Abelli ever would. But now, I just needed to get the heck out of here.

"Okay, well . . . I'll see you around."

I couldn't think of a less idiotic response, so I only took a step to go around him—but, before I could, something grabbed my wrist. *He* grabbed my wrist. His grip felt like a band of fire; rough, calloused fire. A cool breath of fear mixed with something boiling hot leaked into my bloodstream.

He stood a couple feet from me, his grip the only thing connecting us. "Write up a list of your sister's hobbies. Likes and dislikes, shoe size, dress size, and anything else you think will be useful. Yeah?"

"Yeah," I breathed. How many men had he killed with the hand wrapped around my wrist? It wasn't a hard grip, but it was heavy, firm, immovable. It made me aware of how much smaller I was, how unnerved and out of place I felt. How I couldn't leave unless he chose to release me.

He watched me with an inquisitive gaze. My heart felt close to stopping and my skin was burning up. It was inappropriate for him to touch me, future brother-in-law or not. My papà could come out of his office any moment, but this man didn't seem to care. I did, though, especially after the scene earlier.

"I'll give the list to you on Friday at the engagement party," I managed to say and tried to pull my wrist away.

He didn't let me go. My pulse fluttered when his thumb brushed my knuckles. "I was under the impression the Abellis could afford more than a fifty-cent ring."

I glanced at the ring on my middle finger. It came from one of those vending machines and had a purple round-cut jewel in the center. The thought of it sobered me.

"Sometimes the cheapest things are the most valuable."

His gaze came back to my face, and we looked at each other for a moment. His grip slipped down my wrist, palm, fingers. The rough pads of his fingertips brushed my softer ones, and made my heart skip a beat.

"I'll see you at lunch, *Elena.*"

He left, disappearing into my papà's office.

Cazzo . . .

Leaning against the wall, the ring was a heavy weight on my finger. I could take it off, put it somewhere it couldn't haunt me, but I knew I never would. Not yet.

His grip still burned like a brand on my wrist as I left the hallway.

Once again, he'd said my name in the most inappropriate way.

CHAPTER
Three

"Murders came with smiles, shooting people was no big deal for us Goodfellas."
—Henry Hill

Elena

BILLIE HOLIDAY PLAYED SOFTLY FROM THE OLD POOL RADIO. CONDENSATION dripped down crystal glasses, and silverware glinted in the bright sunlight. It was a hot July afternoon, but the steady breeze was the perfect interlude.

Lights wound around the wooden slats of the patio cover, and my mamma's rose bushes were flourishing. The chairs were soft and the food was good, but it could only be so comfortable having lunch with a bunch of strangers. However, the seventies ad sitting across from me didn't seem to share the same opinion.

"Anyway, the cop let me go and he didn't even take my coke—"

"Gianna." The word was a low warning from Nicolas's spot at the table.

She rolled her eyes and took a deep drink of wine, but she spoke no more.

I wondered why Nicolas had chastised her and what their relationship was. Siblings? They did appear to find each other annoying, but I was sure I'd heard somewhere that Nicolas was an only child. Gianna's senior citizen of a husband sitting next to her hadn't said a word, except for some oddly-timed chuckling. I was beginning to think he was hard of hearing.

Gianna *was* my polar opposite. Where I was quiet, she spoke with abandon and laughed loudly. Where I was demure, well . . . she'd stuck her gum to her cloth napkin before eating her pasta without twirling it around the fork. I was a little jealous of her carefree approach to life.

Tony sat on her other side. He leaned back in his chair with his jacket unbuttoned looking bored, but I knew him better than that. I'd seen that smug way he scratched the scruff on his jaw like he was angry and amused at the same time. And that never meant anything good. He was handsome, but if I wasn't his sister I wouldn't touch him with a ten-foot pole. His recklessness was dangerous for anyone involved, especially himself. He caught my uneasy look and shot me a wink.

Low chatter and the scraping of silverware filled the yard, but beneath that lay a tense air that wouldn't dissipate, an uncomfortable vibe the breeze wouldn't take with it. Everyone seemed to be easily chatting amongst themselves, so maybe it was just me. I brushed it off.

Gianna didn't stay quiet for long, though she no longer spoke about 8-balls of coke. She changed the subject to horse racing. That was an acceptable conversation many joined in on. It wasn't like this was a drug-free zone—in fact, many people came through this house on a daily basis with drugs on them—but out in the open, it was *Cosa Nostra* etiquette to pretend we were the classic example of a white-picket-fence family. Even if our homes were surrounded by an iron gate and security instead.

I was happy to see that Adriana had shown up instead of boarding a plane to Cuba. She sat next to her fiancé and Papà at the other end of table.

Maybe I was a coward, but I was glad I didn't have to sit near Nicolas. I was the perfect hostess and had a polite response for anything—as inappropriate as the comments could sometimes be when people were drinking—but with him, words were at a loss for me. I felt tongue-tied around him, tilted off my point of gravity, and truthfully just *hot*, as though a blush permanently warmed my skin.

It might be unpleasant speaking to him, but it was too easy to look in his direction. If not for his size, he could easily fit Adriana's pretty-boy preferences when he had a sober expression on his face. He was tan, his hair was almost black, and I couldn't help but notice that his biceps were defined through his shirt. My future brother-in-law was even more handsome beneath bright sun. It was unfortunate his personality didn't match.

What I found the most intriguing about his appearance, however, was the dark ink that showed through his white dress shirt. It was vague, but I thought it went all the way from his shoulder to the gold watch on his wrist. Nicolas Russo had a full sleeve. I *knew* that gentleman look was all smoke and mirrors.

He glanced over and met my gaze as if he'd felt me observing him. From five chairs down, the impact of an indifferent stare still found a way to touch my skin. The way he shouldn't have said my name played on a loop, deep and suggestive, in my head. Just so I didn't look like a coward, I held his gaze for a breathless second before looking away. I had the sudden feeling that for my future health . . . I shouldn't interact with this man anymore.

"I hear you have a recital coming up, Elena," my uncle Manuel said from a few seats down. His voice had become nothing but a memory of bloodshed due to the part he played six months ago. I drank a sip of wine, tasting nothing but guilt and resentment.

Every pair of eyes shifted to me, all twenty of them, but I was only aware of one of them.

"Yes." I forced a smile. "Saturday."

"You dance?" Gianna asked. "How fun! I've done some dancing but"—her voice lowered—"we're probably talking about two different things."

My eyes twinkled. "Tap, you mean?"

Her laugh was light and airy. "Yes, definitely tap. Have you always danced?"

"Yes, since I was a child."

"Are you any good?"

I laughed at the forward question. "Truthfully, no."

My mamma muttered something in disagreement from down the table. She had to disagree—it was part of being a mother—but I was mediocre at dance and I didn't have a problem acknowledging it. It was something to do. Something to fill the monotonous time. I used to love it as a child, but now it was just a sleeve of the dress that didn't fit.

Conversation quieted, and Gianna pushed her broccoli around on her plate like she was seven and didn't like vegetables. Her husband chuckled at absolutely nothing. She rolled her eyes and took a large gulp of wine.

Lunch continued with meaningless chatter, good food and drink, but the tension never dissipated. It sat there, uninterrupted. Like an echo before the words were even spoken.

My brother leaned back in his chair, a *ring* sounding as he ran his finger around his wine glass. Adriana ate as though a large man she didn't know and was marrying in three weeks wasn't sitting next to her.

Papà mentioned he'd bought an old shooting range, and conversation on that drifted down the table like a domino effect. They'd just served tiramisu for dessert, and I was ready for this lunch to end. But unfortunately, that uncomfortable tension was about to twist its way out of the inevitable.

It began with an innocent suggestion between the men to visit the range. And then I watched it play out like a bad dream. The Russo sitting to the left of me grunted sardonically. I'd learned his name was Stefan, though he'd hardly said more than a word.

The *ring* from my brother's wine glass faded off. Tony's dark gaze centered on the man. "Don't think I caught the joke, Russo."

Stefan shook his head. "Just got better things to do than watch a bunch of Abellis miss targets."

"*Uh-oh,*" Gianna said under her breath.

I closed my eyes. The day my brother let this go without a fight would be the day the sky fell.

"Tony, don't . . ." Benito warned from his seat beside my brother. He was always the voice of reason in that duo. But Tony didn't even glance at his cousin—instead, he smiled at Stefan Russo and it wasn't nice at all.

My chest tightened, and I looked down the table to get Papà's attention, but he was in conversation with Nicolas and my uncles.

"Not sure what you're talking about," Tony drawled. "I didn't miss—what was his name? Ah, yes, Piero . . .?" My brother's eyes flickered with dark enjoyment. "Hit the bullseye on that one."

Tony's amusement faded into a deathly quiet that even the family and guests at the head of the table noticed. Everything went static, like a still-shot in a magazine.

I never saw it coming.

My pulse leapt into my throat as an arm clamped around my waist, pulling me to my feet. My head was forced to the side as a cold barrel pressed against my temple.

Shouting rang out in Italian. Chairs fell backward to the patio as everyone jumped to their feet. Guns rose in every direction.

I heard my papà ordering commands, but my heart drowned out his voice. *Bu-bum. Bu-bum. Bu-bum.* The beat resounded beneath a cold sheen of fear.

I hadn't lived a picturesque life, no matter what my red front door and golden knocker conveyed. I'd seen my papà cut off a man's finger when I was seven. I'd watched my uncle shoot a man in the head, his face sideways on the bloodstained carpet, eyes open. I'd seen knife wounds, bullet wounds, so much *red*. But through all that, I'd never had a gun pressed to my head. Never felt cold metal against my temple. Never felt as if my life could be gone, just like that.

The cold in my veins froze to ice.

Nicolas's voice cut through the drumming of blood in my ears. It was low and smooth, and I grabbed onto it like a life raft. "Put it down, Stefan."

"He was the one who killed Piero!" The barrel shook against my head, and my lungs constricted, but I didn't move a muscle as I stared at the hedges lining the iron fence.

"Tony!" my papà snapped. "Don't."

I glanced at my brother, only to stare at the end of a barrel. He was going to shoot the Russo behind me, but with my heels on the man didn't have much height on me.

"You're a poor fucking shot, Tony. We all know you'll hit the favored little Abelli!" Stefan's heated voice vibrated against my back.

"Put. It. Down." Nicolas's words carried a calmness with a hint of animosity, like the ocean before a storm.

One second, two seconds. Stefan was hesitating—

Bang.

Something warm and wet hit my face. My ears rang as the voices around me sank underwater. The man's arm fell from me, and a dull *thunk* sounded as he hit the ground.

The newscaster's voice replayed in my mind, *murder* spilling from red lips, again, and again. Numbness flooded me. Sounds rushed in, pulled out of water with heavy chains, dripping wet.

"Sit the fuck down! *Now!*" my father's voice rang out. "We're going to finish this lunch, goddammit!"

It took a moment for his words to process and to realize that everyone sat stiffly in their chairs but him and Nicolas. My future brother-in-law's heavy, unreadable gaze touched my skin as I stared at the gun in one of his hands.

"Elena! Sit!" Papà snapped.

I dropped into my chair.

The warmth of blood dripped down my cheek. Red had splattered across my chair and part of the white tablecloth. A dead Russo's feet touched my own.

I sat there, pulling my gaze from a staring Gianna to Tony, who ate his dessert with relish.

"Elena." The small warning came from my papà, and because I was told to, I put a forkful of tiramisu in my mouth and chewed.

Placing my hand on the back of my hat, I glanced up at the clear blue sky.

Circumstances aside, it really was a beautiful day.

CHAPTER
Four

"This thing of darkness I acknowledge mine."
—William Shakespeare

Nico

THE GUNSHOT ECHOED IN THE AIR, AND THE TENSION WAS LOUDER THAN silverware against porcelain plates. The Abellis cast me cautious glances, while my family kept their eyes downcast on their desserts, stiffer than the chairs they sat on.

Leaning back, I rested a forearm on the table and focused my gaze on the cigarette I rolled between my fingers. The anger was strong enough I had to choke it down. It burned in my throat, in my chest, and marred my vision with a red mist.

My eyes skimmed up an inch to find Luca, my underboss and only reliable cousin, wiping a hand across his mouth in a poor attempt to hide his amusement. My gaze darkened, conveying I might just go for shooting two cousins today. He sat back in his chair, his humor fading.

He'd just won a bet that we couldn't get away without any altercations today. And won *double* because anything involving the Sweet Abelli had been a bonus. My family gambled on everything—*everything*. Any possible chance to gain a buck, they exploited it.

I owed him five fucking grand. And I was putting the blame on a little black-haired prima donna, because if I thought about her brother right now I'd end up putting a bullet in his goddamn head.

There are some relatives you don't like—ones you might shoot on your own terms if given the chance. But being forced into it . . . that rubbed me the wrong way, like the lash of a horsewhip. My jaw tightened as venom crawled through my veins.

My papà had a fondness for kicking me in the ribs when I acted without thinking.

My mamma used to smoke at the kitchen table in her nightgown after she and my father would scream the house down.

With my ribs burning and the cigarette in my hand, it wasn't lost on me that the apple really doesn't fall that fucking far from the tree. And I'd guess that those who'd known Antonio Russo—even my own family—would be hesitant to think of that as anything but unfortunate.

I was a mold my father and the *Cosa Nostra* created. As bad a combo as a barrel of gunpowder and a little flame. Where my papà had lacked in my rearing, my mamma tried to fill in the cracks. She *tried*, through dilated pupils and frequent bloody noses. The late Caterina Russo did her best to teach her only child to respect women. Truthfully, it had never really stuck. It was hard to respect a mamma you had to pick up off the floor some nights. Not to mention, I'd had most things I'd wanted handed to me since I was old enough to ask for them. I didn't need charm and respect to get women—my impending wealth and position had done that for me since I was thirteen years old.

Luca's mamma was the first to man up and shoot me the tiniest scowl. My family could be as pissed as they wanted, but I'd appreciate at least one fucking thank-you for stopping a bloodbath from ruining a perfectly good Sunday.

Jesus. It was just Stefan anyway.

Nobody liked Stefan.

The truth was, not every man could handle being a Russo. My nonna used to say our blood ran hotter than most. Though maybe that had just been an excuse to justify why all of her male offspring were entitled, greedy, and possessive of things that weren't theirs. A Russo wanted what he wanted, and once he did it was practically his. Most likely through a variety of illegal ventures. But maybe she was onto something, because it fucking felt hotter than it should.

I'll Be Seeing You by Billie Holiday filled the spacious backyard, the soft piano notes invading a tense atmosphere full of clearing throats and shifting gazes. I rolled the cigarette between my fingers, trying to quell the itch. I only smoked when I was too pissed off to see straight, or the rare occasion—unsettled.

Salvatore left the table to send the servants home. They all knew who employed them and were connected to the *Cosa Nostra* in some way—but it was a sure bet the dead man lying on the patio, his blood running through the divots in the bricks, was too much for some of them.

I'd only caught part of the conversation that set this in motion, but it was clear Tony had been gloating over killing Piero, another idiotic cousin of mine. I hadn't known Tony was the one to do it, but I was hardly surprised. Hardly moved either. I'd addressed Piero's death like I would a Zanetti's: with two fingers of whiskey. You do stupid shit, you get killed. That's how the world works, and my cousin had done more than enough.

In all honesty, I thought Stefan was going to put the gun down. But at that point I hadn't cared. A flash of anger had pulsed in my chest from my cousin's disrespect, and, oddly enough, burned even hotter at the fact he was threatening the Sweet Abelli. The annoying feeling rushed over me that only I could threaten her—so I fucking shot him and watched the blood splatter against Elena's white dress.

Tony had had a hard-on for seeing me dead ever since his friend Joe Zanetti saw the end of my .45 enough years ago I thought it was irrelevant now. I'd assumed Tony and I would have some issues, but I'd underestimated what a fucking idiot he was and that he'd bring them to lunch. I guessed the idea that I'd be fucking his sister was chafing him a bit more than my usual presence would.

I tapped my cigarette on the table, and before I could stop myself I glanced to where the Sweet Abelli sat. My eyes narrowed. I'd only owe Luca twenty-five if it weren't for her.

Blood dripped down her olive skin, yet she ate her dessert because her papà had told her to. I wasn't usually a sadist, but *Jesus*, it was kind of hot. A reluctant rush of heat ran to my groin.

Talking about sadists, my gaze found my cousin Lorenzo a couple seats down. He was staring at the girl like it was his job. And not any job I'd given him—because he was good at turning those to shit—but like a vocation or something. You'd never know looking at the man nor talking to him, but the bastard had an inclination for S&M. Knowing that and watching him stare at Elena Abelli, a sliver of irritation ran through me.

She probably liked it sweet and vanilla.

Probably preferred the man to get on his knees and beg a bit.

Lorenzo would.

I'd rather shut my dick in a car door.

She'd glared at me at church today, and I'd wondered what the Sweet Abelli could have against me. I'd known the nickname before I even met the girl. It was an innocent pet name that became well-known—well, among men—because not only was she sweet, she had the sweetest body around.

I'd heard more about this girl's ass in the past couple years than I ever needed to. And truthfully, I'd grown sick of it. When something was overhyped, it was always a letdown. I guessed the joke was on me because this was not one of those times.

I had always tuned out of conversation when she came up. I'd never seen her, but when my idiot cousins would waste time talking about the same pussy like it was what I paid them to do, it was an annoyance. Her name had become an irritation, like some kind of Pavlovian conditioning. So, when her papà had told me she was unfit for marriage, I hadn't even asked why. I'd signed the contract for the other one.

Then I saw her at church.

Son of a bitch.

My cousins would check out any woman under fifty. *Any* woman if she had just one decent attribute, so of course I had never believed the hype.

Talk about a man's wet dream.

Her body . . . fucking centerfold-worthy. Her hair was a weakness of mine: black, silky, and long enough I could wrap it around my fist twice. The thought had flitted through my mind unwillingly. And at *church*. Jesus.

It was the soft, innocent expression of hers, though, that seemed to burn through my skin and straight to my dick. It was so damn *sweet*, and I knew that's where her little nickname had come from. Couldn't be from Little Miss Glare's personality.

I'd observed her from the back of the church for far longer than I should have. I'd watched as she gave the same smile to every man in the congregation who came up to her, like it was a queue to see Her Majesty.

I was six-foot-three—hardly inconspicuous—but she wouldn't notice me for another thirty minutes, at which time she would glare at me.

The Sweet Abelli was sweet to everyone but me. I could have laughed, if for reasons unknown to me, it didn't piss me off. It was the first time since I'd become Boss that anyone had blatantly disrespected me. Maybe it was juvenile, but I wanted Elena Abelli to know I didn't care for her much either.

No woman with that much male attention could ever be anything but stuck-up and shallow. By her pink designer heels, I could see she liked to spend her papà's money. Her sister was wearing flip-flops. I'd probably save millions of dollars by marrying her instead.

Adriana was a little strange, but attractive. If you took her away from her sister, she was stunning; if she stood next to Elena, she'd blend into the wallpaper. This scenario worked for me just fine. I'd rather not have a wife all my cousins were jerking off to.

It wasn't like I cared much about who I married. It was time to take a wife, and in my world that meant profits. Salvatore had a little dispute with some Mexicans that was starting to grow into a problem. He'd grown soft in his old age. After the wedding, I'd help him find the root of the issue and deal with it the way I'd been taught: with a bullet through the head. This alliance was making me millions richer, not to mention would allow me control of most of the city.

A wave of awareness ran down my spine when Elena's gaze settled on me from across the table. It was a warm and annoying consciousness on the side of my face. I was going to ignore it, but I found myself glancing at her anyway. The back of my neck itched, but I held her stare until she looked away.

After her glare at church, I'd taken it upon myself to find out why she was unfit for marriage. Turns out the Sweet Abelli ran away, got sweet with some man.

I knew her lack of virginity wasn't the reason Salvatore hadn't offered her to me. It was only an excuse. Salvatore didn't want me to have her, though I could hardly blame him. If I were him, I wouldn't give my daughter to me either. It was easy to understand why Salvatore had little trouble offering his other one.

Adriana sat beside me in a black dress, one leg crossed over the other. Her brown shoulder-length hair covered her face as she leaned forward and doodled something on her palm with a pen.

I hadn't said a word to her since she'd shown up to the table late. To be honest, I'd almost forgotten she was sitting here. I guessed it was time to get to know my future wife.

"What are you drawing?"

Adriana hesitated, but then turned her little palm around and showed me.

"A rabbit." It wasn't a question because that's what it fucking was.

She pursed her lips and pulled her hand away to continue. "Mr. Rabbit," she corrected in a tone that would have normally pissed me off. But I was already at my limit, so I shrugged it off and planned exactly what I was going to do to her brother.

"Right or left?"

Tony's jaw ticked but he didn't say a word, just sat in the chair across from his papà's desk like he was at a board meeting. Blood dripped from his lip onto his white dress shirt, though he still wore a darkly entertained expression.

So I hit him. Again.

A burn traveled through my cracked knuckles.

His teeth clenched, but he took it without a sound. Tony was one of those men who were so high on their own shit they couldn't feel pain. He'd fucking feel something before I left this room.

Rays of sun shone through the blinds into Salvatore's office, lighting dust particles in the air. All the guests had filed out, and it was safe to say this lunch was a failure. Which only meant more lunches and parties I'd have to attend. None of the families wanted to risk acquainting everyone at such a large event, because shit like today could happen, before escalating into a bloodbath with women and children present.

Luca stood in front of the door, his cold eyes focused on the back of Tony's head. Benito and another of his younger cousins, who was close to Adriana's age, leaned against the wall with their arms crossed, while Salvatore sat behind his desk with a contrite expression.

I could start a war for Piero's death if I wanted, which was probably why Salvatore was going along with this. That, and the fact that his daughter's life had been threatened due to his son's stupidity.

"You fucked up, son," Salvatore said, clasping his hands on the wooden desk. "I warned you and you went and caused trouble anyway. If something would've happened to Elena, you'd be floating in the Hudson. You should feel lucky."

"Lucky," Tony mocked. He ran a hand across his jaw before saying, "Left."

Satisfaction filled my chest.

Right, it is.

CHAPTER
Five

"There are three sides to every story. Mine, yours and the truth."
—Joe Massino

Elena

I PADDED DOWN THE CARPETED HALL TO THE DISTANT BEAT OF THE MISFITS leaking from under my sister's door. As soon as I entered my room, I left a trail of clothes to the bathroom. Bypassing the mirror, I turned the shower on hot and climbed in.

It burned.

Something had to wash this memory away. Today took me back to six months ago. It was the last day I'd had someone else's blood splattered against my face.

The hot water spilled from the faucet, matting my hair to my face and shoulders. I imagined it was paint—the red running down my body and swirling into the drain. If only guilt was so easy to get rid of.

I closed my eyes.

Shouting. Cold barrel against my temple. One second, two seconds. Hesitation—

Bang.

My eyes flew open.

That gunshot hadn't been in my mind.

The back of my neck prickled. Hopefully it was only Tony

shooting another one of Nonna's vases. But until now, I hadn't thought of the consequences Tony might face after the trouble he caused . . .

I hopped out of the shower and dried off as fast as I could. Leaving my hair wet and uncombed, I threw on a t-shirt and shorts before running down the stairs. The marble floor was cold against my feet as I took the turn toward my papà's office, and once again, I collided with something solid.

A lungful of air escaped me. I'd been going so fast I would have fallen to my butt on the floor, but an arm wrapped around my waist as I teetered backward and steadied me. It was an incredibly warm and heavy arm.

"Jesus," Nicolas muttered with annoyance.

My stomach tightened as it pressed against his. The contact made me tingle everywhere, but I didn't have time to analyze the feeling more. I was spun out of his way and left to watch Nicolas's back as he continued down the hall.

His underboss's cold indifference touched me as he passed, and I was suddenly and surprisingly glad I'd run into Nicolas instead.

A burning sensation remained around my waist, and my heartbeat fluttered from the impact and the worry creeping in. "Did you kill my brother?"

"Should have," was all Nicolas said before the front door shut behind the two men.

I inhaled in relief, but it was short-lived when Tony left my papà's office and swayed down the hall like he was drunk. He was bare-chested and his dress shirt was wrapped around his hand. Blood dripped bright red to the marble floors.

My brother was tall, slightly brawny, and covered in scars. From the two bullet wounds to an innumerable amount of others that I could only guess the cause. Probably from the illegal fights I knew he participated in.

Tony didn't say a word as he passed, but I followed him into the kitchen. With the swinging door pressed against my back, I watched him grab a bottle of whiskey from the cupboard and struggle to open it with one hand. He eventually managed by holding it against his chest and twisting. He took a long pull before sitting at the island. "Go away, Elena."

"You need to see Vito." He was the vicar at church, but also had medical experience to patch up wounds. It was the Lord's work, after all.

"I'm fine." He took another pull on the bottle, spilling some down his bare chest.

He wasn't fine. He was smearing blood across the countertop. And he'd appeared drunk before he started drinking like someone had just broken his heart.

"I'll call Vito." I went for the cordless phone near the fridge.

Tony glanced at me with a remorseful expression. "I'm sorry, Elena. Didn't know it'd go that way. Honest."

My heart squeezed. "I forgive you."

He laughed weakly. "You shouldn't."

Tony usually had a smug look on his face, but when he smiled—a real smile—it drifted away and he became pretty charming. This was the brother I loved, even if I didn't get to see him often. Sometimes it felt like you needed to be the worst you could be to survive in this world.

I didn't know why he'd killed whoever Piero was, but I would pretend it was self-defense. Tony had been thrown into this life as a young man, and while my chains were tight, so were his in a sense.

"Can't help it," I replied.

He shook his head when I began dialing. "Don't call Vito. I'm fine."

"You're not fine. Tony, you really don't look so good." His tanned complexion was sweaty and pale.

"I'm *fine*, Elena."

I sighed. It was just like Papà to leave Tony bleeding without calling for help. I hung the phone back on the hook because my brother had said it in *that* voice. Even if Vito came, Tony wouldn't have anything to do with him. Too stubborn.

I crossed my arms and leaned against the counter with my hair still dripping water to the floor. "Why don't you like Nicolas?"

He snorted and took another drink. "Lots of reasons."

"Well, what's the number one?"

"He fucked my girlfriend."

My eyes widened. "Jenny?"

Another pull.

"Did she tell you?" I asked.

He shook his head. "He sent me a picture."

Ouch.

"Are you sure it was her?"

"Butterfly. Lower back."

"Oh . . . well, that was rude of him."

Honestly, it was hard to feel sorry for Tony. He'd cheated on Jenny with that servant Gabriella and I wouldn't doubt others. I didn't take Nicolas as a man to sleep with other men's girlfriends for the hell of it, though, and I had a feeling . . . "What did you do to him?"

A not-so-nice smile tugged at Tony's lips.

And there it was. There were always two sides to every story.

He took another pull, and with a frown I watched the blood drip down the side of the island and collect into a small pool. Drinking was only going to make him bleed more. I pushed off the counter and pulled the bottle straight from his lips. Whiskey splashed down his chin and chest.

His eyes narrowed, but his next words were slurred. "Jesus, Elena." He looked wasted, or really close to passing out.

I unwound the shirt from his hand and recoiled. "*Oh my god!* You have to go to the hospital, Tony!"

A bullet-shaped hole went straight through his hand like the barrel had been placed directly to it. I covered my mouth, the urge to gag rising in my throat. As I backed up to find Benito, Tony passed out. He fell sideways out of his chair, leaving a smear of red across the counter, and landed with a heavy *thunk* on the kitchen floor.

Crap, crap, crap.

"Benito!" I yelled.

"Why are you shouting?" Adriana asked as she breezed into the kitchen in galaxy leggings and a sports bra.

"Your fiancé shot Tony!"

"Dead?" She raised a brow, focused on picking the best apple out of the bowl on the counter.

"Where's Mamma?" I asked.

She shrugged, peeling the sticker off a green apple.

I sighed. *Fine. If they want to play this game . . .* I nudged open the swinging door and shouted into the hallway, "I'm calling 911!"

On cue, Benito, Dominic, and my papà pushed their way into the kitchen.

Papà narrowed his eyes on me, but then noticed his only son lying on his back in a lot of red. He spoke quietly to Benito—he always spoke quietly unless he was mad—and then my cousins hauled Tony up, one under his arms and one by his ankles, and carried him out of the kitchen.

"Not Vito," I told my papà. "The hospital."

"Yeah, yeah, Elena. They're taking him," he said dismissively, his gaze coasting over the blood on the floor.

I eyed him, wondering if he was telling me the truth. My papà never took any of us to the hospital without a fight.

He glanced at me, noting my suspicious gaze. "It's just as good as a hospital," he snapped.

Ugh. I had no idea where they were taking my brother. Most likely a doctor Papà had on his payroll.

"Hey, has anyone seen my drawing pencils?" Adriana interrupted.

CHAPTER
Six

"Behind every great fortune, there is a crime."
—Lucky Luciano

Elena

I MIGHT NOT HAVE HAD A GOOD REASON TO DISLIKE NICOLAS RUSSO IN THE beginning, but after meeting him, after he shot too close to my head, and after he put a bullet through my brother's hand, I now had substantial motive to immensely dislike him.

The whys of it all didn't matter.

Tony had been gone all night. It wasn't until I'd gotten back from dance practice twenty minutes ago that I learned he was going to be okay. He was given a 75 percent chance of having full function of his hand again.

Apparently, Jenny had volunteered to move into his apartment and help him out. My mamma told me this with a roll of her eyes. She really didn't like Jenny. And after hearing she'd cheated on Tony with Nicolas, I wasn't sure what to think about her either. Granted, I would have dumped Tony years ago if I was her, but I didn't understand sticking around if you weren't going to be faithful. It made me believe she was only around for one thing.

I sat cross-legged on the couch, watching a documentary on recent humanitarian crises, still dressed in my sweaty leggings and an off-the-shoulder top. It was one of the hottest days of the summer so far, and Benito had left the windows down the entire drive home. He'd said the wind did great things for his hair, and so I never got to cool off. I pressed a cold water bottle to my face.

The front door opened and my papà's voice filled the foyer. A rush of awareness ran from my nape down the length of my spine. I realized Nicolas was here before I even heard his voice, deep and indifferent. A strange dance began in my stomach.

Even though I stared at the TV, I had no idea what was happening because I was hyperaware of every noise coming from the foyer.

As their steps went by the living room's double doors, a cell phone rang.

"Take it," Papà said. "I'll be in my office."

Since it was silent, I imagined a nod from Nicolas. My papà's footsteps drifted down the hall.

"Yeah?" Nicolas drawled. A couple of seconds passed before, *"Motherfucker."*

I tensed. It sounded like he was going to kill someone, and his steps were coming straight for me. Before I knew it, he reached over my shoulder and stole my remote.

"Hey," I protested.

He didn't respond; he only changed the channel. *Breaking News* flashed on the bottom half of the screen, and the blonde newscaster went over the details of a large drug bust at the border.

Nicolas stood behind me, close enough my ponytail brushed his stomach. His hands gripped the back of the couch on either side of me as he leaned slightly over my head, his attention on the TV like I wasn't even here. It was invasive and rude.

My pulse drummed in my ears as my heart tripped up in what could only be called anticipation. My body's unwilling reaction brought a rush of annoyance in. I didn't like this man—heart fluttering or not—and I suddenly didn't care how inappropriate it would be to talk back to him.

"Yours?" I asked smoothly. "Bummer."

A tug on my ponytail. "Watch it." His words were low and distracted.

Warmth spilled into my chest, like I'd just gotten away with playing with fire. I wanted to do it again. Was this how people became addicts?

"There are seven other televisions in this house, Russo."

Another tug on my ponytail, but this time he pulled it all the way back so I was looking at him upside down. His eyes narrowed. "I'm beginning to wonder if this Sweet Abelli even exists."

I swallowed. "You shot my brother."

Was his fist . . .? It was wrapping around my ponytail. Once. *Twice.* His gaze flicked to the TV. "He deserved worse."

This man was going to watch the news with a fistful of my hair? *My God.* Maybe it was due to my head being at an awkward angle and my blood not circulating as well, but my brain wasn't getting enough oxygen. And the fact that he smelled so good, like clean soap and man, made the corners of my vision hazy.

"You're not a judge and jury," I breathed.

His gaze came down to me. "He almost got you killed, yet you stick up for him?"

"He's my brother."

His expression hardened. "He's an idiot."

My mamma's voice filtered into the room from down the hall, and slowly, he unwound his fist from my hair and took a step back.

A moment later, she entered the room.

"Nico, I didn't know you were coming today." Mamma's tone was tight. She didn't like that he'd shot Tony either, but she must have known it was coming and hid in her room all night. "Will you be staying for lunch?"

"I'm sure he's got plenty of stuff to do, Mam—"

"That sounds great, Celia."

"Great." Mamma sounded like she meant the opposite. I was so glad to have her back on my side. "I'll prepare a spot for you then."

"Thank you."

Her steps grew faint as she left the room.

"You know what pisses me off?" His tone was dark, but somehow it only awoke a thrill beneath my skin.

I knew the answer to this question.

"Assuming?"

I focused on the TV, pretending not to care about what he was doing, but my heart faltered when he moved close behind me. I held my breath as he slowly set the remote back in my lap, and then right at the hollow behind my ear, he whispered, "Smart girl."

A shiver ran down my neck, but then he left with a parting word.

"Don't fucking do it again."

The sun burned hot and heavy. I imagined if I lay on the brick patio, I would be as well-done as my steak.

"Really, Celia," Nonna complained. "It's hotter than blue blazes out here and I can still see a bloodstain on the patio."

I'd changed into high-waisted shorts and a short top that bared a sliver of my midriff, and a drop of sweat still ran down my back.

"Some fresh air is good for you," Mamma replied.

"So is edible food," Nonna muttered, pushing shrimp around with her fork like they were still alive.

I kept my eyes on my plate as I ate, mostly because Nicolas sat directly across from me. He wore no jacket, and he'd rolled up his white dress shirt. I was right. Black ink started at his wrist and disappeared into his shirt. It wasn't often I'd met men with tattoos—at least, not ones so obvious. The only thing I could make out was the ace of spades tattooed on the inside of his forearm. I guessed he accepted the nickname "Ace," which I'd heard he was called. I might have read a few articles on him myself.

He sat next to Adriana, and they both seemed like they'd always done it. She'd even given him a look because his leg was touching hers. It was strange to imagine them as a couple, yet I'd seen them exchange words, which I'd believed would be a difficult feat in itself. I thought Mr. Rabbit had even been brought up. I'd assumed they wouldn't be good for each other at all, but I was beginning to wonder if I'd been wrong all along.

Papà and Mamma were discussing something between themselves and Nonna was picking at her food, when Adriana suddenly said, "It's called manspreading."

Nicolas's gaze flicked to my sister. "What?"

"Manspreading. How you're sitting."

He didn't respond, only sat back, rested his arm behind Adriana's chair, and then, like he was merely getting comfortable, stretched his legs out a little further.

My sister's expression hardened.

All right, maybe I spoke too soon about them working well together.

"You know, Nico," Nonna started, "I don't blame you at all for shooting Tony. He's had it a long time coming and his papà hasn't done a thing." Papà grunted, apparently now listening to the conversation. "That boy has shot four of my vases. Don't know what I'd do if he ruined another." She sounded like it was the most grievous thing Tony had ever done.

"Glad to hear it," Nicolas drawled.

Mamma shot her a dark look, and my nonna smiled triumphantly at her plate. These two were all I needed to see to know I would never live with my mother-in-law.

I chewed my lip, hesitating. I'd been waiting for the right moment to ask Papà something and now seemed like the best time. He was always easier persuaded around other people, most likely because he didn't want to come off as a controlling jerk.

I'd hardly left the house for anything but dance in six months. Surely he couldn't punish me forever?

"Papà," I started, "one of the dancers is having a pool party on Sunday in celebration of the Summer Recital. And I was wondering if I could go . . . ?"

"Which girl is this?" he asked.

I shifted under his eagle-eye stare. "Well, actually . . . his name is Tyler."

Nonna harrumphed. "Since when are you into beta males, Elena?"

I shot her a look for giving Papà the wrong idea.

She pursed her lips and focused on poking at her food.

The table went quiet while he gave it some thought. I swallowed as Nicolas's gaze warmed the side of my face.

Papà took a drink and set his glass down. "I want the address and the owner's information. And you'll take Benito."

I let out a small breath. Was I being forgiven? Guilt pierced through my chest because I knew I didn't deserve it. "Thanks, Papà."

"I'm going inside before I melt," Nonna said, getting to her feet. "This was the worst day to eat outside, Celia. Don't know what you were thinking."

CHAPTER
Seven

"We don't break our captains. We kill them."
—Vincent Gigante

Elena

"**M**ERCY." MAMMA GRIMACED, AS I'D JUST EXPLAINED THE PLOT OF HER book club novel. "I don't even feel bad for not reading that one."

She hadn't read a single one of them—*I* had.

"Okay, I have to go," she said, putting a heel on with one hand and an earring in with the other. "Your papà and Benito are out, but Dominic is in the basement. Oh, and help your sister pick out her cake flavor. *Tua zia Liza* needs to know today. Please, Elena!"

I sighed and climbed off my parents' bed.

"Leaving!" Mamma's voice drifted out of the room.

I heard a faint "Finally" from my nonna as she passed the doorway with her servant Gabriella in tow. She'd gone on her afternoon walk, or, more likely, sat on the patio for five minutes of fresh air while gossiping.

A couple of moments later, I pushed the kitchen door open. Adriana sat cross-legged on the counter with two plates of cake before her. Her elbows rested on her knees and her fists were under her chin, while only wearing her yellow polka-dot bikini.

"What are the flavors?" I asked, coming to stand before the island.

The sun was the only light in the room, casting the windowpane reflection across the counter.

"Pink Champagne and Luscious Lemon." She said it like the options were really Tasty Garbage and Rotten Apricot. She was going to drag this out for as long as she could. Asking my sister to make a decision was like requesting her to write out the equation for time travel.

I tried both by scooping some up with my fingers. "Definitely the lemon," I said, opening the cupboard for a glass.

I didn't normally have dance practice on Tuesdays, but with the recital coming up we'd had it every day. My thighs burned as I stood on my tiptoes to get a cup from the top shelf. Benito and my other male cousins were all taller, yet they always took the glasses from the bottom shelf just to annoy the girls in the family.

"I was leaning toward Pink Champagne," Adriana groaned.

"Then Pink Champagne it is," I said as I filled my glass from the fridge water dispenser.

She shook her head. "No, now it doesn't seem right."

"The lemon, then."

"That one doesn't seem right either."

I sighed. My sister could drive a saint to curse. I leaned against the fridge and eyed her over my glass. "Why are you in your swimsuit?"

"Was on my way to the pool, but Mamma stopped me and said I can't leave the kitchen until I decide."

After a moment of thought, a smile pulled on my lips. "Mamma left."

Adriana's gaze, warm and hopeful, popped up from the plates.

An hour later, with the cake flavor still undecided, *Don't Stop Believin'* played on the pool radio. The sun was hot, sparkling off the blue water as my head emerged from beneath. The cool liquid ran down my shoulders as I waded to my sister, who wore sunglasses and lay still on a floaty. She was a diva in the pool. In other words: *boring*. I tipped her.

She came up sputtering, pulling her sunglasses off and pushing the dark hair from her face. "I don't know why you can't just let me . . ." she trailed off.

The pool sat at the side of the house, allowing a view to the front gates. My gaze followed hers to see a lawn care truck coming down the drive. *Oh no.* Before I could say a word, she pulled herself out of the pool.

"Adriana, don't," I warned. My stomach twisted. I wasn't sure how she'd seen Ryan this long without Papà finding out. She'd falsified her class schedule, putting an extra time slot down that she could spend with him, but seeing him at the house was too risky.

She turned to me, her gaze soft and pleading. "I just want to talk to him."

"And say what? That you're still getting married in three weeks?"

"And whose fault is that?" she snapped.

Ouch.

She was never abrupt with me like this. We might not have talked much lately—because what would we talk about? Her wedding?—but she'd never been hostile with me.

"I haven't done anything you haven't done," I told her.

"I know. I just need to talk to him. You would want to talk to—" she glanced toward the ring on my finger under the water, "—*him* if you could, wouldn't you?"

Would I? I didn't know. Maybe that was the reason guilt felt like a heavy weight I carried around daily. It'd all been meaningless. It wasn't even for love. And I was the only one who'd gotten out alive.

"The cameras," I warned her. There was a security system downstairs that Dominic only had to glance at to see what was going on outside the home. I took a deep breath and tried to ignore the unease that swam in my veins. "The living room. Talk to him in there so you can see if anyone comes down the drive."

The gardener came on Tuesdays and Fridays for lawn care and to clean the pool, so the truck wouldn't raise Dominic's suspicion. Let's just hope my cousin was immersed in Skyrim like he usually was and wouldn't show his face upstairs. Thankfully, Benito wasn't here; he had a sharper eye.

My gaze found Ryan, who stood next to his truck, looking in our direction. He wasn't even wearing his lawn care t-shirt, but a button-up and jeans. I groaned. *What the hell is he thinking?*

Adriana beamed. "Thank you, Elena!"

Then she was running toward him.

As I lay on my back, arms out, the sun warmed my front while the cool water licked at my sides. My eyes closed. I wondered what it would be like living here without my sister. How long I would coast through the halls until I got the same fate as her. I wondered if my papà would let me take classes this upcoming semester, though I was sure I'd blown that for myself.

I'd been pulled from all writing and political classes six months ago. I was free from a job, all responsibilities if I wanted, but even as the water held me up, slowly turned me in a circle, I might as well be drowning. Drowning in a past mistake I could never fix, but one I could try to make amends for. One I *would* amend, in the only way I could.

The quiet purr of an engine broke through my thoughts.

My eyes flew open.

Swimming toward the side, I grasped the edge of the pool and watched a shiny black car park next to Ryan's truck. I didn't know who it belonged to, but soon enough the door opened and the worst person who could show up stepped out.

A cold sweat drifted through me. Disaster loomed in the distance. More blood. Young, lifeless eyes. *No.* It wasn't going to happen again.

I pulled myself out of the pool and headed toward the front of the house, ignoring the itch to go in the opposite direction. Nicolas held a manila envelope in one hand and shut the car door with his other. My skin buzzed with a cool sensation, and my bare feet paused at the end of the walkway.

I stood there in a white bikini, soaking wet, while my heart beat a mile a minute.

When his gaze finally came up to me, he stopped in his tracks. We stared at each other. He was only wearing black dress pants and a white short-sleeve shirt. I swallowed. It felt like he was more underdressed than me. Black ink covered one arm, while the other was smooth tanned muscle. Warmth rushed to the pit of my stomach and spread through me like fire.

My breathing shallowed as his gaze trailed the drips of water running down my body. Each drop that hit the concrete was another match lit in the short space between us. His attention settled on my face, his gaze narrowing.

"Is this how you welcome all your guests?"

I blinked at his rude tone. I couldn't exactly say I'd ever stood half-naked in front of an unrelated man and had him angry with me for it.

"Some." I tried for nonchalance, but it sounded more breathless than anything.

He gave his head a shake, letting out a small breath of amusement. He wasn't amused at all, though, that much was clear by the way a muscle in his jaw ticked. It wasn't often I was an irritation, and I wasn't sure if I liked it or not.

When he headed for the front door, ice crept through me. I took a step forward. "Nicolas, wait."

He stopped, glancing at me sideways.

"Papà isn't here," I rushed out.

"Aware," was all he said while heading for the door again.

My stomach dipped.

Without thinking about it—because I would've chickened out—I hurried and stepped in front of him. He stopped short and glared at me.

My heartbeat wavered like a plucked string. Without my heels on, his presence was larger, more intimidating. "You can't go in. It's not . . . proper without my papà home." There wasn't a chance my father had invited this man over while he was away. How did he even get past the community gates? But I already knew Nicolas did what he wanted regardless of rules, and my papà must have realized that before the marriage contract was signed.

His gaze sparked. "You have a second to move before I do it for you."

"Be my guest. You'll get all wet."

Somehow, I thought that was a great comeback, but it only made us both aware I was half-naked and soaked. The breeze grew hotter, the air denser.

His jaw tightened as he took a step forward. I didn't move. His white shirt almost brushed my white bikini top. My breasts tingled in anticipation and drops of water tickled as they dripped down my midsection. His body heat was a living thing, sinking into my skin and urging me to step closer, to press my body against his.

I couldn't breathe when he leaned in, his voice low against my ear. "You're lucky I have shit to do today." The rough sound ran the length of my neck, goose bumps following. I couldn't help but think: *What would he have done if he didn't?*

His fingers brushed mine as he slipped the manila envelope into my hand. "Put it on your papà's desk." He took a step back, and my entire body burned in the aftermath. "And don't fucking go through it." I wished I could say his tone doused me with cold water, but it didn't.

My gaze narrowed as I looked up at him. The sunlight made his amber eyes even more golden. "Your business with my papà is the last thing on earth I would concern myself with."

His voice darkened. "Good."

We stared at each other for another moment. He jingled the keys in his hand and took a slow step back, before turning around and heading to his car. I stood there and watched him, because his back was as nice as his front.

Nicolas opened his car door, calling out, "By the way, it's Nico. Nobody fucking calls me Nicolas."

As he backed out of the drive, I reminded myself to keep calling him Nicolas. I headed into the house, dropped the folder on my papà's desk, but, before I could leave, my gaze was pulled to the small safe in the corner of the room. With a tight throat, I walked toward it and tried the handle even though I already knew the outcome. Locked.

Guilt made me grasp onto the tiniest shards of hope.

I checked each drawer of his large mahogany desk, though, once again, knew I wouldn't find what I searched for. My papà had all of his private bank information in this house locked down, but one of these days he had to trip up.

One of these days this family would pay restitution for the

innocent life they'd taken.

I walked out of his office to watch Adriana shuffle Ryan out the front door.

I crossed my arms when I saw her swimsuit top tied awkwardly to the side, her bottoms on inside out. While I was saving her ass, she was having sex? What a little . . . *ugh*.

When he was gone, she leaned against the door, looking pale and relieved.

I pursed my lips in disappointment, turned around and chimed, "Lemon," as I headed up the staircase.

CHAPTER
Eight

"Give a girl the right shoes, and she can conquer the world."
—Marilyn Monroe

Elena

I stopped short in Adriana's doorway and closed my eyes in disbelief.

"Papà is going to kill you," I told her.

"Good," she muttered, adding a long arc with her paintbrush to the canvas that leaned against the wall. The painting would be a rainbow if it wasn't all black.

My sister had been brooding since Ryan came over. She went to her classes, but otherwise stayed in her room. The week crawled by with her casting a black cloud over the house with her emo paintings and sappy music. I was beginning to feel guilty again, but there wasn't a part of me that wanted to put myself in her place. I'd rather have a husband who wasn't so rude, wasn't such a womanizer as I'd heard, and truthfully less handsome. Maybe that sounded odd, but to me it made perfect sense.

Laughter filtered up the stairs, and I closed my eyes once more. Adriana's engagement party had started five minutes ago, and she currently sat cross-legged on her floor in overalls, covered in paint.

I could see Papà's temper not far in the distance, and I would feel its heat just because I was such an easy target. Adriana never reacted when our papà raged at her, and it annoyed him, so he turned it on me.

"What on earth could you be thinking right now?" I headed toward her closet, not looking forward to digging through costumes to find the rare dress she could wear.

"That I hate my fiancé. He's rude, and you've seen him, right? Can you even imagine us having sex, Elena?"

I paused, gave my head a shake, and continued pushing clothes on hangers aside. "Um, no. I'm not going to try to imagine that."

She sighed. "A couple of hours ago I realized I would have to have sex with him."

I made a noise of acknowledgment, not surprised it had taken her this long to come to that assumption. The obvious was like the hidden secrets of the world in Adriana's eccentric mind. Surprising, as she'd always aced her schoolwork and had more friends than I could ever hope for.

"And I kept thinking, maybe there's a reason he manspreads so much? He *is* big. Then I began to worry, so I started looking up pictures—well, videos—of men his size, naked, and that only made me worry more."

"You were watching porn," I said, deadpan, standing in the closet doorway and watching her paint Mr. Rabbit beneath the black rainbow.

She tilted her head to eye her masterpiece. "Yeah, I guess that's what it's called."

"*Adriana!*"

My sister groaned, and I looked toward the door. Mamma wore a red cocktail dress and an angry expression. A slew of Italian flew past her lips as she snatched the dress from my hand and then smacked Adriana on the back of the head. "Shower, now!"

Adriana grumbled and got to her feet.

"And *porn!*" More Italian. "What were you thinking?"

A laugh escaped me.

Mamma shot me a glare, and I turned it into a cough. She had always shown up at the most inopportune times. We couldn't get away with anything.

"Elena, go pacify the Russo. Lord forbid he starts shooting the guests again."

"Me? What am I supposed to do?"

All I received were a few sentences of berating Italian that didn't even address the current topic at hand. When my mamma went off, she'd talk about everything but what she was currently mad about. This time, it was how she broke a favorite porcelain dish earlier, Nonna complained about her lunch again, and the gardener hadn't shown up today. Which was definitely for the best . . .

Guests trickled in the front door as I made my way down the staircase. I wore a pink choker maxi dress, heels with a bow that tied around my ankles, and my hair down, pinned to one side. Even though I didn't approve of this marriage, it didn't mean I wasn't going to take the opportunity to dress up. Frankly, it was the highlight of my week.

"Elena!" my cousin Sophia squealed as she came through the front door. "Squealed" was the best way to explain it. She was nineteen with a constant mischievous expression.

"I've missed you!" She threw her arms around me, and I took a step back at the impact.

"I just saw you at church Sunday," I laughed.

"I know." She smacked a "mwah" on each of my cheeks and pulled back. "But so much has happened since then." She hadn't been here for the lunch incident, but I understood my family well enough to know that my three-year-old cousin Caitlin would be able to recite the entire event like she'd been present.

"Where's Sal?" I asked. Her older brother was a male version of her.

"He ran into Benito out front. You know, 'man talk'." She rolled her eyes. "All right. I'm going to go find us some alcohol. Then we need to talk about this Nico I've been hearing about."

"Check out the bloodstain on the patio. That's all there is to tell," I told her.

"That's not what I've heard. Mamma said he's hotter than David Beckham."

"I don't know who that is."

Her mouth gaped. "You're living under a rock, Elena. Too many books, not enough TV."

"The quote of the century," I mumbled wryly as she saw another cousin, squealed their name, and left me there.

For a moment, I stood alone in the foyer. The windows and patio doors were open, allowing the summer air to flow through the house. It was a beautiful night, and I was praying it didn't end up like the last time we'd had the Russos over. Tony wouldn't be here, so we had a much better chance.

I turned to find Papà, to tell him there was an issue with Adriana's dress and that she was going to be late, and to let *him* relay that to Nicolas, but, before I could, the front door opened once again. Bitterness crawled up my throat, but it was now too late to get away.

Nicolas Russo had the worst reputation of any man I'd met, hands down. Though, somehow, I'd found the courage to be myself around him, not the Sweet Abelli everyone used to know and expected me to be forever. But just as it was when someone got sucked into their old habits by the people they hung out with, I was tumbling back into the abyss of fake smiles and fake words, and I didn't know how to get out.

"*Elena.*"

Warm air brushed my skin as the front door shut, and I longed to be on the other side. But instead, I smiled politely. "Oscar."

Mid-thirties, with dirty blond hair and expensive suits always worn with a colored tie, Oscar Perez was handsome in a classic and charismatic way. He never lacked female attention, yet he always lavished his on me. He worked for my papà and was often around for parties, but since we'd had nothing going on I hadn't seen him in months, since before the incident. It was one of the biggest reliefs, but unfortunately, all good things have to come to an end.

"Don't you look as beautiful as always," he told me, giving me a kiss on each cheek and lingering too long. "*Demasiado hermosa para las palabras.*"

I didn't know what he'd said, but I assumed it had something to do with my symmetrical face.

I stared at his light blue tie, the color of his eyes.

I hated it.

He was the fairest Colombian I'd ever met, and for some reason I resented his blond, comely appearance. What a lie it was.

"Thank you," I said, trying to take a step back, but his hand went to my lower back and drifted to the top of my ass. My stomach tightened with unease. He was lean but tall, and his presence consumed me like a bad aftertaste.

He'd always been subtly inappropriate—his fingers just grazing things they shouldn't. Close enough to make me uncomfortable, but not too close to get shot by my papà. If he went further, would my father even believe me now?

Oscar pulled back to look me in the eye, but his hand didn't leave me. Something crawled under my skin. I realized at this moment why I couldn't escape the expectations people had for the Sweet Abelli with anyone but my sister's fiancé. Nicolas Russo was safe. He was marrying my sister. There was no chance I'd have to marry him, no chance my actions would alter how he would treat me as a wife. Most men walking through these doors could be a potential husband to me. Why make it worse on myself?

Oscar's fingers tightened on my lower back, and he spoke in my ear, "I hear you've gotten into trouble since the last time I saw you."

My heartbeat drummed. He'd always been inappropriate, but politely inappropriate, if that made any sense at all. He'd never brought up something so personal and invasive.

His saccharine voice took a cruel edge. "I was very disappointed when I found out, Elena. You can understand why, can't you?"

There was one thing that could mean—my worst nightmare—but I wouldn't accept it, didn't believe it. I wasn't going to call him a liar, though.

"Of course," I breathed.

I didn't realize how tightly he'd been holding me until he let me go and I fell back a step, my line of vision focused on his ugly tie. It took a second to realize we were no longer alone, and the heavy presence against my back could only be one person.

Oscar glanced warily behind me, before looking back at me with a fake smile and bitterness dancing in his eyes. "I'll see you at dinner,

Elena." He kissed the top of my hand, eyeing my cheap ring with a grimace, and then disappeared into my home like a snake on the loose.

I stared at the door, while his insinuation resounded in my mind. Resentment crawled into my chest, creeping to wherever it resided. However, maybe Oscar Perez was what I deserved . . .

Slowly, I turned around, my gaze traveling up a black vest, black tie, to a gaze just as dark.

"If that was the Sweet Abelli, can't say I'm impressed."

Where Oscar's presence was a dark, looming shadow, it felt nothing compared to Nicolas's larger, warmer one. His pulled you in, didn't send you away. It was infinitely more dangerous.

The reminder of my spineless behavior still permeated the air, and I couldn't flip the switch so fast. "Excuse me," I breathed, taking a step around him, but he reached out and grabbed my hand.

I didn't get a chance to even weigh his expression before he was pulling me to the front door. His rough palm practically burned mine, spreading a warm sensation in my lower stomach.

It took a moment to find the voice to speak, and once I did, it sounded more breathless and uncertain than it ever had. "What are you doing?"

He was mad. He had to be to touch me in the middle of the foyer with guests around every corner.

He ignored my question. "Where's my list?"

My brows knitted, and then I remembered I was supposed to write that. "I, uh, forgot about it."

Under the warm glow of the porch light, I heard Benito and Sal laughing near one of the cars in the drive, but it was too dark to see. Nicolas's grip was soft but strong, and so there was no other choice but to follow him down the stone path toward the side of the house.

I had no idea what we were doing, but it was either go with him, or back inside where Oscar roamed free. It was an easy choice, though surprising considering I'd only seen one of them shoot their family member in the head.

Nicolas stopped near the corner of the house, released my hand, and leaned against the brick wall of my home. A second later, the orange flame of a lighter cast his face in gold tones as he lit a cigarette between his lips.

"You smoke?" It was a stupid question, as he was now blowing out a breath of smoke and watching me with a lazy expression.

"Sometimes," was all he said, his shoulders tense. He glanced up to look at the security cameras above our heads. He was in a blind spot, leaning against the wall. I was probably front and center on the screen for Dominic to see. What would people think if I was, once again, caught alone with a man I shouldn't be with? A rush of anxiety shot through me, and I stepped to the side and out of the camera's view.

Nicolas's gaze was heavy, angry even, and I wasn't sure what I'd done to him. I glanced at the star-lit sky. It was beautiful, but I didn't believe he'd brought me out here to enjoy it with him. In fact, it looked like he'd prefer I wasn't here at all.

I sighed. "Why am I out here with you?"

The night was dark, but I still saw a bitter expression cross his face. "Saw that prick push you around, touch your ass. Was wondering if I could get away with the same."

My heart stilled for a split second before I narrowed my eyes. I had my reasons for putting up with Oscar, but I didn't have to deal with this from a brother-in-law. I took a step to leave, but a rough hand grabbed my wrist.

"Stay." It wasn't a suggestion but neither was it demanding. Why did he want me to stay when he was clearly angry with me? He was rude and confusing. And who told him he could hold my hand, pull me around, and make me feel warm all over? I imagined Nicolas Russo had gotten whatever he'd wanted since he was young, and, being the only child, he didn't even have to share.

I let out a shallow breath and pulled my wrist out of his grip. It was stupid, but I was going to stay. I told myself it was only because I needed to get to know his character for my sister's sake. Not because his mere presence made something hot unravel inside me.

I eyed his cigarette. It looked small and harmless in his hand. I didn't know what it would look like in mine, but I was beginning to wonder.

He must have noticed my expression, because he pulled the cigarette from his lips and handed it out to me. He wanted to share? He watched me with that hooded, looking-into-the-sun expression, not saying a word. My pulse fluttered.

It'd been six months since I'd even touched a man—that must be why I was having such schoolgirl notions about handholding and cigarette-sharing. Male contact wasn't a normal thing for me, and even before this ring graced my finger, it hadn't been then.

I took the cigarette from him, and he watched me as I brought it to my lips and inhaled. The coughing was instantaneous, my eyes watering.

Dark amusement ghosted through his gaze before he reached forward and took it from me, his fingers brushing mine.

"I wasn't finished," I protested, still coughing a little bit. If I was going to smoke, I was going to do it right. Maybe I was a perfectionist, but I couldn't leave anything halfway or poorly done.

I watched him put his lips on the cigarette where mine had been. Thank God it was dark, because my cheeks grew hot. This man had barely said anything to me that wasn't rude, short, or demanding, yet my body reacted to everything he did like it was magic. *Che palle.* I was crushing on my future brother-in-law.

He handed it back to me. "Not so much this time."

I listened to him and only inhaled a little bit. A couple of seconds passed before smoke smoothly escaped my parted lips. A languid rush filled my bloodstream, my head feeling light.

The breeze was warm, the song of the cicadas steady, while I shared a cigarette with a man I knew nothing about.

"My mamma's going to kill me," I said softly, followed by my cousins' low laughter drifting on the light breeze.

Nicolas dropped the butt, blew out a breath of smoke, and stepped on it. "You tell your mamma everything?"

I looked up at the starry sky. The answer was no; I never told anyone much. Nothing that mattered anyway.

"She'll smell the smoke," I said, gazing at the constellations. I glanced at him to see he'd been watching me. I flushed, every inch of my skin growing hot.

"Come here." Something soft and charming wove through his deep voice.

My heart skittered to a stop.

This was how this man got women: by only saying, "Come here," in that tone. Nonetheless, I couldn't say I felt cold when he was rude either.

I had always done what I was told, especially by the Made Men in my life, though not a single step I took in his direction was because of that. I was a moth moving toward the flame, until I stood close enough for my wings to ignite.

I held my breath when his hand rested on my waist. His grip tightened as he pulled me forward until my chest brushed his. My pulse beat in my throat, and his hand was so hot, spreading warmth to the pit of my stomach, that I hardly noticed him leaning in, brushing his face against my hair.

"No smoke." The words were smooth with a rough edge.

His palm slid from my waist to my hip before he pulled away, leaving a trail of fire down my side. He pushed off the wall, and I took a step back and out of his way. Walking away, he stopped and turned to me. His voice was cool, indifferent, and laced with that commanding tone he'd mastered.

"The list? I want it tomorrow, *Elena.*"

CHAPTER
Nine

"What do you mean, like do I carry a membership card that says 'Mafia' on it?"
—Willie Moretti

Nico

TEMPTATION IS HALF-NAKED, INNOCENT, AND DRIPPING WET.

And I am my idiot cousins.

Those were the two conclusions I'd come to this week with an irritating sense of acquiescence. I was practically up to my neck in work, and yet I could only focus on one goddamn thing.

Elena Abelli, of course. So *fucking* wet.

The way she'd stood there, dripping water to the concrete while staring at me with those soft brown eyes and that sweet expression. Her long, wet hair and a body you'd see on a porn star. *Jesus*, it couldn't be real. That's what I'd convinced myself, but then it followed me, got in my way even, and told me what I couldn't do.

It was regrettably real. Every perfect square inch of it.

For an unknown reason, the idea of her greeting guests looking like that dug under my skin. Was her papà letting her run around half-naked while men were over? And as her soon-to-be brother-in-law, could I tell her to go put on some fucking clothes?

I hadn't ever wished a girl would get dressed, especially one with an ass like Elena Abelli's. Frustration clawed at my chest, because I knew when irrational responses went through my head it meant one thing, and it usually wasn't good for either party involved.

The night was lit by tiki torches and the sparkling orange lights above the Abelli's patio table. The atmosphere seemed to be easy enough, though that was probably because all the Abellis stayed on one side of the yard and all the Russos on the other.

A servant poured Adriana her sixth glass of wine, and I reached out and took it from her, setting it on the other side of my dessert plate.

Her gaze burned a hole into my cheek.

"You're not fucking old enough to drink," I told her.

She sighed, mumbling something about having to drink to forget the videos—whatever that meant.

We were supposed to be "getting to know one another," as her mamma suggested, but we'd hardly said a word to each other and I couldn't find it in me to care. Mostly because I knew where her sister stood and was concentrating on not letting myself look in that direction. The girl had the entire male population of New York kissing her ass, and I didn't care to be included in that circle jerk.

Nevertheless, a flash of pink in a corner of the yard caught my attention, and I couldn't stop myself from flicking an unwilling glance to her. She was playing croquet with her girl cousins and Benito. And just like a prima donna, she still had her heels on. I'd thought my perception of her personality would be a big enough repellent, like a thick cloud of bug spray or maybe a little mace. Unfortunately, it didn't do anything to turn me off. Not when I looked at her, and especially not when she spoke with that soft, warm voice that soaked through my skin and ran straight to my groin.

I now understood my cousins' fascination.

The fact that I could be lumped into the same group as those idiots . . . ridiculous.

I knew what this was. I was a Russo. We wanted what we couldn't have, and what I couldn't have was Elena Abelli in my bed just one damn time.

"You don't like my sister?" Adriana asked.

Jesus, she was a bit perceptive. I would have to remember that.

I took a sip of whiskey. "I like your sister just fine."

"Hmm," was all she said, like she didn't believe me but didn't give a shit either.

This was how our conversations seemed to go. Short and apathetic. I couldn't decide if we were perfect for each other, or if she'd drive me crazy with her idiosyncrasies.

My gaze found that blond prick talking to one of Elena's uncles. I didn't know the man, but I knew I wouldn't help him if I saw him bleeding out on the street. A burn radiated in my chest from only looking at him. I'd barely stopped myself from smashing his face against the front door earlier. Elena Abelli was not my business, regardless of the way the Russo blood in my veins burned a little hotter in her presence.

"Yankees or Mets?" Adriana had poured all the salt out of the shaker and was now drawing caricatures in it.

"Red Sox," I responded dryly.

"Boxers or briefs?"

"Commando," I lied.

Her gaze dropped to my dick, only to look away a moment later and purse her lips. "This game is boring."

Amusement filled me. This girl was fucking weird. And I was aware that's why Salvatore had offered me a daughter in the first place. "Unfit," he'd said about Elena. *Unfit, my ass.* Not a single man in the *Cosa Nostra* would turn Elena away because of her lack of virginity. Salvatore didn't want to give up the favored Sweet Abelli, at least not to *me*. He probably thought he'd gotten one over on me.

I'd take the weird one. At least she would be entertaining. She was also the smartest choice. Who knew how many men Elena had been with? I was Don. If I married a woman who'd been fucked by a few others in the *Cosa Nostra*, it would look bad. And, honestly, I never was that great at sharing. I'd have to kill all of them and I already had enough on my plate.

Luca leaned against the wall by the open double doors, sharing a look with my cousin Ricardo who sat at the edge of the party quietly observing the scene. Luca held up two fingers, nodding toward the girls on the lawn. Ricardo shook his head. After a few more silent exchanges, they both nodded.

At least tonight seemed to be dull enough for bets on stupid croquet games rather than as eventful as it was last Sunday. I sure as hell wouldn't be the one to ruin it by cracking skulls against doors.

I flicked a glance at Elena to find her gaze already on me. It was the same way she'd looked at me when she said, "You'll get all wet." I tried to ignore the heat running to my groin. The words had been innocent, the thought not crossing her mind that any man would let her get them as wet as she wanted. And not with fucking pool water either.

At first, I thought whoever nicknamed her had never even met her, but as I spent a little more time observing her it started to make sense. She looked tense when she stood up to me, like it was new for her, like she expected me to wrap my hand around her throat and squeeze. A thought I'd had, though probably in a different context.

The Sweet Abelli was trying to grow some wings.

Thank fuck.

Something in my chest rattled with satisfaction when she listened to me without hesitation. The hot-blooded male in me wondered how obedient she really was. And the Russo wanted to know how much she would let me get away with.

I had already touched her more than I should. Had only shared my cigarette with her just so I could see her lips where mine had been. I'd imagined those little pink fingernails around a specific part of my body, rather than holding a smoke.

I'd only touched the girl's waist, and the warmth and softness of it was still burned into my palm.

The whole goddamn situation was fucking annoying.

The blond prick grabbed Elena by the arm as she walked past, pulling her in to say something in her ear. Animosity crawled through me. Leaning back in my chair, I rested my forearm on the table and away from my gun, because I had the sudden urge to shoot another man in the Abellis' backyard. Elena's papà glanced at the exchange, though hardly seemed concerned.

My tongue ran across my teeth, a deep, unsettling ache unfurling in my ribs.

Elena nodded tightly before the prick dropped his hand and let her go. She disappeared inside.

"What's his name?" I asked Adriana, nodding toward the blond whose mere presence had become tiresome.

"Oscar Perry—no, Pretzel." Her brows knitted. "No, that doesn't sound right either. Oscar something. God, I'm hungry for pretzels now."

"What does he do for your papà?"

She frowned. "I don't know. Kind of a creep, though. He's always all over Elena."

I let out a dry breath. "Who isn't?" They greeted her at church like she was Mother Mary.

"True, but she doesn't care about any of them. My sister is in love."

My gaze narrowed. "She's what?"

"In love."

Something dark and unwanted slithered through my veins.

Adriana's wide eyes came to me like she just realized she'd said too much. She tipped her entire glass of wine back. I hadn't even noticed her acquire another.

I shook my head, agitated. "You puke tonight, I'm not holding your hair. I don't do that shit."

"My sister will," she said, like she was planning on throwing up. "Are we done getting to know each other then?"

"For now."

"Thank God," she muttered, getting to her feet and drunkenly drifting away to join one of her loud cousins. The girl had already introduced herself to me. Well, she'd come up and said, "Mamma was right. David don't got a thing on you," before winking and then disappearing. Strange fucking family.

I accepted another glass of whiskey from a server's tray, ignoring my cousin Lorenzo who came to sit next to me. He pushed his jacket open and shoved his hands in his pockets. Who the hell knew where he'd been, but I'd rather he be anywhere but staring at Elena Abelli. Just the idea itched beneath my skin.

In a moment of silence, Lorenzo's gaze followed some Abelli jail-bait's ass as she walked across the lawn. "What'd he do to you?" He nodded toward the blond prick I guessed I hadn't been secretive about wanting to put a bullet in.

"Pissed me off," was all I said, swirling my glass of whiskey.

"Must have been bad, then. Takes a lot to piss you off. Let me guess, he insulted your mamma?"

"No."

"Papà?"

"No."

"Your most handsome cousin? Six-two, dark-haired, big cock—"

"Lorenzo?" I said dryly.

"Yeah?"

"Fuck off."

Lorenzo laughed, slapped my shoulder hard enough to slosh some whiskey over the rim of my glass, and then left.

Told you, fucking idiot cousins.

CHAPTER
Ten

"Whether we fall by ambition, blood, or lust, like diamonds
we are cut with our own dust."
—John Webster

Elena

IT WAS SILVER, TINY, AND REFLECTIVE. I COULD ALMOST SEE MY FACE IN IT. Gianna's dress, of course. Long feather earrings, green heels, with her hair piled on the top of her head and no makeup but red lipstick made up her ensemble tonight.

" . . . If you're going to do it, do it with a male stripper. Trust me on this one." She was talking to my fifteen-year-old cousin Emma, who sat at the kitchen island sipping punch through a straw while looking bored.

All my aunts conversed about Adriana's bachelorette party as I sat off to the side and across from Nonna at the table, with a cup of coffee in front of her. We'd only heard that tiny bit of Gianna's conversation before my family's noise drowned out the rest.

I shook my head, slightly amused, but more unsettled. The words Oscar Perez had whispered in my ear earlier sank to the pit of my stomach. He'd pulled me aside once more to tell me to smile, that it would complement my *belleza*—whatever that meant. I didn't speak Spanish and I never wanted to. The beautiful language sounded harsh and invasive from his lips. I hated when someone told me to smile, as if a smile of mine belonged to them and not me.

He never had clarified why he'd be upset that I ran away and slept with a man, but there was only one reason I could ascertain: He thought he was going to marry me. It was hard to imagine Papà would agree to it considering Oscar wasn't even Italian, but why else would I have sat next to him at dinner when I never had to before?

"You are unhappy."

My gaze coasted from the scratches in the wooden table to Nonna's brown eyes. I shook my head. "No, I'm not." I would never let a man like Oscar Perez steal my happiness.

"You are not a good liar, *cara mia*."

I didn't respond, uncertain of what to say.

"The littlest problems seem so great to those who are young," she lamented. "I used to worry like you, you know. Do you know what it got me? Not a thing. Do not waste your time on things you cannot change." She stood up, bracing a hand on the table. "I'm going to bed."

"Goodnight, Nonna."

She stopped, turning to me. "Do you know what you need to do when you are unhappy?"

I didn't want to argue with her that I was *not* unhappy, so I raised a brow. "What?"

"Something exciting."

"Like?"

"I don't know. Maybe smoking cigarettes with handsome young men."

Ugh. A smile pulled on my lips. Only she would think of Nicolas as a young man.

"Goodnight, *tesoro*." Nonna winked.

The candle's flame danced, a bleak reminder of false smiles in the orange, mesmerizing light. Sheer curtains blew in the light summer breeze, and a lamp cast a soft glow against the wall of shelved books. Frank Sinatra leaked under the library door so quietly it could be a distant memory of a similar night half a century ago.

I sat with my legs folded against my side in a seat by the fireplace, a book lying on the arm. I hadn't read more than two pages until I'd given up and rested my head against the chair and stared at the candle filling the room with the smell of lavender. My heels lay forgotten on the floor, the white bows unraveled across the red oriental rug.

I'd escaped the kitchen as soon as I could, my mamma's talk about the wedding an annoying noise that became louder and louder until I needed silence. It wasn't even about Oscar Perez anymore. It was about words unsaid and a future uncertain.

Like the hard shell of a coconut, the Sweet Abelli shielded the real me from the world. It couldn't be cracked without strong tools. Lowering that barrier bared a part of me not many had seen—a me that *felt*. A vulnerable me. I wasn't sure why I let Nicolas Russo see that side. Maybe it was because his indifference made me believe he didn't want to crack me.

My eyes shot up when the click of the library door hit my ears, and, as if my thoughts had conjured him, Nicolas stepped in.

When his gaze came up from the floor and he noticed me, he stopped short. For a second, I thought he was going to turn and leave without a word just because I was here. His stare was an indifferent, condescending one—like he'd come into *his* library to find a servant in his chair. The man really wanted nothing to do with me. Well, I didn't like him either. Truthfully, it was mostly because he didn't like me.

His gaze narrowed. "Why aren't you at the party?"

"Why aren't *you*?" I countered.

He ran a hand down his tie, watching me in a calculated way, like he was weighing the pros and cons of my presence. It didn't look like there were many pros.

Making up his mind, he shut the door and headed to the mini-bar, never answering my question. He poured a drink, and I tried to pretend he wasn't here, that his presence hadn't filled the room, making my mind now useless. Nonetheless, I found myself watching him, every smooth move as he filled a glass tumbler with whiskey.

My skin lit like a live wire, the fabric of my dress felt heavy, and the breeze from the open window brushed my shoulders. As he walked past, I pretended to be engrossed in the little black sentences before me, but in reality, I didn't take in one word of John F. Kennedy's assassination. History, facts, they made me feel better in a time of doubt, because someday I would be nothing but a memory, just like them.

He sat in a gray armchair by the window and pulled out his phone. He leaned forward, his elbows resting on his knees. He'd unbuttoned his jacket, showing his black vest that hugged his flat stomach. His tie hung askew from pulling on it, and the visual suddenly made me wonder: *What does he look like in the morning, all disheveled?* I swallowed.

He might be able to pull off his suit like a gentleman, but once again the red, busted knuckles of the hand holding his phone told me his appearance was just a façade.

Light scruff covered his jaw, and his hair was as dark as his suit, the top thick and messy. He was intimidating, with a heavy presence and a glare that burned, but when he wore a soft, sober expression like now . . . he didn't even have to look at me to make me burn.

He glanced over and caught my gaze. "You've got to work on that staring."

My pulse fluttered in my throat, and warmth rushed to my face.

His eyes fell to my cheeks.

And then he did something I never expected. Maybe it was from disbelief, or maybe he thought I was ridiculous. I didn't know, and I didn't care. He laughed. Softly, *darkly*. The kind of laugh that has no good intentions. The kind of laugh the walls don't forget.

Warmth curled low in my stomach, and I couldn't help it, I stared even more. He had white teeth and sharp incisors, just like the villain he was. When he glanced at me sideways, with dark mirth in his gaze, a flame pulsed between my legs.

"*Jesus*," he said under his breath, running a hand through his hair.

I leaned my head against the chair, my teeth tugging on my bottom lip. He glanced at me one more time as his laugh faded, his amusement disappearing into a tense atmosphere that sparked. A warm breath of air breezed through the window and I shivered.

I didn't know how long we sat in the same room, in silence, not far apart. Time wasn't a factor. The moment was recorded each time he shifted, looked up from his phone, took a drink, glanced my way when I'd flip a page or brush my hair off my shoulders.

I thought I was doing well, that I was turning pages at an equivalent of what someone would if they were reading them. But I was thrown off when his gaze pulled up from his phone and rested on my face. It settled there for a moment, before running down my bared neck and shoulders. My breathing stilled when it trailed over the curves of my breasts and down my stomach. And I flushed when it went lower to my thighs, tracing my legs until it reached my pink-painted toenails peeking out of my dress.

He was doing the staring now, but I didn't have the courage to call him out on it. I'd been stared at enough times I'd gotten good at ignoring it, but not once had it ever made me feel like this. Over-heated, itchy, *breathless*.

Whitney Houston's *I Will Always Love You* seeped under the door, and I could hear Benito belting out the words. He was the first to start the karaoke, and ironically, it was always to iconic love songs. My cousin wouldn't sleep with the same girl twice unless she had double-Ds. His words, not mine.

When he mangled his next line, a soft laugh escaped me. I let myself glance at Nicolas, expecting some amusement, but my laughter faded when I found him already looking at me. The darkness in his eyes shaded his sober expression.

The music and voices outside the door became indiscernible noise as blood drummed in my ears. He got up, set his unfinished glass of whiskey on a side table, and headed to leave. He stopped by my side. The ability to breathe ceased to exist when his thumb ran down my cheek, as light as satin and as rough as his voice. He gripped my chin and turned my face toward his.

We looked at each other for seconds that felt like minutes.

"Don't follow men into dark corners." A spark flickered to life in his eyes. It softened when his thumb skimmed the edge of my bottom lip. "Next time, you might not get out alive."

With the warning hanging in the air, his hand slipped from my face and he left the room without another word.

I rested my head against the armchair and breathed normally for the first time since he'd walked through the door. I didn't know what that was, why it felt like I had a continual live wire under my skin in his presence, but I didn't want to analyze it. I knew it wasn't a good thing. Anything that stops your breath can't be good for you.

My gaze fell to his drink on the table.

I was out of my mind.

I was *burning*.

I closed the book and got up from my chair. Walking around the side table, I twirled the tumbler on the lacquered wood between loose fingers.

The remaining liquid sat on the bottom, golden and forgotten.

I never did like whiskey.

But I brought it to my lips . . . and I drank it anyway.

CHAPTER
Eleven

"If I can stop one heart from breaking, I shall not live in vain."
—Emily Dickinson

Elena

THE WHISKEY WAS A MEMORY OF WARMTH IN MY STOMACH AS I SAT ON MY haunches before my sister's TV stand. *"Fright Night, Evil Dead,* or *Night of the Living Dead?"* I placed the movies on my lap and waited for a response.

Adriana's muffled words sounded from the bed. *"Sixteen Candles."*

My eyes widened. *"Sixteen Candles?"*

"Mmhmm."

This was bad. *Very* bad.

"You're absolutely sure?"

A sigh. "Yes, Elena."

"Okay. . . let me go get it."

I eyed my sister like she'd grown two more heads as I headed out of the room. However, she only looked drunk and tired, covered by a *Star Wars* blanket.

I returned from my room a moment later, popped the DVD in, and climbed into bed next to her. Stealing half the blanket, I pulled it over the dress I didn't have the energy to change. Soft light flashed from the TV in the dark room as we watched the movie in silence.

"Elena?" Her voice was quiet.

"Yeah?"

"What do you think of Nico?"

I hesitated.

"I'm not sure," I finally responded.

"I talked to him a bit tonight."

"You did?"

"Yeah. It wasn't so bad. He's a little rude, but I don't hate him."

I focused on the movie because I didn't know what to say. I was glad for my sister, that she found something to talk about with him . . . However, my chest tightened in a strange way.

"Elena?" she said softly, grabbing something off the nightstand.

"Yeah?"

She handed her cell phone to me without looking. "Please send it. I can't."

I took the phone and read the text already typed out to Samantha— well, that was the codename for Ryan. A simple "Goodbye" was all it said.

My throat constricted, but I pushed the little button that could change lives and break hearts with nothing but an electronic word. I did it for Ryan's sake, and wished I could go back and do the same for another's.

"Done," I whispered.

We lay side by side and watched a girl fall in love.

One of us already had, and the other knew she never would.

I sat at the kitchen table, legs crisscrossed on the chair, watching a raindrop make its way down the windowpane.

"No, no, no!" Mamma tossed the wooden spoon on the island, having just tasted the red sauce Adriana had prepared. Mamma's sweatsuit was purple today, and her hair was half-up like it always was. "Now you've gone and killed him."

Adriana sighed, her expression tightening with frustration. "How have I killed him again already?"

"That sauce is so bitter he would keel over."

Amusement filled me. The last pot of sauce, Adriana had taken too long and poor Nicolas died of starvation.

Mamma shook her head. "*Incredibile.* I don't know how you went on this long not knowing how to cook *una semplice salsa di spaghetti.* I should pull you from those classes you take and make you spend the time in the kitchen."

Adriana leaned against the counter. A white apron covered her *Hamlet* t-shirt that was longer than her shorts, and a yellow bandana kept her hair back from her face. "Elena isn't a good cook either."

I frowned.

"Elena is not getting married in two weeks!"

The soft patter of rain hitting the windows filled the room, a quiet discomfort replacing any words. The need to ease the tension rushed over me. It was what I was good for, after all.

"I doubt she will kill the man, Mamma. If he can survive being shot a number of times like I'm sure he has, then he should outlive Adriana's cooking."

"Three times," Adriana piped up.

My brows knitted. "What?"

"He's been shot three times."

"*Mamma mia,*" Mamma scolded. "Do not talk of such things."

A certain interest ran over me, and, ignoring Mamma, I asked, "How do you know that?"

My sister's sparkling gaze came my way. "I asked him last night."

"You what? *Adriana!*"

I sat forward in my chair. "And he told you?"

"Well . . . not exactly. I asked him, and he only looked down on me like I was annoying him. But then Gianna, who was overhearing the conversation, told me three times."

"Do you have a brain in your head? Why would you ask him something like that?"

Neither of us looked in Mamma's direction. A smile pulled on our lips. We were now playing a popular game to see who could shock Mamma enough she'd storm from the room, berating us in Italian. It usually began with ignoring her a few times.

"Is Gianna his sister?" I asked, though I was 99 percent sure he was an only child. She could have been a cousin, but somehow, I knew she wasn't.

Adriana laughed. "No. Stepmother."

My jaw dropped. "She's younger than him!"

"A year," Adriana confirmed.

"My God. Can you imagine sleeping with a man more than twice your age?"

"*Elena!*"

Adriana's gaze widened. "You think she had sex with his papà?"

"Stop with this talk."

I pursed my lips. "Well, they were married. They at least had missionary—"

"*Basta!*" Mamma headed for the door, tossed her apron on the counter, and spewed Italian about her heathen daughters the whole way.

Our laughter filled the kitchen.

"I can't believe she's his stepmother," I said, before adding, "Or, was."

"I know." Adriana stuck her finger in the sauce and tasted it, grimacing. "But I don't think they have a mother-son relationship."

"No," I said, "more like the other way around."

Adriana shook her head. "No, not like that either."

"What do you mean?"

"I would bet my entire costume collection they've slept together."

My eyes widened. "Really?"

"Yep," she said, wiping the island down.

My sister was usually quiet, blending into the background at parties and events, but that only made her skilled at reading people—when she took the time or cared about doing it, anyway. She was probably right. How very . . . blasphemous. Though, I wouldn't have expected much else from the boss.

I hopped off my chair, headed to the pot on the stove, and tasted a little from the wooden spoon. Bitterness exploded in my mouth. "Wow, that's, um . . ."

Adriana laughed while struggling to reach a cup on the top shelf. She hopped and growled when she still couldn't get it. She turned around, giving up, her gaze narrowed.

"Benito and Dominic are downstairs," I told her. "They're probably hungry."

"Why would I care—?" She paused. Understanding filled her eyes and then she pushed off the counter. "I'll go tell them lunch is ready."

Red and orange streetlights blurred beyond the drips of rain running down the glass. The sky was dark, pretending to be night when it was only six o'clock on a summer's day.

Benito's phone flashed and buzzed in the console, *again*. Ironically enough, Benito reminded me of Manny Ribera from *Scarface*, in looks and personality. I could count on him flirting with at least one woman everywhere we went, like clockwork.

"Read it, Elena."

"No," I protested. "The last time I did that I saw something I didn't want to see."

"Then don't bitch at me for checking it."

Ugh. I reached forward and read it. "From 'Blonde Angela.'" I didn't blink twice to see that he had to mark his female contacts by more than their names, probably because there were simply too many. He wouldn't want to mix them up. "I don't want to see you anymore," I read blandly and set the phone back in the console before a "goodbye" picture could be received.

His brows furrowed with one hand on the wheel. He wore black pants and a white dress shirt, no tie. It was a casual day for him. There was a high possibility he took longer than me to get ready in the mornings.

Mamma and Papà had a dinner planned with one of my father's connections, and I'd told Nonna not to worry about coming because of the rain falling like it never had before. So, it was just Benito and me, and he would only drop me off like he usually did, before driving to whatever girl's house in the meantime. Not Angela's now, though.

My cousin sighed and ran a hand through his dark, gelled-back hair. "As a woman, Elena, how would you interpret that text?"

I paused. "Well, I think it means she doesn't want to see you anymore."

"And that includes sex?"

"Yep."

He frowned. "Dammit."

"Double-Ds?"

"Yeah," he said sadly.

I copied his tone. "Shame."

He pulled up to the curb outside the theater, reached across me, and pushed the door open. "Go kill it, cuz. Be back at nine."

"Thanks." I hopped out of the car and grabbed my duffel bag from the backseat.

"Elena." Benito's expression was serious as he leaned over and stretched his arm across the passenger seat headrest. "You think her text applies to oral, too?"

I rolled my eyes. "God, you're disgusting."

He grinned. "Break a leg!"

With my bag over my shoulder, I headed inside and said hello to a few other dancers on the way. It wasn't a large theater, but it was upscale—like my papà would ever allow me to dance in a hole in the wall. Sparkling lights, cream walls, and gold and red accents. It was a beautiful auditorium. I loved the flash of it all: the makeup, the dress, the friendships I'd gained—as shallow as they were—but for me, dance was merely a great form of exercise. The small amount of passion I'd once held for it was fading away, and I wasn't sure how long I'd continue with it.

A brush of air rushed over me, followed by a deep voice. "Say you'll go out with me."

Without looking at the man matching my steps, I shook my head, a smile pulling on my lips. "No."

"Sushi?"

I wrinkled my nose.

"Okay, no sushi. Italian?"

"Ha ha," I laughed.

"Are you coming tomorrow?"

Tyler was lean, like most dancers were, with dirty blond hair and a crooked smile. He was cute, polite, but not my type. He was a friend who wanted more, and for his sake I'd never let anything happen. I'd learned my lesson.

Sometimes I wondered how he would react if I told him the truth about my family. I doubted he'd still ask me out every time he saw me. Anyone could put together who my papà was if they merely Googled his name. My classmates at the all-girls school I'd attended had found out early on, and I'd practically been a pariah. Adriana had made lots of friends in her drama circle, but I never found the same.

"Yeah, I'm coming," I said. "I'm bringing my cousin, if that's okay."

"Oh, yeah. That Benito. Your family aware women don't need a chaperone anymore?"

I smiled. "They're aware. They just don't care."

Chatter grew louder as we reached backstage where ten or so other dancers congregated.

"Last offer," he said firmly. "Cheeseburgers. Bring Benito with you. We'll make it a threesome."

I laughed. "I don't think he's into guys."

It was his turn for a "Ha ha," as we parted ways.

CHAPTER
Twelve

"Every savage can dance."
—Jane Austen

Elena

I LEANED AGAINST THE ALLEY DOOR, THE METAL HARD AND COLD AGAINST MY back. Mist fell, mixing with the sweat dripping down my bare midsection. Tire noise, sirens, and an occasional laugh from a close bar filtered into the alleyway.

"You've got the right idea." Sierra stepped outside and pulled her blond hair off her sweaty face and into a bun.

The red curtain had opened and then closed, some laterals, spirals, and stag leaps in between, and the recital was a success. The dance was based on a man who died for love—a modern Romeo & Juliet tale. I played Death.

The performance was slow and dramatic, but it had a beautiful, haunting tone. Why must everything have a happily ever after? Aren't the most memorable, poignant moments of history tragic? I had always appreciated sad endings. I was a realist, not a romantic.

I talked to Sierra for a little while about her two-year-old son and being a single mom, and then decided Benito was probably growing tired of waiting for me.

"I'll see you later, Sierra. Tomorrow at the party, if you're coming."

"Yes, I'm coming! My mom's watching Nathan. Please tell me your hot cousin is coming."

I groaned with a playful roll of my eyes. "He'll be there."

"Great. See you then." She winked.

I threw on an off-the-shoulder top and grabbed my bag before heading to the front. I'd just made it out the stage doors when an arm draped around my shoulder.

"I know I said last offer, but I forgot I haven't suggested Chinese yet."

I shook my head with a smile, but truthfully, there wasn't a chance I was walking all the way to the car with Tyler's arm around me. I loved Benito, but I could never forget he worked for my papà. It was his own father, my uncle Manuel, who was responsible for the death that haunted me. Benito had done nothing but watch, and I held no belief he wouldn't let it happen again.

Just as we reached the front hall and I was about to slide Tyler's arm off my shoulders, my heart stilled and so did my feet.

Nicolas stood near the doors, leaning against the wall with his hands in his pockets. With his black suit lit by sparkling lighting, he could pass as a handsome gentleman. One only needed to glance up and see the dark look in his eyes to know it was only smoke. What worried me the most was that his stare, edged with venom, was aimed at Tyler.

My stomach twisted, and I shrugged Tyler's arm off. He seemed to notice Nicolas's presence at that moment.

"Family?" he asked hesitantly.

"Um . . . yeah." It was sort of true, I guessed. I wasn't going to explain all the details with Nicolas's burning gaze in this direction. He must believe that since he was marrying into my family it was now his obligation to deal with any men who came my way.

Frustration crept up my back. I had plenty of male cousins and uncles and a temperamental brother—the last thing I needed was another man butting into my life. I imagined everything Nicolas did, he did it with his all, because not even Benito would wear that expression over a man having his arm around me.

"So . . . I'm guessing Chinese is a no?"

"Just go, Tyler."

"All right." He took a step back, probably put off by my tone. "I'll see you tomorrow then, Elena."

The worry tightening in my chest released when he left, still alive. I swore all the men in my life were psychotic. It was at moments like this when I hated it. I'd only wanted out at one point in the past. When it felt like I was nothing but a beautiful girl trapped in a world of forced smiles, with a grim future in the distance. The parties, the dancing, the fake laughs—it all exploded, until I stood alone for the first time in a city I'd never truly experienced.

It didn't take long to realize I didn't belong, that I was already stained by the world I was raised in. That a man with a clean conscience and clean hands would never fit me just right. I'd destroyed a decent man's life, and while he'd touched me in places I'd never been touched before, I'd wished he did it a little rougher. I'd wished he was tainted by the darkness, as the men I was used to were.

Everyone knew you didn't fall in love with a man in my world, like the one who stood before me now. Not unless you wanted your heart shattered into a thousand tiny pieces. No, I'd never fall in love. Truly, I'd never expected to. You didn't mourn something you'd always known you couldn't have.

At least this man wasn't mine. He was too distracting, too fascinating . . . I'd never make it out alive.

I adjusted the strap on my shoulder and walked toward him, my heart beating to every step I took. I stopped a few feet from him. With that look in his eyes, I wouldn't put myself in this man's reach for anything.

"Your papà know you're kissing men on stage?"

I faltered, my clammy hand tightening on my bag. Nicolas must have been here long enough to catch the end of the show. Where in the world was Benito? This man was going to kill me by the look of it.

My feet shifted. "I didn't kiss anyone."

Technically, it was a lie, but I was going to talk myself out of this. Because after Nicolas had overheard Tyler ask me out, and the fact that it was Tyler who I'd kissed—well, this might seem worse than it was. To the men in my family's ears, it would sound like I'd gotten naked with the man. I told you—*psychotic*. Apparently, Russo men were the same.

Nicolas pushed off the wall and walked within a foot of me. "Yeah? Why don't you explain what it was you were doing then?"

My cheeks grew hot. "I was Death. I was . . . sucking his life away."

Maybe that was the wrong way to explain it, because his expression grew even darker. I thought "sucking" might have done it. Ugh. His stare crept under my skin, flustering me.

"It was completely platonic," I said.

His gaze sparked. "You put your lips on another man's and suck, it's never platonic."

He made it sound so dirty when it had really been a dry, unmoving kiss. Anger simmered in my veins. Who was he to tell me who I could kiss—Mr. I'll Sleep with My Stepmom and Other Men's Girlfriends?

Frustration rose in my throat, mangling any possible comeback, so I only brushed past him. He grabbed my duffel bag off my shoulder as I passed. His gaze was still heated, but he followed me out the doors.

The mist fell steady, and I blinked it off my eyelashes as I searched for his car. It sat at the curb, all black and shiny. I wasn't getting in it; I'd wait for Benito. I stood on the sidewalk while Nicolas tossed my bag in the backseat.

He shut the door and turned to look at me. "You gonna stand there all night or get in the car?"

"Where's Benito?"

He opened the passenger side door. "He's got some business with your papà."

From past experience, that meant something bad was happening in New York tonight. I was surprised Papà had sent Nicolas to chauffeur me, considering his lack of trust with me and men. But I was also a little uneasy he felt he needed Nicolas to take me home.

I'd always felt safe and it was probably nothing, but if there was a reason Papà needed to worry about my safety I was glad he'd sent Nicolas. The man had a million enemies and he had stayed alive this long.

Though, the idea of being locked in a car with him made my stomach flutter with nerves. I imagined I'd feel similar right before jumping out of a plane. I didn't know why he created such visceral reactions in me, but when he said, "Car. Now, Elena," I'd never disliked anything more.

I wanted to make him say *please*, but as my gaze coasted to his, the dark storm that looked back at me changed my mind real quick. I walked past him and got in his stupid car.

My frustration mixed with turmoil. What would he do with the information about Tyler? I didn't think Papà would care so much about a stage kiss, but with his arm around me, asking me out . . . my stomach turned. That could sound bad.

I was resenting Nicolas Russo so much right now that I tried to ignore the warm, masculine scent filling the car. Sandalwood, clean skin, and a certain danger that made my pulse drift between my legs. I tried to ignore the way it invaded my senses and made the corners of my mind fuzzy. It hit me like a shot of liquor, and I distracted myself with buckling my seatbelt.

When he sat in the driver's seat and shut the door, the car felt infinitely smaller. Quiet enough I could hear my heartbeat and warm enough the heater had to be on. Was it his body putting out that much heat?

Mist hit the windshield, running down the glass and blurring the outside world. I was alone with him in such a small space. The fact resounded in my mind, playing havoc on my nervous system.

Without a word to me, Nicolas typed out a text. Probably to my papà. I could only imagine it read something like: *Package picked up safely.*

My fingernails dug into my palms.

How did I even address him? I'd never found it so difficult to speak with someone before, but all rational thoughts flew away when he was near.

"Nicolas." I hesitated. "Maybe we started off on the wrong foot . . . at church last weekend. I didn't mean to glare at you, truly."

His gaze flicked to me. A hint of amusement played in it, though it wasn't normal amusement. This man did everything a little dark.

My cheeks warmed. "And I wanted to say I apologize. I was uncertain about the marriage in the beginning, but now . . . I think you and Adriana will be . . . good together." I forced my sweetest smile.

It didn't get me the reaction I wanted.

He let out a sardonic breath and tossed his phone in the center console. "Glad to hear it, but I'm still telling your papà about your romance with the dancer."

My smile and stomach fell.

He put the key in the ignition and started the car. A metal song played quietly on the radio. I couldn't help but notice it was the same station Adriana listened to sometimes.

"Wait," I rushed out, putting one hand on the gearshift as if I could stop him. He glanced at it and then back at me, his gaze conveying he would remove it if I didn't. "I'm telling you, there is nothing going on with Tyler. It wasn't even a kiss! I was merely . . . taking his life away. It was completely platonic."

He didn't say anything, but his stillness made me believe he was wavering.

I swallowed. "Nicolas, please . . ."

His eyes sparked. "What's my name?"

I paused, opened my mouth but then closed it. I didn't want to say it. Nicolas Russo had a reputation. Nicolas Russo was a stranger. Nicolas was distant. I didn't want to call him Nico. It would flow too easily off my lips. Sound too good on my tongue.

We sat in tense silence for a moment, before he gave his head a shake. "Usually, when someone wants something, they appease the one they're trying to persuade. A basis of negotiating." He told me this like I was stupid, and I flushed in irritation.

"There's no negotiating with a cheat." The words were out of my mouth before I could stop them.

He ran a hand across his face, wiping off a hint of amusement. "Touché." Glancing at me sideways, he gave me an appraisal, maybe impressed I had the guts to say what I did. Licking his lips, his deep, serious voice rushed over me. "So prove it to me."

My brows knitted. "Prove what?"

"That it was platonic."

"How am I supposed to—?" My stomach erupted with butterflies when it dawned on me. The shock of what he wanted me to do settled in the space like an elephant in the room. "You're serious?"

"Deadly."

It was this moment right here that his reputation became clear to me. His cousin's death hadn't done it. The articles of his pursuits hadn't done it, but his cool, indifferent expression as he laid this trap for me did.

He was waiting for me to say it would be inappropriate. Then my "it was platonic" excuse would crash and burn before my eyes.

I didn't know why he cared so much about Tyler, but I was betting he'd gain a little male satisfaction from keeping his future sister-in-law away from non-Italian men. Benito always stayed in the damn car—why couldn't he have picked me up today?

I wasn't going to fall into his trap. That meant I could only call Nicolas Russo's bluff.

"Okay." My calm response filled the small space, like even the air hadn't expected it.

The tiniest flicker passed through Nicolas's gaze. He scraped his teeth across his bottom lip, maybe in surprise I hadn't walked into the hole he dug for me. The action only made me stare at his mouth. Warmth filled my stomach.

"Okay," he finally responded, his eyes darkening around the edges.

What.

He thought I was bluffing. I wasn't bluffing—he was supposed to be. Nicolas was playing with me. He wanted to see me squirm—I could see that leaking through his cool expression. It sent the burn of frustration through me.

"Okay."

We stared at one another.

Neither of us was willing to admit we'd been bluffing. Mine for the sake of Tyler's well-being and his for the sake of his giant ego. Unease rattled in my chest. I didn't think I was getting out of this.

"If I do this, you'll keep it to yourself?" I unbuckled my seatbelt and his gaze tracked the movement.

His jaw ticked in thought, but the tension in his shoulders told me this was the last thing on earth he wanted to do. Maybe he shouldn't underestimate his opponents then. His gaze came to me, one nod of his head, and those butterflies in my stomach took flight.

I told myself to get it over with, but the tingles of nervousness and expectation that vibrated under every inch of my skin slowed my movements.

I rested my hand on the console, planning not to touch him anywhere I didn't need to, and leaned in. He watched me with an expression like he was in line at the DMV. Five inches away, four, three . . . I jumped the gap.

My lips touched his to *Snap Your Fingers, Snap Your Neck* playing on the radio. Soft and warm, his scent was concentrated and mind-numbing. I hadn't even moved my lips, only pressed them to his, but a moan climbed up my throat. I kept it locked inside.

I couldn't breathe; every inch of my skin was on fire.

Just like I'd done with Tyler, though nothing like it at all, I inhaled a breath of air from the slight part between his lips. One second, two seconds, three. I stole his breath, yet my head grew light as if he took mine.

I could hear nothing but the drumming of my blood in my ears. Feel nothing but the softness of his lips and the tingles beneath my skin. A heaviness settled between my legs.

Then I did something I shouldn't have done. I couldn't resist, couldn't even think about stopping myself: My lips closed around his top one for a wet, warm moment. It was merely a pull on one of his lips, a tiny taste of what it would be like to truly kiss him. I pulled away, fell into my seat, and stared forward.

"See," I breathed. "Completely platonic."

His gaze burned my cheek for too many seconds. Though he must have agreed, because he only put the car in drive and pulled away from the curb.

CHAPTER
Thirteen

"I like to be myself. Misery loves company."
—Anthony Corallo

Nico

THERE WERE TWO RULES I ALWAYS FOLLOWED.

Never leave the house without my .45.

And never put myself in a position I knew I couldn't get out of.

I had more enemies than the President of the United States, and I'd only survived this long by following those two simple rules. I'd never been tempted to break them—up until I was locked in a car with Elena Abelli.

Gas station fluorescent lights flickered and buzzed above my head. Mist fell from a dark, starless sky, each drop sizzling on my skin. I was fucking burning up. I took my suit jacket off and tossed it in the backseat. Pulled on my tie and leaned against the car door. I inhaled, smelling nothing but rain and gasoline, and listened to the tire noise from the expressway.

I could have laughed, though I wasn't amused at all. The smallest sexual interaction I'd ever had with a woman had gotten to me so much I had to pretend I needed gas just so I could get the fuck out of that car. Heat crawled beneath my skin, and I rolled up my long sleeves.

Elena Abelli pressing her lips to mine was in breach of rule number two. I'd known it wasn't something I could handle, yet like an idiot I'd let my dick guide me. It hadn't killed me, but fuck, it felt like it. I was more worked up than I'd ever been. I swore, straight lust in all its itchy, burning glory rushed through my veins.

I put a cigarette between my lips and slipped my hands into my pockets. I wasn't going to light it. If I did, I'd have to admit she unsettled me, and I refused to do that over a fucking grade-school kiss.

I leaned against the car for far longer than it took to fill up the five dollars' worth of tank space. I paid at the pump—couldn't go in because I had a fucking hard-on.

The mist began to cool me down, but before I knew it, I was sucked back: her soft lips on mine, her shallow breath in my ears, the tiniest brush of her tongue, hot and *wet*, before she pulled away. *Fuck* me. Heat raced straight to my groin.

I didn't know how I'd managed not to grab her nape, pull her closer, slide my tongue against hers and taste the inside of her mouth. It hadn't felt like a want at the time—it felt like a *need*. And that realization gave me the strength to hold back. After the night before, especially. I'd thought she was materialistic and shallow, yet she watched documentaries, read history, and was reserved. I wanted to know what she did during the day and what kind of thoughts consumed such a pretty head.

A car door shut behind me.

I turned to see Elena looking at me over the top of the car. She wore a high ponytail I should've never wrapped around my fist. Now I could never forget how silky it really was.

She cocked her head toward the gas station. "Bathroom."

I nodded once, then gave her my back, because the last thing I needed right now was to watch her ass as she walked away. She was wearing leggings—enough said.

I'd underestimated her. I'd thought she would refuse to reenact the stage kiss, therefore giving me a leg to stand on by calling that "platonic" excuse bullshit. Truthfully, I didn't give a fuck if it had been. It pissed me off.

I wanted to make her squirm after I'd spent the entire week trying to drive her half-naked body from my mind. Except she didn't squirm; she undid her seatbelt and laid one on me. She called it platonic, while I had been one second from losing my grasp on self-control and touching her everywhere she'd let me.

Shit, was she irritating—a little nuisance that had wiggled beneath my skin. She was supposed to be wallpaper, but I couldn't stop my gaze from finding her whenever she was in the room.

In the library the night before, she'd stared at me unashamedly, and fuck if it hadn't made me feel itchy as shit. When I couldn't take it any longer, I'd called her out on it and she hadn't even said a word, only continued to watch me with the softest brown eyes I'd ever seen as pink tinted her cheeks.

Never thought a blush could get me so hard.

Watching her with Tyler made me wonder if he was the man she was in love with. She hadn't hesitated to kiss me to protect him. My teeth clenched. The ring on her finger was from a man. I'd bet money on it. Tyler? Or the man she'd run away to be with?

Jesus, why did I care?

I wasn't going to worship Elena with the rest of the male population of New York. I'd stand on the sidelines and watch the idiots pine for her attention. I ran a hand across my face, pulled the cigarette from my lips and dropped it in my shirt pocket.

As I twisted the cap on the gas tank, my attention coasted up to see Elena walking toward the car, her steps quick and her eyes toward the concrete.

My gaze narrowed. I'd learned how to read body language over the years. It was good to know when someone was going to shoot at you in the middle of a meeting. And Elena's posture raised all my alarms. Avoiding eye contact, tight shoulders—she was stressed.

"Elena," I said, trying to get her to look at me.

She didn't stop at my voice. She climbed in my Audi and slammed the door. My chest burned, and without realizing how I'd gotten there I stood on her side of the car.

"What happened?" I demanded as soon as I opened the door.

She shook her head. "Nothing. Can we go?"

Maybe I'd believe that if she wasn't such a fidgety mess. But nah, not even then. Everyone knew that when a woman said *nothing* she was fucking lying.

"Yeah."

Her gaze shot to me, and now I *had* her. Now I could see the turmoil swimming in those eyes.

"Yeah?" she whispered.

"Yeah. After you tell me what the fuck happened."

She sighed and rested her head against the seat. "Nothing. I just want to go home."

I dropped to my haunches, grabbed her chin, and turned her face to mine. "I'm not leaving until you tell me what happened."

Her teeth tugged at her bottom lip, and she averted her gaze. "I don't want you to make it a big deal."

"Won't." *Depends.*

"Promise you won't do anything."

"Promise." *Lie.*

Those soft brown eyes met mine, working their way into my chest. "The cashier . . ." She swallowed. " . . . Well, he told me I had to buy something because I used the bathroom. And then I told him I didn't have any money on me, and . . ." She hesitated.

"Jesus, spit it the fuck out," I snapped. Anger crept beneath my skin, slow but *searing.* "Did he touch you?"

"No!" she responded too quickly. "It's not that big of a deal . . . he just threatened he would if I didn't leave."

A deathly stillness fell over me. "You're lying."

She tossed her head, trying to shake off my hand.

My grip tightened. "Where?"

Her eyes came to mine with a spark. "He smacked my ass and told me I could pay another way, all right?"

I had to take a second to swallow down the burning rage so I could form a coherent sentence. Could this woman go anywhere without men losing their goddamn minds? The irrational part of me grew agitated, pounding at my chest and shaking the bars of its cage.

I ran my thumb down the indention in her chin. "Which hand did he use?"

Her gaze widened. "No," she breathed. "You promised!"

Her voice was distorted by the rage rushing through me, drumming in my ears. Red crept into my vision, until she was covered in it. I closed my eyes, took a deep breath of gasoline fumes, and then stood.

"No, don't. Please, please, don't, Nicolas," she pleaded.

"I'm just going to talk to him."

"No, you aren't—"

I slammed her door.

A frustrated noise came from inside.

One lone black man was at the pump, filling up his old beater. A gas can sat on the oil-stained concrete; the one I had watched him fill while Elena was inside getting fucking *groped*. I grabbed the container and headed toward the station doors.

"What the fuck you think you doin', man?"

"Some friendly advice," I said without turning around. "Might get the fuck out of here if I were you."

It took him two seconds to put it together.

"Aw, *hell* no," I heard from behind me. A door slammed shut and a car drove off.

The 'P' on the Pronto sign flickered in and out. A bell chimed as I entered the harshly lit gas station with dirty, peeling laminate. The cashier stood behind the counter reading a magazine. He looked to be in his forties, with a balding head. His red, starched t-shirt said "David" in yellow.

"You the only one here tonight?"

The clerk flicked a gaze up, the end of a pen bit between his teeth. He pulled it out before saying in a heavy Long Island accent, "Yeah. What's it to you?"

I ignored the question and looked around the dump. "Nice place you got here. You own it?"

The clerk glanced at the gas can in my hand. "Yeah."

"Must be your livelihood, I imagine."

His expression turned stiff. "I don't know what you want, but I'm not interested."

"Can't afford new floors, nor to replace your sign out front. I'm sure all income is going straight home. Wife . . . kids, maybe." I undid the cap, and then sloshed some gasoline on the dirty laminate.

The clerk dropped his pen, taking a step back. "What the fuck are you doing?"

"The girl that just came in here?" I gave my head a shake. "Wrong girl, David." Gas splashed a shelf of postcards.

"I'm calling the cops." The clerk's voice shook. Out of the corner of my eye, I noticed he didn't reach for the phone. I glanced at the man to see he was focused on my forearm—on the ace of spades tattooed on the inside.

An amused breath escaped me. "I swear, this lack of anonymity ruins all my fucking fun. Should've never gotten the tat."

"I didn't know," the clerk blurted. "I didn't fucking know who she was!"

"I wanted your hand," I said, walking down aisles, sloshing gasoline on shelves, cooler doors, the rack of porn mags. "But that's a fucking mess, really. Don't have the right knife on me to do a good job."

The clerk stood, frozen and sweating.

"You got insurance, David?"

He swallowed. "Of course."

The smell of gasoline fumes consumed the gas station. I tossed the now-empty can on the floor and grabbed a Zippo lighter off a shelf. Ironically enough, one with the ace of spades on the sides. I thought for a moment about the location and class of the joint. "Hartford?"

"Y-yeah."

I placed a cigarette between my lips, a dark smile pulling on the corners. "The correct answer is you *had* insurance."

"Wait," he pleaded. "Fuck, I'm sorry. Let me apologize—"

His words became white noise in my head, a gurgling, annoying sound. Standing in front of the glass doors, I lit the cigarette between my lips. A cherry glowed at the end, and nicotine flowed through my blood.

With the lazy, autocratic stare I was known for, I told the wild-eyed, frozen clerk, "If you got a back door, you better find it."

A breath of smoke from my lips and the clerk was gone, slipping on gasoline all the way to the back room. Before he reached it, I flicked my cigarette to the laminate, silently hoping David wasn't quicker than he looked.

The bell dinged above my head as the old glass doors shut behind me. I slipped my hands into my pockets. Cool mist hit my face while the heat of a fire brushed my back.

The old Pronto lit up like a fucking Christmas tree.

CHAPTER *Fourteen*

"Heard melodies are sweet, but those unheard are sweeter."
—John Keats

Elena

"PAPÀ, I'D APPRECIATE IT IF NEXT TIME YOU WOULD SEND ANYONE—*anyone* at all—but Nicolas to pick me up."

I stood in my papà's office doorway, my duffel bag hanging from my shoulder. As soon as Nicolas had pulled into the driveway and I'd seen my father was home, I'd hopped out of the car and came straight here.

I had already been humiliated enough by the incident. I wasn't a girl who wanted to be saved or avenged. I just wanted to forget about it and put it behind me. But I couldn't do that because Nicolas had burned the entire gas station down. There would always be charred remains—and possibly a *body*—reminding me. I'd never seen the cashier come out. Sure, he was a disgusting creep, but did he deserve to *burn* to death? My throat tightened.

Papà set his pen down and gave me his "I'm listening" expression for the first time in a long time. "And why is that?"

I crossed my arms, saying simply, "He's psychotic, Papà."

At that moment, my back tingled in awareness, and my father's gaze coasted above my head. Apparently, Nicolas now came in and out of my house like he owned it.

I hadn't said a word to him the rest of the drive home, though he'd hardly tried to instigate a conversation. Between him threatening me about Tyler, kind of kissing him, and watching the gas station light up in my side-view mirror as we drove away, I was more frustrated than I'd ever been.

That kiss had made me hotter for more than I'd ever felt before, and he hadn't even touched me. I hated how it made me feel. How it made me realize that the man whose life I'd ruined was based on a meaningless, even *passionless*, motivation.

Papà's brows rose when he took in my words, and then, surprisingly, he laughed. "Well, Ace, I've never heard such an accusation from my daughter. What do you have to say about it?"

Nicolas stood so close my ponytail brushed his chest. He had no boundaries, I noticed with annoyance, while at the same time I tried to ignore the heady pull to step backward until my back touched his front.

"The cashier groped her," he said indifferently. "So I burned down his place of business . . . and maybe him."

Papà's gaze hardened. "Who's stupid enough to touch my daughter?"

Oscar Perez, and every time you invite him over . . .

"A nobody now, if he even made it out."

"Good," Papà snapped. "Let's hope he didn't."

I didn't know why I had even tried.

"Nico, we need to talk if you have some time. Elena, go check on Benito in the kitchen and make sure he's still alive."

My eyes widened. "What?"

"He was shot tonight. Though, maybe you aren't so concerned about that as you are about who drives you home."

I frowned.

Turning around, I was frustrated enough with his barb that I forgot Nicolas stood so close. I bumped into him, and then braced my hand on his stomach to steady myself. Heat burned through his white dress shirt and into my palm. God, he was a furnace. My fingers unwillingly curled into the muscle before I stepped back.

"I'm convinced they should call you the Clumsy Abelli instead," he said, annoyance coating his tone.

My gaze sparked. "Cute."

A hint of a humoring smile pulled on his lips, but he only grabbed my wrist, pulled me impolitely out of his way, and then shut my papà's office door behind him.

I shook off the tingling warmth left behind from his grip and walked down the hall toward the kitchen. It didn't take long to realize that Benito was going to live. Pushing the swinging door open, I stopped in my tracks, a blank gaze taking in the horror show.

Benito leaned against the counter with a hand towel pressed to his shoulder, while Gabriella—who wasn't even supposed to be here this late—kissed a corner of his lips, cooing something too low to hear. I imagined something like, "Poor baby."

It was a little cringe-worthy, but that wasn't the reason I turned around and headed back to my room. That's because her hand was in his pants. My cousin was getting a handjob in the kitchen, and while it was seriously unsanitary, I didn't have the energy to tell them to get a room.

Later, I lay in my bed staring at the ceiling, at the lone glowing star left from years before. Because every time I closed my eyes, all I saw was fire reflected in an amber gaze.

Every time I closed my eyes, all I felt was the wrong man's lips against mine.

"I told you we didn't have to go, Benito."

"I know, and I said it isn't a big deal, Elena."

I sighed and fell back in my seat. I'd been excited about the pool party, but after the night before, I wasn't confident it was a good idea to spend any more time around Tyler. Especially now that I'd seen how easy it was for Nicolas Russo to destroy a man's life in five minutes flat.

Urban development and eleven o'clock morning sun blurred through the car window as we sped uptown. Benito drove with his uninjured arm, his fingers tapping on the steering wheel to the beat, while singing along to *How Deep Is Your Love* by the Bee Gees. Typical behavior for him, but he'd been awfully quiet the whole drive . . . I watched him for a moment, a frown tugging at my lips.

"Are you on painkillers?"

His brows pulled together. "I only took three this morning."

"You mean, like right before we got in the car. *That* this morning?"

"Yeah, with some orange juice." He said it like that tidbit was important. I closed my eyes. Benito was high. He should've known those painkillers Vito supplied were in doses large enough for a horse, and he'd taken *three*.

I rubbed my temple. "You shouldn't be driving."

"And what?" he scoffed. "Let you drive? You don't know how."

"No, I was going to say we should have just stayed home." I trailed off, staring in confusion when he took an exit off the expressway. "What are you doing, Benito? You can't get off here."

"Can now. The marriage, Elena."

How could I have forgotten? As I drove on Russo streets for the first time, it was beginning to feel real. My sister was marrying Nicolas. My throat felt tight.

"What are we doing here?" It felt like I was visiting another world, when it was only a part of New York City I hadn't seen. It made me realize how sheltered I was. The only other countries I'd been to were Italy and Mexico. The former was to visit Mamma's parents and family over there; the latter was for yearly vacations, though I thought that was just a guise for Papà's business meetings with Mexican cartels.

"I just have to drop something off at Nico's."

I swallowed and tried to will my body into complacency, but I couldn't stop the rush of anticipation from zinging beneath my skin. I gave my head a small shake in frustration. The truth was, I was incredibly attracted to my sister's fiancé, whether I liked it or not. And I *didn't*. The idea that I might get to see him from the car window was enough to have me on edge. I hated it, but I didn't know how to turn it off either.

The city passed before my fresh eyes as we drove deeper into Russo territory.

We lived in a classy, spacious community in Long Island. The only neighbor you could see from the backyard was Tim Fultz. He owned a law firm Papà laundered money through; at least that's what Benito told me once. He was a nice guy, besides. Our neighborhood was quiet and private, and I'd always assumed Nicolas resided in something similar, but he didn't. He lived in the middle of the Bronx, in a red-brick home with a small white porch and a private drive that went to a garage in the back.

Benito pulled into the drive, drove to the back, and parked next to Nicolas's car. The detached garage door was up, and two vehicles sat inside, one with its hood open. They were both black, just like Nicolas's soul. I didn't know a thing about cars—who could blame me? I'd never even been taught to drive—but I was aware these were classics. One was a Gran Torino. I only knew that because I'd seen *Gran Torino* not too long ago. Benito had cried, though he would never admit it. And since seeing a man cry was the saddest thing in the world, so had I.

My heartbeat jumped when Nicolas stepped out from behind the hood, wiping his hands with a rag. He wore dark jeans and a plain white t-shirt. I'd never seen a man covered in grease who looked this good. I let my head fall against the seat.

"Son of a bitch. I'm bleeding again."

Sure enough, a red stain had bled through Benito's white dress shirt. We were going to a pool party, but he wouldn't be swimming or dressing down. Where would he put his gun?

"Didn't you get stitches?"

"Yeah." He pulled the keys out of the ignition. "But I split a couple open."

Stupidly, I asked, "Doing what?"

"Gabriella." He smirked.

"Yeah, about that . . ." My nose wrinkled. "Can you keep it away from the kitchen?"

His gaze narrowed before filling with amused clarity. "I know we all have our kinks, Elena, but you're my cousin. Find someone else to watch."

I rolled my eyes, opened the door, and got out before I knew what I was doing. I didn't want to sit in a hot car, not while my skin was already warmer than normal from being in a certain man's proximity.

Nicolas leaned against the garage, towel in hand. His gaze found mine, narrowing at the edges, before coasting to Benito, who handed him a manila envelope. These men sure loved their manila.

"Hey, man, can I use your bathroom?"

Nicolas's attention fell to the bloodstain, and then he nodded once. "Second door on the left."

"Thanks," Benito said, heading inside.

Nicolas and I stood there, watching each other. His gaze went to the white bikini strap I wore underneath a pink cover-up dress, paired with wedge sandals. It was a cute ensemble, but I only got a squinted condescending stare.

I frowned, crossing my arms defensively.

He looked at me for another second before heading back into his garage. I stared at his white-clad muscled back until he dipped his head under a car hood and ignored me. Quite the host, this one.

It was one of those days the heat grabs on and doesn't let go. We'd had a cool summer up until a week ago, but with the start of August tomorrow it seemed to be hitting us all at once. The sun burned hot and unforgiving, enough to make my olive skin redden if I stood beneath it long enough.

Something about the relentless heat and watching Nicolas wipe the sweat off his neck with the collar of his t-shirt made a warm haze permeate the corners of my mind.

A fan whirled near the door. A baseball game filtered out the open window of the neighboring house, and a small TV played the news in the corner of the garage. I wanted to catch the highlights, but it was too quiet, and to get closer I'd have to walk within the two feet of space behind Nicolas. I hesitated.

With the idea that I was being ridiculous, I made up my mind. Every nerve ending tingled as I squeezed past him to get to the wooden workbench and stool. I grabbed the remote and turned up the TV, but it took much longer than it should have to find the volume button. I was attuned to every movement, every noise behind me. Connected to him like static electricity. A drop of sweat ran down my back, and goose bumps rose on my skin.

I tried to watch the news, but it was like reading with Nicolas around: impossible. I pulled my hair into a ponytail while pretending to listen to the blonde newscaster's words.

I could feel his gaze on my bare shoulder blades as I twisted the tie around my long strands. Breathless. Itchy. *Hot.* I should have gone to church today because this was the wrong way to feel in the presence of one's soon-to-be brother-in-law. But I'd stayed home, or I'd be late for the pool party.

My nails dug into my palms. Why did I have to be attracted to this man? If given the choice, I'd rather be infatuated with fifty-year-old, married Tim Fultz. Maybe if I spoke to Nicolas, his terrible personality would make this strange attraction fade away. It was worth a try . . .

I turned around, leaned against the workbench, and ignored the nerves coursing through me about starting a conversation with him. "Your place is . . . nice. Not at all what I expected."

He side-eyed me with a look that made my heart stutter, while working on something beneath the hood of the Gran Torino. "And what did you expect?"

I swallowed under his attention. A few words from him were more exciting than they should have been. "I guess I expected a little more . . . fire and brimstone."

His gaze turned darkly entertained. "Hell."

"Or padded rooms . . ."

He wiped the side of his face with his sleeve, his focus on his work. "For thinking I'm a psychopath, you don't seem to fear being alone with me."

"I can scream. Loudly."

He glanced at me, like my words had an entirely different meaning—like he might like to hear me scream. My breathing became shallow.

The baseball game from the next house over filtered in, and I glanced out of the garage. Nicolas had a chain-link fence, no privacy . . . for someone in his profession, it wasn't normal. "Your neighbors are so close," I noted.

His expression sparked with dry amusement. "What, you think I shoot someone every time I eat lunch?"

I lifted a shoulder, biting my bottom lip.

He stared at me, and me at him. This conversation was doing nothing to ruin his appeal. He was slightly sweaty, grease-stained, and tattooed. None of which I thought I could appreciate until now. This strange attraction sank so deep, my cells shifted and grew heavy as they soaked it in.

"The only acts of violence I've committed this week have somehow revolved around you," he pointed out.

"You mean last night when you promised you wouldn't do anything? Was that one of them?" My words were sweet as I tilted my head.

"Wasn't it you who called me a cheat, *Elena?*"

I wasn't even sure how he did it, but my name rolled off his lips in a low, suggestive drawl that ghosted across my skin like a shiver. Heat ran between my legs.

"Don't say it like that."

"Like what?"

I grew flustered. "You know what you're doing. Stop."

He walked toward me with a car part, setting it on the workbench. My entire side tingled at his proximity a couple feet away. I turned in his direction and leaned my hip against the table. I didn't know what I was doing in here, watching him work, but it was almost . . . thrilling. Like living on the edge. Who would rather sit in the car?

He took a similar-looking part out of a box. I couldn't believe he did his own mechanic work. I guessed even men like him had to have a hobby.

"What are you doing with Benito?" His tone seeped with indifference, but interest shone through.

"We're going to a pool party."

After a moment, he said, "Tyler Whitmore's, I imagine."

"Yeah—" I froze. I knew this interaction was going over too smoothly. "Why do you know his last name?"

"You can find out anything these days, Elena." He said it with a dark edge, while wiping his hands off.

My teeth clenched. "I didn't ask how, I asked *why*."

His gaze came my way, hard and intimidating. "I'm marrying into your family. That makes your business now *mine*."

"No, it doesn't." My eyes narrowed. "That makes Adriana's business yours, not mine. I have plenty of men in my life already."

"Guess you got another." His words were deep. Smooth. *Final*.

I opened my mouth to say something—something about how much I disliked him—but before I could work out my thoughts into coherent words, he told me, "Maybe rethink what you're about to say."

I closed my mouth. He was so confident, unconcerned, while my stomach twisted with worry for Tyler. The last thing anyone wanted was their full name on Nicolas Russo's radar. Frustration clawed beneath my skin. He'd come and butted into my life like he had a right to. He would make a disaster of it.

I couldn't keep it in.

"Have you always been unhinged? Or is your controlling, delusional nature a product of inadequacy?" I said it sweetly. Sweet as *poison*.

He continued tinkering with his part, his gaze staying focused like he hadn't even heard me.

I had to admit, it felt good to get that off my chest. Great, actually—

A cool rush of shock flooded me as he grabbed the back of my neck and pulled me within a foot of him. My heart was in my throat and my eyes squeezed shut, because I didn't want to see how he was going to kill me. All I felt was warm skin and a tug on my dress, and then his hand slipped from my nape and he was gone.

After a couple seconds, I opened my eyes to see him walking away with a part in hand.

I stood there, frozen.

"Never really thought about it," he drawled. "But I guess I've always been."

Feeling something out of order, I glanced down.

My lips parted in disbelief. He cut my bikini strap.

I had a feeling this wasn't even because of the comment; he just didn't want me to go to that party.

Benito's voice filtered into the garage, though I couldn't see him over the car. "I used your kit under the sink to fix a couple stitches. Hope you don't mind."

I tried to catch my breath and collect myself while they talked for a moment. I slipped my bikini top off under my dress—it was worthless now. I wasn't a girl who could go without a bra. Not to Benito's standards, but close. I'd have to cross my arms the whole way home and tell my cousin my strap broke. He'd believe me, and he wouldn't even notice anything. Men were oblivious.

"You ready, Elena?" Benito asked. "Let's go."

"Coming."

As I passed Nicolas and noticed that Benito was preoccupied with texting next to his car, I tossed my bikini top under the hood. "Don't psychopaths like souvenirs?"

The tiniest hint of amusement pulled on his lips, and one grease-stained hand fisted the white fabric before I left the garage.

Benito sat in the driver's seat, sunglasses on. "Sorry I took so long. 'Bout fucking passed out fixing a stitch."

As I imagined, he never noticed my missing bikini top. Didn't ask questions about the broken strap. He only took me home. But before we reached the red front door, his suspicious gaze burned my face. "What's on your neck?"

I wiped the spot, coming away with a smudge of grease. Unease leaked into my blood. "Um, I don't know."

He didn't respond, didn't hear my heartbeat ricocheting in my chest. Though, something dark crossed his expression before I could disappear upstairs.

I didn't ask to get manhandled by Nicolas Russo, by my sister's fiancé. But the one unfortunate truth I was scared Benito might read on my face was . . . I *liked* it.

CHAPTER
Fifteen

"I want to live my life, not record it."
—Jackie Kennedy

Elena

I WAS BEGINNING TO THINK THIS ATTRACTION WAS MY PUNISHMENT FOR *HIM*. This was karma. While *he* had touched me, I'd wished for someone else, and that someone came in the form of my sister's fiancé.

The rest of Sunday passed with nothing but humidity, icy air-conditioning, and thoughts on my mind. Before *him*, I was a virgin, had never even kissed a man. An entire world of lust and sex had always been there, but I was unaware until I'd stepped into a low-income apartment holding the hand of a man I hardly knew. He didn't know the Sweet Abelli, and, to me, that was all that mattered.

When I walked out the door, with that broken chain lock and a cheap ring on my finger, it was as a different woman, with a stain of red I could never remove, and a deeper, *darker* desire in my blood. Once you set foot into that hazy, carnal corner of the world, you couldn't go back. The ingenious part was that you didn't even want to. I attributed this to my problem and came to terms with the small fact that I was losing my mind.

When I'd heard my future brother-in-law in the foyer a few minutes ago while doing laundry to pass the time, I'd gone out of my way to cross his path. I hadn't needed a drink of water, and I certainly hadn't needed to wear the tiniest pair of shorts I owned while getting it. I was close to crossing a line, but I didn't know how to stop myself from toeing the edge.

I understood my attraction to the man. His hands were rough, his voice deep, his presence commanding . . . he checked all the boxes I needed but didn't want.

Whenever he was near, an invisible string pulled me toward him, vibrating with the promise of a thrill if I gave in to the heavy tug. I hadn't known I had such a lack of self-control until him. The part that gave me a bitter taste was that I didn't even want to show restraint.

At least I knew I couldn't step over the line completely. It took two for that to happen, thankfully.

Nicolas had been on the phone in the foyer as I'd walked past him. His gaze had coasted from the marble floors, up my thighs, over the ridiculous shorts I was now regretting, and then to my face. He'd looked at me like I was gum on the bottom of one of his expensive shoes. It was a mystery how I could be so attracted to him.

Since that brief, wordless interaction, I'd been trying to conceive a plan to get over this all-consuming interest in everything Nicolas Russo.

I could ignore him. However, I'd already told myself I would do that, and look where it had gotten me: in the kitchen drinking a glass of water I didn't need, while wearing tiny shorts you could call underwear. I could go to Confession and then pray for the good Lord to save me, though with my luck, Father Mathews would tell my papà.

The most feasible option was to try to turn the attraction on to someone else. That might cause issues in itself, but at least I wouldn't be lusting after my sister's fiancé. The problem was, if this were possible, I would have already done it.

Frustration ran through me, and I dumped the rest of the water into the sink. I was being ridiculous. I just needed to put the attraction behind me. Mind over matter. Easy, right . . .?

I didn't have so much faith in myself after all, so, Monday evening, as we were on our way to Don Luigi's to have dinner with the Russo family, I posed a hypothetical situation before my nonna. It had to be vague—very much so—otherwise she'd easily put it together with her astute ways.

"Nonna," I started hesitantly, "say you've . . . wanted this . . . dog."

Her nose wrinkled from her spot in the town car. "I would never get a dog. I have allergies."

Dominic sat between us, texting. He was my quietest and broodiest cousin. And he smoked too much weed. I could smell it on him now.

Benito drove, singing along to *Rocket Man* by Elton John with his Aviators on, even though the sun had already fallen below the skyscrapers. Mamma sat in the front seat, fixing her makeup in the mirror and complaining when Benito went more than three miles per hour over the speed limit. Adriana had ridden with Papà and Tony, surprisingly. I was sure my father just wanted to chastise her about all the stuff she shouldn't do while married to Nicolas.

"Imagine you weren't allergic and you did want one, Nonna. But you want your . . . neighbor's dog."

"We're not getting a dog, Elena," Mamma said.

"*Cazzo.* I know." I only spoke Italian when I wanted to curse. I hardly ever swore, except for *damn*, *hell*, and maybe *ass* with a *hole* on the end now that I'd met Nicolas. But that was mostly inner monologue, so it didn't count. "It's hypothetical," I said. "Now, say your neighbor's dog is so . . . cute, and you want him—er, *her* for yourself."

"I think, if I could, I would rather have a cat," Nonna answered while looking out the window.

"Fine," I sighed. "A cat, then. You want your neighbor's cat—"

"We're not getting a cat, Elena," Mamma said.

Oh my god.

"I know. I said it's hypothetical—"

"Why does it smell like skunk in here?" Nonna's brows knitted.

I didn't miss Benito shooting a sharp glare at Dominic in the rearview mirror. He wasn't supposed to smoke weed; it altered the mind and slowed reflexes. Papà would be mad if he found out.

"Well"—Nonna picked a piece of lint off her skirt—"it must be that perfume you wear, Celia. Seems to ferment after a while."

Benito choked, and Dominic ran a hand across his almost amused expression while still focused on his phone. I thought Nonna picked on my mamma a lot of the time just because she got laughs from the boys.

Mamma shook her head, probably planning to drink enough for five tonight. She loved wine. And soap operas. If only one of her kids had played soccer.

"Now, what were you asking, Elena? You want a pet?" Nonna opened her clutch purse for candy, most likely. She only put chocolate and Kleenexes in there, of which she reused and reused like they'd quit making them.

"She's not getting a pet," Mamma said sternly.

Nonna shifted haughtily on the seat. "Well, I've heard pets do wonders for depression. Maybe you should be concerned about your daughter's mental health."

"She is not depressed."

"She wants an animal! In the house. What more needs to be said? Really, Celia . . ."

I tuned them out like the knob on the radio until all I heard was fuzz.

Looked like I was on my own with this one.

Black and white pictures of Old Bronx hung on the walls. The round tables were covered with red and green checkered tablecloths. A wooden bar ran across one wall, which my mamma headed straight for. Booths took up the other, where a few Russo women congregated. The light fixtures were originals, casting the room in a soft, warm glow. It was the kind of restaurant you would dine at to converse and get drunk, but I only stood by the door uncertainly.

I was in a Russo restaurant, in Russo territory.

I felt like a fish out of water, and by the way my two cousins stood by me, eyeing the place with their hands in their pockets, I imagined they felt the same way.

I'd met a few of the women who occupied the booths, but not enough to feel comfortable sitting near them, and I wouldn't go join the men at the corner of the bar for anything. I noticed Nicolas among them; it wasn't just his height that made him stand out, but his mere presence.

Warmth spread through me when his eyes landed on mine. He had a way of looking at me that made me feel like I was indecently dressed. He glanced away, responding to the man he was speaking to, and I let out a breath.

"What are you doing blocking the doorway?" Nonna muttered, pushing her way through me, Dominic, and Benito. "Kids these days. Typing on those phones all the time their brains have rot . . ." Her voice trailed off as she headed to a table to sit down.

Warm air brushed my skin as the door opened. Adriana stomped in, her eyes a dark storm. I stared at her attire—she wore a yellow t-shirt dress with black Converses. It was a cute ensemble, but this was a black-tie dinner, no matter the low-key Italian restaurant. I wore a black glitter maxi, and I wasn't even the bride.

Her expression was equal parts fury, equal parts despair.

"What's wrong?" I asked her.

She opened her mouth, closed it, then waltzed to the bar and pulled her petite frame onto a stool. Mamma had a glass of wine to her lips when she saw Adriana. Her eyes widened, her face darkened, but then she shook her head like she couldn't deal with it at the moment and headed in the opposite direction.

Walking up to the bar, I met gazes with the young male bartender in a white shirt and black waistcoat and ordered a beer. He raised a brow at my choice of drink.

Benito was four years older than me and had always had the downstairs fridge stocked with beer. I drank with him secretly in my teen years when Mamma would've scolded me about it. I'd grown to like it more than the tartness of wine. At the time, I thought it would be the most scandalous thing I'd ever do. Boy, did I wish that were true.

"Why did the turkey cross the road?" I asked without looking at my brooding sister, who was sipping on a shot of what looked like vodka. I had no idea how she did that, and briefly wondered if my mamma had had an affair with a Russian. He would've quickly been a dead Russian if so.

"To prove it's not chicken." Her response was dry.

Crap. I must have used that one before. I used to tell her silly jokes when she got upset about something, though it didn't look like it would work this time.

"Okay." I tried to up my game. "Why do bananas use suntan lotion?"

She didn't answer, only sipped her vodka.

"So they won't peel!" I exclaimed it with so much cheer it hurt my own ears.

The bartender chuckled and slid my beer across the lacquered wooden bar to me. My sister, though—she didn't blink.

I sighed. "Oh, come on. He thinks it's funny."

"He doesn't. He just wants to sleep with you," she deadpanned.

My eyes widened and then shot to the bartender who was within earshot. I expected a blatant refusal, but he only lifted a shoulder with a smirk before helping another customer.

He was either the bravest man in the room or the most idiotic to hit on a don's daughter.

I blushed, shook my head at my sister, then brought the bottle to my lips and took a drink. It was cold, refreshing, with a hint of bitterness. "Do you want to share what the problem is, or try to drink it away?" I leaned against the bar and settled in, because I already knew her response.

"Drink it away."

And so, we drank.

CHAPTER
Sixteen

*"I see nothing in space as promising as the view
from a Ferris wheel."*
—E.B. White

Elena

MY HEAD FELT LIGHT AS MY SECOND BEER SETTLED INTO A WARM PUDDLE IN
my stomach.

I was only tipsy and had already exchanged alcohol for water. I never drank too much in public; it loosened my tongue, to the point I feared what I would say or do. What if I told everyone what I was thinking? The Sweet Abelli and alcohol didn't mix. I wasn't ready to jump headfirst into the world as myself, didn't know if I'd ever be. When you're groomed and praised for being a certain way your entire childhood, sometimes there's no escape.

Adriana didn't share the same opinions on the matter. She was drunk, very much so. Thankfully, she was usually quiet while intoxicated, and appeared to only be eating much more and with less decorum than she did sober.

More family had shown up and filled most of the restaurant. Russos sat with Russos and Abellis with Abellis. Though, Adriana sat next to Nicolas and his uncles and their wives. I knew his mamma had passed when he was a teen, and his papà had been killed when the

Zanettis shot up one of his nightclubs. Unsurprisingly, it was because Nicolas's father had cheated them on a business deal.

It was strange not having Adriana at our table, but I guessed she was going to be a Russo in less than two weeks. A discomfort tightened in my throat.

I sat next to Tony, who seemed to be in good spirits. He had a bandage on his right hand, though, and kept asking me to get his drinks for him, to pass this or that, and to cut his steak. He always asked with too much enthusiasm, as if he liked his new condition. I was feeling for Jenny, cheater or not.

My parents, Nonna, Dominic, and Benito also sat with us. The men kept the conversation monotonous with talk about work—Papà owned many different establishments, from strip clubs to laundromats, though the latter was probably a cover-up for the packaging and distribution of drugs—or about their bets on men in their illegal fights.

Gianna ran the conversation in the room, making Abellis converse with Russos and vice versa. She looked like Barbie today. Thin-strapped pink dress, high ponytail, and light pink makeup. She was charismatic, independent, and now that I believed she'd slept with Nicolas, I watched her more than I should have. I was fascinated with the idea that she knew what it was like to sleep with him. Though, the more I thought about it, a foreign feeling—a wave of something unpleasant—slithered through my veins.

Envy.

That's what it was.

I wasn't only attracted to the man, I was jealous of the women he'd been with.

I groaned out loud.

All eyes at our round table came my way, forks of dessert halfway to their lips.

"Indigestion?" Nonna questioned.

"Yeah," I responded without thinking, and pushed my chair back. "I'm going to use the restroom."

I didn't even realize what I had said until I was walking away from the table and heard my brother and cousins' soft laughter behind my back. *Men.*

I had the bathroom door open three inches when I heard my name between the sound of the running faucet and toilet flushing.

"Look, all I'm saying is that she's known to be this Sweet Abelli, but really it's only because she gets sweet with a lot of men."

A bitter taste filled my mouth.

The voice belonged to a Russo woman. Valentina. Married to one of Nicolas's cousins, though I didn't know which. She was tall, statuesque, with strong Sicilian features. Hard to miss or forget.

"You're just jealous because Ricardo's been staring at her all night," another woman replied. It sounded like Jemma, Nicolas's cousin. She was close to my age, maybe a little younger, with light brown hair and eyes. I'd only spoken to her once, but she'd seemed like a nice girl.

"I don't care what Ricardo does. I have Eddie," Valentina replied. I heard a rustle like someone was digging through their purse, then silence, maybe reapplying makeup. "They killed her lover, don't you know? Some man from Staten Island."

"They're going to kill yours too if you don't shut up about it," Jemma said.

Valentina scoffed. "Ricardo and I hardly sleep together anymore. What does he expect me to do?"

"Stop. I don't want to hear about you, my brother, and sex in one sentence."

"Fine, *prude.*"

I let the door close quietly. I hadn't known my nickname was so popular until I'd met the Russos. I wondered if that's what everyone believed—that the Sweet Abelli was easy and sweet about it.

My stomach turned. I didn't care so much about what others thought of me, but the rumor hit closer to home than I wished. A man was killed because I'd made the mistake of sleeping with him, and now I was lusting after my sister's fiancé. Her comment struck the right nerve.

The girls exited the bathroom with a fresh wave of perfume and didn't even notice me standing in the shadows.

I leaned against the wall as the past came to the surface.

I'd met him at the carnival.

Warm breeze, sun, and laughter from the Ferris wheel high above. Smells of fried funnel cakes, popcorn, and cotton candy. At least, that's what I imagined it to be in the heat of summer. Instead, it was as empty as a Sweet Abelli smile. Nothing but snow, concrete, and the whistle of cold wind.

He worked at a mall nearby as a security guard, as well as two other part-time jobs to support his mother and younger sister, who I could only imagine were struggling to get by while mourning a son and brother. The awful truth was, I didn't even know his name. I wouldn't tell him mine, so with a smile he'd told me he wouldn't share his until I shared mine. Now, he'd never get to tell another anything.

He was blond, charismatic, and easygoing. I hadn't known such light-heartedness existed, and it had charmed me in a way. However, I was raised and deeply embedded in a different world altogether. A world that ended his life.

The most bitter part was that the guilt was fading, like the image out of a rear-view mirror as the car drove away.

I leaned my head against the wall, tilted it up, and twisted the ring on my middle finger. *He* gave it to me as a lark. However, now it had become a promise to myself to make restitution for my mistake. And I wouldn't take it off until I had.

A familiar awareness brushed my bare skin.

I rolled my head to the side to see Nicolas standing at the end of the corridor, his hands in his pockets and that lazy stare all mine.

"And here I thought I'd never see you out of pink."

His deep voice touched my ears, and I shivered from the sound filling the silent hallway. *Never see you out of pink.* My mind took that to a dirty place, where I wore nothing and he looked on. My breasts tightened as warmth ran a languid path between my legs. I swallowed and pushed the breathlessness away.

I hardly ever wore black, but I was feeling edgy tonight. Maybe because I knew he would be here and I needed the strength black could offer to pretend he didn't exist. He'd only ever seen me in white or pink—it wasn't a surprise he looked at me like I was a ridiculous girl most of the time. But that was for the best. If he had returned this fascination, I could only imagine the chaos it could bring, and I wasn't starting another scandal. Ever.

Still leaning against the wall, I pulled up the hem of my dress until my hot pink heels were showing.

A hint of a smile pulled on his lips, and he wiped at it with a thumb before sliding his hand back in his pocket. Butterflies erupted low in my stomach. If I ever cursed—*really* cursed—it would be to describe how handsome he was. It deserved a salacious word, otherwise no one could understand the magnitude of it.

"What do you know Sweet Abelli to mean?" I asked, my expression thoughtful. I had to know if I was considered a whore to the entire *Cosa Nostra*. Living in naivety wasn't my style, no matter how much I disliked the truth.

He raised a dark brow, maintaining a ten-foot distance. "You want me to say it?"

I gave my head a slow nod, pulling my bottom lip between my teeth.

How bad was it?

His gaze sparked with dark amusement, though a small amount of bitterness leaked through. "One of the sweetest pieces of ass in New York, easily."

I blinked. Swallowed. Made a *hmm* noise to hide my breathlessness. That's just what he knew it to mean, not necessarily what he believed, right? Still, I couldn't help a weight from forming between my legs. My dress from feeling abrasive and hot.

This attraction burned, and before it scarred me forever, I needed to treat him differently. If I regarded him like family—which he would soon be—maybe then it would fade away.

I pushed off the wall and walked toward him. The old restaurant's atmosphere held a charge. I suddenly wondered if the feeling was merely a reaction between two combustible forces, or if my crush had sunk so deep into my skin the air was thicker to breathe in his presence.

With an exhale that could be construed as relief, I said, "Well, that's not as bad as I was assuming." I stood in front of him, within arms' length. A feeling of significance rushed me whenever I was in his company, like I had the attention of the most popular boy at school.

The past still gripped me, enough that the present seemed easy, courage not difficult to find. I stepped closer and ran my finger across the edge of his jacket button.

His voice held a variety of his natural darkness; this one was rougher, not in the least amused. "What did I say about assuming?"

Somehow, his demanding, bossy nature only made my cheeks warm. How easily this man told people what to do and expected immediate obedience. A silver spoon must have fed him his entire childhood.

"I had good reason to believe it was something else." I pushed the black button through its hole, undoing his jacket. He watched me, and every inch of my skin burned like I was standing too near to a fire.

"I'd love to hear your half-baked reasoning." His tone told me the opposite.

"So, what do you want?" I opened his jacket, revealing the black vest beneath that hugged his stomach. "Just checking up on me?"

His words were laced with harshness. "Your sister is drunk and you encouraged it."

"Oh, so I'm in trouble, then?" I reached into his vest pocket and pulled out the cigarette I knew would be there. I'd seen him put it between his lips or roll it between his fingers like he was trying to quit. "Take it up with my papà. I'm an Abelli, not a Russo."

I went to turn around, but he grabbed my wrist.

"You're not going outside alone."

"I saw some kitchen staff go out there." I tried to shake off his grip, but that only brought his attention to my hand. His gaze darkened on my ring like he wanted to pull it off. I curled my fingers protectively because I believed he might just try it. When his grasp slipped from my wrist, I headed toward the back door.

"You're not going outside with the kitchen staff."

Treat him like family, right?

"Nicolas, go find someone else to boss around—"

I froze, my heartbeats slowing like they'd been dropped in molasses. He held me by the ponytail and kept me from taking another step, like it was a leash. My breath stopped when his front pressed against my back. He felt so warm, so good, I could have groaned if I had the air to do so.

With a small tug on my ponytail, my head tilted to the side and his lips brushed the hollow behind my ear. "Tell me what to fucking do again."

My neck would be the most sensitive part of me if the obvious didn't count. Goose bumps rose on my skin. His gravelly tone ran the length of my nape before trailing down my spine and between my legs. My back arched on reflex.

"You're not going outside alone. And not with the kitchen staff either."

With half-lidded eyes and a hazy mind, it took a moment to comprehend his words. I blinked, trying to clear my head.

"Do you have a lighter?" I was going outside, whether he liked it or not. My question left the suggestion open that he was invited, though I didn't know why. This moment here proved I couldn't treat him like family.

He gripped my waist and pushed me forward a step. He must have let my hair go and I hadn't even noticed.

When he opened the alley door and humid August air brushed my face, I hesitated.

With his back pressed against the door, he held it open, his hands in his pockets. His stare was edged with something heated—maybe annoyance. He didn't want to be out here with me.

The Sweet Abelli would have considered his feelings. I didn't have to be her around him, though.

I stepped out to smoke with Nicolas Russo.

CHAPTER
Seventeen

*"The best and most beautiful things in the world cannot be
seen or even touched—they must be felt with the heart."*
—Helen Keller

Elena

THE PAST HELD A SIMPLISTIC CHARM IN MY HEART, BUT THAT DIDN'T MEAN I couldn't see the beauty in my complicated present. Urban development stretched to the sky, its pollution blocking the stars, but beneath it the magic of humanity lived on. There was good in the world, and I couldn't understand how the blonde newscaster only focused on the unpleasant.

The alleyway was still, the kitchen staff having already dispersed. Tire noise, honking, and sirens were steady in the background, but even louder than that was the soft, harmonic lilt of a saxophone.

My heels clicked on the asphalt as I took a few steps toward the music. A certain reality settled on me: I didn't have a spellbinding love story to bring to this world. The honest truth was, I only forced myself to enjoy tragic endings because I knew mine wouldn't be far apart.

Warmth brushed my bare back, the whisper of a thrill trailing behind. I turned around to find Nicolas standing so close I had to tilt my head to meet his gaze. He took the cigarette from my fingers, put it between my lips, and then, with the metallic *clink* of a Zippo lighter with an ace of spades on the side, the mesmerizing glow of a flame flickered between us.

"This is the last cigarette you're smoking, so enjoy it."

I smiled, and as he lit the cigarette, I puffed slowly so I didn't cough and come off as a rookie once again.

"Something funny?"

A soft laugh escaped me. "Yeah. You."

With a pensive stare, he pulled the cigarette from my lips, brought it to his own, and inhaled.

I tilted my head, regarding him. "So, can I call you my *fratello* now?" I didn't know why I'd said it, but it had just slipped through my lips as easily as air. Nicotine ran through my veins and lightened my tongue.

He looked at me, blowing out a breath of smoke above my head. We were standing so close his sleeve touched my arm. So close his presence obliterated mine. And there was nothing that felt familial about it.

He handed me the cigarette. "No." It was a hard *no*, not one you debated with.

"Why not? You will be."

His jaw ticked. "I'll be your *cognato*, not your brother."

"Same thing, really. You already have the controlling brotherly act down."

His expression told me he wasn't amused and he wasn't going to participate in this conversation.

"You can call me your *sorella*. Maybe a sibling is what you need to realize the world doesn't revolve around you."

He let out a breath of amusement, but it sounded like he wanted to choke me. "Smoke your cigarette and shut up."

I turned around to hide the ridiculous warmth that rushed to my cheeks and walked a few steps from him. The soft clicks of my heels in tune with the saxophone's lilt was hypnotic. The nicotine must have been mixing with the alcohol in my system. Or maybe I was just drunk on his presence.

Spinning around, I leveled my gaze on him. "You don't have

to babysit me, you know. I don't usually get assaulted twice in one weekend."

He leaned against the back door, his gaze sparking with sarcasm. "Just once, then?"

"Just once," I repeated, a smile pulling on my lips.

"I'm not your babysitter."

"Could've fooled me."

His expression darkened around the edges. I didn't know why I was practically poking him with a stick, but the filter that was usually in place had drifted away with the last saxophone note.

His tone was rough and dry. "Keep opening your mouth, *I'll* assault you."

I didn't believe he meant the sexual variety, though that's how I regrettably decided to take it. I brought the cigarette to my lips and inhaled. His gaze met mine through a breath of smoke.

"I'll be sure to tell my next attacker that only my *cognato* gets to assault me." Somehow, a suggestive nature filled the alleyway so heavily a passerby couldn't miss it. My expression was thoughtful, though my heartbeat played the conga in my chest. "I'm sure you're running out of ways to ruin men's lives, anyway."

"It's called a repertoire, Elena. They can be used again."

"Hmm. And what's next on the list?"

"Who's being assaulted?" His voice was bland, like we were talking about the weather for the third time.

I lifted a shoulder. "Me."

His gaze went cold, but his tone stayed impassive. "The entertainment for tonight would be watching him bleed out."

Nothing about his expression told me he was exaggerating. "Well, it wouldn't be a normal evening with you around if there wasn't some blood involved." I paused. "Though, I guess you did all right at our last supper."

The smallest yet darkest smile pulled on his lips. "Guess I did."

Butterflies erupted in my stomach. That mischievous, wicked smile was the exact reason women liked bad boys.

Cazzo.

I needed some air.

Bending down, I put the cigarette out against the concrete before tossing it in the restaurant's dumpster. Butts and trash already littered the alleyway; I didn't want to contribute.

Nicolas still leaned against the door, and so I stopped in front of him and waited. He held out his phone to me. "My list. Write it now."

I frowned at the cell phone and then looked at him.

His expression was serious, and truthfully, with this attraction spiraling out of control, zinging under my skin like electricity, I didn't have it in me to argue with him. I grasped the phone and took a few steps back. There wasn't any way I could think with him standing so close.

I opened his notes and typed in Adriana's dress size, shoe size, and even bra size. He didn't look like a man to skirt around details. When it came to her hobbies and likes, I couldn't help myself.

Acting

Cult horror films

Gardening

Not you

I smiled, but then his phone pinged and it fell from my lips.

I stared.

Who was he? *Benito?*

The image was of a woman, naked. Blond hair, coy smile, big breasts.

Jenny.

I glanced at him to see he was only waiting for me to finish. I turned the phone around. His gaze stayed on mine for a second before giving it a glance. Not a blink.

"This is Tony's girlfriend," I accused.

"Is it?"

I couldn't tell if he was amused or annoyed. Couldn't tell if he didn't know who this was, or if he was playing stupid. Did he get so many random pictures of naked women he couldn't tell them apart? Anger sparked in my chest.

"Stop sleeping with her," I said coldly.

Now his darkness was the amused variety.

My grip tightened on the phone. "It's wrong."

He lifted a shoulder. "Tit for tat."

I paused. "You don't have a girlfriend." *You have a fiancée . . .* though that usually didn't mean much to a man in this life.

"Did."

Oh.

A strange discomfort curled in my chest.

I blinked, trying to sort this out. "You guys are sleeping with each other's girlfriends to, what? Get back at each other?"

Not a word from him, and his gaze told me there wouldn't be one.

"He loves her, Nicolas, whether he knows it or not."

His expression turned to ice. "You're a champion for love, are you? Personal experience, maybe?"

What?

My eyes narrowed. I didn't know what he meant, but I was too angry to care. "You're marrying his sister, so it's not fair anymore." I had no idea what I was saying, but I wasn't taking his side.

His laugh was dark.

He didn't like me taking sides. Did he think I'd pick his?

A sudden thought, a need to know, came to me, and it escaped my lips before I could stop it. "Are you going to be faithful to Adriana?" My heart thumped to an awkward beat. That was the most invasive thing I'd ever asked anyone, and it left a foreign and regretful aftertaste on my tongue.

His gaze leveled on mine, not liking my question either, but he kept his words deep and smooth. "Does she expect me to be?"

Of course she didn't.

Not one woman expected that in this world—not when work for a man was considered going to a strip club. Not when money and power corrupted. And not when women like Jenny threw themselves at rich and attractive men. It was why I didn't want a husband as handsome as him. He didn't even have to work to be unfaithful—it would sit right in his lap.

I shook my head, this conversation chafing me with frustration.

"You're evading. Answer the question." Maybe if he said the words, showed me how disloyal, dishonest, he was, then I could put this fascination for him aside. I was more interested in his reply than even my sister would be.

He pushed off the door. "You answer *mine*."

My response was calm and suicidal. "You can have your phone back after you answer my question."

His condescending stare burned me, and then, with the tiniest shake of his head, he came in my direction.

My heart leapt and I backed up, but then my bare back hit the alley wall and the cool concrete sent a shiver down my spine. I was trapped, cornered, and frazzled enough I couldn't think clearly. Didn't think at all.

I dropped his phone down the front of my dress.

He froze two paces away. Stared at where his phone had gone. And then ran his tongue across his teeth in a type of roguish disbelief.

"You honestly think that's going to stop me from taking it back?"

I had no idea why I'd done it. For once in my life, I wished for the Sweet Abelli to save me. Her calm, collected ways wouldn't have gotten her into this mess in the first place. I swallowed down my breathlessness.

"That would be inappropriate."

Both of our gazes dropped when the phone fell from my breasts to my stomach, before catching on the tight fabric near my hips. His phone was stuck below my navel.

His eyes came back to mine. "From what I've learned, kissing is platonic these days. Reaching up your dress can't be much worse."

My stomach fluttered. "You're *not* reaching up my dress."

"Three seconds, Elena." His words were short, pissed. I knew he meant I had that long to give it back to him.

I didn't know what I was doing or when I'd suddenly acquired a death wish, but my gaze met his for a consecutive three seconds. Quietly and maturely, I said, "You haven't answered my question."

His stare flicked to the concrete, and when it came back to me burning hot, I knew I was in trouble. A surge of expectation leaked into my bloodstream but was doused with unease when he took the remaining steps toward me.

His shoulders blocked the alleyway, his heavy presence slowing my breaths. He wasn't gentle. With his amber gaze on mine, he gripped a fistful of my dress near my thigh and tugged it up, jerking me in the process.

He fisted the fabric, skimming it up my legs. Every inch of my skin sizzled, and an empty ache formed low in my stomach. When he made contact with my bare thigh, I had to bite my lip to hold in a whimper. His palm was rough and hot enough to burn. And God, a man had never smelled so good. I wanted to nuzzle my face in his neck so I could get more of it, all of it.

It wasn't lost on me that I was criticizing him for being unfaithful to Adriana while fantasizing about him doing the same thing with me. The thought was only fleeting because his presence, his warmth, brushed it aside.

I didn't know if he had slowed, or if this moment was so significant I was experiencing it in slow motion, but it quieted, the sound of my ragged breaths filling the alley. A slight breeze made its way through the sliver of space between us, making me aware of how hot I was. I'd never felt warmer in my life.

He pressed closer against me, his jacket brushing my arms, his watch cold on the smooth skin of my inner thigh. One hand was braced on the wall beside my head, trapping me, but what he didn't know was that I didn't want out.

Once he'd touched bare skin, his gaze hardened, before flicking down as if in reluctance. The empty ache between my legs pulsed. I couldn't help but to part my thighs, to imagine him slipping a hand between them. Cupping me over my thong. Pulling it to the side and pushing a finger inside of me. My palms lay flat on the cold, concrete wall on each side of me, and a buzz sounded in my ears.

His jaw tightened, and his fingers gripped the inside of my thigh. Sparks ran from the heat of his hand straight to my clit, all my blood drumming in that area. He'd only have to run a palm across the fabric to realize how disturbed I was, how wet this was making me. How much I wanted him.

But he didn't do any of that.

He only grabbed his phone.

His thumb brushed over the thin string of my thong on my hip, pulling it down a bit before his hands left me. As my dress fell to brush the asphalt, his voice was rough against my ear.

"You already know the answer."

He stepped back and tilted his head toward the door, in a way of telling me to get there, now.

Too breathless to do anything else, I headed in its direction, a whisper of an ache trailing behind.

CHAPTER
Eighteen

"No one will ever kill me, they wouldn't dare."
—Carmine Galante

Nico

THERE WAS NO BETTER PLACE FOR ME THAN AT THE HEART OF THE *COSA Nostra*. Like the last piece of a puzzle, my existence was a perfect fit.

No matter if I were a lawyer's son, a doctor's, or a janitor's, I would have found my way on the wrong side of the law doing the one thing I loved to do: hustling.

I was Antonio Russo's son, no one else's, and for that reason I was damn good at what I did. My papà used to have a saying: *Non può provare il dolce chi prima non ha provato l'amaro.* It was a way of telling me there was no room for regrets in this world, that a man had to taste the bitter before he could taste the sweet.

I'd heard it when I was seven, as I looked at the first dead man I'd ever seen: eyes open, blood pooling on the warehouse floor.

In my profession, regrets were easy to come by. They piled up, each one weakening a man's resolve. I didn't regret much, and up until recently I had only one that followed me around. I regretted fucking Gianna while she was still married to my father. Most recently, and more so than even that, I regretted signing the contract for Adriana.

I wanted her sister.

In my bed.

Against the wall.

On her knees.

I'd involuntarily gone over what it would take to get out of the contract, knew exactly what I would do. My family was known for breaking agreements—it was what got my papà killed, in fact. Not the best incentive, but I didn't fear the Abellis. Didn't fear anything at all, honestly, which would probably be the cause of my eventual demise.

I wanted Elena Abelli, and starting a feud just so I could have her was beginning to sound less and less like a bad idea every time she was near. But I wasn't going to go through with the twisted plan my mind had created.

I wanted to fuck her.

I didn't want to marry her.

My wife was only supposed to be a woman I could respect and who'd have my children. Not one I was so fascinated with I couldn't think straight. In this life, I couldn't afford the distraction. Didn't want the attachment. And she'd fucked with my head already.

Though, as regrettable as it was, I couldn't help but to be interested in everything that came out of the girl's mouth. It was getting to the point she couldn't make a move without my notice, no matter how much I tried to stop myself.

I didn't know why she spoke so freely and obstinately with me, though it was probably because she now considered me to be a fucking *brother*. If only she knew that when she talked back to me, I wanted to cover her mouth with my palm, back her up against a wall, and then watch the shock in her soft brown eyes as I slid my hand beneath that tiny pink thong she was wearing. Fucking *pink*. For some reason when I saw that, my control shook *hard*.

If I'd started, I wouldn't have stopped.

I would have fucked her up against an alley wall, and I had a tenacious feeling it wouldn't have been enough. It was the Russo blood in me. It wanted what it wanted, and fuck everything else.

The alley door shut with a click behind me, pulling me from my thoughts. I buttoned my suit jacket and followed Elena down the hall, that silky black ponytail within arms' reach. When she'd spun around in the alley, it hit me in the chest. I had to tell myself it wasn't a fucking leash because after I grabbed it earlier, I now wanted to pull her around by it, straight to my bed whether she liked it or not.

The cut of her dress was low, baring smooth olive skin, while only thin strings crisscrossed her back. The black fabric hugged the curve of her ass, leaving nothing to the imagination but what it would look like bare.

Jesus, what I could do to that ass.

Not fucking helpful, Russo.

I forced my gaze away, and ignored the heat running straight to my dick.

Without another word to me, she entered the main room and headed toward her sister and nonna who appeared to be playing a game with crayons on a kid's menu.

The atmosphere was light, the chatter friendly, which I should have been relieved to see—but frankly I would've welcomed a little animosity right now. I was worked up, my shoulders tense with pent-up sexual frustration.

Tony sat with his back toward me, laughing with his cousins. We'd yet to engage each other tonight. I knew we would have to get on eventually, and so I'd invited the idiot to come along. Right now, with this frustration chafing beneath my skin, I was glad I had.

I headed to the bar and sat next to Luca. I needed a drink. Just one, to take the edge off. The last time I'd gotten drunk was six years ago and I'd fucked my stepmother. Lesson learned.

Luca side-eyed me with an amused expression as he took a drink of his beer. He apparently knew I wanted Elena, just like every fucking other man in New York. It was more entertaining, I supposed, because I wasn't quiet about disliking her before I'd even met her.

"Fuck off," I gritted.

His chuckle was quiet.

A few moments later, I nursed my whiskey, vaguely listening to my cousin Lorenzo talk about the horse he'd bet too much money on.

"I'm telling you, the odds on this are good . . ." Lorenzo trailed off, staring at what had to be some girl behind my back. "Jesus Christ, I want to marry that woman."

A wave of agitation ran through me because I knew who he spoke of, but I only swirled the whiskey in my glass before taking an annoyed sip.

I heard Elena laugh softly at something Tony had said behind me. I bit down on the liquor, swallowing. She was so loyal to her idiot of a brother—the one who'd almost gotten her killed. My teeth clenched.

I needed an outlet for this before it exploded.

It was either fighting or fucking. And since I knew the latter would be tainted right now by everything Elena Abelli, the former would have to do.

I slipped my phone out of my pocket.

Then I forwarded the photo of Jenny to Tony.

And waited.

Truthfully, I hadn't had a girlfriend. She was more accurately a steady fuck, which was the closest thing to a girlfriend I'd had. I didn't think Elena would give me as much sympathy if I'd said that, so I . . . fibbed, like the *cheat* I was. Tony had slept with Isabel, making sure I found out, and so out of mere principle I'd fucked Jenny. It was kind of embarrassing how easy it'd been.

I hadn't spoken to Jenny for more than a year now. With her recent contact, I assumed Tony must not be able to get her off as well with his left hand as he could his right.

"Uh, Ace . . ."

I swirled my whiskey. "Let it happen."

"*Okay*, boss." Lorenzo took a step back.

Luca shook his head and left his seat.

I shouldn't have done it. I didn't start shit in public. But I was afraid of what I would do if I didn't. If I ran into Elena Abelli again tonight . . . I'd lose my goddamn mind.

A sudden wave of tension brushed my back before a dull pain exploded in the side of my head.

"Tony!" Celia gasped as the glass tumbler shattered and pinged as it hit the floor.

The room fell into silence.

I couldn't help a corner of my lips from lifting.

Thank God that fucker was reckless.

CHAPTER
Nineteen

"Imperfection is beauty, madness is genius, and it's better to be absolutely ridiculous than absolutely boring."
—Marilyn Monroe

Elena

"STUPIDO!" MAMMA REPEATED THE WORD THREE TIMES, HER VOICE resounding in deaf ears, before muttering in Italian that all of her children were stupido as she left the kitchen.

"Fuck, Elena. Stop." Tony winced.

I pulled the cotton ball away from the nasty cut on his face. "You can hit Nicolas with your injured hand, but you can't take a little burn of alcohol?"

And to think that I had waited on him all night when he could throw punches like he was 100 percent. He was regretting it now, with his tight expression and the red seeping through the bandage on his hand.

God, he looked awful.

There was nothing more gruesome than watching two men pummel each other half to death. Especially when you had the odd feeling of not knowing who you wanted to win. Tony . . . right? I swallowed, feeling like a traitor.

After Tony had shattered a glass against his future brother-in-law's hard head, Nicolas had wrapped an arm around my brother's neck and slammed him to the floor. The heavy *thunk* still resonated in my mind.

Nonna had looked up from her game of tic-tac-toe with my sister and sighed. "Finally, some entertainment."

Adriana had taken a sip of wine, her expression lightening since whatever news she'd received earlier, and, oddly enough, bet my nonna fifty bucks on Tony. Apparently, Nicolas was part of the reason she was upset.

Papà had only sat back in his chair and watched, and so had Nicolas's uncles. No one was stepping in, and for all I knew they were going to fight to the death. The thought settled unpleasantly in my stomach until I couldn't watch it any longer. I waited outside, in front of the restaurant, with Dominic.

I wasn't sure how it had started, but I imagined Tony had found out about the picture, or maybe Jenny had admitted she'd been with Nicolas recently.

And this was the aftermath.

Red marks covered Tony's bare torso, the beginning of bruises forming on his ribs and back. Blood spilled from a nasty cut on his face, from his nose, his lip, and dripped down his chest.

He leaned back in the island chair, dressed in his shoes and dress pants, texting.

"What's the cut from?" I was unsure of how such a ragged wound from the corner of his eye to his hairline had been the product of a fistfight. Though, I guessed it was a pretty severe one, as though they'd both been saving all their aggression for it.

"Broken chair leg."

My eyes widened. "He hit you with a chair leg?"

What a cheat.

"Yeah. After I hit him with it."

Oh.

Truthfully, I didn't know why I was even trying to help Tony. He hadn't exactly been the best brother as of late. It made me feel like a pushover, but for as long as I could remember I'd had this mother-hen gene I couldn't get rid of. It was an urge to help I couldn't ignore. I didn't know where I'd gotten it. It wasn't from my mamma and, as Nonna used her cane to push open the kitchen door and then thanked Tony for winning her fifty bucks, not from her either.

My skin also danced with an edginess that tonight had left behind. I had to do something to stay busy, otherwise thoughts of *him* came to the surface, making me feel hot all over. And, to be clear, it was the *wrong* him I thought of.

I crossed my arms, still wearing my dress and heels. "Well, did you get some hits in? Because it looks like you took the brunt of it."

A sarcastic gaze flicked to me before he glanced back to his phone. "I got enough."

"Please tell me you aren't texting Jenny."

"I'm not texting Jenny," he said dryly.

He was texting Jenny.

"You both cheat on each other. Don't you think it's not the healthiest relationship to be in?"

He set his phone on the island and ran his hand through his hair. "I love her, Elena."

A little lump formed in my throat. "Sometimes love isn't enough, Tony."

"Of course not," he responded with a serious tone, and I thought we were going to have an intelligent, meaningful conversation for once, but then he opened his mouth again. "Good sex has to come with it."

I sighed.

He laughed and ran a hand down his chest, smearing blood as he did. "You're a good sister, Elena. Now come give your big brother a hug."

"No." I frowned. "You're sweaty and bleeding."

"A hug is the least I can do."

"The least you can do is not—no, Tony, don't!"

He squeezed me in a bear hug and made a show of wiping his nasty man-ness all over me. I groaned, wrinkled my nose, and tried to fight my way out of it.

He sucked in a breath. "*Fuck.*"

I froze. "What?"

"Broken rib, I think."

I winced and pulled back just as Papà pushed the kitchen door open. He glanced at my first-aid supplies on the counter and then at me with disapproval, telling me not to coddle Tony. His gaze went to his son, eyeing him with that judgmental stare he was good at.

"You look like shit."

Tony chuckled. "Thanks, Pops."

The door swung shut, and then Papà's voice filtered through it. "Office, *now*."

Wide awake, with all my synapses still firing, I dragged my feet to my room. As the hot shower water sluiced down my skin, I wondered how bad Nicolas got it. Who was cleaning his cuts? *Gianna?* An unpleasant weight pulled on my chest.

In a restless daze, I combed my wet hair and then pulled on some panties and a tight t-shirt that said, "Sleep Tight, I Bite."

Lying in bed, the gothic band Type O Negative leaked from Adriana's room and into mine. A good sister would have gone to ask her why she was upset, but I was beginning to learn I was a selfish one. I closed my eyes, wishing I could only flip a switch to get rid of this attraction for her fiancé.

When I opened them, I still felt it—a fascination so deep in my skin it was like it had always been there, lying dormant. My breathing turned shallow as I relived the night: his presence brushing mine, his deep voice in my ear, his hand on my thigh, pushing my dress up and up.

Warmth ran between my legs, leaving an emptiness behind I was scared only he could fill.

I had it bad.

So bad.

I wanted this man like I hadn't even known you could want a man.

Throwing the covers back, I slid out of bed and padded to the dresser. I pulled a Zippo lighter out of my clutch.

With the scratchy sound of the flint, a flame danced before my eyes.

After the fight, I'd gone back inside to retrieve my purse and found the lighter on the floor. It was his, with an ace of spades on the side.

I took it as easily as he took my sanity.

Climbing back into bed, I lay there and flicked the Zippo open and closed, filling the room with a flame for a man I shouldn't have.

Before I snuffed it out.

CHAPTER
Twenty

"A woman is like a tea bag—you can't tell how strong she is until you put her in hot water."
—Eleanor Roosevelt

Elena

"I'M GOING ON A RUN!" I YELLED DOWNSTAIRS. A SLEEPY GRUMBLE SOUNDED in the dark man cave before I slammed the door.

I liked to pretend I could leave the house and run in our gated community alone, but I couldn't. So, I sat on the staircase and took my time lacing up my sneakers.

It was early—eight o'clock, maybe—and a couple servants were moving around, cleaning an already clean house. There was always someone here. When I married and owned my own home, I didn't want servants. I wanted to walk the halls naked. Hopefully that would be enough incentive for my husband to agree.

A moment later, Dominic appeared, his thick hair mussed from sleep and his broody expression even broodier than usual. He wore a sleeveless t-shirt, running shorts, and shoes. I knew underneath there would be a gun strapped to his thigh.

Gabriella came around the corner, carrying some sheets. Her eyes brightened when she saw me. "Oh, good, you're running! I'll start with your room then. Your nonna yells at me when I go in hers earlier than ten."

Her dark hair was in a messy pile on the top of her head, and her smile was infectious. I couldn't help my own.

"Yeah, you'll have to maintain a queen's schedule with her."

Gabriella had vivacious good looks and a coquettish personality. I'd wondered if the men in my family were taking advantage of it, but I knew I was wrong as she walked up to Dominic—who was texting, go figure—stood on her tiptoes, and whispered something I could only imagine was dirty in his ear.

He never pulled his gaze away from his phone, but a grin tugged at his lips. "Later," was all he said.

She dropped back to her heels with a shy smile, and then excused herself as she made her way past me up the stairs.

Him, too?

"Unbelievable," I muttered once she was out of earshot. "You don't even have to look at a woman to get laid."

I received the tiniest bit of amusement from him as he slid his phone in his pocket. "Let's go, before it gets hot."

We ran the entirety of the gated community. I waved to Tim Fultz as we passed, who was getting into his car for work at the law firm. The rest of the properties were quiet, the people who could afford them spending half the year on vacation, or still in their beds with a small hangover and an expensive prostitute. I noticed Ryan mowing one of their lawns and a bitter feeling ran through me.

By ten o'clock, as we were within sight of the house, the sun beat down harder than ever. Sweat made a lazy path down my back, and my lungs burned. Jumping into the pool sounded better than any idea I'd ever had.

"I'll race you home," I panted.

"No." Dominic maintained a steady pace, but his shirt was soaked with sweat.

"Come on, chicken."

"If I were five that might have worked."

"I'll tell Papà where your stash of pot is."

He blew out a sarcastic breath, shook his head, and then sprinted.

"Hey!"

With burning thighs, I picked up the pace until I was side-by-side with him. I shoved his shoulder for cheating, managing to push him over a step. Though, I soon realized he wouldn't return the gesture, considering Papà stood on the front porch with an unfamiliar man, their eyes on us.

Nicolas's car sat in the driveway, and when he stepped his big body out of it my heartbeat faltered, which created a domino effect of flutters in my chest.

Dominic slowed, apparently thinking it wasn't appropriate to race his cousin in company. I met him stride for stride until my feet touched our front lawn.

Dominic put his hands on the back of his head and sucked in deep breaths. "Son of a bitch," he complained, panting.

"Too much smoking," I told him, choking on air because I was trying to inhale it so fast.

He raised a brow, in a way of asking me what my excuse was.

"Mamma's cookies," I told him unashamedly.

He laughed in that quiet, thoughtful way of his.

My thighs were on fire, but I resisted the pull to drop to my knees. I would have made a show of falling to the lawn any other day, but *unfortunately*, we had company. I believed if I told myself Nicolas's presence was unfortunate, it would eventually feel that way. Grasping at straws was all I had.

My hair stuck to my sweat-soaked face, and my heart pounded without a pause. I rested my wrists on the top of my head, trying to catch my breath while my eyes unwillingly coasted to Nicolas. He wore a gray suit, white undershirt, and black tie. He looked like a million bucks, just as he always did. I had the sudden desire to wipe some of my sweat on him.

He flicked a gaze to me as he strode down the walkway. His expression wasn't very nice for the half-second it landed on me. There wasn't a kink in his step, and, from a distance, he didn't appear to have been in a table-smashing fight last night. Tony was probably still sleeping downstairs, recovering. He'd spent the night, and I could only hope it was because he was thinking about his relationship with Jenny.

Papà's voice pulled me from my thoughts. "Elena, come here."

I groaned internally. That was the classic "Come meet this man" tone. Glancing at Papà, I tried to convey that I wasn't dressed to meet someone, but he only gave me a blank look, his demand withstanding.

Dominic rounded the house to the back door and I burned with jealousy.

With a sigh, I headed to the porch and closer to a certain soon-to-be brother-in-law. My sweaty skin became a live wire.

I stood next to my father and his guest, but only vaguely heard my papà's introduction because Nicolas was a few feet away. He leaned against a porch column with his hands in his pockets, his gaze warm against my face. A red mark marred his cheekbone, and it looked like he had a cut on the edge of his bottom lip.

That gentleman look went up in smoke . . .

I turned my attention to Papà's guest. "It's nice to meet you, Christian."

I had the uncanny ability to subconsciously take in information, especially when it came to my father's introductions.

I glanced at Christian's face and then paused.

Because *holy* handsome.

Dark hair, piercing blue eyes, with soft yet angled features that were the epitome of masculine magnetism. But there was something cold about him. Maybe it was how his watch fit his wrist, how straight his tie was, how his suit was pressed, and how confident his stance was. The man was a perfectionist—I'd bet money on it. When he smiled, the cold look transformed into charm, if not a bit indifferent. He was so unbelievably handsome I found a blush warming my cheeks.

"I should have come a little earlier and gotten my workout in with you. Looked like you were giving your cousin a run for his money," he said.

The wheels in my head spun. This man was charming, had a cultured if not slightly cavalier tone, and was a real Adonis.

I smiled shyly. "Well, Christian, I run at eight in the mornings." It was an invitation and, surprisingly enough, Papà didn't even blink.

His expression stayed appeased. I wasn't sure if that was a good or bad thing.

Christian laughed, running the thumb of his right hand over the watch on his left. "I'll have to keep that in mind." His gaze warmed, remaining a sliver detached. "It's been a pleasure, Elena."

Papà said something, but the cogs were turning in my head too loudly to hear. As Christian and my father headed inside, I turned to watch them go.

Christian was going to snuff out the flame I held for Nicolas.

He was the first intriguing man I'd met since my sister's fiancé, and I was going to do everything I could to get to know him better. Hopefully, my crush would transfer over like a bad transaction—which it would be, if that dangerous perfectionist vibe was anything to go by.

Flicking my gaze to where Nicolas had stood, my attention halted on him when I realized he was still here.

He was giving me the rudest look I'd ever seen, and for him, that meant something. "Since when do you run every morning?"

How did he know I didn't?

I blinked. "Since right now."

His jaw ticked, and he flicked a dark gaze toward the side before focusing it on me. I realized that was Nicolas Russo's way of rolling his eyes in disgust.

What the heck was his problem?

"He's a cop."

I couldn't help the little nose wrinkle.

Well, not ideal, but I guessed I could work with it. He didn't look like a cop and I could usually tell. Even when they were crooked, they still didn't fit. He was FBI, maybe. No way he was a street cop. They never came to the house, and the fact that Christian had must mean he was high-profile and didn't fear getting spotted by any surveillance. Only the dark side of the world knew how corrupt the government was. Maybe it was why I was so interested in politics—my life was immersed in it already.

After a moment, I lifted a shoulder. "Okay."

His gaze sparked. "Stay away from him."

I paused, not understanding his sudden temper. Maybe this was about last night. Was he that mad about the phone incident?

"I didn't tell Tony about the photo, Nicolas."

"I know," he said with heat. "I did."

My eyes narrowed. "Why would you do that?"

"I wanted to beat the shit out of your brother."

I blinked, not expecting such a candid response, and then let out a half laugh. "Well, was it as satisfying as you had hoped?"

"No." The word was dark, full of meaning and underlined with something magnetic that tingled in my breasts. He glanced at my hand by my side and then back at me. "Not very faithful, are you?"

I was taken aback, even though I didn't understand. "What's that supposed to mean?"

Instead of answering me, he pushed off the column and ran a hand down his tie. "He's not fucking Italian. There's no chance for you and him."

Back on the Christian kick, were we?

Nicolas took a step toward the open front door, apparently done with this conversation.

My papà hadn't seemed to have an issue with what I'd said to Christian. Why was Nicolas making such a big deal of it? Frustration swelled in my chest and the words slipped from my lips before I could stop them.

"Who said I'm thinking about marriage?"

He halted, his dark gaze practically assaulting me.

Wrong thing to say.

"I swear to God, Elena, if I find out you've let some man touch you, I will deliver his hands to you in a box."

I swallowed.

"And I do not. Fucking. Bluff."

He slammed the door behind him.

CHAPTER
Twenty-One

"I can resist anything except temptation."
—Oscar Wilde

Elena

THERE COMES A POINT IN LIFE WHEN YOU KNOW THAT WHAT YOU WANT TO do is wrong, and you have to decide whether to avoid the temptation or do it anyway.

I was doing it anyway.

Nicolas's words should have left a puddle of dread in my stomach. However, they had the opposite effect—sinking into my skin and sending a breathless shiver all the way to my toes.

The man was rude, arrogant, and slightly psychotic.

The logical part of me didn't like him. But the carnal part—*God,* did it want to give him anything he wanted.

Which was a serious problem.

Only made all the more serious by the fact that his statement had sounded suspiciously like jealousy. The idea had left a thrill behind even as he slammed the door in my face.

It left a dangerous, *dangerous* desire to know for sure.

What I was doing was manipulative and slightly juvenile, but I didn't have time to spare. I wanted this new man's interest and I wanted it fast. Although, I might have been challenging the possibility of

Nicolas's jealousy more than anything.

I had to know if this wasn't embarrassingly one-sided.

I didn't know what I would do with the results, but I wasn't thinking that far ahead. All I knew was that I *needed* to know.

So I was testing it.

Teasing it.

Taunting it.

It included a bathing suit, a scene inspired by *Fast Times at Ridgemont High*, minus the nudity unfortunately, and a certain male's attention.

Water dripped down my body as I pulled myself out of the pool, wrung my hair out, and sat on a lounge chair.

A light breeze blew through the yard, and the radio played seventies rock quietly. As I leaned back on my hands and let the sun warm my skin, I realized I was as weak as my face was symmetrical. What I was doing could have been innocent enough, but *why* I was doing it was for all the wrong reasons.

I'd wanted to swim before Christian, Nicolas, and Papà came out to sit at the patio table with paperwork before them, but it became a priority *after* I'd noticed they had.

I wore a light pink one-piece. Papà would kill me if I strutted around in a bikini while he had guests over. But I liked to push it, especially because it was the only thing I could get away with. It was the most risqué one-piece I owned, with only two strings crisscrossing my back, and it was slightly too small, the fabric often riding up my ass.

Papà sat with his back to me, Christian at the end of the table, and Nicolas facing me. The latter's gaze was warm and thrilling each time it touched my skin. He leaned back in his chair and tapped his pen on his papers, his eyes coasting to me every once in a while.

I didn't know what I was doing. I'd never tried my seductive wiles before now. Before I met Nicolas, I only wanted to be as inconspicuous as possible.

Truly, I wasn't acting on rational thought.

I was running on some kind of innate feeling that pulsated in my chest and manipulated my actions.

Occasionally, Christian would glance my way, though it was more detached, as if he appreciated a woman's form but that was all. I guessed I would have to win him over with my personality, then. Cop or not, he was intriguing enough to get to know. With Christian, the darkness lingered under the cold, whereas Nicolas wore his on his sleeve. I wasn't sure which was worse.

They knew one another. I could tell by the way they sat near each other, how easily they communicated. They were friends. I couldn't envision anyone volunteering to be Nicolas Russo's friend, but Christian did look the part if I had to imagine one.

As I stood and pulled my hair out of my ponytail, the heat of two gazes settled on my back. It was most likely due to the fact I had a wedgie baring half my ass. A shiver coasted down my spine.

This probably wasn't doing anything for the women's movement, but there really wasn't one of those in the *Cosa Nostra*.

With the warmth of their eyes still touching me, Papà's voice trailed off as if he'd noticed. He was going to yell at me any minute. I could feel it in the air.

I sighed, grabbed my towel, and started for the door, neglecting to fix my wedgie. Glancing at Nicolas before I headed inside, I swallowed. His pen rested against his lips, and his gaze followed me, simmering with anger.

I wasn't sure what that reaction meant. He could be annoyed I was splashing around while he was trying to work. God, what was I even doing? Once I was in the safety of the house, away from my distracting future brother-in-law, my actions felt ridiculous.

The house was quiet. Adriana was at her last class of summer theater, Mamma was probably in her room bingeing on soap operas, Nonna on *Jerry Springer*, and the boys were in the basement, their laughter filtering up the stairs and into the kitchen.

Tony was always involved with Papà's work, but my father was probably giving him the day off, considering the good beating he'd taken last night and the fact that Nico had been the one to give it to him.

I paused. *Nico?*

Merda.

I padded barefoot to the counter to grab a glass. Swimming always made me feel like I was dying of dehydration.

Opening the cabinet, I stared at the empty bottom shelf. It was getting to the point I was about to put a lock on the entire cupboard, of which only the women in the house knew the code.

Sighing, I stood on my tiptoes and struggled to reach the glass far back on the top shelf. As I was about to give up and climb the counter, I felt it.

The hair on the back of my neck rose.

Nico's body heat brushed my back as an inked forearm reached above me, grabbed a glass, and then set it on the counter next to me.

I tensed, my gaze focused on busted knuckles and an ace of spades tattooed on tanned skin.

Anger rolled off him, and in the dark kitchen it sent a cool mixture of fear and anticipation buzzing through me. Dropping to my heels and grasping the cup, I breathed, "Thanks." I tried to move away from him, but I was forced to step back when his hands gripped the counter on either side of me, trapping me.

My heart drummed so fast it stole my breath.

"You know what happens when you dance around men looking like this?"

I swallowed and shook my head.

"They don't respect you." His voice was rough and so close to my ear it sent a shiver down my neck.

"Who said I want their respect?"

His grip tightened on the counter. "You want him to fuck you?"

I blinked. "What?"

"Christian," he growled.

"And if I do?" I asked quietly.

"My earlier statement is withstanding."

I inhaled slowly, trying to think clearly in his presence.

"Do *you* respect me?" I had no idea where it came from, but it was there now, lingering in the air with a heavy insinuation.

He didn't answer.

A wave of shock rolled through me when the pad of his finger traced the hem of my swimsuit bottoms that still bared too much of my ass. My breath stopped when his other hand slid up my side and gripped my waist, beneath my breast. My nipples tightened, tingling in expectation. Heat pulsated between my legs, and I fought the desire to grab his hand and slide it up until he palmed my breast. I swayed, fighting the need to lean back against him, to feel his body against mine.

His finger slid under my bottoms, gliding over the curve of my ass where it almost met thigh. All the blood in my body sizzled when he came too close to a taboo part of me. Though, it was probably only taboo to me since no one had ever touched me there before.

Wetness pooled between my thighs. The desire for him to touch me, to slip his fingers inside me right here in the kitchen, was so strong I inched up on my tiptoes and arched my back, urging his hand lower.

He cursed roughly and pulled the fabric out from between my cheeks. His hand slid around my hip, grasping my waist to match the other one. They were so close to my breasts I was losing my mind. I fell back until I was leaning against him, and my entire body sang like it never had before.

My nerve endings buzzed and sparked like rain on a live wire. He was so warm and *hard*. His erection pressed against my lower back. Nicolas Russo was turned on, and I'd never experienced a single thing more thrilling.

My head rested on his chest, and the buttons on his dress shirt tickled my bare spine. I brought my hand to my waist and slipped my fingers between his. Our breathing filled the kitchen.

When I heard my brother's laughter from downstairs, I realized how dangerous this was. Anyone could come in.

"You want me to respect you?"

It was a loaded question, but I only knew one answer. Only wanted one thing from this man, and only needed it once so I could know what it was like.

I shook my head.

I wanted him to disrespect me. *Every* inch of me.

His hands tightened on my waist almost painfully, as if he struggled to keep them there. He nuzzled the back of my head, but his voice was suddenly as cold as ice. "You like it when men disrespect you?"

A chill passed through me.

My hand still rested on his, and he gently spun my ring with a finger until the jewel faced downward. His teeth scraped my ear. "Or maybe you just like to get them all worked up, panting after you."

His lips brushed my neck and goose bumps broke out along my body.

"So, which one is it?"

I was a slut or a tease.

Those were the options he'd given me—what he thought of me. Frustration expanded in my chest.

"Both."

He stilled, before making an angry sound in his throat and shoving me away from him.

I grasped the counter, catching myself, and then spun around.

His gaze flared. "Looks like you're as big of a *cheat* as I am, Elena."

What was that supposed to mean? That was the second time he'd insinuated I was somehow disloyal.

Ice trickled into my veins when someone appeared at the top of the basement stairs. *Gabriella.* She looked between us, back and forth, then smiled awkwardly and hurried from the kitchen.

I wasn't in a position to analyze why she had been down there with three of the men in my family, and even if I were, I didn't care to dwell on it. The relief was palpable that she hadn't entered a moment sooner.

"Go upstairs and change, Elena." Nico's voice was hard and uncompromising.

Did he honestly believe I would do what he said? God, he was so full of himself.

My eyes narrowed. "No."

He ran his tongue across his teeth, and before I understood his intention, he had an arm around the backs of my thighs and my feet left the floor. A breath whooshed out of me as he tossed me over his shoulder.

"Guess I'll have to do it for you then," he bit out as he carried me to the door.

"Okay! Okay, I'll do it."

When he didn't put me down, I struggled and tried to wiggle out of his grip. His arm tightened around my thighs like a vise and I couldn't move an inch. He pushed open the swinging door and panic flooded me.

"Stop!" I hissed, hanging upside down. "I said, I'll do it."

"Ask me nicely."

My teeth clenched. "Please, put me down."

He dropped me to my feet in the foyer. His eyes flicked to the staircase, in that commanding way of telling me to get there.

"There's something seriously wrong with you," I told him as I walked away, my heart beating so hard against my ribcage it hurt.

He released a sardonic breath. "You haven't seen anything, Elena."

Truthfully, that's what I was worried about.

CHAPTER
Twenty-Two

"That was the beginning of the end of our thing."
—Anthony Casso

Elena

"COME IN!"
The door of the penthouse on the twenty-second floor swung open, and Gianna stood on the other side. I didn't believe that even someone who knew Gianna would be able to guess what she would wear next.

Tonight, it was a small black dress with a hem cutting diagonally from one hip to the opposite knee. Tall red pumps. Fishnet stockings. Wavy hair that was half-up, tied in two knots on the top of her head, and no makeup. Really, she didn't need it.

"You're early!" she exclaimed. Her eyes shone a little too bright, her pupils too large. She was high. Cocaine, most likely.

"I've brought some bruschetta and seafood salad," Mamma said, moving into the kitchen with a tiny bowl of tomatoes while Benito struggled with everything else.

Adriana and I stayed in the hallway, hesitating.

Why was Gianna answering Nicolas's door?

A sliver of something unpleasant curled in my chest, and for a split second, I didn't like Gianna. The feeling was so strong and sudden I had to inhale a breath to push it away.

It was an unreasonably jealous reaction I shouldn't have had, *especially* after yesterday. The problem was, I could still feel his hands on me, like I'd been branded for life. The only other man who'd gotten as close as Nicolas had a warm, gentle touch which faded to memory only seconds later. What I would give to reverse the two.

Adriana stepped into the apartment, her eyes taking it all in. "So, this is going to be my prison cell."

Mamma gasped and spun around to shoot her a look. *"Adriana!"*

My sister walked further into the room with me following behind.

Gianna laughed. "Thankfully, this prison comes with great amenities. I'll give you a tour!"

Apparently, Nicolas owned a few properties in New York and he'd chosen this one for Adriana. It wasn't as quaint or as homey as his red-brick house, but it was upscale in every meaning of the word.

It was modernly decorated, with white and silver marble floors, lots of glass tables and chrome finishes. The lighting was dim and romantic, twinkling off the wall of glass that showcased the city. It was breathtaking, but I knew my sister would hate it.

"I hate it," she said sourly, examining the view.

"Oh, come on," Benito responded, throwing an arm around her shoulder. "It ain't so bad. Look, it's even got a pool."

It did. The blue water lay still, the railing nothing but glass before a two-hundred-foot drop.

"If you like it so much, then you live here," Adriana said.

"Don't think Nico likes me like that."

A hint of a smile tugged at my sister's lips.

Gianna and Mamma took the tour by themselves, my mother's "oohs" and "ahhs" drifting down the hallway.

Nobody else had arrived yet, not even the groom.

He was probably planning to leave Adriana here and to only show up when conjugal visits were necessary. My cousin Cici, who lived in Chicago, got the same fate. Though, she didn't despise it so much because she hated her husband.

With the thought of "conjugal visits" sticking around like a bad aftertaste, I decided I needed some alcohol. So I went in search of some.

My head was in the fridge when I heard him behind me.

"Look at you, snooping through my shit. You'd think I was marrying you instead."

His voice sent a shiver down my back, but I ignored it and grabbed a wine cooler off the shelf.

Closing the fridge, I turned around.

Nicolas stood on the other side of the island, his gaze on me as he dropped a folder next to Mamma's appetizers. He must have come straight from work, because he only wore a black button-up shirt and pants. Not dressed for a party. His hair was messy, like he'd been running his hands through it, and I had the sudden desire to do it myself.

I leaned against the fridge. "Thank the good Lord for small miracles, huh?"

His gaze was averted as he took off his watch and set it on the island, but a small smile pulled on his lips.

My pulse pattered to an uneven beat. I'd come to the conclusion that even if I were to marry this man, he could give my heart nothing but tiny fissures and cracks—*it* didn't know that, though. Or maybe it did, and the heart only took chances the brain would not. Thankfully, I'd always been a realist and usually reacted to the latter's cues.

However, an entirely different part of me controlled my actions regarding him: base instincts. This was how the human species kept populating. Unyielding attraction and lust. And Mother Nature wouldn't let me forget there was a male in his prime nearby.

We'd been doing something we shouldn't have yesterday. It wasn't like we'd crossed a direct line, but we'd undeniably dipped a couple toes on the other side. It would be much easier to dip a few more the next time. It was a dangerous slope, and I just needed to stay away from it completely.

I had no idea how he would regard me now—now that I'd asked him to *disrespect* me. I planned to pretend it had never happened, but my body hadn't forgotten. It sang in his presence, my stupid heart warming and not knowing what was good for it.

As he came around the island, I tipped my wine cooler out to him in a gesture asking him to open it.

He watched me as if he definitely remembered I'd asked him to disrespect me yesterday and he wouldn't pretend otherwise, though his expression was indifferent, like it was nothing new to him. I was positive it wasn't. I'd had his phone for two minutes max and received a naked picture. I couldn't imagine what I'd see if I had it all day.

He took the bottle from my hand and twisted off the cap. Right before he gave it back, he took a drink while looking at me all the while. My stomach erupted with butterflies from sharing with him, but I ignored the ridiculous feeling.

I swallowed when he returned it to me and headed to the sink. My brows knitted as I looked at the half-empty bottle. How did men take such big drinks?

Leaning on the fridge, with the bottle resting against my lips, I watched him wash his hands.

His eyes came my way, running from the hair I'd straightened and wore down, to my gold dress that stopped mid-thigh. His eyes narrowed slightly, like he didn't like it at all. When his attention landed on my white heels, it traveled back up my body slowly, and I knew he was looking for the pink.

Danger. Playfulness. *Fever.* A mixture of them all filled my chest, trickling through my bloodstream and straight between my legs. Beneath the light pink thong that suddenly felt heavy, hot, and damp.

A little lightheaded, I scraped my teeth on the bottle, biting down.

His gaze darkened.

Was the air growing warmer?

Cazzo.

Brother-in-law. Brother. In. Law.

As my eyes fell downward, I paused.

The water was running pink.

He was washing blood off his hands.

"Good day at work?" My tone was sweet and sarcastic.

He flicked an amused gaze to me. "And look at how well you play wife. Starting to think I got the short end of the stick."

My eyes followed his to see Adriana sitting on the floor, cross-legged in the corner, playing what looked like a game on her phone. She was at least dressed appropriately in a yellow halter dress and flats. It would take blackmail to get her in heels.

The TV sounded from behind the low wall that separated the kitchen from the living room, and I imagined Benito was settled on the couch with his arms resting across the back as he always had them. In the background, my mamma was squealing about how big the shower was.

I tilted my head. "I think we do much better as *fratello* and *sorella*, don't you?"

He licked his lips, running his teeth across the bottom one thoughtfully, but it looked like he was thinking about all the *wrong* things.

Those butterflies took flight.

"If you say so, *Elena*."

"I do, *Ace*."

He dried his hands and tossed the hand towel on the counter. Just like a man not to hang it back up.

"You been reading up on me?"

"Maybe." I lifted a shoulder. "But no one knows why they call you Ace. Can you kill a man with a playing card?"

That amused him. "Why does it have to be about killing? Maybe I'm just damn good at cards."

I raised a brow. "Are you?"

My heartbeat raced as he walked toward me, because it felt more like a *stalk* than anything.

"I'm all right." His expression hinted at dark amusement, like he knew something I didn't. He stepped within a foot of me, braced a hand on the fridge above my head, and then leaned in until I could see nothing but him.

I held my breath.

His gaze was thoughtful, as though he wondered if he could trust me with his secrets, whether he wanted to.

"You didn't read much about me," he guessed.

I shook my head.

He ran a thumb across my chin, right below my bottom lip and down the small indention. "First man I killed, I shoved an ace of spades down his throat."

I swallowed as he took a step back and walked away from me.

"Name's been with me ever since."

"What about her?"

"Bitter and bisexual," Adriana answered blandly, taking a sip of wine from her seat beside me at the island.

"How can you tell she's bisexual?" I asked.

"She's checked out Gianna's boobs *and* Benito."

I paused. "Well, her boobs are kind of distracting."

My sister tilted her head, regarding Gianna's breasts. "Yeah, I guess you're right."

The penthouse was full of about twenty Russos I hardly knew. The women stood in a corner, talking amongst themselves, and the last thing I wanted to do was small talk. Adriana should have been getting to know them better, but she never did anything by the book.

Papà was speaking to Nico, who had just come out of his room freshly showered and dressed in a black suit. Mamma's smile was fake—she was doing a poor job of feigning interest in Nicolas's aunt's conversation. And Adriana and I sat here, playing a game where we judged people by two words, only because Mamma took my sister's phone—and therefore *Angry Birds*—and yelled at her to get off the floor.

So far, Adriana thought everyone looked bitter and had some kind of secret sexuality. I didn't think she was giving this game her all.

She still hadn't shared with me why she'd been so upset last night, and that could mean two things: she'd given it some thought and decided it wasn't as bad as she initially believed; or, the one I was concerned about—she'd decided not to listen to his demands. How would

Nicolas deal with that? My stomach tightened.

"Your turn," Adriana said, picking at the label on my empty wine cooler.

At that moment, the door swung open and a groaned "Why?" escaped my lips.

Tony stood on the other side of the door with Jenny. Her blond hair was down, her dress was tight and navy blue, the same color as her eyes as they landed on us. "Ohmygod, hi! It's been forever since I've seen you!"

Adriana rolled her eyes. She hated fake cheer, or really, just cheer in general. It wasn't my favorite either, but I understood *fake* better than anyone.

I nudged my sister's shoulder, silently telling her to be nice.

Jenny's screech brought everyone's attention to the door. Nico's gaze landed on her while speaking to my papà. I didn't know what I expected, but it wasn't for him to glance away to finish his sentence, uninterested.

Tony headed to Benito and Dominic, who hung out near the mini-bar, and Jenny came straight to us. I tensed as my brother walked by Nicolas, and then let out a breath when there was no altercation. They only glanced at each other with indifference. I'd never understand men.

"I'm so happy for you, Adriana," Jenny said as she reached us. "Your wedding is so soon." It looked like Jenny wanted to hug her, but my sister's expression made it clear she didn't want to be touched. Jenny took an awkward step back after coming too close.

I tried to lighten the mood and smiled. "How are you, Jenny? I hear you're graduating culinary school soon."

"Yes, but I don't think I'll ever be as good a cook as Celia." She said it loudly enough for my mamma to hear, who only pursed her lips and sipped her cocktail.

I swore Adriana muttered, "Suck-up."

Truthfully, nobody liked Jenny.

Papà frowned when he saw her, and Mamma pretended she wasn't here. My father's reason was that she wasn't Italian or connected to the *Cosa Nostra,* and therefore a liability. Jenny knew what my family was involved in, though she never let on she did. She wasn't faithful to Tony, which meant she didn't love him. In this life, there was only one reason a woman from the outside would stick around with a man she didn't love: money.

Jenny was a gold digger.

A nice one, but a little gold digger, indeed.

Tony was paying for her classes, her apartment, and the diamond bracelet on her wrist.

I'd always tried to give her the benefit of the doubt, but after seeing her very naked on Nicolas's phone a couple nights ago, I realized I was wrong.

She grew up in the foster system, in a poor home. I couldn't dislike her for trying to make her life better any way she could, but I didn't like that she was pulling on my brother's heartstrings for her own gain.

I never confronted anyone, though.

No one besides Nicolas Russo, anyway.

"Well, you're definitely better than Adriana and I combined," I said with a laugh. Nico's gaze found me, lingering, and I swallowed. "You'll have to give us some pointers some time."

"Oh, I'd love that!" Jenny exclaimed.

Two quiet knocks sounded on the door, and Gianna pulled herself away from a conversation with Valentina Russo to answer it.

When I saw it was Christian standing on the other side, I sat straighter in my chair. Brown hair combed back, in a navy suit and red tie, his countenance appeared welcoming. Only his icy blue eyes seemed to fit with the cold resonance he carried around.

Every woman in the room turned to stare—even my mamma's eyes widened on him. They might as well have taken their panties off and thrown them at him it was so obvious. Nicolas's gaze warmed my face, but I refused to look at him.

Once Gianna noticed who it was, her head rolled with annoyance, and she tried to shut the door on him.

With one hand and indifference, Christian easily kept it open.

Gianna turned to walk away, but he stopped her by grabbing her wrist, and then pulled her closer.

I watched, enraptured.

I didn't want Gianna to be involved with Christian because *I* needed him, but there was something compelling about the dressed-to-the-nines agent and the walking fashion disaster that was Gianna. They were so different, and yet . . . maybe not so different at all.

Gripping her chin, Christian looked into her eyes with scrutiny. He shook his head with a slight grimace, before shoving her face away. Gianna muttered something that looked to be *stronzo—asshole—*and then stomped away on her stilettos.

Christian must have noticed she was high, but it didn't look like Gianna cared at all what he thought. So, what was their relationship? Maybe she was his stepmother, too. She was married to a man three times her age, though I noticed she never wore a ring.

Adriana's gaze landed on Christian, before she announced, "Perfectionist." She paused, tilted her head. "Straight as an arrow."

Well, at least that was on my side.

CHAPTER
Twenty-Three

"Judges, lawyers, and politicians have a license to steal.
We don't need one."
—Carlo Gambino

Nico

I WAS POURING A COUPLE FINGERS OF WHISKEY NEAT WHEN ADRIANA CAME UP beside me. I eyed her as she grabbed the vodka decanter and then filled a tumbler three-fourths full.

She glanced at me, looked away, and then flicked her gaze back to me when she noticed my attention. *"What?"*

"Maybe try to hide your alcoholism from me from now on."

"Let me continue my classes and I will."

"Would you rather be safe, or happy?"

She blinked as if it were a much more complicated question. "Both, I think."

"Unfortunately, that isn't a choice."

Her sigh was put-out. "It's not my fault a lot of men want to kill you."

A lot was probably an understatement.

"And now you."

Her brows knitted. "What?"

"They'll want to kill my wife too," I said, before adding, "Probably rape you a few times first."

She frowned. "Like you're going to do to me?"

Somehow, I knew she was going to say that. I stared at her, my expression impassive. She pushed a strand of caramel-colored hair behind her ear. She had golden specks in her brown eyes, like Elena's. In a disturbing way, I hoped there were other similarities.

"You're not even going to say you won't rape me?" She sounded annoyed, bringing her drink to her lips while looking out the floor-to-ceiling windows.

I admired the view with her. "No."

"Why not?"

"Not very good at keeping promises."

She choked on a sip of vodka, glancing at me with wide eyes. "I'm going to die," she muttered before disappearing.

Dry amusement filled me, and I gave my head the tiniest shake. That meeting with my future wife went well. I hadn't raped a woman in my life and wouldn't start now, though, for some reason, I'd felt like sabotaging the conversation. Probably because I was already agitated, and the night had just started.

Elena stood in the kitchen talking to Lorenzo, with her complete attention on him. Her long hair was pin-straight and she wore a gold dress that hugged her every curve. It was *way* too fucking tight and receiving enough stares from my cousins to piss me off. Even Luca had glanced at her with a knowing smile and then tipped his beer to me in an obnoxious gesture.

Lorenzo was making a besotted idiot of himself. The man was a cold-blooded killer, yet he appeared to be a nervous mess talking to Elena Abelli. He was currently rubbing the back of his neck and fucking *blushing*—and just imagining Elena tied to Lorenzo's bed in some kind of fucked-up BDSM scenario made that Russo blood burn me from the inside out.

"That went smoothly." Gianna's tone was dry, apparently having overheard my conversation with Adriana. "Why did you have to invite *him*?"

Her pupils were so dilated only a sliver of dark brown surrounded them. A wave of displeasure ran through me. It sucked me back to age fifteen when I found my mamma's lifeless eyes wide open.

"Who?" My question was indifferent, but I already knew.

Her gaze narrowed. "Christian."

"It's none of your business who I invite to *my* apartment, Gianna."

I wouldn't have invited him if I'd had a legitimate reason to do so—and more than Elena practically drooling over him yesterday. The asshole had a pretty face, and it annoyed me more than I cared to admit that it had interested Elena.

"I don't want him here, Ace." She watched Christian talk to my uncle Jimmy with a sour expression.

"Ask me if I care," I answered dryly.

Gianna had hated Christian since the moment she met him. The FBI part was at the top of the list of reasons why, but she was also the agent's opposite in every way. She scoffed at his perfectionism, while Christian grimaced at her lack of decorum.

Elena's soft laughter filtered through the room, hitting me in the chest.

My jaw tightened.

Lorenzo was not that fucking funny.

"That's the wrong sister you're staring at. The right one is over there." Gianna pointed a white-painted fingernail at Adriana, who sat on the couch next to Benito with her legs pulled up beside her. "She's probably recovering from your threat of rape."

I let out a dry breath when Adriana giggled at something on Benito's phone. "She looks real traumatized." There was something cold and fearless about her, but apparently the idea of sex with me was unappealing enough she believed she would die from it. Maybe it was a good threat I could keep in mind, because I thought I might need a strong one with her.

Truthfully, I'd thought about sleeping with Adriana a complete total of zero times. All thoughts of sex had been about her sister, especially after she'd arched her ass against me yesterday in the universal way all men understood as a go-ahead.

She hadn't been shy about letting me know she'd let me touch her, but I couldn't help an inkling of awareness from settling in when she'd placed her hand on mine and I'd felt that ring of hers. She loved some man. Wore his cheap ring on her finger like it was a diamond.

Bitterness had run through me. She wanted to get off and she was going to use me to do it. When I realized that, I'd felt something I had never felt in my life: like I was expendable. And that pissed me off.

Nonetheless, *Do you respect me?* had followed me around all day and night in that soft, sweet voice of hers. Everywhere I fucking went.

There was always some vice that eventually killed a Russo.

Irrationality. Idiocy. A penchant for unprotected sex with cheap hookers. My father's was monetary greed.

I was beginning to think mine was Elena Abelli.

I wanted to fuck her and ruin her for anyone else. I wanted to crush her wings and then put them back together again so she'd become dependent on me. I wanted her to *need* me. That dark, possessive, and dangerous feeling crawled through me every time she crossed my path.

Elena Abelli was my vice, and fuck if I'd let it kill me.

However, the urge to try to fuck her out of my system was consuming me, regardless if she wanted me to be someone else. It was an itch I needed to scratch. And when I was done with her, she'd never remember another.

Gianna shook her head while looking down on me, although she was a foot shorter, even in her heels. "That's an awful idea," she said.

"What?"

"Sleeping with Elena."

Jesus.

Elena's papà stood three feet away, though he was too deep in conversation to have heard.

"Gianna," I warned.

"What? It's what you were thinking."

"And what am I thinking right now?" Gianna thought she was clairvoyant when she was high, which was a lot of the time.

She pursed her lips. "That you want to strangle me."

My brows rose in accord as I took a drink of whiskey.

"I don't understand how I had sex with you," she said, observing the party with a sigh.

I didn't either, though I could only feel relieved that she'd been the one to start it. Truthfully, we'd been so drunk, there was hardly a memory to go with the deed.

My gaze landed on Tony, who appeared to be getting talked down to by his mamma. It was only a diverting amusement that he'd brought Jenny, who was currently trying to sell my aunt Mary Kay.

Gianna began to drift away, but before I knew what I was doing, I grabbed her arm and asked, "And why would it be such a bad idea?"

I didn't look at her, but I felt her sad smile.

"Because you'll fall in love with her," she said. "And she won't love you back."

Elena

The chatter was low, Elvis Presley's *Can't Help Falling In Love* a little quieter. The soft lighting sparkled off the glass view of the city, and Nicolas's black-suited form only highlighted it as he stood near the bar.

I didn't know how it had happened, but I was drunk. Lolled into a sense of warmth and complacency, and I couldn't stop myself from heading toward what had to be a gentleman. The problem was, if I stopped to ask this one for help, he'd most likely take advantage of me. Or maybe that was only wishful thinking . . . He'd probably only give me a rude stare.

"I didn't expect you to like Elvis Presley."

I was assuming just because I could.

Nicolas glanced at me with a half-lidded amber gaze that always sent my pulse racing. "Every time you've assumed, you've been wrong."

I took the remaining steps toward him, eating up the electricity that spanned between us with each click of my heels. "That's not true."

I stood by his side, perusing the liquor decanters. Close enough my shoulder brushed his chest. Close enough my skin danced with awareness.

"Yeah? Then what have you gotten right?"

I reached across him for the gin, pretending that my arm grazing his didn't affect me at all, when in reality it sent a rush of warmth low in my stomach. "I assumed from day one that you were an asshole, and I was right." I paused with my hand on the decanter, not believing that had come out of my mouth.

A hint of a sly smile pulled at his lips, almost as if he was thinking about something inappropriate. "Is that the first time you've said asshole?"

"Yeah. Did I use it right?" I tugged off the lid and poured some liquor into my glass.

"Could've been better."

I frowned, a little affronted. The first time I used a curse word to insult someone and it was lame? Maybe I didn't have it in me. I glanced at him, and a sudden wave of shyness overcame me when I noticed he'd been watching me.

"How so?" I added some tonic water and lime to my glass.

"It was pretty unmoving." He had one hand in his pocket, while the other brought his glass to his lips as he looked around the room.

"How would Nicolas Russo do it, then?"

His gaze settled on mine. "If I was going to insult you, I'd make sure to leave you thinking about it for a while."

I stirred my drink, feeling like stirring up something else. "So show me."

His eyes narrowed. "You want me to insult you?"

I nodded, took a sip, and then licked the gin off my lips. My breath turned shallow when his gaze fell to my mouth and darkened.

"Thought I did that yesterday."

"Really? I've already forgotten."

The tiniest bit of amusement crossed his expression, and he ran his tongue across his teeth, a calculating stare coasting around the room. We were sort of secluded, the guests closest to us having their backs turned. Although, when I was in his presence it always felt like we were alone.

He shook his head. "I'm not going to insult you."

"Why? Are you *acting* like a gentleman tonight?"

"Nah. Just don't care to."

I scoffed. "That's because you don't have a good one—"

A breath of shock escaped me when his rough palm gripped the side of my throat and he pulled me to him. His lips pressed against my ear.

"You look like a *slut* in that dress, Elena."

A violent shudder rolled through me.

My eyes closed as his warm, masculine scent sank through my skin and sent a hum through my veins.

His words softened. "Only good for one thing, and it's *not* running your pretty little mouth."

I couldn't breathe with his body pressed against my side, his dirty, insulting words in my ear. He ran a thumb down the goose bumps on the back of my neck, and then his grip was gone. I stared blankly as he grabbed his drink and walked away, leaving me with a parting word.

"That's how I would do it."

CHAPTER
Twenty-Four

"You can be the moon and still be jealous of the stars."
—Gary Allan

Elena

"**M**AMMA, DOES THIS DRESS MAKE ME LOOK . . . EASY?"

My mother sipped her cocktail with a straw, a crease forming between her brows. "Well, *cara mia* . . . you did sleep with a man you couldn't have known very well."

"Mamma!" Adriana scolded.

There were few moments in my life when my mother and sister's roles switched, but it *had* happened.

"I didn't ask if I *was* easy. I asked if I looked easy," I sighed.

The truth was, this dress *was* tight. And by "tight" I mean that I didn't try it on at the store and when I finally got around to putting it on it fit two sizes too small. But it was just too pretty to stay in my closet.

"You don't look easy, Elena," Adriana assured.

Benito sat next to her on the couch, his arm resting across the back. He gave my dress a cautious expression and scratched his jaw. "Well . . ."

"Ugh, just forget it."

I headed through the throng of people toward the patio area and pool. The chatter dissipated as I walked out the double doors and into a hot, still night. The terrace was empty; the only company tall buildings and their yellow lights filling the horizon.

I crossed my arms over my chest and glanced at the nighttime sky. "No stars," I said quietly. I had a feeling they would be visible at Nicolas's red brick house.

"Scorpius." The voice was cool.

Christian's presence brushed my side as he came to stand beside me. "Scorpius is there." He nodded to where my gaze was focused, with a flat gray sky staring back.

"And there?" I pointed a little to the left.

A small smile pulled on his lips. "Aquila."

I had a feeling he could name every constellation and each star they were made up of. It suddenly felt like he was completely out of my league. *Cop* or not.

A sigh escaped my lips. My head was light, my inhibitions unhindered by the alcohol I'd consumed.

"Don't enjoy parties?" he asked.

"No, I do. Honestly, I'm shallow in that regard."

He laughed. The sound was deep and rough, and a shiver coasted down my spine. He even laughed like an Adonis.

"How do you know so much about the stars?" I asked.

"Grew up in an old farmhouse in Iowa. Sometimes there was nothing to do but stare at the sky. Got tired of not knowing what I was looking at."

"Well, that was a decent explanation, but it was a lie. Try again."

I blinked. That would have never come out of my mouth a year ago. I would have accepted the lie and moved on. Maybe I only needed to become an alcoholic for the courage to free myself from my childhood chains.

I saw the tiniest smile out of the corner of my eye. "Studied astronomy abroad. Wanted to impress French girls right into my bed."

"Even more unbelievable. Have you seen yourself?" With that face, this man wouldn't have to impress anyone.

Another smile. "How did you know the first one was wrong?"

"You're colder than the Arctic. You don't become that way in a friendly small town. That's city living, most likely on your own. No wonder you found yourself on the wrong side of the law."

Small shake of his head. "Heard a lot about you, Elena Abelli. Can't say you're what I was expecting."

I didn't even want to know what this man had heard about me. I seemed to be a popular subject, and I didn't believe it was for any good reason.

"Haven't you heard? Assuming will only get you killed."

"Sounds right out of Ace's handbook," he said wryly.

A sliver of uncertainty curled in my chest. He knew there was something going on between Nicolas and me, though I didn't know what myself. What a twisted web I was tangled in.

"Christian, do you drink?"

"I do."

"I'm going to use the ladies' room and then make one. What would you like?" I finally looked from the sky to him. Wide shoulders in a navy blue suit outlined the brightly lit horizon.

His presence was comfortable but distant, like he stood on a different terrace another world away. His gaze met mine, and I waited for that zing of chemistry to settle in, but all I felt was scrutinized by icy blue eyes in a handsome face full of secrets.

He ran a thumb over his watch, in a thoughtful tic I'd noticed he had. "I'll get the drinks and meet you back out here."

His gaze flicked to the left and so did mine. My papà watched us through the glass in the living room, not with caution but interest. All of a sudden, I knew. This had been set up.

Disappointment sank like lead in my stomach. I wanted control of some things in my life—this conversation one of them—but as my papà gave me a "behave" expression, I knew it had all been contrived.

Although, if Papà was considering Christian, that meant he hadn't settled on Oscar Perez. The possibility released some of the pressure closing in on me. I would take Christian over that creep any day.

"That sounds great." I smiled the Sweet Abelli smile.

Feeling tipsy, with too many thoughts on my mind, I headed inside.

My feet froze when I saw Nicolas leaning against the hallway wall. One hand was in his pocket while the other held a cigarette he played between his fingers. He wore an expression most people would run from.

I had no choice but to walk past him, so I swallowed, and then forced one foot in front of the other when I wanted to head in the opposite direction.

His gaze burned as it followed my every step. My heart raced, and I prayed for anyone to step around the low wall and save me from this man.

My skin danced with unease as I walked by him, but apparently, he was only trying to kill me with his expression because he didn't say a word. His silence seemed to be worse than his demands; at least I knew his intentions then. Once I'd made my way past him, I stopped, turned, and snapped, "What?"

"What did I tell you about Christian, Elena?" His voice was low and calm, but it carried a deadly edge.

I hadn't considered his current mood could be due to the fact I was talking to Christian on the terrace. We'd only been speaking, and in view of everyone. Was he serious?

"I don't know. I must have missed it." My response was sarcastic, and he didn't like it at all if his narrowed gaze was anything to go by.

"Then let me remind you. Stay the fuck away from him."

"I told you before, and I'll say it again: I'm an Abelli, not a Russo. You don't get to tell me what to do."

"I'm growing tired of you not showing me the respect a don is due," he bit out.

"And I'm fucking tired of men!"

His gaze grew lethal. "Watch your fucking mouth."

I couldn't believe what I had said, but I was drunk, frustrated, and just damn tired of trying to force myself not to feel a certain way. I could still taste the curse word on my tongue and it felt strange, sinful, *liberating*.

"No Christian."

Two words. He expected me to listen to those two commanding words.

I shook my head. In my mind, it was Christian or Oscar. The easiest decision I'd ever had to make.

"No."

He slipped the cigarette in his pocket, and my pulse leapt when he took a step toward me.

I backed up and was only aided when a soft yet consuming grip came to my throat and he lightly pushed me. I fell back a step until I hit the wall. It was an aggressive move, but the way he did it so gently, so absolutely, made something flutter in my chest and spread throughout my body. Want. *Need.*

He stepped closer until his vest brushed my dress, and my breasts tightened in anticipation. I couldn't breathe with him so close, his hand around my throat, and the idea that anyone could come down this hall. People were drinking; they'd have to use the restroom.

He braced a palm on the wall beside me, and I'd never felt so consumed in my life. His head lowered, lightly resting on top of mine.

What is happening?

My heart burned.

"Nicolas," I breathed. "This is inappropriate."

His thumb caressed my neck, causing my pulse to hitch.

"Platonic," he rasped.

My insides melted, my lips parted, and my vision grew hazy. I wanted to taste that word straight from his mouth. A laugh from around the wall filtered through the buzz in my ears. I shook my head to clear it, but his face was so close to mine I couldn't think.

"No," I panted. "It's not. Please let me go."

"No. Christian." His tone wasn't nice, even though his touch remained so. It was a strange play on my senses.

And then I realized what this was.

Blackmail.

He was going to hold me here until I complied. He knew being caught like this would unnerve me more than it ever would him because of my past.

Frustration tightened in my lungs. The longer we stood here—him holding me in an intimate way—the further the panic spread through my blood, itching and chafing. I pushed against his chest in a last-ditch effort, but it was like trying to move a brick wall.

"Okay," I whispered. "No Christian."

He must have been satisfied with my answer, because he stepped back.

A second later, someone came around the corner. Ice crawled up my throat. Benito stopped when he saw us, his eyes narrowing to slits.

Nicolas and I stood a couple feet apart now, though we were both alone, and my wide doe eyes had to give everything away. I forced a smile, and Nicolas gave my cousin a look of dark indifference before I sprinted into the bathroom.

Leaning against the door, I exhaled a breath of relief.

I was not going to marry Oscar Perez.

Now that I knew there was an out, I let myself hope for the best. And I wasn't going to lose the chance because of Nicolas Russo.

I used the restroom, went straight to the terrace beside the pool, took my gin and tonic from Christian, who must have noticed I liked them—a good quality in a man—and swallowed a large drink for courage.

Then I talked to him. Animatedly. Like it was 100 percent my choice and not done by my father's interference. Like I hadn't gotten blackmailed not to.

Christian was amused by it all, appearing to know everything I did, and I wouldn't doubt it. He was perceptive, and *hot*. He only got hotter the more I drank, but, for some illogical reason, I couldn't push Nicolas out of my mind for a second. I was continually aware of his presence, even with this insanely attractive man's avid attention.

My gaze caught on Nicolas's through the glass. He watched me, his hands in his pockets, while talking to Luca. His expression was un-expected: indifferent and calm. Like the exchange in the hall hadn't happened.

What a confusing man.

He'd told me he didn't bluff, and unfortunately, I would soon learn he really didn't.

Five minutes later, my cheeks felt hot from my fifth drink of the night, and I was beginning to think I'd imagined Nicolas's temper as well. Christian was easy to talk to, though I wondered how much of what he said was the truth. I listened as he told me about a cabin he owned in the Rockies, where the stars were incredibly bright.

"Sounds beautiful," I commented. "I would love to see it."

"See what?"

My shoulders tensed at Nicolas's deep voice behind my back.

"My cabin in Colorado," Christian responded, while I said, "None of your business," at the same time.

"You sound angry, Elena." Nicolas's voice was tainted with something dangerous. "Maybe you should cool off."

My brows knitted. "What? No—"

I never got to finish what I had to say.

Because, with one hand on my side, Nicolas pushed me into the pool.

CHAPTER
Twenty-Five

"What is drama but life with the dull bits cut out."
—Alfred Hitchcock

Elena

WHILE I CLIMBED OUT OF THE POOL, SOAKING WET, THEY STOOD A FOOT apart staring at one another.

Christian's lips tipped up as he brought his drink to his mouth, but his gaze never left Nico's.

"*Elena!*" Mamma gasped, running onto the patio. "What happened?"

Everyone's eyes touched my skin through the glass, and it felt like I was on display at the zoo.

My teeth clenched. "I fell."

"*Madonna!* How much have you drunk?"

"Apparently more than I thought," I muttered.

Her hesitant gaze ran to Nicolas and Christian, who were the two most ungentlemanly men I'd ever met—the former for pushing me into the pool, and the latter for not helping me out.

Gianna came rushing outside with a towel, and Christian flicked a slow gaze to her over his glass, like the glance was equal parts involuntary and unwanted.

"Thank you," I mumbled, accepting it.

"I think I have something for you to wear." She grabbed the heels I'd pulled off so I could get out of the pool. I should have thrown them at Nicolas's head, but by that time I had the entire party's attention.

As I followed Gianna inside, everyone stared at me with wide eyes—well, all the women. I expected the worst from my papà, but he wasn't even looking at me. His attention was on the two men on the patio, his expression darkening.

My stomach dipped.

How many had seen that it was Nicolas who pushed me in? And why would he do something like that? I guessed Russos did what they wanted when they wanted. Papà should have known from the beginning not to get involved with Nicolas.

I followed Gianna into a room that looked like a spare, while drying my hair with a towel. She dug through a bag on the bed, and something twisted in my chest. Was she planning on spending the night? Ugh, why did I even care? Nicolas had pushed me into a damn pool. I didn't like him at all.

Gianna found a pair of red shorts that had white trim on the edges and up the sides, and a plain white t-shirt. The outfit was from the seventies, right off Farrah Fawcett. I was beginning to wonder where Gianna shopped.

I accepted the clothes and a sports bra—thankfully, Gianna was close to the same size as me in the breast department—and turned around to change.

"Thank you. I'm sorry for the inconvenience. I guess I'm just . . . clumsy."

Ugh.

Gianna laughed. "You don't have to lie. I saw Ace push you in."

I paused with my dress around my waist while I pulled the t-shirt on. "How many saw?"

"Oh, mostly everyone."

Of course they did. I blew out a breath, shimmied the dress down my hips, and then pulled the shorts on.

Turning around, I saw Gianna lying on the bed, her feet on the floor and her arms stretched above her head. It was an unladylike pose the Sweet Abelli would have never imitated. And I envied her for it.

"Thank you for the clothes again," I said. "I'll wash them and return them to you."

"Keep them."

Silence morphed between us, and I had an urge to fill it.

"Does he usually push girls into pools?"

She laughed, sitting up. "No, definitely not. He would have to care to do that."

I paused, not knowing what to say considering she'd insinuated he *cared* about *me*. *What have I gotten myself into?* All I knew was that I needed to undo it.

"It's not like that." I wanted to sound firm, but I came off more uncertain than anything.

She smiled, but her eyes conveyed years of hidden torment, before saying quietly, "It never is."

A few minutes later, I learned that everyone had in fact witnessed my sister's fiancé pushing me into the pool. Apparently, this was hard for even the Russos to understand, because the women—Valentina, especially—regarded me with scrutiny, like they'd finally noticed I was at the party. Jemma, however, looked at me with sympathy, as though I'd gotten into something that would eventually kill me. I didn't know what to think about that one.

On the way out of the apartment, I ignored Adriana's drunk and curious questions, Benito's angry gaze on the back of my head, and my papà's and brother's stone-cold silence. Before I stepped out the door, I glanced back.

Nico's hands were braced on the island, and he watched me, his gaze a warm caress on my skin. I'd met his stare enough to grow used to it by now, but tonight something was different. It wasn't rude. It was pensive, calculating, slightly devious. Like he was contemplating doing something he shouldn't.

I swallowed, tore my gaze away, and didn't look back.

I assumed I would be grilled on the way home, but nobody said a word to me. My mamma talked about the wedding that was next weekend, and my papà responded accordingly from the driver's seat.

Adriana fell asleep, her head resting against the window.

Tony wrapped an arm around my shoulders, giving me a squeeze. I listened to the tire noise, watched the yellow light fly by and cascade through the glass and into the car.

Through it all, I still saw the calculating expression on Nico's face, still felt the caress on my skin.

And I knew it like the sky was blue, he'd been thinking about *me*.

It was Thursday afternoon. Hot sun burned on concrete, while the smells of fresh bread and garlic filled the air outside Francesco's green double doors.

My gaze focused on the ground as I walked from the car to the restaurant, because the strap on one of my heels had come undone. I tried to fix it, hopped on one foot, and when I began to tip sideways a strong hand gripped my waist from behind and steadied me.

"You're a walking hazard, you know that?"

I tensed. His deep voice rushed over me and filled my insides with a warmth it shouldn't.

As I stepped away from his grasp, his palm skimmed from my waist to my hip. A burning caress. It felt obscene when he touched me, like he had his hands in much different places than only on my side. The feeling was frustrating because I couldn't stop it, nor could I turn off the thrill that buzzed beneath my skin when he was near.

My eyes narrowed but I kept my mouth closed. I'd gone over how I would deal with this man: I wouldn't. *Don't engage him.* It was the best I could come up with.

When I continued to walk awkwardly with my strap dangling against my ankle, an amused breath came from behind me.

"The silent treatment, huh?"

My teeth clenched. He thought this was funny. How could I be so confused and twisted up about him, while he thought it was all amusing? I spun around, retorting, "You pushed me into a pool! Why should

I talk to you?"

Light blue shirt, gray waistcoat and pants, black tie, stupidly hand-some face. I swallowed. *Why did I engage?* It was too late to go back now.

He ran a thumb across his bottom lip, his gaze falling to coast over my strapless nude dress and pink heels. *"You're* the little liar, Elena."

Of course he'd turn this around on me; he was too good at that. *"Me?* You tried to blackmail me!"

"If you would've listened to me in the first place I wouldn't have had to."

Was he serious? His gaze remained stoic. Ugh, he *was.*

I turned around, and when I almost fell again, I braced a palm on the hot brick wall and managed to buckle my shoe with one hand.

"Where's your cousin?" he asked, typing something on his phone. "You shouldn't be out here alone."

Benito had only dropped me off at the door to go park, and Mamma and Papà had driven separately with Adriana. But that was none of Nicolas's business.

"Quit the brotherly act. I already have one."

I said it just because I thought it bothered him.

His jaw ticked. "Inside, Elena."

"Ask me nicely," I retorted, mocking him from the time he'd said it to me.

His gaze came up from his phone, amused, dark. "If you don't get your ass inside, Elena, you'll be the one screaming *please.*"

My God . . .

"That was inappropriate," I breathed while heading to the doors.

"Perfectly platonic," he parried.

It was then I realized I'd really screwed myself over with that word.

The red-lettered Closed sign was visible through the window near a few shelves of fresh bread, but when I pushed the door open, I was im-mediately greeted with, *"Mia bella ragazza!"*

A smile tugged at my lips. "Zio."

My great uncle grasped my face and pressed a kiss to each cheek. He smelled like oregano and nostalgia. Some things will forever have that smell no matter if they never left to begin with.

Francesco Abelli lived on the tamer side of the *Cosa Nostra*. Every cent laundered in our family name was a product of this dress pants and shoes, wife beater and apron-wearing sixty-five-year-old. When he wasn't cooking books, he was running this restaurant.

"Have a seat near the windows. *È una bella giornata.*"

It wasn't *that* beautiful of a day. It was hotter than Hades, but he probably hadn't set foot outside. He lived upstairs.

I took a seat at the table and poured myself a glass of water from the pitcher. Blinding sunlight streamed through the large window. It was an awful spot to sit, honestly, but Zio's word was as final as Papà's, no matter if everyone was miserable because of it.

Benito came in and took a seat, clearing his throat and pouring himself some tea. My eyes narrowed on him as I sipped water through a straw. "You got a hickey on your neck."

He rubbed the spot, muttering, "Told her not to do that."

I shook my head, not wanting to know how he'd gotten some action in between parking the car and now.

Fifteen minutes later, Mamma and Papà sat across from me, Adriana on my side, and Nico on my other. Mamma frowned when she realized my sister and Nico weren't sitting beside each other, but neither the bride nor groom seemed concerned. Tony, Benito, Dominic, Luca, and my uncle Manuel shared a table next to us, talking amongst themselves.

Mamma glowered and blinked against the bright sunlight, and Papà blocked it by reading his menu, though he knew it by heart.

Lunch wasn't a tense affair like I'd expected it to be after the note last night left off on. However, the oddest thing about it was Adriana. She seemed distant, like she was here but her thoughts were a mile away. She only stared out the window, when she was known to always keep her hands busy.

Papers were strewn about the table as Mamma went over the

last of the wedding details with Nico, asking for his approval on some things.

"And will there be a honeymoon?" Mamma asked.

Unease danced beneath my skin to a foreboding tune. I shifted in my seat.

Nico ran a hand across his jaw, glancing out the window. My gaze followed his into the street, Long Island pavement and sun.

A tickle played in my awareness when I saw a black town car on the road, going slower than normal. And by the time I saw the tattoo *MS* on the driver's face, Nico's voice filled the restaurant, "*Giù!*"

Down.

Shouts broke out. *Giù, giù, giù*, over and over again like a messed-up recording with a myriad of voices. Alarm came on the air so thick I could taste it on my tongue.

And then a lungful of air escaped me as I was taken to the floor. A heavy body covered mine as glass shattered in an unmistakable pattern. *Gunfire.* My heartbeat drummed in my ears, and I couldn't discern it from the bullets flying above me.

I knew who lay on me, tried to match my breathing to his as the chaos played on. A feeling of safety enveloped me while the restaurant became a battleground for New York's scorned criminals.

It felt like it went on forever, before a stillness fell over the room that carried an echo of gunfire.

"*Stai bene?*"

I heard the words, but my thoughts were focused on red. Blood dripped to the wooden floorboards in my line of vision.

Hands grasped my face, turning it.

"Are you okay?" Nico repeated.

I nodded, the ringing in my ears fading.

His hands and gaze ran down my body, checking anyway, but I didn't feel it because all I saw was the *drip, drip, drip* of red. Anguish tore into my chest, cutting my consciousness down to only emotion. I pushed Nico's hands away.

"Get off me!"

"Stop." He gripped my wrists. "Everyone's all right."

I blinked numbly. "Yeah?"

"Yeah." He ran a thumb across my cheek. "Breathe."

I inhaled a steady breath, and it was then that I heard their voices. They were all checking in, and I hadn't been able to hear it over the horror of that dripping blood.

Benito was the one bleeding. He groaned, "Son of a bitch," while holding his arm. "The same fucking arm."

Papà spit Italian over the phone and Mamma was crying. Adriana sat up, surrounded by broken glass and disorder. Just as sirens sounded in the distance, the restaurant fell into silence, as though the shift in the air touched everyone's skin.

And then my sister stared ahead and muttered two little words that would change both of our lives forever.

"I'm pregnant."

CHAPTER
Twenty-Six

"The die is cast."
—Julius Caesar

Elena

SOMETIMES THERE'S NOTHING TO SAY.

Sometimes words will only clutter a space already filled with an unpleasant truth.

I sat next to my sister on the couch while we both numbly watched an episode of *The Office*.

The funny moments, all the "That's what she saids" passed without even a smile.

My mamma had taken a bottle of wine and a Xanax up to her room, and she hadn't made an appearance below stairs in hours.

After we gave our vague statements to the police—we'd been schooled on how to talk to cops at age four—we came here and hadn't left the living room since. Our Uncle Marco and Dominic, his son, were both in the house, but since the incident at Francesco's, the rest of the males in the family had been absent.

Red.

It was now dripping somewhere other than my uncle's restaurant.

And I felt no remorse about it, just numb.

It was two a.m. when they decided to show up. The light in the living room flicked on, and the sound of steps and voices filled the foyer. Weight pressed down on my chest.

Papà came around the couch. His shirtsleeves were rolled up and his suit jacket was off, which he was never seen without, even on sweltering days like today. Not a good sign. I swallowed when I noticed the blood splattered against his white dress shirt.

Marco, Dominic, Manuel, Tony, Benito—who must have discharged himself from the hospital—Luca, and finally Nicolas filled the room. My gaze followed Nico, but he didn't give me a glance. He still wore the same outfit from lunch, and his expression was unreadable as he leaned against the TV stand.

His fiancée had been impregnated by another man. Any Made Man would take that as a personal and *grave* insult, but as he finally flicked a thoughtful gaze to me, for some reason I wondered if that was even what was on his mind.

Eight men stared at my sister. They were going to try to intimidate the name right out of her.

"Phone," Papà barked.

Adriana sat cross-legged on the couch in the white dress she'd worn to lunch, while I'd changed into shorts and a tee. She didn't even look at our papà or acknowledge his demand. That had him grinding his teeth.

I grabbed her phone that sat on the couch between us, stood, and handed it to my papà. We'd already deleted every speck of Ryan's existence from it.

Papà handed it to Dominic, who began searching through it.

"We'll find out who it is, Adriana, so you might as well tell us," Marco said. He was starting with a softer approach, but my papà wasn't going for it.

"You'll tell us, Adriana. *Now.* Or I swear to God you won't see daylight again."

My sister crossed her arms, her eyes flashing with defiance. *That* strategy would never work with Adriana, and Papà knew it. I thought one day he believed she would magically become compliant.

"We won't kill him," Marco said. "There's a baby involved, it's different." He didn't say it, but we all heard it: Different than *me*. Different than my situation.

When hope flickered in Adriana's gaze, my stomach twisted.

"He's lying," I blurted.

Angry male eyes shot to me.

I swallowed, giving Nicolas a glance, but he still seemed to be a mile away.

Uncle Marco shook his head. "No, I'm not. We're not going to kill him, Adriana. I promise."

The glint of hope in her eyes grew a tiny bit more.

Panic flooded me. I knew that look in Benito's gaze, in my brother's. *Lie. It's all a lie.*

"They're lying, Adriana," I urged. "Don't believe them."

My pulse leapt into my throat as the back of Manuel's hand came toward my face. I flinched, expecting the blow. When only a brush of air touched my cheek, I opened my eyes to see Nicolas's hand wrapped around my uncle's wrist.

"Hit a woman in front of me and you won't be alive to do it again," Nico growled.

Seconds passed before Manuel ripped himself from Nico's grip and took a step back, his face red with disdain.

Papà watched the exchange with neutrality, but something close to displeasure played behind his eyes when he looked at Nico. My papà had never hit me—his distaste was for another reason than Nicolas stepping in, but I wasn't sure what.

My mamma's brothers had always been mean, except Marco. He was gentle, reserved, but at the slightest infraction, he was nothing but a wolf in sheep's clothing on the hunt.

"Elena," Papà barked. "Leave."

I had never stood up to my papà before. However, I knew my sister; she was tough but gullible. She wanted to believe in her fairy-tale, so she would. And it would be the death of her prince.

I didn't move.

"*Elena.*" My papà's tone was colder than the Arctic and tinged with disbelief.

I was pulled by the desire to listen, yet my feet were frozen to the floor. I now stood on cheap apartment carpet, watching a similar scene play out before my eyes.

Papà flicked a gaze to Tony, who, with a look of contrition, came around the couch to me.

"I'm not leaving," I protested.

"Come on, Elena. Let's go." Tony reached for my wrist, but I jerked it away. He sighed, before wrapping an arm around my waist and lifting me.

"Adriana, don't do it," I pleaded as Tony half carried me, half walked me with one arm to the door. "I promise you they're lying."

I knew the kind of guilt this carried around—let alone the heartbreak—and I couldn't allow Adriana to live with the same.

Once my feet were in the hall, Tony shut the door, leaving me alone on the other side. I let out a noise of frustration, before smacking the wood with my palm. Sliding down the door with my thighs pressed to my chest, I listened to their voices seep through the cracks.

I waited and waited for the name Ryan to escape my sister's lips.

It never did.

Nico

A clock ticked. Ice clinked in a tumbler glass. Cigar smoke hung in the air. And a certain distaste emanated from Salvatore sitting behind his desk.

I occupied a chair in front of it, leaning back with one elbow on the armrest. I was pretty sure he hated the way I sat like I was bored, so I'd continued to sit that way.

I wasn't sure how long we'd been in his office, remaining silent, while Salvatore smoked his cigar, but something was building, and it wasn't from me. Truthfully, I enjoyed the atmosphere. I could survive on tense, awkward silences alone.

"You can't have her." The words cut the quiet like a knife through the air.

My gaze found Salvatore's through a haze of smoke. "I didn't say I wanted her."

He let out a sardonic breath, shaking his head. "Cut the shit, Ace. I know you want Elena, and she's not on the table."

My jaw ticked. I did not like being told what I couldn't fucking have. "I don't think you get to tell me what's on the table, Salvatore. You fucked me over."

Technically, his daughter fucked someone, but it was the same thing in our eyes. He'd breached the contract.

Salvatore puffed on his cigar one last time, before contemplatively putting it out. "Elena isn't a possibility, even if I wanted to give her to you." His gaze came to me, showing me that he didn't. "She's engaged."

I stared at him with indifference, while my chest twisted with aversion before going cold enough to burn.

I'd thought a lot about this situation, what I could get out of Salvatore for breaking the contract, what I *wanted* the most. It started with an E and had long black hair. It was also my vice.

I wanted it, but I couldn't let myself have it.

Nonetheless, now that I knew she belonged to another man, something violent spread through my veins like an internal case of frostbite.

My irrational side began speaking for me. "Contract signed?"

Salvatore nodded, a glint of satisfaction in his eyes.

I watched him closely. I bet after that little incident with the pool and me shoving Elena into it, he'd locked that man's signature right down.

I had nothing against Salvatore, but there was something about sharing the same title with a man close to half his age he didn't like. And I was fucking richer than him. He didn't like how far my reputation stretched, and the details of said reputation. But after today, he knew he couldn't afford to get on my bad side. We'd found the Mexicans involved with the drive-by, but there were still a few members that needed to be taken care of.

Frankly, I had more men on the streets than Salvatore. Even men on his, who I'd used to find the men responsible for today's shooting. Salvatore hadn't liked it when I'd used that card. I didn't play by the rules, and the straight-laced don didn't trust me. He needed me, though. I thought that was why he disliked me the most. He also just really didn't want my Russo hands all over his favorite daughter.

"Who?" The question escaped me, and I fucking prayed he wouldn't answer.

His gaze narrowed as he took a sip of whiskey. "Oscar Perez. Colombian."

We stared at each other, and the cold bit into my chest.

"This problem with the Mexicans has fucked some of my connections with suppliers. Oscar has been an . . . acquaintance for a while. He has good product, but he wants Elena."

Salvatore was trying to convince himself, it sounded like. Oscar was the kind of man the godly-rich with a twisted sense of ennui bred. Fitted with a malignant stain he'd try to rid with Elena.

I got up, buttoned my jacket, and turned to leave. "We'll talk about this tomorrow. It's late."

"And Adriana?" he said as I opened the door.

I hadn't shown much desire in getting revenge on the man who dared to fuck Nicolas Russo's fiancée, but only because I'd been fighting the possibility of her sister.

"Her phone records. They've contacted each other," I replied, before walking out.

I didn't care so much about who Adriana had slept with while engaged to me.

It was just the fucking principle of it.

Elena

It was eight o'clock in the morning as I sat on the couch, in a pink over-sized Yankees t-shirt and shorts. I ate a bowl of Cap'n Crunch while the blonde newscaster filled me in on current events.

I watched the news every morning and night. There wasn't much in the world that was reported on that I didn't know about, from the Korean child labor crisis to the botchy Botox injections being given in L.A.

When a familiar face appeared on the screen, my pulse stilled. And when the words "Oscar Perez" followed by "found shot execution style in front of his apartment," passed the reporter's ruby red lips, I choked on my cereal.

Not ten seconds had gone by, before "SON OF A BITCH!" came from my papà's office.

My eyes widened.

As I was sinking into the couch with the relief of Oscar's death, the noise of Nicolas entering the foyer with my brother filtered into the room. They were talking about Adriana's phone records. My heart dropped. If the report showed all of my sister's messages, it would take little effort to find Ryan.

Tony and Nicolas had found something in common now? Disgust twisted in my stomach.

They headed past the living room doors to my papà's office, while I watched the news, narrow-eyed and simmering.

Papà's anger drifted down the hall like fog, and I wondered if I was going to hear gunshots, but another five minutes passed before his shout filled my ears.

"Elena! My office, *now!*"

I hesitated, but then got to my feet and padded barefoot toward his office. Dread sank into my skin with each step.

I knocked on the doorframe before entering the room. Papà was behind his desk, Tony sat in the chair across from him, and Nico leaned against the wall near the window.

I stood in the middle of the office, my fingers playing with the hem of my shirt. The sun warmed my clammy skin.

"Congratulations," Papà bit out, his eyes a dark storm. I swallowed, having never seen my father so angry. "You're getting married."

A cold sensation crawled down my throat and filled my lungs.

Slowly, I glanced at Nicolas to see he watched me with indifference. Keeping his gaze, I let out a shaky breath and asked, "To who?"

but I already knew. I hadn't imagined this outcome, and I wasn't sure why.

"To Nico."

My heart beat so fast I fought not to choke on it.

Silence filled the room—deep and loathing from my papà, thoughtful from my brother, and apathetic from my no longer future brother-in-law but *fiancé*.

The silence I felt was instinctive, like how prey quiets to avoid capture. A survival instinct kicked in, and I shook my head.

"No," I whispered.

A spark flickered through Nico's eyes.

My papà shuffled some papers on his desk. "It is done, Elena."

That must be the contract in his hand.

Nicolas could sign for me, and "it was done?" Of course, this was how it always worked, but something tasted bitter about Nico doing it.

This news was like a slap to the face. How could I process him being my sister's fiancé to *mine* in less than five minutes?

That wasn't only it.

I had never wanted a husband like him. He was everything my body thought it needed and everything my brain knew it didn't. I would lose myself in Nicolas Russo, and I wouldn't know where to come up for air.

My heart would fall for him and he would crush it beneath his feet. I could live a loveless life. I couldn't survive a broken one.

I gave my head another shake. "Papà—"

"Enough, Elena! It is done. Now, go pack a bag. You're staying with him until the wedding."

My eyes widened.

"*What?*" I breathed.

He directed a sarcastic gaze at me. "It's not like you're a virgin, Elena."

"Papà," Tony snapped.

His words pierced my chest. I knew he was pissed and was directing it at me, but it hurt all the same. "How could you allow this? Do you think that because my reputation is already stained you can just rip it to shreds?"

"You can blame your poor reputation on yourself and your fiancé. After this issue with your sister and your . . . past, I agreed to his terms."

What he meant was that Nicolas didn't trust me not to fool around with other men behind his back before the wedding. Papà apparently didn't have much say on the matter, considering the contract was broken on his end.

I didn't know what to say, but I wasn't ready to accept this.

"I don't know how to cook," I blurted, before looking at Nicolas, who still leaned against the wall, his hands in his pockets.

"I have one," was all he said in a deep, thoughtful voice. I had a feeling he didn't entirely want this marriage either, so why had he agreed to it?

"I like to shop. I spend way too much money." It was true, but I also donated to the local shelters just so I wouldn't feel so bad about my spendthrift ways. So I guessed that meant I spent even more.

"I have it."

Was he only going to speak to me in three words now that he owned me?

"Enough, Elena," Papà cut in. "Go."

A frustrated sound traveled up my throat, but I kept it locked in. "I don't want this," I told my papà, my voice quiet. I avoided Nicolas's gaze, though it burned my cheek like a rash.

"It is done." Papà copied my tone, but his words were final.

So I left his office, headed to my room, and, while packing a bag, I contemplated how I could ever survive Nicolas Russo.

CHAPTER
Twenty-Seven

"Lust will be the death of us."
—Unknown

Elena

THERE WAS NOTHING BUT SILENCE. IN FACT, THE QUIET SEEMED TO EAT AT me the entire drive. And the worst thing about it was his car smelled so damn good. The events of today hit me like whiplash, leaving a numbness behind that only his masculine scent seemed to penetrate. Instead of the prickling feeling of panic, his close proximity and the idea of his hands on me were driving me insane.

It was as though my body focused on the primal aspect I'd been craving so I wouldn't be traumatized by the event. A protective mechanism.

I was equating marrying Nicolas to severe trauma.

Truly, it didn't seem far apart.

There was a difference between lusting after a man and wanting him to be the father of your children. The idea pulled me in two resilient directions: thrill, and terror.

The feelings were so tenacious I remained only numb, leaving room for one thing. Warmth hummed between my legs, my skin a nesting ground for electricity and ice.

My mamma had watched me walk out the door with Nico

carrying my bag, her eyes wide as if I were being sent to the slaughterhouse. Even my sister had rushed down the stairs, mouthing, "I'm sorry," before the door shut behind me. Papà never came out of his office, and Tony and my cousins only watched Nico like he was stealing something.

I wanted to stay detached from this man, as indifferent as I possibly could, but as the city passed before my eyes in a blur of concrete and bright sun and we grew closer to his place, impassive was not a word I would even recognize.

When we pulled up to a familiar red-brick house, my throat grew tight. "Why not the penthouse?"

"Expecting something more lavish?"

My eyes narrowed. "What? No. I just expected the penthouse. That's what you chose for Adriana."

"It's not what I choose for you."

I tensed. He wasn't letting me forget he owned me now, and it cut through the numb haze that caged me.

I didn't know what to feel: nervous, terrified, determined to keep some autonomy, or aroused by the possibility of his hands on me. It became a mixture of all four, dancing along my skin as I got out of the car.

Nico grabbed my bag from the backseat, and I followed him into the house. It was larger than it looked from the outside. The back door entered into the kitchen, with steel appliances, gray granite countertops, and low lighting.

An office sat to the right of me, the cherry desk visible through the cracked door. Except for that and a small bathroom and laundry room to my left, the space was an open floor plan, with a staircase running upstairs. You could watch the flat-screen TV while standing at the island. It was simple, masculine, and comfortable.

I swallowed when he shut the back door with an unmistakable click. I was still in shock about this turn of events and didn't know how to process it completely, or at all. I was going through the motions while my thoughts lagged behind.

He dropped my bag into an armchair and then his keys on the

kitchen counter. This place might look the epitome of comfortable, but I had no idea how I would ever feel that way in his space.

I stood planted next to the door, while he poured himself a drink from the minibar near the front windows. A strong feeling consumed me that if I moved, something would attack me—maybe him. The curtains were closed, and only small shards of light got through, leaving the room dimly lit.

It was nine o'clock in the morning and he was drinking whiskey. I prayed he wasn't an alcoholic. He might have stopped my uncle from hitting me last night, but knowing a few alcoholics, especially on my mamma's side, nothing about them was predictable.

He wore all black, and the way he looked at me from across the room made me fully aware of his reputation. He was the most dangerous man in the city, and soon I would have to call him Husband.

He watched me as he leaned against the small bar, and the longer he did it my heart pumped faster, pushing nerves through my veins.

The thoughts I would have processed over a matter of time all rushed in at once. I wondered how many women he had been with, what he expected of me. I wasn't a virgin, but I wasn't far from one. I'd had sex with one man, and only enough to fill a weekend. I was inexperienced and worried he would chew me up and spit me out.

He pulled on his tie while walking into the kitchen. He set his tumbler on the island, then looked at me. "You gonna stand near that door all day?"

I swallowed and nodded.

With his hands braced on the counter, he gave his head a small shake. My stomach fluttered when he glanced at me, his eyes molten.

"Come here."

I didn't think it was possible for any woman to ignore that command from him. I had an awful, awful impulse to listen.

With an erratic heartbeat, I took the short steps toward him.

As soon as I reached him, he grabbed my nape, threaded his fingers into my hair, and then buried his face in my neck. He made a masculine noise of satisfaction that I could feel deep in my stomach, before it settled into a weight between my legs. I rocked back, not fighting

him, but shaken with this lightning bolt exploding in my chest and fizz-
ing through my veins.

My breasts pressed against his hard, warm abs and a shiver rolled
through me. He ran his face up and down my neck, as though he was
savoring my smell, or maybe languishing in the fact that he'd caught
his next meal.

"Fuck. You feel good," he groaned against my throat.

He wrapped an arm around my waist and lifted me, setting me
close to eye-level on the island. The counter was cold against my thighs
as he stepped between them, forcing them further apart.

My heartbeat drummed in my ears, and a cold sensation crept
through me. *Fear.* He pressed his lips to my throat, kissing a slow line
down it. Each one sent a sizzle between my legs, and I tilted my head
to give him more access, a moan escaping my lips.

This man had changed roles from a tempting someone I couldn't
have, to owner, lover, and fiancé. The whiplash had given me no time
to act but on instinct alone. I wanted him, but at the unknown, a cool
breath of fear dripped into my subconscious.

I grasped the edge of the counter on both sides of me, trying to
ground myself to earth somehow, while he worked my neck with slow
kisses and scrapes of his teeth. As his presence consumed my own, my
reservations dissolved into smoke.

His large hands ran down my sides, from underneath my breasts
to low on my hips, his thumbs brushing bare skin beneath the band of
my shorts. It was a maddening sensation, and I was dying for him to go
a little further, up or down. To just freaking pick one.

His erection pressed against the inside of my thigh, and if he
would only step forward a few inches, it would be right where I wanted
it, *needed* it.

I swayed, my eyes heavy-lidded, when a solid grip came to the side
of my neck to hold me still while he pressed hot, wet kisses to my
throat. My head fell back on a moan, my hair skimming the countertop with the next nip of his teeth.

His hips lined up with mine, his hands grasping the top of my ass,
and then his hard-on pressed against my clit in a slow roll that stole

my breath. A quiet growl fanned against my neck, while an emptiness pulsed between my legs.

He only ground against me once, when I needed it over and *over,* before he pulled back. His hands left me and grasped the counter beside my own. I'd yet to even touch him while stuck in this dream-like state.

His gaze was more black than amber. "Take off your shirt."

Each bossy, gravelly word was a slow hum in the empty ache between my legs. The cold sense of fear snuck its way back in, cutting through the haze. A part of me needed to comply, to do everything this man asked of me. To give him anything he wanted, but I couldn't. Not yet.

With a shaky breath, I shook my head.

His gaze narrowed at the edges.

"Promise not to kill the father of Adriana's baby and I will."

His expression hardened even more. "I don't like ultimatums."

"It's not an ultimatum. It's an . . . incentive."

He shook his head and started to pull away from me, but I grabbed him by the belt loop. "Please . . ." My voice was throaty, sounding different to my ears. It was coated in thick, deep lust, and he paused, his attention all mine. "For a wedding present."

He glanced down at my finger hooked through his belt loop, his jaw ticking with thought. After a moment, he said, "You'll take it all off. Whenever I ask you to."

Elation zipped through me, and he must have noticed because his voice took an edge. "And I'm still beating the shit out of him."

I nodded with hesitation. Not an ideal situation for Ryan, but I knew this was much better than death and I wasn't going to push my luck. "What about my papà?"

"I'll talk to him."

"How do I know you aren't lying?"

"Guess you'll have to trust me."

Maybe it was stupid, but I did trust him—on this matter, anyway. My finger slipped from his belt loop, and a huge weight released from my shoulders. Maybe I was taking my sister's situation personally, or maybe I thought righting this wrong would erase mine. It wouldn't, but at least Adriana didn't have to live with the heartbreak and regret.

Nico grabbed his drink and leaned against the opposite counter, taking a sip of whiskey like he was settling in at a strip club. Though his expression appeared as if he were standing in line at a grocery store checkout.

Now, fear rushed like an icy river beneath the surface of my skin. My breath came out in shallow pants as I reached for the hem of my t-shirt. With an erratic beat of my heart, my shirt hit the floor. The quiet noise of fabric on hardwood sounded loud and suggestive as the still kitchen air met my bare midsection. My breasts pressed against the fabric of my bra, tingling in expectation. Before I had a chance to think it through, I unclipped the back of my bra and dropped it to the floor.

A blush spread from my cheeks to my chest as his burning gaze caressed my bare breasts. The silence filled with the drum of my heartbeat.

His posture remained indifferent, but his eyes singed like paper around the edges. He ran his tongue across his teeth and flicked his gaze from me before taking a sip of whiskey. I didn't know why, but I had the feeling he was trying to shake his attraction off. He didn't want to want me. I didn't know how I was supposed to take that, but for some reason a rush of confidence spread through me.

I had never undressed for a man before. The only one I'd been with had done it himself, but I should have known Nicolas Russo would demand I do it for him. I *wanted* to do it for him, whenever he wanted.

Grabbing the waistband of my shorts, I pushed them down my thighs, letting them drop to the floor. I sat there in only a hot pink thong while he stood across from me, in a button-up and tie.

His attention was now all mine and the thrill of it stole my breath.

Slowly, without taking his gaze off mine, he set his glass on the counter and walked the short steps to me.

"I haven't finished," I breathed, but he didn't hear or didn't care.

I shivered when he gripped my neck, sliding his hand upwards into my hair. His hold on my nape pulled my face to his, so close his breath touched my lips, warm with a hint of whiskey. Nerves vibrated deep down, because he was going to kiss me. But when he leaned in to brush his lips against mine, I turned my head.

He went still, his body tensing.

I avoided his gaze. "You can have anything you want, Nicolas. Anything . . . but that."

There was only one way to protect myself in this situation. I couldn't lose myself in this man, when I could already feel the pull of how easy it would be. I needed to maintain my autonomy, my distance. My heart didn't need any more incentive to fall into his clutches. I knew I couldn't keep sex from him, knew I wasn't that strong, but I didn't have to make love to him.

I *couldn't* make love to him and then watch him do it with someone else. And I already knew he had no desire to remain faithful, from what he'd told me in the alley that night. I couldn't share myself with someone so carelessly, so indifferently, especially now, after my past mistake. So I could only give him a part of me—the only one he would want—and hope I would survive.

I didn't expect him to argue, or to even care about my refusal. Kissing was romantic in a way, and I couldn't see him wanting to share that with me.

My hands still gripped the counter on either side of me, and when he glanced at my left, the one with the ring, his gaze turned black with contempt. I could taste his sudden animosity on my tongue. Anger wasn't a reaction I'd expected from him, but I guessed telling this man he couldn't have something was only a way to make him want it more.

"Spread your legs." His command was cold, rough, and rattled the existing fear.

With an unsteady inhale, I complied.

His palms ran up my legs as I did so, his thumbs pressing into my inner thighs with a harshness that made my stomach tighten in an unexpected way. His rough hands felt so absolute against my soft skin.

Legs spread, cool air brushed my panties and I was suddenly aware of how wet they were. His gaze touched me there, warm and thrilling yet still tinged with anger.

He yanked me closer by the back of the neck until my bare breasts pressed against his chest. My breathing was erratic as he growled in my ear, "You're so goddamn hot it pisses me off." And then he nipped my neck, hard.

I yelped at the short pain, but it turned into a moan when his thumb pressed down on my clit through the fabric of my thong. His grip tightened in my hair, forcing my head back, and then he sucked a nipple into his mouth. A spark ignited in my lower stomach, the flame spreading through my body like wildfire.

He brushed his thumb over my clit, up and down, while holding a fistful of my hair so I couldn't even look down. He groaned from deep in his chest and switched breasts, licking and then sucking with a slight scrape of teeth. An embarrassing sound escaped me, but I was so hot everywhere I didn't care.

I leaned back on my hands, my hips starting to rock under his touch. His mouth was so hot as he licked and played with my full breasts, until I thought I would die from it. When his hands left me, protest screamed in my veins.

With a dark gaze that wasn't entirely angry anymore, he fisted my thong at my hip and pulled it down my thighs, dropping it to the floor with the rest of my clothes.

I spread my legs once more, past the point of rational thought. His gaze fell between my thighs. He gave his head a shake, running a hand down his tie. "Fuck." That's all he said, before his arms wrapped around the backs of my thighs, he jerked me to the edge of the counter, and then his head lowered between them. I shuddered under the first hot, wet touch of his tongue. A deep rush of pleasure flooded me, a stronger wave rolling through me at every soft, slow lap he took from the entrance to my clit.

This dangerous man was being surprisingly gentle, reverent, in what he was doing. Something touched me in the chest.

However, he wasn't that docile.

His arms held me so securely I couldn't move my hips an inch, while he took his time licking me, like he was doing it for himself and not me.

"Oh, God," I moaned, digging my hands into his thick hair,

running my blunt nails against his scalp. I'd said this man's name a handful of times since I'd met him, but I found it slipping from my lips when he swirled his tongue over my clit before sucking.

He tensed, and I realized too late he didn't like it when I called him Nicolas.

"What's my name?" he rasped before his tongue pushed into my entrance.

I made a throaty, porny noise I never knew I was capable of.

When I didn't answer, his mouth left me, and his smoldering gaze found mine. His words were sharp. "What's my name?"

"Nicolas," I breathed.

His eyes flashed, and then a feeling of fullness came over me when he slipped one finger inside me. Pleasure ignited, the wick burning through my bloodstream. He held his finger still and I tried to rock, but his grip around one thigh was immovable.

"Name?" he pressed.

I shook my head, hating this game. I had "Nicolas" on the tip of my tongue, but when he pulled out his finger and then plunged two inside me *hard*, I choked on it and it unwillingly came out as "Nico."

A tremor went through me when his mouth found my clit, licking and sucking while his fingers moved in and out of me, again and again. He did it so leisurely, making deep noises of satisfaction every once in a while.

He was taking his time, slowing down when the pressure built, driving me mad until *"Please,"* escaped my lips. Then his fingers curled inside of me, the flame growing hotter.

When he slowed again, I shook my head in panic, my hands tugging at his hair. I didn't know what I'd turned into, but all I found myself repeating was "Please," over and over. He finally gave me what I wanted. His firm laps steady, he fingered me faster, harder, until there was nothing but deep, hot pressure.

His dark gaze found mine.

My last thought before the final *please* left my lips and the pressure exploded through my veins like an inferno was: *He loves to be begged.* The fire dissipated into a languid heat, spreading tingles throughout.

As I lay against the counter, slack, I pulsed around his fingers, and he only made out with my inner thigh and continued to slowly move them in and out until it stopped.

I let out a shaky breath, running my fingers through his hair, not ready to let it go. It was the only part of him I got to touch.

That was the first orgasm I'd ever had with a man, and I hated to admit it for my future health, but it was the most addictive thing I'd ever experienced.

When his hands ran up my thighs, nerves came to the surface.

Did he want me to reciprocate?

Or did he expect sex?

A shyness overcame me as I sat up, and I was sure, as he braced his hands on the counter and met my gaze, that he could see it all.

He'd yet to even shed his tie while I sat naked in front of him. After the heat settled, it all appeared so much more obscene.

"You'll call me Nico from now on. No more of that Nicolas bullshit."

I nodded hesitantly. All my *pleases* still echoed in the kitchen, his words cutting through them with an abrasive knife.

I didn't know what I expected then, but I knew it wasn't for him to turn his back on me, leave the house, and then shut the door behind him.

I exhaled, falling against the countertop.

Merda.

I was in over my head.

CHAPTER
Twenty-Eight

"I am as bad as the worst, but, thank God,
I am as good as the best."
—Walt Whitman

Elena

THE TICKING OF THE CLOCK BROUGHT MY GAZE TO IT AS I SLIPPED OFF THE island. I'd been engaged to Nico for only one hour, yet I already felt turned inside out, as if he'd stolen a few of my layers and I'd never get them back. I knew I made the right decision not to give him every piece of me. If I did, the inevitable would happen, and I'd be nothing but dust beneath his feet while he ruled New York's underworld.

I traced the rim of his whiskey glass, the air-conditioning cool against my bare skin. I leaned on the counter and sipped the liquor, hoping it would numb the abrasive feeling of his scruff against my neck, hoping it would make his clean, male scent disappear from my nose. It didn't.

When the sound of the garage door opening met my ears, I glanced toward the noise. I wondered if he would leave me here alone, but when I didn't hear any engines starting, I imagined he was only working on his cars.

I tossed back the rest of the warm whiskey and set the glass on the counter, but before I could walk away, my eyes caught on some paperwork. Hesitation flooded me, but I took a step forward and grabbed the top paper between two fingers.

I stared at my fiancé's private bank account information, my heart beating with confliction. Vacillation at the wrongness of my intentions. Yet, I felt the hope of absolution, no matter how small it might be.

This life I was born into might be dark, but it was transparent. The *Cosa Nostra* was only a candid version of the Outside's politician smiles. I knew this world, knew its darkness, knew its light. And I knew that I was good, but sometimes even the good has its shadows.

Before I could think more about it, I pulled open cupboard drawer after drawer, searching for a pen and paper. When I found them, I copied the information down and slipped it into the bottom of my duffel bag.

You can only sink or swim.

You can't swim in the underworld, but I'd always heard drowning was the best way to go.

After dressing, I took a tour of the home. I found three bedrooms upstairs and dropped my bag on the queen-sized bed of one that had to be a spare. Cream walls, white duvet and furniture. It was understated elegance, and I knew Nico hadn't been the one to decorate it.

A bay window with a seat below took up the far wall and looked over the backyard and garage. My fingers touched the glass as my gaze found Nico whose head was beneath the hood of one of his cars in the drive. Only his side profile was visible, but my heart thumped to an uneven beat. He wore a white t-shirt, his button-up and tie lying in a pile on one of the lawn chairs.

I wondered who did his laundry. He said he had a cook, but it was close to lunchtime and no one had arrived yet. I really didn't know how to cook. It was a travesty for an Italian woman, I knew, but I partly blamed it on my mamma for never teaching me. She was a perfectionist in the kitchen and would slap our hands if we took one misstep, so it had always been easier to stay out of her way.

Heading out of my new bedroom, I stopped in front of the master. With gray walls and mahogany furniture, it had a masculine touch. The large bed was unmade, and dress shirts and ties lay over the back of a chair, some fallen to the floor. It looked like a messy king lived in here. I had an impulse to clean it, but I quelled it and moved on. I didn't know how he would feel about me going through his things and I didn't want to. I might have to live with him, but this was an arrangement—not a real marriage.

However, when I thought of my other options, I couldn't help but feel relief from Oscar Perez's death. I could guarantee that if I were sent to his home for the day, I wouldn't have been lying languid on his counter from an orgasm I didn't have to reciprocate. My skin crawled at the thought of him touching me.

I would kiss whoever killed him.

When I opened the fridge, I was relieved to see some pre-made meals I only had to pop in the oven. There were handwritten notes on the top of each saying what they were in a feminine scrawl. So, he did have a cook. I was going to feel like less of a woman if I had to have some other woman make my meals now that I was getting married. I guessed I would have to put learning how to cook on my to-do list, though it wasn't as if that was exactly full.

I put a casserole in the oven and then searched the house for a phone.

As I stood at the island and pulled my hair into a ponytail, my brows knitting from the unsuccessful search, the back door opened. My pulse slowed.

Nico stepped inside, his gaze running from the floor to me. God, that plain white t-shirt would be the death of me. Grease stained his arms and hands and he was sweaty to a hot degree. I finished tying my hair up, and then dropped my clammy hands to my sides.

He eyed me as he passed a couple feet away, like it was a natural thing for me to be in his home, but he wasn't sure whether he liked it. I had the distinct feeling he didn't and suddenly felt unwanted and out of place. It seemed as though his presence occupied the whole kitchen and there was no room for me.

I stood there, watching his back as he grabbed a glass from the cupboard and filled it from the faucet. His dark hair was mussed, brushing his collar, and I grew warm remembering I'd had my hands in it not an hour ago.

"I thought we talked about that staring thing." His voice was deep, slithering down my spine with a rough caress. He emptied his glass in one drink without turning around.

"We didn't talk about anything." My response was quiet. "*You* talked and just assumed I was listening."

"You were listening," was all he said, bracing his hands on the edge of the sink.

A heaviness filled the air and my lungs. Uncertain. *Suggestive.* Each silent second was the tick of a bomb soon to detonate. This weight in my chest, this thrill beneath my skin that thrummed when he was near, wouldn't be good for me. He didn't even want me here. All my reservations about this engagement came to the surface.

I shifted. "Can we talk?"

"About what?" There was a tightness to his shoulders I couldn't miss.

"About . . . us?"

"Is that a question, or do you have something to say?"

"I have something to say."

He finally turned around, crossed his arms, and leaned against the counter.

"Go ahead, then."

I swallowed. "I'm sure my papà would forget the marriage contract if you asked him to."

His eyes sparked with dark amusement. "I'm sure he would."

I paused, not expecting his response. I'd believed my papà had been the one to pressure Nico into this marriage—that his anger was for another reason entirely. I just hadn't known how to start the conversation any other way.

"So . . . have him do it."

"Now, why would I do that?" he drawled, though his voice was edged with something not-nice.

My brows pulled together. "Why wouldn't you?"

His gaze turned to ice. "Good question."

I knew I'd walked myself into that and sort of deserved it, but I still bristled from his insinuation. If this was how all of our conversations were going to go, I would go insane before we even got married.

I hesitated, not understanding any of this. "We won't do well together," was what came out, when I wanted to say: *You're the only man I've met who could do me permanent damage.*

"You seemed agreeable enough to me earlier." His expression had *kitchen island* and *naked* written all over it.

I couldn't stop the heat from rushing to my cheeks at his crass reminder, but also because I was quickly losing control of this conversation and growing more flustered by the minute. "That's different and you know it. If that's what this is about . . . you don't have to marry me for it." It made me sound easy—especially with what he knew of my past—but I didn't care. "We made a deal," I said quietly, remembering my promise to take my clothes off whenever he asked. "And I'll uphold it."

The air filled with a bitter current that made me regret my words. He let out a tense breath before running his tongue across his teeth. "And why is it you're so against marriage?"

"I'm not against marriage."

I didn't mean it to be so cutting an insult, but he read the insinuation that it was marriage to *him* I was against. I swallowed as his expression turned even stormier, a muscle moving in his jaw.

"So, what happens when your papà marries you off? Will you still fuck me when I tell you to?"

I chewed my bottom lip. If I said no, he wouldn't protect Ryan anymore, and I couldn't risk it. "We made a deal."

As darkness pooled like liquid lead in his eyes, I realized how that sounded. Like I wouldn't honor my vows, and as I was currently engaged to this man, it sounded *really* bad. The stressed silence made it hard to breathe.

When he took a sudden step toward me, my heart jerked. I took one back and bumped into the island.

He stopped. Bitter amusement crossed his face with a tiny shake of his head. "Jesus."

It wasn't like I feared him overly much, but my mind was spinning, my body reacting on instinct. And when a man like that stalks toward you, it's only natural to retreat.

I held my breath as he took the remaining steps, until he was only an inch away. He smelled like man, clean sweat and whiskey. The scent sank its way into my skin, embedding itself deep.

He braced his palms on the counter on either side of me, stepping closer until his presence touched me everywhere. He leaned in, his lips brushing my ear. "Why are you afraid of me?"

"I'm not—"

I jumped when his hand came down on the counter beside me, the loud slap filling the kitchen. My heart pounded, and I was sure he could hear it.

"You're not, huh?" he asked with a sardonic tone that should have frustrated me—but his closeness, this exchange, had my blood flowing. In a strange way, heat pooled between my legs.

He gripped the side of my neck, tilting my head until I looked him in the eyes. His voice was deep, soft, yet laced with frustration that he even had to say it. "I'm not going to hurt you."

He said that now, but I'd heard stories of how a don dealt with a thief.

"That much I can promise you, Elena."

The words found their way into my chest, seeping into the cracks and filling it with warmth. This man's voice turned my resolve to ash. However, I then read between the lines, and what he meant was: *That's all I can promise you.*

I didn't know why it mattered—it wasn't like I had anything to offer him but betrayal.

"But this marriage is going to happen."

"Why?"

I couldn't help but think I'd been his second choice. He'd chosen Adriana over me, had he not? Why did he want me now? Was I merely a convenience?

"I need a wife. You need a husband. And I think we both know you don't want your papà in charge of choosing for you."

A convenience, then.

He was right. I never did have much faith in Papà in that department. I believed he really had encouraged Oscar's suit, and it didn't take a psychologist to understand that man's character. I was ready to be out from under my father's thumb, though I was unsure if being under this man's would be worse.

If Nico could treat this marriage like an agreement, then surely so could I. I hesitated, his closeness pushing my reservations deeper into my subconscious with each second.

I had no idea if I was making a mistake, but as much as I liked to believe I had a choice in this marriage, I did not. He was merely humoring me by pretending to care about my opinion.

"Okay." The quiet acquiescence filled the small space between us.

"Okay," he repeated, running his thumb across my chin and, at the hint of amusement passing through his eyes, I knew he left some grease there.

My stomach fluttered, but then dipped at the dark tone of his next words.

"I said I'll never hurt you, Elena, but if I find out you've touched another man, there is nothing in this world that could save him."

CHAPTER
Twenty-Nine

"Every new beginning comes from some other beginning's end."
—Seneca

Elena

"**O**H, CARA MIA! *È COSÍ BELLO ASCOLTARE LA TUA VOCE!*"

"It's good to hear your voice too, Mamma," I responded dryly, even though I'd only been gone for a few hours. The tiniest bit of amusement rose in me.

Before Nico took the stairs two at a time, like he hadn't threatened to kill any man who touched me, he'd handed over his cell phone when I said I needed to call home. I didn't want his hand grenade of a phone, but apparently it was the only one in the house.

Mamma went on a tangent of, "How could your papà agree to this?" and "All my wedding plans, ruined!" for a solid five minutes. "You're living with him, not married! It's *osceno!*"

"It wasn't my choice," I mumbled.

"We're only pushing the wedding back a week. I'm not letting that Russo get the cow for free."

I closed my eyes. "Mamma, that's not how the saying goes."

"Who cares how it goes! He shoots my son, decides to marry one daughter, then steals the other! *Non ci posso credere.* How am I going to plan another wedding in time? And this arrangement? *Disonora la famiglia, lo è—*"

"You don't have to plan it. Email me the list of what needs to be done and I'll do it."

She was crying now, through unintelligible Italian. *"Mia figlia . . . sposata."* A switch flipped. "Fine. We'll go to the dress shop tomorrow."

I sucked in a shallow breath. I was getting married.

It felt so strange to my ears.

We went over a few wedding details, and then I asked about a couple of easy recipes I could experiment with. I wrote down the recipes on a notepad as I stood at the island, doodling when she went off topic, which was often and mostly about her unwed and pregnant daughter. I wanted to talk to Adriana and quell her worry about Ryan, but I wouldn't until I knew for sure that Nico wasn't lying to me. I wouldn't raise her hope just to crush it.

I glanced toward the back door when it opened, and hesitation ran through me as I met a cold gaze. Luca halted, one hand on the handle, and then he stared at me for what felt like a minute. He shook his head, a small smile pulling on his lips as he took his cell phone out of his pocket and began texting while walking to the couch.

I swallowed, somehow feeling like I was the subject of that text, and then responded in the negative to my mamma's "What am I, talking to a wall?"

As Luca sat on the couch and turned the TV on to a ball game, I finished writing down the recipes.

It wasn't until I said goodbye and hung up that I realized Mamma believed Veal Milanese was an appropriate meal for a beginner. I sighed and then thought with some kind of masochistic inclination that I could invite Jenny over to help. Ugh.

Nico came down the stairs, hair wet, in a white dress shirt, gray tie, and pants. He paused, his eyes narrowing as he saw Luca lounging on the couch with one arm resting on the back, before continuing his descent.

The timer on the stove went off, and I pulled the baked rigatoni out of the oven. My mouth watered as garlic and basil filled the kitchen. It took a lot to ruin my appetite—apparently more than marrying a murderous don.

As I filled my plate, Nico's presence brushed my side. I glanced at him and smiled as I could only imagine women had in the fifties.

"Hungry?"

A hint of amusement pulled on his lips. "Nah, I have a lunch meeting." His gaze fell toward his cell sitting on the island. "You don't have a phone?"

I shook my head. I didn't want to explain that it was taken from me six months ago, but Nico must have read it on my face. Something obscure sparked in his eyes. I wondered if he would ever question me about it, about *him*, but he only said, "We'll get you one tomorrow."

Truthfully, I hadn't missed my phone. My friends were limited to my family. Outsiders could never truly understand me. I was a mold the *Cosa Nostra* had created, a triangle trying to fit in the square of society.

"Help yourself to anything in the kitchen," he said, before adding in an amused drawl, "Though, I can see you've already done that."

"When does your cook come? I would like to meet her." Maybe she would be kind enough to give me some pointers, though that might not be such a great idea, because as soon as I learned I would want to find her other employment. The idea of having my own home to run was an unexpected thrill, no matter if I had to share it with Nico.

"Isabel comes Mondays and Thursdays. She cleans too."

She'd been here yesterday, yet his room was such a mess? Maybe he was weird about his things. I shook it off.

"Do you have a computer I can use? I need to help Mamma with some of the wedding details."

"There's a laptop in my office. You can use that. And"—he pulled out his wallet and tossed a black credit card on the counter—"for all that money you spend."

I didn't like the personal nature of spending this man's money. Especially with the idea of his bank information already in my duffel bag upstairs. "I don't need it. I have my papà's," I replied, pulling my bottom lip in between my teeth.

"You'll use mine from now on." His tone was non-negotiable as he put his watch on.

Translation: *I own you now, not your papà.*

I nodded, but then stilled when the pad of his thumb pulled down on my bottom lip until it escaped my teeth. "Don't tempt me," he said with a harshness that touched my skin. It wasn't lost on me that he spoke of the kissing variety of temptation.

My breath caught somewhere in my chest. How much I wanted to run my tongue across his thumb, to pull it into my mouth. It was an itch I could hardly stop, and I knew he saw the desire on my face.

His eyes burned like coal, and his thumb brushed across my lips, daring me to do it. A shiver rocked through me. I wasn't that brave and we both knew it. He took a step back and slipped his hands into his pockets, leaving a warm imprint on my lips.

He glanced at his cousin, who sat with his elbows on his knees watching the game.

"Luca will stay here with you. In my *office.*"

Luca's broad shoulders tensed under his white dress shirt. "Ace—"

"If you need to reach me, you can use his phone until we get you one tomorrow," he told me, grabbing his keys from the counter.

Luca stood to his incredible height that had to be six and a half feet. "I'm not a babysitter, boss."

I stared forward, saying a silent prayer that Nico wouldn't leave this man with me.

"You are until I can find a gay cousin," Nico returned dryly.

I closed my eyes.

It was safe to say that wouldn't happen, considering the *Cosa Nostra* was a worse advocate for the LGBT community than they were for the women's movement. It was a work in progress.

Luca's jaw ticked.

Nico opened the back door, but then paused. "Elena?"

"Yeah?"

"Burn that shirt." He then left without another word.

I glanced down at my pink Yankees t-shirt. I guessed Nico was a Red Sox fan.

We really wouldn't work out now.

Luca eyed me like he wanted to wrap his big hands around my throat and squeeze.

Nerves played beneath my skin.

"There's no TV in his office," he said eventually.

I blinked, realizing he was asking me in the most arrogant way I'd ever encountered if he could watch TV out here, even though Nico had told him to go in his office.

I really didn't want to spend my day around this man. He was that unnerving, but if he was going to be here for a while, I didn't want him to have to hole up in Nico's office. It would make me feel guilty all day.

"Well, I guess what he doesn't know won't hurt him."

Instead of thanking me, he nodded toward the food on the counter. "What's that?"

I sighed, grabbed my plate, and slid it across the island in his direction.

Nico

I sat back in my chair and cracked my knuckles. It wasn't until then that I recognized the restlessness that ghosted under my skin.

I didn't know how I was going to get through the work day with Elena in my home, willing to take off her clothes whenever I asked her to. The idea was a constant in the corner of my mind, and it was the exact reason I didn't want to marry her. I sat in front of five men who would kill me if they could, in the conference room of my club, and I couldn't think about anything but how she had looked naked in my kitchen, how smooth her skin was, how she'd tasted.

She tasted better than hustling.

I hadn't planned to do it. I was going to get something else out of

Salvatore for fucking me over, but when he'd said Oscar Perez . . . the irrational burn concerning Elena had seared through my veins. So, I found out where he resided and then I shot him in the goddamn head. I'd tried to pacify myself with that, but Salvatore would just pawn her off to someone else, and I knew for God only knows what reason I couldn't fucking handle it.

"Here's an idea, why don't you—"

"Here's an idea," I cut Rafael off, my voice remaining impassive. "Why don't you get the fuck out."

A tense air crept through the room on hands and knees. I couldn't listen to his stupid proposition for one more second.

The Mexican drug lord's tanned complexion turned red and blotchy. "It was only business advice, from one man to another," he seethed, standing.

"If I wanted business advice from a man poorer than me I would have asked for it."

Rafael slammed the conference room door before the three of his men could make it out behind him.

"Are we done here?" I asked the table.

With tight countenances and some shifting gazes, the men all got to their feet and headed out of the room.

"Well," my uncle Jimmy said from the seat beside me, "someone needs to get laid, and it ain't me."

An understatement if I ever heard one.

It'd been close to two weeks now and the urge was beginning to burn, to bubble over until it became an absolute necessity. Even I knew I became a jackass when I abstained from sex. I couldn't even remember the last time I'd gone this long. There was no particular reason for the lapse, except for the annoying notion that I'd acquired a sudden hard-on for long black hair and, lately, I'd only come across one who had it.

"Not good business, going and pissing off our suppliers," Jimmy said, lighting a cigar and leaning back in his chair.

"It was a stupid venture and you know it."

"Bad deal, what you did to that Perez, Ace." He shook his head.

So the man was a little more prominent than I'd first presumed. There would be people who'd miss him. "The only thing I regret is that I didn't make it last longer."

I glanced down the table to see three pairs of eyes on me. Lorenzo rocked in his chair, looking at me like I'd kicked a puppy, while Ricardo and Dino—a capo of mine—sat beside him, their keen attention on me as well.

At that moment, Gianna breezed into the conference room. My eyes narrowed, taking in her tight black dress that all club waitresses were mandated to wear, but she violated the dress code with her choker necklace and high pigtails.

She stopped by Lorenzo's side, holding out her palm. Without looking at her, he reached into his jacket and pulled out a wad of bills, setting it in her hand. She licked her finger and then began counting it like Lorenzo would short her. He was a Russo—he would.

"And what was this bet?" A dark edge crept into my voice.

Lorenzo scratched the back of his neck. "Whether or not you'd marry Elena instead of her sister, boss."

My jaw tightened.

Gianna pursed her lips and held out her hand again. Lorenzo sighed, reached back into his jacket and dropped the rest of the bills in her palm.

"Thanks, Lo." She spun on her heel to leave.

"Wait a minute," I said.

She stopped in front of the door, her shoulders tensing.

"You're not working here."

She turned around, glaring at me. "Why not?"

"Because you're a train wreck, that's why. Once you can pass a drug test, then I'll think about it. Return your uniform before you leave."

I should have known not to give her a choice of who to marry after my papà passed. The capo was too old for the business, let alone to control Gianna. Which was undeniably the reason she'd chosen him.

Her smoky eyes went steely around the edges. "Fine." And then, in classic Gianna fashion, she grabbed the hem of her dress and pulled it off in one defiant swoop.

I gave my head a small shake, annoyance running through me.

Lorenzo rolled back so he could get a better look at her in only a black bra, thong, and heels. Ricardo whistled, and Jimmy chuckled before coughing on some smoke.

Gianna was hot, and she knew it. Even her tasteless style seemed to draw men in more than turn them away. But she'd been little more than a pain in my ass since my papà had died. And it looked like she was angry enough she was going to hurl her dress at my face.

"Try me," I warned.

A frustrated noise escaped her. She chose the safest option and threw it on the floor, before turning on her heel and marching out of the room.

Lorenzo let out a low whistle at the sight as she left.

With regret, her bare ass was making me think of another bare ass, and a rush of heat ran to my groin.

"Fork it over, Ricky," Jimmy said, puffing on his cigar.

Ricardo tossed some cash across the table, before giving me a nod and leaving the room.

"You too, huh?" I asked.

The moment with Elena on my kitchen counter was starting to replay on a loop in my mind. Her little sounds, her smell—*fuck*, I needed to get laid.

Jimmy collected his money. "Who do ya think made the bet? It's been going since your engagement party."

I wasn't even surprised I'd been that transparent.

I was another man pining after her.

Fuck me.

But she was mine now, whether I liked it or not. And I didn't. She was fucking distracting. She had a body I wanted to bury myself in and never leave, and it was why I was forcing myself not to go home tonight. I had to have some control where that woman was concerned. Had already told myself I wouldn't touch her until the wedding, just to prove to myself I could. But then she was in my space . . . and fuck, I couldn't do it.

She'd barely stepped in my door before I had her naked on the kitchen counter.

The funny part of it—though arguably not funny at all—was that she didn't want anything to do with me. I was hung up on this girl, badly, and she was in love with some other man. Something green burned through my veins like a lit wick, and I ran my hand across my jaw.

They'd killed the man she was with when she ran away, but they weren't found in a compromising position and neither did the apartment belong to him. It was possible they killed the wrong man and her lover was still alive. At least, that's what I heard through the grapevine, and regardless of how much I ached to, I wasn't digging further.

I'd always considered my morals to be slightly lower than mediocre, but it was at this moment I knew I was far, far below redemption.

Because innocent or not, if that man wasn't dead and he crossed my path, his lifeless body would be unrecognizable.

CHAPTER
Thirty

"If I get married, I want to be very married."
—Audrey Hepburn

Elena

THE TOUCH WAS INNOCENT. HIS HANDS WERE BRACED BESIDE MINE ON THE countertop, grazing my own, yet the warmth that flooded me felt like the letting of sunlight into a dusty, dark room.

"What's this?" His drawl ran down my spine as he stood behind me, his body trapping mine against the island.

"It wouldn't interest you." I bit my lip.

This morning I'd awoken to the sound of rain on glass, the *drip, drip, drip* seeping into my subconscious. I'd lain in an unfamiliar bed, though slept better than I had in a while. It was eight a.m. when my fiancé decided to come home.

I didn't know where he was last night, *who* he might have been with, but I decided it didn't matter. This was the start of my new life with him, and I'd known it would be this way.

I'd spent yesterday going over the list Mamma had emailed me, while Luca watched TV and pretended I wasn't here. I'd assumed he'd slept on the couch, because I hadn't once heard the unmistakable creak of the old wooden stairs.

He was in Nico's office now, watching sports news on the

computer. I'd wondered why he couldn't do that yesterday, but came to the assumption the couch was probably much more comfortable than the desk chair.

"I'll let you know what interests me."

"Wedding stuff," I said. "You know, the details that will tie us together for the rest of our lives?"

"Sounds like you're trying to scare me off."

"Is it working?"

"Nah, I'll take my chances." The amusement in his voice did strange things to my nervous system. How could he be so nonchalant and insistent about marrying me, and why did that hold a certain charm to it?

His fingers brushed mine as he pulled the printout of my mamma's email closer. He had nice hands, I noticed. Big, masculine, with clean, blunt nails. I wished I could find something I didn't like about this man, but it seemed it would have to be with his personality and not with his appearance.

His body grew closer to pressing against my back with each second as he read my mamma's list like I wasn't trapped in front of him.

"How do you feel about pink?" I breathed.

One of his hands slid to my waist, searing my skin through the pink scalloped dress I wore. "Never thought about it before," he drawled, "but I think I like it."

Warmth ran to my cheeks. "Good," I supplied. "Because you'll be wearing a pink tie."

He let out a breath of amusement. "I don't mind, but it will probably annoy Luca. Did he bother you yesterday?"

"No, he was a perfect gentleman. Didn't push me into a pool or anything."

"He stayed in my office?"

I hesitated, because I was a terrible liar. "Of course."

"Hmm." His hand slid from my waist to my hip, his fingers gripping my flesh with a firmness that set my pulse aflutter. Pressing his lips to my ear, he whispered, "I don't believe you."

I inhaled. "You expected him to stay in your office all day and night?"

"Yes," he said, like he wasn't asking for much. "Tell me what you did."

"We played monopoly and shared an ice cream cone."

I could feel his smile on the back of my neck. "Little liar," he drawled.

"You don't have a coffeemaker," was all I could think to say.

"I don't drink coffee."

"You're not human," I breathed.

His palm ran from my hip to my lower stomach. Heat curled inside me with the smallest amount of pressure from his hand. Each finger burned through the fabric while his lips brushed the nape of my neck. My insides were melting, dissolving into nothing but memory as he softly bit down and then licked the skin. I gripped the edge of the countertop, a moan crawling up my throat.

"Why are you dressed to go out?"

I sucked in a shaky breath. "I'm going to the dress shop with Mamma at ten."

"Are you now?" He ran his face across my bare shoulder, his scruff teasing my skin. "Who's taking you?"

"Benito's picking me up."

It went silent for a moment, and I suddenly wondered if he would tell me no. Would he be strict? Irrational? All the horrid possibilities came to mind as I finally realized I was putting my future in this man's hands. I hardly even knew him. I *wanted* to know him, just so I could understand how he would react. At least, that's what I told myself. I wanted to know what he did last night. What his middle name was. Who he had loved or who he *did*. I wanted to know everything, and that made my chest ache with the inevitable break.

"You'll take a burner phone until I can get you a new one."

I exhaled. In relief? I wasn't sure. It was hardly enough to understand his character, but it was something.

"Nico, it's not necessary to have Luca stay here with me. I don't need a babysitter."

A strained quiet crept between us before he stepped away.

"Your past says differently."

I tensed, somehow not believing he'd said that.

I got my first glimpse of Nico that morning. He walked into the living room, pulling off his tie, and I couldn't help but notice he wore the same clothes he had on last night. Swallowing the bitter taste in my mouth, I said, "I'm not going to run away." I did that once and it wasn't liberating; it was the biggest mistake I'd ever made.

His gaze was a lit match in a pitch-black room. "There's nowhere you could go that I couldn't find you."

A cold shiver rolled down my spine at the indifferent tone of his voice, because I believed him. Though, an edge to his expression made me believe he wasn't only leaving one of his men with me for my safety or the fact that I might try to run.

I paused when the realization hit me. Did he believe I was involved with another man? It would make sense with the way he'd implied more than once that I was somehow unfaithful.

Did he think I was that stupid? I would have to be incredibly foolish to be in a clandestine relationship, especially after what happened to me before. No offense to Adriana—she thought with her strange heart, not with her head.

Annoyance bubbled to the surface.

This man could sleep with whoever he wanted. My throat tightened as I imagined he'd done just that last night, and I was babysat so I didn't do the same? It was the way this life worked, I knew. But I'd only understood it from afar, not personally from a man I would soon call Husband. From a man I would share a home with.

Annoyance turned to bitterness and spread through my blood like poison.

I would never have a husband of my own. I would always have to share him. And that truth felt so real, so raw at that moment, tremors of resentment ached in my chest.

My eyes narrowed, just like they had at the church when I'd first seen him.

His gaze imitated mine.

I had no desire to inform him there was no other man. It didn't matter if there was, anyway.

My heart would never be his.

It was the one thing in my life that was mine, and I would never sign it over.

The entire ride to the dress shop, Nonna and Adriana watched me with blank, non-blinking expressions. Benito stayed silent in the driver's seat, and Mamma talked, over-animated and nervously, about the wedding.

Where most girls dreamed about their wedding and how perfect it would be, I viewed it behind a murky film. As if the dress in the store's window was behind a finger-smudged pane of glass. My wedding wouldn't be based on love, but a mere transfer of power from my papà to my husband.

Although, as my heels clicked on the pavement and my breath went shallow with each step, something danced under my skin. Vibrated in my veins. Excitement. *Yearning.* With a sad flame of hope flickering beyond.

The glass was crystal clear, a gorgeous white dress showcased behind it.

I didn't love the man I would marry. *Couldn't.* Placing my finger to the glass, I left one smudge against the false hope this window gave.

My mamma held the door open, her eyes narrowing as she examined me. "One day with the Russo and I think my daughter's gone *stupida.*"

"With your genes?" Nonna muttered, walking inside. "What else did you expect?"

I shut the door with a quiet click behind me. Awareness brushed my skin from my head to my toes as Nico flicked a gaze my way from his seat at the island.

His elbows rested on the counter, his gun taken apart in front of him. The way he cleaned the piece in his hand was thoughtful, as if he had a lot on his mind—or maybe he was just meticulous about his gun.

"Did you find a dress?" His tone was light, not tainted with the anger I'd expected.

The tension in my shoulders eased. My frustration had faded with the hours of the day, but with the way we'd left things earlier, I didn't know what to expect when I returned.

I leaned against the door, feeling the toll of the day all at once. When I thought of my dress, a smile came to my lips.

"The perfect one."

"Perfect, huh?" he drawled.

"Uh-huh." And then, because this conversation seemed too stuffy and formal, I said, "It was very expensive."

It rewarded me with the tiniest smile.

"'Course it was."

It wasn't as if its price had any bearing on my decision. When I saw it, I knew it was the one. Love at first sight with a dress. I had reservations about our marriage, but today I realized the wedding would be my only one. I wasn't going to throw it away because the union might not be the love story of the century.

We'd found four pink bridesmaid dresses, instead of the yellow ones Mamma had chosen for Adriana. And considering my sister's bridesmaids were made up of me and three of our closest cousins, I didn't have to make any changes to the wedding party. Maybe that should have been depressing, but to me it just seemed convenient.

I kicked off my heels. "Mamma cried."

"Did she?"

"I guess *sobbed* is more accurate," I sighed, remembering the scene.

"Shame I had to miss it."

This conversation was easy, relaxed, though I couldn't help but notice his movements were slightly tense. I chewed my lip, padding into the kitchen. I grabbed a glass from the cupboard and filled it from the faucet as if I did normal things around this man all the time and didn't care about his presence. In reality, my spine tingled with a violent awareness.

While trying to think of something to say, my attention caught on the new appliance on the counter. Something heavy sank in my chest.

"You got a coffeemaker?"

"Can't have you turning into anything nonhuman."

That was thoughtful of him . . . and I hated it, because I couldn't remember the last time someone had thought of what I needed before I had to ask for it.

I swallowed the lump in my throat.

"The phone on the counter is yours," he said.

My gaze flicked toward the device, and I picked it up. In all honesty, I'd enjoyed the freedom of not having a phone for the last six months. "I don't think I want it," I told him.

"It's yours, Elena. Keep it on you at *all* times."

I wondered if this would be an inappropriate time to ask him to say please.

"Ace," I read when I came across his name already programmed in my contacts. "Awfully presumptuous of you to put your number in my phone."

I turned my head to see a small smile pull on his lips, but his gaze was focused on his work. "You're a sure thing, *wife*."

"Wife" should have been a sweet pet name for any man to call his fiancée, but the sardonic possessiveness of his tone ruined it. However, six months ago I'd realized I didn't like sweet. Heat spread through me.

"I'm not your wife yet," I told him.

"Semantics." He glanced at my pink cheeks. "I've never seen a woman in the *Cosa Nostra* blush until you."

He didn't need to remind me.

"Does it bother you?"

"Not at all." He pulled his gaze to his work, running a thumb across his jaw in a thoughtful way.

My breathing turned shallow, and I took a step toward the island, grasping the countertop. "Thank you for the coffeemaker and the phone."

Sitting across from me, the dim lighting made his eyes look like burnt gold. "You're welcome."

Tension crept between us, finding its way between my legs and settling there like a heavy weight. I wanted to thank him in an entirely different way. I wanted to see what was beneath that white shirt. I wanted to know how much little effort it would take for him to hold me down. I wanted to put out this fire inside me that had been there since I'd met him. I wanted *him*.

His gaze found mine, and the gold blackened around the edges. My pulse pirouetted to a strange dance.

"You're coming to work with me tonight."

His indifferent tone broke the tension until it scattered to the corners of the room.

I exhaled. "Why?"

"I need Luca and I don't trust anyone else to stay with you."

I ignored the way that made me sound like a two-year-old. "Are you expecting trouble tonight?"

"I expect trouble every night."

My brows pulled together. "And you want to drag me into it?"

"I'm not going to let you die." His gaze flashed with dark amusement. "I'm just getting started with you."

CHAPTER
Thirty-One

"One can't paint New York as it is, but rather as it is felt."
—Georgia O'Keeffe

Elena

THE CLOSEST THING I HAD TO NIGHTCLUB ATTIRE WAS A PAIR OF SKINNY JEANS and a loose, strappy top. It was white and shimmery, and the sleeves were cut on the sides, leaving thin strings connecting them to my wrist. Paired with my white heels that still lay near the back door, it would be passable.

As I stood in front of the bathroom mirror, I frowned at the curling iron in the second drawer. When I'd bathed this morning, I found cherry blossom shampoo and soap already in the shower. Some woman visited enough she stockpiled toiletries. What would I do if he brought her home while I was here? Something bitter twisted in my stomach.

I tried to figure out why it bothered me so much. If it were Oscar Perez who brought another woman home, I would feel lucky for the reprieve. Though, with this man . . . the idea made my throat tighten with an unexplainable feeling.

I used the curling iron. And then I freshened my makeup but kept it light.

I was near the back door, slipping into my heels, when Nico came downstairs. I wished my uncertainty about that stupid woman's shampoo would have dulled the sensation of how my body reacted to him. It thrummed at seeing him in a black suit with a sober expression that burned through my skin. His handsomeness was so classic it made me believe he could fit seamlessly into any time period.

I couldn't hold on to resentment or anxiety of what he may do in the future. I wouldn't live my life like that. I would just have to take it one day at a time and let the inevitable work its way out when it did.

"How did I get ready before you?" I teased, leaning against the back door.

His lips tipped up as he grabbed his keys off the counter and then typed something into a security system keypad near his office door.

Hesitation settled in me when he didn't respond. He'd seemed more distant since our conversation this morning. What did I expect? I was sure he thought I was involved with some man, and I had never made it clear that I wasn't. I'd told him I didn't want to marry him, and I wasn't a virgin, which I was sure he wanted since he picked Adriana. Or maybe he just preferred her?

Why did he even want me?

He could have anyone he wanted. Any virgin from here to the west coast would be delighted if they could get past his reputation.

I realized then that I wanted him to want me.

Where a deep attraction had hummed for him since I'd met him, there was something else coming to life, pulsing like a weak beat on a heart rate monitor. I could almost hear the *beep* echo in my ears. Almost feel the thrum in my chest. But it wasn't of me.

It felt like man, clean sweat and whiskey.

Twinkling urban lights. High heels and short dresses. Too many drinks and meaningless sex hanging like an inevitable in the air. Nightlife was in full swing as we made our way into a side door of the club.

I'd never been to a nightclub before. Had never been one of these girls who waited to get into my fiancé's club. Who might've even had sex with him for all I knew. Some unease curled in my stomach. How could I ever please him when I was sure he'd been with much more experienced women? It was a hit to my womanhood imagining I would bore him in bed. He hadn't even tried to get me there—had just given me an orgasm like it was an engagement present and left.

I chewed the inside of my cheek in thought. The idea that he might not want to sleep with me only made me want it more. Just his hand on my arm and his presence by my side warmed me from the inside out.

Nico guided me down a red-carpeted hall. The lighting was low, and the air carried a hint of fresh cigarette smoke. Wasn't it illegal to allow smoking in one's establishment in New York? A smile pulled on my lips. *His most heinous crime, I bet.*

An electric beat pulsed through the walls as purple and blue strobe lights flickered into the hall like they'd escaped the dance floor. We went down a set of stairs and then stopped at a heavy metal door. Nico stood so close behind me his jacket touched my back. Over my head, he knocked five times in a heavy rap with a short pause in between each.

A moment later, the door swung open and a dark-haired hostess in a tight black dress stood on the other side. *"Signor Russo."* She smiled brightly at him, but then her smile fell as her eyes came down and regarded me. Her gaze narrowed, fake eyelashes and all. She did a great job with her makeup, I had to admit, but the way her lips curled in disgust like I was a cheap prostitute was blatantly rude.

Ugh. My first day out with Nico and I was the most unpopular woman in the city.

I would have brushed it off before, not having the guts to confront it in any way. Nonetheless, I was now marrying a don. I couldn't let myself be run over by waitresses. It felt a little ridiculous, like I was playing immature games, but I reached back and slipped my fingers in between Nico's.

He stilled as if I surprised him, but after a second, his fingers tightened around my own. And then I felt a light smack on my ass to get me moving. The gesture made me warm everywhere, but thankfully it didn't reach my face.

I didn't look at the waitress again, though I believed she got the picture. He could do whatever or whoever he wanted, but not in my presence. There was a certain amount of respect I was due, and I didn't think even Nico would deny me that.

I dropped his hand and stepped onto a short steel staircase. I blinked, taking it all in.

A thick atmosphere hung in the air that I wouldn't have expected in a place like this. For starters, it looked like there were maybe two women in the room, including the one at the door. The gross majority were men, from suits to board shorts and polos.

Poker tables were distributed around the large area, with players occupying seats in front of them, all in different stages of betting their life savings away.

I followed Nico down the stairs, observing the obvious illegal gaming hall. A card game ended, and as the players stood, all five lit a cigarette and headed to the corner of the room.

"Are they not allowed to smoke at the tables?" I asked Nico.

"They can. Most times it's a tell so they wait until the game's over."

Interesting.

I liked to know weird stuff like this.

I fired questions at him all the way to his office, from how much the House made in one night (roughly twenty grand) to why there were only two women (they were distracting).

The gambling was serious enough that distractions weren't wanted in any way. Nobody paid me an ounce of attention as we walked toward the back of the room. The men at the tables were statues of concentration, and the ones smoking were sweating from their losses or too busy texting about their winnings.

His office was a perfect square with a blue, stylish couch, a mahogany desk with a couple chairs in front of it, a flat-screen TV, and a minibar. I set my clutch on the glass coffee table, while he pushed a button on his keyboard to get the computer started.

The walls were concrete, but with the gold and blue oriental rug and nothing but one piece of artwork on the wall, the room was somehow warm and comfortable.

I studied the painting that sat behind a shiny piece of glass. Pastel colors and bold yet refined sweeps of a brush. I wasn't an artistic person like my sister, but I recognized the work. I'd watched a documentary about the downfall of modern art. That what we consider art today is a poor example of the talent and heart of art in the past.

"I didn't take you to have a soft spot for Monet," I said, glancing at him.

His attention was on his computer, but a small smile pulled on his lips. He stood with one hand braced on the desk while hitting keys with the other. Either he had this place under his command much like a mad scientist with their destructive red buttons, or he was a very unproductive typist.

"My mamma was a fan."

My stomach warmed at the deep way *mamma* rolled off his lips. "She had good taste."

He laughed quietly. A bitter note showed through, and he wiped his amusement away with a palm like he'd just realized what he'd done. It felt like I was about to wade into deep waters, but I couldn't stop myself from going deeper.

I raised a brow. "You don't like Monet?"

"I have it in my office, don't I?"

"That's not why you have it in here."

His shoulders tensed, and he pushed his keys a little harder. "You analyzing me?"

I gazed at the soft, pastel strokes in the painting. "There's a saying amongst us women: Don't trust a man who isn't good to his mamma."

His gaze burned into my cheek. "You think I was bad to my mother?"

I wasn't sure how I recognized I wouldn't get to know him easily, that I might have to get him worked up to do so. He wasn't someone to sit around and share his past with others, his fiancée included. I needed to know the man I would marry. There was a part of me that just wanted to know, so I lifted a shoulder. My heart danced at the unfamiliar game I was playing.

"Am I supposed to think differently?"

He let out an unamused breath, but he didn't say another word. He didn't try to defend himself, and my stomach tightened with the need to assure him that wasn't what I thought. *Was it?*

An itch began in my throat to apologize for what I'd insinuated as he walked across the office to leave, and I turned to see him open the door.

"James will be right outside if you need something. Stay here. I shouldn't be gone long."

"Nico, wait. I shouldn't have said—"

Nicolas called into the hallway for a Lucky. Glancing back at me, he said, "No, you're right. You shouldn't trust me. I've already lied to you since we've been in this room."

I swallowed. "About what?"

He paused with a hand on the doorknob. "I always just say she was a fan. It's much easier to say than to explain that she was always so high she couldn't tell a Monet from a fucking caricature painted on the street."

CHAPTER
Thirty-Two

"True love stories never have endings."
—Richard Bach

Elena

THE DOOR SHUT BEHIND HIM, AND I WAS CONVINCED I WAS THE WORST person in the world at that moment. I had no idea about his mother. I'd assumed she'd died of cancer or some other illness, but now I wondered if it was an illness at all. I had imagined that in his family, the woman would be the only reliable and steady person to lean on. He didn't even have that.

This painting had been his mamma's, and he'd kept it even though she was probably far from the best parent.

He was good to his mamma.

I needed a drink.

As I took my time making a gin and tonic, a kid of fifteen or sixteen stepped in. Once he shut the door, he stood beside it with a stoic expression. I had a James in the hall and this must be Lucky. The nickname had conjured an image of a beefy man with a shamrock tattoo, not a boy. My fiancé must be initiating this kid, poor thing.

I smiled. "Hello. I'm sorry, I don't know your name."

"Matteo, but everyone calls me Lucky," he said, slipping his hands into his suit pants pockets.

"Why do they call you Lucky?"

"I suppose because I'm lucky, ma'am."

A bit of amusement rose in me. "Nice to meet you, Lucky. I'm Elena, but you probably already know who I am, considering you're my babysitter and all."

He laughed a slightly uncomfortable laugh.

I flicked the TV on and got settled on the couch. For twenty minutes, I watched the news and sipped my drink, with the intermittent commotion from outside and the electro beat pulsing through the ceiling. Nico better be confident his gaming hall wouldn't be busted while I sat in his office. Though, it wasn't exactly a real worry of mine. An FBI agent showed up to his parties; I was sure he had the rest of the force in his pocket.

I sighed. Lucky had only been quietly standing by the door like the good Made Man in training he was. I grabbed a pack of cards off the coffee table and turned the box in my hands.

"Lucky, would you like to play cards with me?"

"Oh, well,"—he ran a hand across the back of his neck—"I'm no Ace."

My brows knitted, unsure of what he meant. "I just thought cards would be a good alternative to us both dying of boredom."

He chuckled. "Um . . ."

"Or are you not allowed to?" How strict was my fiancé with his men?

A corner of his lips lifted. "I'm only supposed to look in your direction when you speak to me."

I guess that answers that . . .

With a sigh, he said, "One game."

He didn't sound so sure, and I hesitated because I didn't want to get him in trouble. But he was already walking to the couch, and the truth was, I didn't want to sit in silence any longer.

"Are you related to Nico?" I asked.

"Cousin," he said. "My papà was his papà's brother."

Lucky was taller than me, but he was lean and wiry. Still a boy. I wondered what Nico was like at Lucky's age. Probably still bossy and used to getting his way.

Poker was the game of choice, and when I told Lucky we didn't have to play for money, he looked at me like I was crazy. I laughed. What a little Russo in the making.

So I played poker with this teen boy and bet money I didn't have.

I lost.

I used to play often. Nonna had a taste for the game, and sometimes when my mamma got a hankering for "family night" we all got together and played.

"Lucky," I said, rearranging my cards, "how did your aunt die?"

"Caterina?" He frowned. "Drug overdose, I think. I was a baby at the time."

I sighed. *Yep, horrible person.*

"Where is Nico tonight?" I was 99 percent sure he wouldn't tell me, but that still left a 1 percent possibility. When his shoulders tensed slightly, alarm ran through me.

"I don't know," he said eventually.

"Yes, you do," I accused.

He glanced at me with wide eyes. "Well, I do, but I'm not going to tell you."

"Why not?" I pretended to be taken aback.

"Because Ace would have my ass if I talked business with you."

"How would he know?"

He only shook his head.

"Fine." I set my cards on the coffee table and then stood.

"Where are you going?" His tone wavered.

"I think I'll go dancing upstairs."

He shot to his feet. "No—wait."

I halted in front of the door with my back to him.

"James is in the hall and you won't get past him," he said.

"But it would look bad that I got past *you*, wouldn't it?"

Three seconds passed.

"Fine." It was a little boy growl.

A smile pulled on my lips.

"He's dealing with the man that knocked up your sister."

I went still, took a deep breath, and then headed straight for the minibar.

"You lost again."

One game had turned into three, and Lucky was either lucky or I was just bad.

I sighed and tossed my cards on the coffee table, watching some scatter to the floor. I was on my third drink and my head felt the effects.

Nico had been gone for almost two hours and the worry gnawed at me. He told me I shouldn't trust him, so how could I trust the promise he'd made me about Ryan?

"That's two grand now," Lucky said, smug.

I groaned in my mind. Russo boys were just as bad as Russo men.

"Two grand, huh?" The voice carried a dark edge.

Lucky shot to his feet for the third time that night. "Boss—"

"Enough."

The kid shut his mouth.

Nico's focus was on me as he walked into the room. Self-assurance seemed to brew under his skin, like he'd gone for a run and instead of perspiring, he sweat cool confidence. His mood was electric and affecting me like a contagion in the air.

"Get the fuck out, Lucky." Nico's voice held a sharp note as he unbuttoned his suit jacket. His cousin headed toward the door. "Leave your post again and I swear you'll be unable to leave your bed for a week."

Lucky said, "Yes, boss," before shutting the door behind him.

"Is there a reason my men don't do what they're told when you're around?"

"Maybe you need to ask nicely," I said, biting my cheek to hide my amusement. "A *please* never killed anyone, you know."

"I suppose not." His gaze sparked with dark amusement. "It seems to be your favorite word under certain circumstances."

I sucked in a breath as warmth rushed to my cheeks. The blush spread throughout my entire body, and to distract myself from it, I changed the subject.

"I lost two thousand." My tone was unapologetic, like I did this all the time.

Nico tugged on his tie, a smile pulling on his lips. "You didn't lose anything. He cheated you."

I paused. "How do you know that?"

"Because I taught him how, that's why."

Lucky, my ass.

"He would've won without the cheating," I admitted with a sigh. "I have a terrible poker face."

An intense gaze met mine, the pressure of it touching my skin. "Somehow, I doubt that." He walked toward me with his hands in his pockets, and it felt as if I was forgetting how to breathe with each step.

I had no idea how to respond to that, or why it felt like it meant something, so I only said, "I don't know the first thing about how to recognize when someone's cheating, either." I had the feeling I would get eaten alive in the Russo family. Even a teen boy had shown me up.

Nico dropped to his haunches before my spot on the couch and picked up a card from the floor. My heart pattered like rain against glass. He was close enough I could reach out and run my hand through his hair.

"Well, we'll have to fix that, won't we?"

In between his pointer and middle finger, he held the card out to me, but before I could reach for it, it disappeared into thin air.

My eyes went wide. "How did you do that?"

"Simple sleight of hand."

The cheating in the Russo family was so extreme that making cards disappear was "simple."

"Show me," I insisted.

His gaze sparked with amusement. "We'll start with the basics first, so I can leave you alone for a couple hours without you losing all my money."

I frowned.

He picked up the rest of the cards, and I noticed his freshly busted knuckles. I chewed my lip as he got to his feet, took off his jacket, and sat in the chair behind his desk.

"You play often?" I asked.

He leaned back, resting an elbow on the armrest. "Used to."

"Why not anymore?"

"Got business to run."

"Lucky made it sound like you were good. But now I can't decide if you were good at poker or good at cheating."

A dark smile pulled on his lips. "Sounds like you got him talking."

Eh. I knew *that* tone, and it wouldn't be good for Lucky.

"Well . . . no. I kind of threatened him and told him I would go dancing upstairs if he didn't tell me what I wanted to know."

"And what did you want to know?"

I swallowed. "Where you were tonight."

"I thought my business would be the last thing on earth to interest you," he said in an amused drawl.

"Some of your business has become personal."

His words were tinged with sarcasm, yet so quiet I barely heard them. "Don't I know it."

I wasn't sure what he meant, but I didn't wonder about it anymore when he said, "He's alive, just like I told you he'd be. Your *famiglia* is taking him into the fold right now."

I cringed. "He'll live?"

"He'll live."

I let out a deep breath of relief and let my head fall against the back of the couch.

"Thank you," I said softly.

"I think we both know I hardly did it to be charitable."

My cheeks flushed as I remembered our bargain. He'd yet to cash in on that. It made me believe he didn't want to. Or maybe he didn't want me to know how charitable he could really be . . .

Nico had some emails to reply to, so while waiting I used my phone to look at wedding table arrangements on my mamma's party planner's website. Out of the options in stock, I narrowed it down to a short round vase with studded pearls around the edges, and a simple one that would sit on a piece of glass.

I sent the pictures to Mamma only to receive a text that said: *They both look like something you'd find at one of those Goodwills.*

The vases were simple and classic and me.

My mamma was loud, proud, and would want her wedding tables to show it. Which was exactly why I didn't want to use what was already purchased for Adriana—my mother being the buyer. I tilted my head and regarded them once more, but still couldn't decide.

Nico had been on the phone for a short time, and I could grow used to his deep timbre in the background, no matter if he was discussing "product," which I was sure was what killed his mother.

Now, he was quiet as he responded to an email, or possibly wrote a report on the next man's life he was going to ruin. I was going to marry this man. I'd never believed I was a woman who needed attention, but at that moment, I wanted his. Undivided, and as thrilling as it always was.

Nerves played beneath my skin, but I got to my feet and walked around his desk until I stood beside him. He flicked a gaze to me and then leaned back in his chair.

"I can't decide on a centerpiece for the tables," I told him.

"Show me."

Instead of taking the phone from my hand, he pulled me onto his lap. My heart raced from the shock of it. His arm was firm around my waist, yet it felt like it was burning me more than balancing me. I steadied myself with a hand on his shoulder. He was so big and warm and hard. I pretended this position didn't affect me at all, but in reality, it took me a moment to remember why I'd come over here.

I turned my head to look at him. My breath shallowed when I realized his lips were only inches from my own. His gaze was warm, seeing deeper beneath my skin with each second.

With his body pressed against mine, warming me from the inside out, the pull to lean in was a physical thing. A heavy tug, as if he were my center of gravity. I could taste his breath and feel his strong heartbeat.

I could jump the gap, just as I'd done in a rain drizzled car once before.

How easy it would be: to bury my fingers in his hair, to run my hand along his jawline, to meet my mouth with his.

I knew it would be the best kiss I'd ever had.

So I only showed him the vases instead.

CHAPTER
Thirty-Three

"Simplicity is the ultimate sophistication."
—Leonardo da Vinci

Elena

HATED HIS CAR, HOW IT WAS INFINITELY HIM. HOW I WAS SUFFOCATED IN HIS space in a way I couldn't find unpleasant.

I hated his car.

But I loved how he drove it.

How his hand fit the wheel, how he sat in the driver's seat with an unpretentious confidence, and how he always drove the speed limit as if to maintain that gentlemanly façade.

It reminded me of the soft sound of fabric hitting the floor, the scrape of teeth on the nape of my neck, the tug of my hair.

My pulse drifted between my thighs, and I pressed my legs together.

I wasn't usually a betting girl, but I would put all of my papà's ill-gotten gains on the idea that this man fucked just like he drove. With complete control and confidence.

Nico remained silent as we drove uptown, streetlights flickering and fading across an unreadable expression. Earlier, he'd picked the simple vase and said, "Less is more," and I had to agree with him.

After that, he'd hardly said a word to me. During his silence, I realized I liked his voice. I wanted to know what he would say. There were whole sentences in that head just waiting to be drawled, and I wanted every one of them. I couldn't and wouldn't analyze why.

The quiet, the pressure between my legs, they started to build until I had to break the tension.

"How fast does this thing go?" I asked.

His head tilted to the side, catching my gaze. He held it for a moment before turning back to the road. "Fast."

I pulled my bottom lip between my teeth, trying to think of how to respond. What I came up with was, "How fast?"

He didn't glance at me, but a small smile appeared.

"Show me." It escaped my lips on a breath, quiet and suggestive.

"No."

I raised a brow. "Why? Are you scared?"

He flicked a gaze to me. Darkness glinted behind an ounce of amusement. "Scared and reckless are two different things."

I didn't know why considering it didn't help my case, but it was a relief he'd said that. I had a rash brother—I didn't want a similar husband. However, I wasn't ready to give up yet; his attention had sparked a thrill inside of me.

"Are you saying you've never shown off with a woman in the car before?"

"That's not what I said."

"So, you have?"

"When I was sixteen, probably."

That was a long time ago, yet I couldn't stop a sliver of envy from finding its way to me. What girl was important enough to him that he'd shown off to impress her? I shook it off. "I'm marrying a Russo. Don't you think I should know what it's like before it's too late?"

The glance he cast my way was nothing but heat. "It's already too late."

My pulse fluttered, but I forced a sigh. "It's okay. If you're scared—"

He shook his head before the car accelerated so fast I fell against my seat. A laugh escaped my lips, yet his only response was a look in my direction, a spark passing through his eyes. I watched the odometer hit 90 . . . 100 . . . 110.

Nico drove like he would if he were going a mere sixty mph: relaxed, not conveying an ounce of emotion. Adrenaline surged and fizzled through my veins. He hit 120 before he had to slow for our exit.

High on lust and life and speed, I rolled down my window and let the warm air brush my cheeks. We pulled into the driveway fifteen minutes later, and I couldn't exactly say it felt like home yet, but something about it did feel *right*.

The adrenaline had faded to chugging along, like a train running out of fuel. It left a hot and cold sensation under my skin, nerves thriving in the atmosphere.

He turned the ignition off, and the soft *pops* and *crackles* of a hot engine filtered into the car through the open window. Hot urban air, silver moonlight, and a heavy tension settled in the space between us. My breaths were labored, each second feeling like a pregnant pause.

I was sure the truth was as clear as the sounds of the ball game escaping the neighbor's window. That I wanted this man. Every time I was near him I lost all poise and control. What scared me the most was that I didn't want control, I wanted him to have it all. I wanted to experience what I was sure a hundred other girls had, no matter that the thought made me burn with jealousy.

He must have known all of this, but I wasn't so sure he shared the same sentiment.

I was a convenience.

His second choice.

It took a moment to realize *Snap Your Fingers, Snap Your Neck* played on the radio. The song was far from romantic, but it was rough and compelling, like the man beside me. It was the song I'd kissed him to. Someone might as well have yelled it into the car, as aware of it as we suddenly were.

I opened my door an inch so the radio would shut off, but I didn't get out. Something pounded in my chest. An unfulfilled need that felt close to bursting. My palms grew clammy.

"Nico—"

His hand came toward my face and my words caught in my throat. As if my body expected a blow, a breath escaped me when his thumb brushed across my lips and down my chin. "Go inside. I have some things to do out here."

The truth was, I hadn't exactly figured out what I would say, and for that reason I was glad he'd stopped me. But as I made my way inside, a heavy weight that felt too much like rejection settled in my chest.

Once I was inside my room, I slipped into my Yankees t-shirt. My body thrummed with indecision, my heart beating with a speed that made me feel alive. I sat in the seat below the window and stared through the glass, at the light underneath the garage door.

I fell asleep before I ever heard the creak of the stairs.

A crick in my neck ached as I awoke curled up on the window seat. Sunlight filtered into the room in rays, lighting dust particles in the air. My mouth watered as the smell of bacon reached my nose. I wondered if Nico's cook was here, though it was Sunday and she wasn't due until tomorrow.

Not fully awake, I made my way into the hallway bathroom, combed my hair, and brushed my teeth. Maybe I should've put on a little makeup now that I had a fiancé I could run into at any moment, but truthfully, I'd never cared much for the stuff.

I padded toward the smell of bacon, and then stopped short at the base of the stairs. Heat curled in my stomach and drifted through my body in one smooth sweep. My heartbeat settled between my legs. A pan was cooking on the stove, but I hardly had a sexual fetish for food. That I knew of, anyway. I'd seldom seen this man out of a suit and tie. Now that he stood at the island without a single stitch on his upper half, it was a shock to my nervous system.

He was more brawn than chiseled, wide shoulders, defined chest, and when he ran a hand across his bare abs, my cheeks grew so warm they could have heated the house. I swore blushing was the bane of my existence.

He flipped a page of the magazine that held his attention. "Thought I told you to burn that shirt," he drawled.

I swallowed, and couldn't think of one thing to say, because it was so early and there was *so* much skin. His ink stopped at the shoulder of one arm, leaving everything else tan, hard, and *ugh*. I opened my mouth, and what came out was, "Why? So we can both walk around inappropriately dressed?"

His lips lifted, though he didn't bother to look at me. "I don't know, seems platonic compared to what you were begging me—"

"Okay," I blurted. "Fine. But I'm not burning my shirt. You'll have to convert." I told him this with all seriousness as I made my way to the coffeemaker.

His response was a dry noise of amusement that let me know that was *not* going to happen.

I worked on getting the coffee started like it required my full attention, because his nudity made butterflies dance in my stomach. However, I got distracted somewhere along the way and ended up staring at his back.

All of a sudden I decided I had a thing for men's backs, though I was uncertain about the gun tucked into the waistband of his sweatpants. No wonder he was still alive—he was never unarmed. There was a small circular scar low on his side, and I wondered where the two other bullet wounds had been.

"Who taught you how to cook?" I asked, eyeing the pan on the stove.

He turned around and leaned against the island, grasping the counter on either side of him. "Are you telling me you can't make bacon and eggs?"

I frowned and shifted my weight to the other foot. "Well . . ."

His smile was sly and charming at the same time. "Starting to wonder what I'm getting out of this marriage."

I bit my lip. "Me too."

He laughed, deep and hearty, and it made my pulse skip a beat. It was only the second genuine laugh I'd heard from him, and I suddenly knew I could grow used to it.

The coffee began brewing, filling the kitchen with a rich and earthy smell. Nico had gotten me the good stuff, though I would have drunk burnt gas station coffee for my fix. Glancing at the clock, it read seven-thirty a.m.

"Does this marriage thing mean I have to go to your church?"

He smiled and then wiped it away with a palm. "Yeah. That's what *this marriage thing* means."

My lips pursed in thought. It wasn't like I had a particular fondness for my church—in fact, I knew our priest was on Papà's payroll. Therefore, I couldn't be honest during Confession, leaving me with all these sins that needed to be absolved. It was a mess on my conscience, really. But I imagined it wouldn't be that different at Nico's church. And I'd also have to be surrounded by Russos . . .

I swallowed. "I guess I better go get ready."

"Nah, not this week. We've got somewhere else to be."

I watched him for a moment while a tickle played in the back of my mind. My gaze narrowed. "I'm sure it has nothing to do with the fact your priest won't approve of me living here before marriage?"

The tiniest flicker passed through his eyes and I knew I was right. He was hiding me from his priest. He wanted to be a respectable Catholic, and even though it was far, *far* from the truth, it was sort of admirable.

"So, I'm like your dirty little secret." It was supposed to be teasing, but it came out more acutely as I realized it bothered me.

"Dirty?" The look he shot me was warm whiskey over ice. "Hopefully."

I inhaled, though my lungs refused to accept it. I didn't know how he could say something like that as if the intensity of it didn't bother him a bit, whereas I needed to break eye contact and brush the moment away.

"I don't need to keep you a secret, Elena," he said, going to tend to his pan on the stove. "I just don't have the patience to listen to what people think I should do with what's mine."

Mine. It drifted through the room, hanging above our heads like a lazy breeze unwilling to depart. Something touched me deep in the chest.

"Yours, huh?"

He stilled, running a hand across his jaw. "My fiancée," he corrected with indifference, as though he'd realized his simple mistake, as though *fiancée* had a different meaning than *mine*. In this world, it did.

"My family's aware you're here and that's all that matters," he said. "They aren't going to say anything."

"Or you'll shoot them?"

He glanced my way, gaze lazy. "Or I'll shoot them."

The frightening thing about it was that I couldn't tell if he was serious or not. A part of me heard the light, teasing tone, while the other replayed him shooting his cousin in the head on a sunny Sunday afternoon.

His stare swept me from head to toe, burning my skin. But when his eyes met mine, something soft came to the front.

I don't keep secrets, Elena.

He was lying to me.

And I could only think of one reason for it. A part of me rebuffed the possibility, while the other went soft and warm inside.

He was keeping me a secret because he worried about my reputation.

Maybe it was for selfish reasons, but my heart still decided to grow twice its size. Guilt deflated it just as fast. I seemed to bring this man more trouble than I was worth. The numbers I'd copied onto paper sat in the bottom of my duffel bag upstairs and heavily on my conscience. "Maybe I should stay at home until the marriage," I offered.

"This is your home."

"You know what—"

"No."

Okay.

Not one for negotiating, it seemed.

He grabbed two plates from the cupboard. "Thought you ran every morning."

I almost didn't hear him over how shirtless he was.

I pursed my lips. "I've decided it doesn't suit me."

He gave me a dark look. "If you decide it *does* suit you, use the treadmill in the spare room upstairs. You can't run the streets like you used to."

My smile was sweet. "You have a way of making me feel so very liberated."

He wasn't amused. "What are your plans for dance?"

I hadn't signed up for another class since the recital and I didn't think I was going to. Although, now I wasn't sure if I'd be able to get out of the house any other way.

"I haven't decided."

He filled two plates while I poured a cup of coffee. This man had given me an orgasm and made me breakfast. The former I had only hoped for, the latter I hadn't imagined. I was beginning to wonder what he wanted with me. I would be a poor excuse of a wife.

He leaned against the counter, giving me all of his autocratic attention. "If you decide to go back, we'll have to find you a new studio."

I paused. "Why?"

"I don't trust your papà's streets."

My eyes narrowed.

He noticed and returned the look. "You're awfully loyal to the wrong people." Annoyance coated his voice.

"You mean my family? Those people?" I raised a brow. "There's nothing wrong with my papà's streets."

The unimpressed expression he gave me said *driveby* loud and clear.

I had nothing substantial to respond with, so I reflected. "Maybe I don't trust *your* streets."

"You won't be an Abelli for much longer. If you're going to dance or whatever else it is you do, you're doing it on my streets." He added with a dark tone, "And forget sucking anyone's life away."

A shiver went through me as I realized I would be Elena *Russo* in a short amount of time. I forced a sigh to hide my unsettlement.

"You're dreadfully totalitarian today."

"Just shy of psychotic, then?" His eyes sparked. "Guess I'd better up my game."

As we stared at each other, three feet apart, something heavy flowed into the kitchen. A languid, hot, and suggestive air. My heart thumped the heavy beats of a drum. He stood there, half-naked, *so* much man. And I knew that if I remained silent, something was going to happen. Everything was going to change. Just before eight a.m. on a Sunday. Unease, anticipation, and a sliver of panic flooded me.

I knew something about the next step would break my heart.

"Please do," I breathed. "So I know what to expect." The words cut through the thick haze, clearing the air.

He watched me for another second. Shook his head. And then pushed off the counter.

"Eat your breakfast. We're leaving in twenty."

"Where are we going?"

He grabbed a magazine off the island and dropped it on the counter in front of me. The advertisement said *Show and Shine Car Show.*

What on earth did you wear to a car show?

"Fashion fades, only style remains the same."
—Coco Chanel

Elena

WITH MUCH REGRET, I REALIZED THAT NICO WAS A MORNING PERSON.
While I needed a good hour or two to drink my coffee and prepare to even get ready for the day, he made breakfast, dressed in jeans and that white t-shirt, and was ready to go with the sun.

Flaw found. Right next to the question of his mental status. Though, I believed the issues went hand in hand.

"You look nice," he told me as we pulled out of the drive.

Like an idiot, I flushed all the way to my hairline.

He laughed quietly and then turned up *Last Resort* by Papa Roach until it was all I could hear.

Throughout the day, *You look nice* was a deep, worn-out recording in the back of my mind. It was such a simple observation, and for that reason warmth filled my chest. I was used to compliments, and maybe that sounded shallow, as though I felt I was deserving of them. But I didn't believe I was, nor did I want them. In my life, the beautiful girls ended up like Gianna: hiding the misery in their eyes with dilated pupils.

I was observant as a child. I wanted to analyze the world and decipher its meaning, but what I found was myself as a little girl standing in front of a mirror where a loveless, empty life stared back.

The truth was, I was a liar. I'd always been a romantic. So deep a romantic that the thought of not finding my own love story felt like I once again stood in that vacant parking lot with nothing but snow and the whistle of cold wind.

I wasn't the smartest girl in the world to blush from his compliment right after I'd used his girlfriend's—lover's, whoever she was— iron to curl my hair and pull it into a ponytail. Nevertheless, with a violence I hadn't felt before, I only hoped the other woman wasn't Gianna. She was my opposite—carefree and uninhibited—while I was so . . . pale in comparison. And with a triviality I doubted we shared, I was concerned about having to wear the same heels two days in a row because they were the only ones that paired well with my summer dress.

During the hour-long drive, I decided on the flowers for my bouquet and arrangements for the tables, while Nico was either on the phone or had the radio too loud for conversation. It was hardly a romantic date, but there was something comfortable about it.

Cars sparkled beneath sunlight as people milled up and down the parking lot. The day heated up like an oven burner, like the sun was angry at the world. In my ignorance, I believed there would be entertainment of some kind. However, the only entertainment was the cars. It was at times like this I was glad my thoughts were private.

Maybe there weren't any performances, but what I experienced was far from monotony. I oftentimes felt like one of the cars to be admired as Nico's attention found me, burning my skin with a distinct gaze that brought one thing to mind. I wondered if he was as attentive with all his women, and then immediately hated myself for thinking it.

"Stay by my side," he'd told me as soon as we got there.

A tenacious part of me wanted to know what he would do if I didn't.

I always was a bit too curious.

As he was busy saying a few words to one of the cars' owners, I slipped away and pretended to be admiring a convertible. It was only thirty seconds later that a large, intimidating presence brushed my back.

His voice was gravel, silk, and *annoyed* against my ear. "Do you honestly think I'm going to follow you around all day?"

I nodded, my heart fluttering like wings. "You have to."

He didn't touch me anywhere, though he stood so close the deep timbre of his words touched my neck. "I don't have to do anything."

The light summer breeze played on my skin as people walked around us, but I was only aware of one of them, one man.

You look nice.

Mine.

"Maybe you want to," I breathed.

Two heartbeats passed. Three.

He could have said he didn't. He could have said anything to deny it, but instead, he chose to let a silence full of unspoken words spread between us.

This tie we shared used to be equal parts thrill and terror. Today, the former was nudging the other away until it was as forgotten as a faded photograph tucked in the bottom of a drawer.

As I often pushed my luck and stepped away from him, growing tired of his car talk with the few people he chose to speak to, I felt his gaze follow my every move, even while he was immersed in conversation. And I realized one thing: I might not be the only woman in his life, but I would be the only one he called *wife*. The revelation was a vigorous thrum in my chest. So consuming a hum I couldn't force myself to feel anything but a deep-seated contentment.

"Nicolas," I said a few moments later, covering my eyes from the sun as I glanced across the lot. "It's just like your Gran Torino."

Nico stopped by my side but was busy sending a text. I'd yet to see this man drunk when I'd assumed he was an alcoholic. However, I was always seeing him work. I was beginning to think *workaholic* was a more likely diagnosis.

"How do you know what model my car is?" he asked without looking up.

"I have a superior knowledge in all things cars." I smiled, because I didn't even know how to freakin' drive.

He glanced at me, amusement ghosting across whiskey-colored eyes. "I'm sure you do." Slipping his phone into his back pocket, he looked across the lot. "That's a '70. Mine's a '72."

I paused. That was awfully perceptive of him, having been too far away to read the paper in the windshield. "How do you know?"

"Wild guess," he drawled.

Hmm . . .

"What year is that red one?" I pointed to the next Gran Torino in line.

He gave the car a glance. "'71." And then a smile pulled on a corner of his lips. "It was the movie, wasn't it? How you know?"

I frowned.

That was the fourth time I heard him laugh. I didn't know when I'd started counting, but now I wondered if I would ever stop.

I soon learned it wasn't a "wild guess" as he'd said. In fact, with some more questioning, I realized he could tell me the make, model, and year of all these cars here with a simple look. He was like a car encyclopedia, though humble enough not to admit it.

I watched him, was fascinated in a way by the few words that he spoke, and I took a mental image when he glanced my way and the sunlight hit him just right. Pierced with that dark, acquisitive gaze of his, something warm started in my chest, and as the day went on it spread further through my being until it was so interwoven I'd never get it out.

"How do you know so much about cars?" I asked him as we walked side-by-side. The sun was a sweltering weight against my skin, and I pulled my ponytail off the back of my sticky neck.

"Kept me out of trouble," was all he said.

I imagined he meant when he was a teenager. What kind of trouble did a young Nico get into?

Guilt felt heavy in my chest when I recalled what I'd insinuated about his mamma last night. My parents were far from the best, but I'd been safe, loved, and cared for as a child. I wondered who'd loved

Nico. I bet his papà had shown him about as much affection as mine did Tony, which was worrisome. And I doubted an addict for a mamma could be very caring and supportive.

"Nico," I said, then hesitated. I wanted to ask him so much. I wanted to know everything, but I knew he wouldn't tell me. So, I settled with: "I'm thirsty."

"Ah, so it's Nico when you want something," he drawled, amused. "Come on. Let's get you something to drink."

I'd never seen my papà leave the house in anything less than a two-piece suit. Yet here this man was in boots, jeans, and a white t-shirt. He still didn't fit in with the crowd. It was like everyone knew he had a gun tucked somewhere under his shirt. Or maybe they could see the *Cosa Nostra* in his eyes.

We sat at a picnic table near the edge of the lot with a bottle of water. Nico finished his in two drinks and then rested his elbows on his knees and watched the crowd. After the driveby I'd experienced not even a week ago, maybe I should be worried about my wellbeing. But the truth was, I didn't think there was another person in this world who could make me feel safer.

When his gaze settled on my face, I tried to pretend I didn't notice. But after a moment with a sputtering pulse, I couldn't take it any longer.

"Why are you staring at me?"

One heartbeat. Two.

His voice was rough and his gaze was steady when he said, "Maybe I want to."

Something soft and warm wrapped around my heart and squeezed.

We stopped in front of the Gran Torinos, and mischief flamed to life in my chest. I strayed to the next car over, examining it like I knew what I was examining. And knowing he owned a '72, I announced, "I think I like the '70 the best."

He didn't look at me, but a sly smile tugged at his lips. "Come a little closer and say that."

Butterflies took flight in my stomach, and I had to bite my cheek to hold in a smile.

It was eleven a.m. on a Sunday when I realized I wasn't only attracted to my fiancé. I was, with a madness that ached, completely and utterly infatuated with him.

By the time we got back to the car, my feet were killing me and the sun had reddened the skin on my shoulders. It could also be said that I was nearing starvation. It was only two in the afternoon, but I was very particular about when I got fed, and now I had missed lunch *and* second breakfast.

As he drove, I rested my head against the window and watched the world fly by. After a moment, I sat up, my brows knitting in confusion.

"Nico, I thought the Capellos owned this part of the Bronx?"

When he licked his lips and didn't say a thing, a disbelieving laugh escaped me. "Oh my god. You're crazy. We can't be here."

He glanced at me, a sly glint in his eyes. "I thought we already established I was crazy."

I glanced out the window and felt like I was a wanted criminal in a foreign land. I couldn't believe I'd been walking so casually only moments ago on Capello streets, the family whom my papà had a neutral but sometimes tense relationship with.

"You're going to get me killed," I announced.

He shook his head before pinning me with a gaze that pooled with intensity. "Do you honestly think for a second I would let someone kill you?"

No. It was an immediate, visceral response in my head.

I warmed from his words, though was uncertain of how to feel. I'd always followed the rules, and the one time I didn't it had cost an innocent man his life. I'd known Nico didn't care much for the law of the land, nor even the rules and etiquette of the *Cosa Nostra*. And today only proved it. I didn't want trouble; this man lived for it.

"It's dangerous," I said.

Silence filled the car. He ran a thumb across his bottom lip and glanced at me with one hand on the wheel. "Trust me?"

The fact that he'd told me not to last night was a loud awareness between us. I swallowed, because the way he'd said it, all soft and rough, burned through my chest and straight to a place I tried to close off from the world. This was him telling me I could. That I *should.*

I had to marry the man.

I didn't have to trust him.

Though not everything is about what we have to do, but what we *want* to.

I glanced outside the glass, at this forbidden part of town he'd taken me to. My stomach tightened at the unfamiliarity of it all, but the warm presence beside me, the strong heartbeat I'd felt last night, the masculine scent, it was all beginning to feel familiar. Necessary.

I never was a very good liar, so I told him the truth.

"Yes," I breathed.

And I'd never been more sure of anything.

CHAPTER
Thirty-Five

"Black as the devil, hot as hell, pure as an angel, sweet as love."
—Charles Maurice de Talleyrand

Elena

W E STOPPED AT HIS OFFICE, AND WHEN I SAW THERE WAS PIZZA WAITING
for me on the coffee table, I groaned.

Nico let out a breath of amusement and headed past me to his desk, where he spent the next hour on the phone. It could have been longer, though I wouldn't know, because with my stomach full and the toll the sun had taken, I fell asleep on the couch. It was a light sleep, where I could still hear his deep and newly comforting timbre in the background.

Three hours later, I awoke to an empty office.

Slightly disoriented, I blinked and then pulled my hair out of its ratty ponytail. I finger-combed it and slipped my heels back on before heading to the door and into the hallway. The card tables were still, the basement silent except for a few soft male voices.

I stepped into the main room and noticed Lorenzo, Lucky, and Luca at one of the far booths, each holding a hand of cards. I wondered how one went about playing poker with a cheater in each seat.

I didn't see Nicolas anywhere, and suddenly grew an itch to check out the club upstairs. I was going to have a rule-breaker for a husband, so maybe I needed to go out of my comfort zone and learn how to get on his level. On the balls of my feet so my heels didn't click, I walked to the staircase and slipped out the door.

The place was elegant yet comfortably decorated. A wide dance floor made of panels blinked from purple, blue to yellow. A long line of red plush chairs sat around lacquered, round wooden tables, with a mirror taking up the far wall. A staircase led upstairs to where I imagined the VIP rooms were. I hoped Nico didn't allow shady things to go on in there, though that was wishful thinking.

After another moment, I decided to head back downstairs before they noticed I was gone. As I took a step to leave, I realized I wasn't alone.

"So, you're the lovely Elena."

I froze.

The voice was unfamiliar, though I'd learned I was a top choice on any gossip list lately, so it wasn't surprising he would know me.

I turned around and met an uncultured yet refined gaze, as though the two battled amongst themselves. Ruthlessness spilled out of his Armani suit, yet his easy looks, urbane wardrobe, and relaxed carriage belied it. I imagined he was a chameleon, effortlessly taking form of whatever façade he wished.

"I'm sorry, I don't think I've had the pleasure."

His quiet laugh sounded like low musical notes left to die on the wind. "No, you wouldn't. I'm only a second son."

While the significance of his statement should have become extinct in the twentieth century, I understood what he meant. I was living proof of the *Cosa Nostra's* old-fashioned ways—my wedding right around the corner.

As a second son, he wouldn't inherit much, not the title nor the business, and he would always be expected to work for his papà and then older brother. He would be forever second best and overlooked.

"I'm sorry to hear that."

He scratched his jaw, amused, and then I thought he muttered, "No wonder he liked you."

I didn't know the man to question him, though the past tense of that statement—*liked*—piqued my interest. I shouldn't be conversing alone with a man I didn't know, but it wasn't like Nico would let someone he didn't trust into his club, would he?

With hesitant steps, I closed the distance between us. This stranger grasped my hand and pressed a light kiss to it. As he did, I said to him, "You seem to already know who I am, though I know nothing about you. You must have a name?"

"You can call me Sebastian." A subtle glint passed through his eyes before he added, "Perez."

Something cold shot through me, and my knee-jerk response was to yank my hand out of his grasp. It was then I noticed the thin accent to his words as Colombian.

He blew out a breath like my reaction was equal parts amusing and annoying. "Third time that's happened. Starting to wonder how I'm going to get laid in this city."

I wavered at the light tone of his voice and statement. However, as I watched him slip his hands in his pocket and turn to look at the place, I realized this man might be more manipulative than his brother. Though, what I wanted to know was how *deviant*.

I wondered if what he insinuated was true—if Oscar had a bad reputation with women. He seemed to have enough female attention that I'd seen, but it was only in our circle, and if he had certain . . . proclivities, I was certain he wouldn't show them to anyone in the *Cosa Nostra*. Not until he locked one of their women down with marriage and stole them away to Colombia, anyway. A fate it felt like I'd missed by a hair.

"You know, he liked you," he said. "He liked you *a lot*."

An unpleasant taste filled my mouth. To be desired by Oscar Perez felt like contracting an STD.

"This is a nice place," he observed, taking a few steps deeper into the club. "Interesting to find you here, though. Thought Ace was marrying your sister?"

I swallowed. "Change of plans."

The simple *huh* that escaped him was coated with amusement.

"You know," he said, "one time when my brother was drunk, he told me your voice was like a woman's soft caress."

"How very . . ." I held in the grimace. "Nice."

He chuckled as though he loved the awkwardness his statement had brought into the room. "He spoke sonnets of you. Would you like to hear the others?"

"I . . . don't think so."

"Good choice. Some of them were . . ." He turned around with a slight frown. "Uncultured."

"You're no longer a second son," I noted.

A flicker of pitch black passed through his eyes. "No."

My stomach tightened. "Is that why you're here?"

As soon as the last word left my lips, a wave of pure tension brushed my back. My body went still, but Sebastian stood where he was, his hands remaining in his pockets as he flicked a gaze to the man behind us.

"Elena. Downstairs." The words were cold and distant. Words of a boss that carried an unmistakable timbre of control. A shiver worked its way beneath my skin. *"Now."*

I turned around to comply.

I knew this breaking the rules thing wasn't for me . . .

Nico didn't give me a glance. He remained focused on the Colombian who stood in the middle of his club and who I was beginning to think hadn't received an invitation.

This version of Nico was all hard lines and an intimidating presence that burned if one stepped too close. I couldn't help but notice that the man I knew caressed me with the same hands the don used to maim.

I passed him and headed down the hall, but something made my feet halt around the corner, the tension thick enough to suffocate. An itch to see how Nico did business. Plain curiosity.

"You have five seconds to explain how the fuck you got into my club."

Sebastian's laugh was quiet. "Straight to business, then?" His tone turned as sophisticated as his suit. "Very well. I put the front cameras on loop and used the good ol' credit card maneuver."

"There are two chain key locks on that door."

I could feel the smile spill around the corner. "What can I say? Maybe you should have gone with three."

Silence met my ears and I could tell Nico wasn't amused. "If you want to leave here with all your body parts intact, I would start talking."

"My brother must not have been a friend of yours."

Impatience crept on the air and I inhaled slowly.

"Perez," Sebastian said. "Oscar." A pause. "You see, my brother was suspicious—straight up paranoid, really—about someone trying to kill him. Can't say I didn't consider doing it myself. I mean, I think I had thoughts about it since I was seven—"

"Point," Nico snapped.

Sebastian sighed. "Well, he was so paranoid he hired a private investigator. Someone who followed him around and made sure no one else followed him." He laughed. "Ironic, no?"

There was an intermission as though he waited for Nico to respond. Nico never did say anything, and I imagined he was only giving the man that intimidating glare.

"Right," Sebastian repeated. "Well, the reason I imagine my brother wasn't a friend of yours is because that PI has some photos of you shooting him in the head."

My pulse skid to an awkward stop. And when all Nico said was, "Don't think you've come to tell me who this PI is," a cool rush of awareness flooded me.

Sebastian laughed. "If I did that, I'm sure he'd be floating in whatever river is closest to here. Besides, he gave the photos to me. Wouldn't have even taken them if he'd recognized it was you. 'Bout had a heart attack when I pointed it out."

"Smart man," Nico drawled. "You, not so much. Tell me what you want before I decide I don't give a shit."

"Let's just say my brother ran the business into the ground. Killed a lot of our contacts with his . . . well, to be frank, he loved women. Fucking them, beating them, cutting them up. It made for bad business. You partner with me and those photos go poof."

Nico let out a sardonic breath. "You realize, starting a new relationship with blackmail isn't the smartest move you could make?"

"Like you would have considered a new supplier another way."

Nico was the one who killed Oscar . . . *Why?*

"You have good shit?" Nico eventually said.

"The best."

"Fine. We'll talk about this later this week, after you make a fucking appointment like anyone else. Where are you staying?"

"Why?" Sebastian's tone was amused. "You want to show me the city?"

"So if I decide to kill you, I won't have to waste my time finding you," was Nico's deadpanned response before I decided I'd heard enough.

Before I left, I paused at Sebastian's next words, needing to hear Nico's reply.

"Tell me," Sebastian said, "why did you do it?"

A heavy silence took over, and my chest tightened at Nico's cavalier tone.

"He had something I wanted."

CHAPTER
Thirty-Six

"There is no great genius without some touch of madness."
—Aristotle

Elena

I WASN'T SURE HOW I KNEW, BUT I DID.

An intuition played in the back of my mind, sending a wave of uncertainty through me. The inkling itched, demanding to be made fact, and before I could stop myself I grabbed my phone from the coffee table and sent Tony a text.

Me: *Did you know Oscar Perez loved to cut women up?*

He responded a minute later.

Tony: *WTF, Elena. No.*

Since he knew it was me, I assumed Nico must have passed my new number on to him. I didn't know what to think about them being all buddy-buddy now. Truthfully, I wasn't sure I liked it.

Me: *You sure? I guess it's common knowledge.*

Tony: *Why would I lie about something like that?*

Time to bait the hook . . .

Me: *Maybe because you knew Papà promised me to him.*

My phone rang in my hand, and I answered it with a simple "Hello."

"What the fuck's the matter with you?" Tony's voice seeped with annoyance and concern. "Do you really think Papà would've agreed to the engagement if he knew Oscar was into that kind of shit?"

Engagement.

The word settled over my head with an unsurprising awareness, and I said, "Thank you, Tony. That's all I needed to know," before hanging up.

My phone chimed a second later.

Tony: *Don't be weird.*

My response was juvenile, but impossible for any sibling to suppress.

Me: *You're the weird one.*

My stomach dipped as a familiar magnetism walked into the office behind my back. Hypnotic and volatile, his presence brushed my skin, sinking into my pores like it owned me. However, it evoked something deep and uncertain as well, like being fascinated by the green sky of a coming storm but knowing that as soon as it hit you, there would be nothing left.

He had something I wanted.

Oscar had *me* . . . and then he was dead.

I wanted to dismiss the idea that Nico had done what I was beginning to think he did, or rather, *why* he'd done it, because just the thought started a kindling in my chest that felt suspiciously like hope.

Without hope, there's nothing to lose.

With it, we're nothing but dominos waiting to fall.

Still, as his presence filled this office, that kindling fed on the warm bravado of it, and grew and grew.

"You get a good look at the club?"

My grip tightened on my phone as though it could ground me to earth. "Quite." I turned around to see him leaning against the corner of his desk, a piercing gaze glued to me.

"I don't think I'm a fan of finding you talking to some Escobar alone."

By his tone that was a *gross* understatement.

"But I can talk to you?" I raised a brow, hinting at how he wasn't a much different man in the regard to ethics.

"Not can." His eyes darkened. "*Will.*"

I wanted to ask him: *If I don't, will you make me?* But the words caught in my throat. There was nothing playful in this office—there was gunpowder and flame. One wrong move and it would detonate.

I couldn't breathe while the threat snuffed out any remaining oxygen. We only stared at each other, both recognizing the distinct longing hanging in the air like the Monet on the wall, but neither addressing it.

Nerves rattled in my veins with a cold whisper.

I wanted to be the best thing he'd ever had. To make him burn as much as he made me. I wanted him to want *only* me with a raw ache. However, I didn't believe I could ever compare to the more experienced women he'd been with. And I always was a bit of a perfectionist—if I couldn't do it faultlessly, I hesitated to do it at all.

"Were you friends with Oscar?" The words fought to be heard in the tense atmosphere.

A grimace flared behind his eyes as he pushed off the desk. "No."

"Did you work with him?"

He grabbed the car keys off his desk and rolled his shoulders, like even talking about Oscar agitated him. "No."

"Not even—?"

"I didn't fucking know the guy, Elena," he snapped.

My brows knitted in a poor attempt to pretend I was taken aback. But really, warm honey filled my heart, creeping through my vessels and veins.

He had something I wanted.

And now I knew it was me.

Nico

Dirty Diana by Shaman's Harvest filtered through the car speakers, fusing with the bottled-up tension rolling off me. If it were possible to put fucking the girl next to me out of my mind for one goddamn minute, this song about a slut named Diana would ruin it.

My self-restraint was pulled taut. I could hear the fibers snapping one by one until it hung by a thread, and my grip tightened on the steering wheel.

I deserved a fucking award for this.

Because nothing physical stopped me from letting go. From slipping my hand between her thighs and pushing two fingers inside her. From fucking her with them and letting her roll her hips against my palm until she came. I wanted it badly enough I could smell her, taste her. My mouth watered, a deep wave tightening in my stomach and burning a downward spiral.

With a flood of lust and anger, I shut the radio off.

Fuck Diana.

And fuck every asshole getting laid right now.

A heavy tension and the quiet rustle of fabric as Elena crossed her legs filled the car. The nervous gesture bared more of her tan, smooth thighs, and my heartbeat pulsed in my dick.

A grimace pulled on my lips and I wiped it away with a palm. I knew what was beneath that dress now. The mental image was burned into my fucking brain. Not only did she have the hottest little body I'd ever seen, it was those dark eyes, soft and innocent, that pierced a hole through my chest. She'd only sat on the island, as though she would let me do anything I wanted to her. Submissively. Dutifully. Fuck me.

She wiped her hands on her dress, pulling it back down, and a dark part of me got off on the idea that I was unsettling her. Tit for tat and all that.

I could make her do whatever I wanted.

I could take it all.

I even knew she would like it.

But something arcane and deeply rooted held me back. Something that gave me the urge to smoke every time I thought about it.

I had to know I wasn't a substitute for some lost love. Had to know she wasn't pretending I was someone else. Had to know it was what she wanted and not due to some kind of obedient trait or sense of duty.

When I found her talking to Sebastian Perez, for a split second I thought she'd let him in, that he was responsible for the ring on her finger. Acrimony had burned in my throat and tasted acidic in my mouth. She was mine. And I'd kill anyone who told me otherwise.

She was staying with me until the wedding because I couldn't stand the thought that Salvatore might try to keep her from me. The idea made my chest ache with something foreign and hollow, and fuck if I was going to sit around for two weeks feeling it.

Nevertheless, I was glad I didn't shoot Sebastian.

I liked the way he did business.

As soon as we pulled into the drive, I turned off the ignition and got out of the car. If I had to sit in there with her for another millisecond I'd crack.

She followed me to the back door, and I couldn't help but to be aware of her every move. Her heel must have gotten stuck in a divot in the walkway, because she started tipping. I took a step back to reach out and steady her but was unprepared for her to fall into me.

I gritted my teeth at the impact. Her entire body pressed against my side, from her tits to her hips, and fuck, did it burn.

Jesus, this girl.

If I lasted the night, it would be a goddamn miracle.

Elena

The click of my heels echoed off the wooden floorboards, and my heartbeat replayed each reverberation against my breastbone.

It had only been days since I arrived here and stood in front of this door. The uncertainty I felt was the same, but something had shifted. The ache in my lower stomach had bloomed to fill every available space in my body. I could feel it—*him*—everywhere, and he wasn't even touching me.

Nico typed something into the security system as I slipped off my heels. Stopping before the stairs, he glanced at me. His gaze was dark, shimmering, with an unfathomable depth.

"You good?"

"Good," I breathed, though I felt close to bursting at the seams if he didn't touch me.

He nodded once before he took the stairs one at a time and left me there, engaged and alone. *Infatuated and burning.* I stood there for a moment, with nothing but the sounds of a settling house for company.

Padding into the kitchen, I filled a glass of water and set it on the island, not taking a sip. I grasped the edge of the counter, closed my eyes, and let the pressure of what I needed from this man build until it felt like it was all I could breathe.

The stairs creaked beneath my bare feet, and I stopped at the top when I heard the shower running from his bathroom. Indecision ate at me, bit by bit, until I felt raw and naked. It would be so easy to let my dress hit the floor and slip into the shower with him. He wouldn't turn me away, though that was never the reason for this waver inside of me.

So instead, I went into the hall bathroom. I turned the shower on hot and washed my hair with some other woman's shampoo. And then I dried it with her hair dryer. In nothing but a towel, I paused in the hallway, the indecision strong enough it vibrated under my skin.

My bedroom door shut behind me and I leaned against it, stared at the ceiling and breathed. My heartbeat played a melody of fear, uncertainty, *need.* I slipped into a t-shirt and shorts and stood in the middle of the room.

He had something I wanted echoed in a deep timbre in my head. It was the last thought I had before I found myself in the hall, right outside his closed door.

Once I opened it, I could never go back. I knew it would change everything, but what I didn't realize at the time was . . . everything already had.

CHAPTER
Thirty-Seven

"You can't blame gravity for falling in love."
—Albert Einstein

Elena

H E DIDN'T LOOK UP AS I OPENED THE DOOR.

But he knew I was here.

He sat on the side of the bed with his elbows on his knees and his gaze on the floor. A dangerous haze permeated the air like tendrils of smoke. It felt as possessive as chains, looked like moonlight, and tasted like obsession.

Silver rays filtered through glass, illuminating his body but not his expression. Now that I was so close to him, breathing his air, feeling his presence that could effortlessly consume mine until I would cease to exist, the bravery that had brought me here disintegrated to dust.

My heartbeat tried to escape my throat, and an icy shiver ran through my blood, leaving my skin hot to the touch. I hadn't known it was possible to want something so much and to fear it in equal measure. Hesitation stopped my feet and tugged at my heart. Nonetheless, I suddenly knew that even if I chose to change my mind and turn around . . . I wasn't getting out.

Every inch of my body burned as I walked toward him. Sensitive as freshly waxed skin, his pants felt abrasive against my inner thigh as

I forced my leg between his slightly parted ones. He didn't look at me, nor did he widen his stance so I could step fully between his legs. My breaths and the drumming of my heart fluttered in the air before silence liquefied them.

I brushed a hand across his neck and into the thick hair at his nape. He let out a quiet, tense breath. A heady warmth poured off his shirtless chest, and I absorbed it like an addict. My fingers laced through the soft strands, gripping a handful like I'd done days ago.

Feather-light, his hands skimmed up the backs of my thighs, and my pulse sparked like crackles in a fire. My breasts were bare beneath my shirt, heavy and tight so close to his face. He only had to lift his head to put his mouth on them, to relieve them of this pressure.

His fingers grew firmer on my thighs, gripping the flesh, caressing it. Something tugged on my stomach from the inside as the fiery heat of his palms burned through my skin. Every squeeze sent a thrum between my legs, settling into an empty ache. My breaths came out ragged and shallow while he remained silent, as though what he was doing deserved his full concentration.

The haze in the air began to thicken, to flare, to *burn* with every inhale.

My stomach tightened as his hands inched beneath my cotton shorts, teasing the curve of my cheeks with a touch I was beginning to believe was singular. His palms slid under the hem and gripped two handfuls of my ass. A throaty sigh escaped as he kneaded the flesh. Tingles, hot and slick, pooled between my legs, and my fingers curled in his hair.

He found my thong and traced the cotton downward. My body hummed in anticipation, but right before he reached where I needed him, he tugged the fabric to the side and let it snap back in place. The movement brushed my clit and sent a sizzling sensation up my spine that knocked me off balance. When my other hand found his nape to catch myself, my short nails trailed down the back of his neck.

He shook his head to throw my touch off like he hated it, and a low growl sounded from deep in his chest. My hand dropped away. I didn't have time to weigh his reaction because his fingers slipped beneath my thong, sliding so low they brushed my back entrance before pausing. The touch was foreign to me, but I was *so* hot I found myself rolling my hips for friction.

A groan poured out of me when his hand slid further downward and one finger pushed inside of me without warning. His rough "Fuck" ran down my spine. He fucked me slowly, in and out, and the pressure built between my legs like too much steam collected in a glass jar.

My head fell back and my palm came up to his neck, my nails running the length of it. When he tensed, I suddenly realized what I did and dropped my hand. However, it was already done. I received a smack on the underside of my ass that sent a toe-curling rattle throughout my entire sex. I didn't think it was a good punishment at all, but then he pulled his finger out of me and a desperate ache remained.

A haze had infiltrated my skin, my mind, my inhibitions, and the corners of my vision. I needed *one* thing, could think about only *it*, and it wasn't physically possible to leave without getting it.

His legs parted, and I didn't hesitate to step all the way between them. His gaze lifted and his eyes met mine; the blaze inside them was liquid lead and darker than shadow. Our lips were inches apart. Close enough we shared breaths. Close enough to kiss.

I realized how weak I truly was at that moment, because if this man told me to kiss him, I would. I would do anything he wanted. But he never did. He only watched me with a narrowed gaze while breathing my air like it was his to take.

"Take it off," he gritted.

He didn't speak of my clothes. He looked at my face, but he might as well have stared at my left hand. Now I understood it wasn't the nails on his neck that had bothered him—it was the ring.

I swallowed and tried to think through the mist he'd created in my mind. I'd told myself I wouldn't take the ring off until I did what I could to make amends. I hated to admit it, but I wanted this moment more than a guilt-ridden reminder. Though, the truth was, it wasn't simply about what I wanted anymore.

I *needed* him. More than morality or honesty.

I knew I shouldn't sleep with Nico, not with my deceit so close on the air I could taste it.

But, as I took the ring off and let it fall from my fingers to the floor, this was the moment I knew I wouldn't be so bad a Russo after all.

Heat and satisfaction rolled off his body. Without another thought, I grabbed the hem of my t-shirt with both hands and pulled it off in one swoop.

He groaned, and before I could even lower my arms, his mouth latched onto my breast, giving it one slow suck while dragging his teeth across the nipple. White heat shot like lightning between my thighs before pulsing in an empty ache. I swayed into him, running one hand around his neck and into his hair.

His hand shoved down the front of my shorts, brushing over sensitive skin and cupping me with a roughness that brought me to my toes. His entire palm rubbed back and forth, a firm pressure against my clit. My head fell back with a moan.

"So *fucking* wet," he growled. He sucked a nipple into his mouth and then slid two fingers deep inside me. Hot, *sweet* pressure filled me, threatening to overfill as he fingered me. Fast and then lazy. Over and over.

Maybe I should have been embarrassed that I was so wet the room filled with the sounds of his fingers pushing in and out of me. But my skin was hot enough it felt like I'd been doused with kerosene and then lit by a match. The fire burned into my lower stomach, creating a blaze that needed to be fed. And if not . . . I would go up in smoke.

"Oh, God . . ." I moaned, digging my nails into his shoulders. I was so close, so *so* close. "God, *please*."

He trailed over every inch of my breasts, kissing them like he would my mouth: with lips and tongue and teeth. His fingers slipped out of me, pulling wetness to my clit, and when he pushed them back in, that was *it*.

Pressure burst into tingles and flame. My veins burned up like a line of gunpowder, shooting flames of light behind my eyes. A shudder fluttered through my body as though three shots of liquor poured straight into my bloodstream, before a languid heat spread.

As I came down, I realized my legs had given out and I sat on his thigh. I hadn't opened my eyes yet when his lips and a deep rasp touched my ear. "Jesus, you're the hottest thing I've ever seen."

Satisfaction still shimmering with an orange glow dripped into my chest like a leaky tap. "Thank you," I breathed, my cheeks flushed enough to singe if touched. His hand slid from my shorts and I shivered at the loss of contact.

His eyes were heavy-lidded, the color black intoxicated. His thumb grazed my lips and his words were coarse like he hadn't spoken in a while. "You're welcome."

He left a streak of wetness across my mouth, and I knew it was of me. I drew my tongue across my bottom lip and licked it off.

His gaze flashed. "Get on the bed." It was a demand, his lazy mood hardening into a harsh one that made my heart thump against my ribcage.

I pulled away from him and crawled onto the bed. It felt like I lay on a cloud of Nico as I got settled on my back. It was too soft to be him, but it smelled like him: warm whiskey, sandalwood, and an unnamable scent I associated with sweet temptation and danger.

While holding my stare, he slipped his sweatpants off, and my cheeks grew warmer even though he still wore boxer briefs as black as his full sleeve. I swallowed as I glanced at his erection that strained through the fabric. Anticipation thrummed to life between my legs. He was so hard, and it was the sexiest thing I'd ever seen.

My body was languid, pliable, and still high on an orgasm, but as this man watched me while he walked around the bed with a volatile darkness in his gaze, my pulse began to tremble in my throat.

Goose bumps spread across my skin as the air-conditioner kicked on with a blast. He opened the nightstand drawer, pulled out a condom, and tossed it on top of the table. My stomach tightened, and a noise of surprise escaped me when he grabbed my ankle and jerked me to the side of the bed.

"These fucking shorts," he gritted, grabbing the waistband and yanking them down my legs along with my thong.

A *somewhat* manipulative part of me knew exactly what he meant. The shorts resembled underwear, and I might have worn them in front of him while he was still my soon-to-be brother-in-law.

He tossed my clothes on the floor behind him. "Were you trying to fuck with me, Elena?"

The orgasm might as well have been truth serum, because I breathed, "Yes."

He grasped my thighs, parted them, and then let out a low curse. His gaze flicked to my face, hardening. "Who *else* do you fuck with?"

The words hit me in the stomach and turned every drop of lust sour. He still thought I was a slut, and here I lay with my legs spread for him? With a glare, I yanked my thighs out of his grasp and stood. "Screw yourself, Nicolas."

His eyes narrowed. "I'd rather screw you."

"Too bad," I snapped, pushing past him.

I didn't make it another step before his arm wrapped around my waist, my feet left the floor, and he tossed me onto the bed. The air whooshed out of me and a breathless annoyance flared. "I'm not a doll you can throw around, and I'm not sleeping with you."

He crawled onto the bed and kneeled between my legs. "No one said anything about sleeping," he drawled.

I hated to admit it, but my body loved his voice and responded by growing warm everywhere. I was *such* a pushover. "Nico—"

"Platonic."

I faltered. "What?"

A sigh escaped me as he ran his calloused palms down my thighs, spreading them. "You want me to stop, you say Platonic."

The word only reminded me of how very *un-platonic* I wanted to be with him.

His fingers tightened on my inner thighs as two tense seconds passed between us. And when I didn't say a word, his eyes grew so dark I could see his blackened soul. He lowered to his stomach, and anticipation fluttered and flared in every nerve ending.

I sighed a half-hearted "Wait," but I should have saved my breath. It wasn't the right word, and while I didn't want to come off as a pushover, I didn't want to say Platonic more. I leaned on my hands watching him, and as he pressed his face between my thighs and inhaled, my head fell back.

I once said that whatever Nico did, he did it with his all.

And God, did he *ever*.

His arms wrapped around my thighs, lifting them slightly, and then he licked me all the way from ass to clit. Steam crawled through my blood, lighting me on fire. I gasped, my fingers fisting the sheets.

It was so dirty, so wrong, so *inappropriate*, but God, maybe that's why it felt so good.

A deep sound of satisfaction came from his throat.

"You're disturbed," I breathed. "Do that again."

For the first time ever, Nico listened to me.

The hot sweep of his tongue sent a violent shiver through me. A mindless haze brushed my thoughts away, leaving lust and insanity behind. I was so *hot*, burning up like a comet falling from space. My hips rolled beneath his mouth as he licked me everywhere he could reach.

Each fiery wave coalesced into an empty ache between my thighs, until I could only feel *empty*.

I needed him. In a *mindless*, archaic, bordering madness kind of way.

And if it made me a slut, I didn't give a damn.

"Nico . . . stop." I learned his compliance was a one-time thing, because as I tried to pull away, he did nothing but tighten his arms around my thighs. However, I then lost track of my end goal for a moment, my eyes rolling back into my head.

So empty.

I yanked his hair as hard as I could, and he finally deigned to give me his attention. The gold in his eyes had burned up, leaving nothing but char. They narrowed around the edges. I didn't say a word, but he must have read what I needed on my face.

He crawled over me, licking and nipping my stomach and breasts as he did. His body covered mine. He was so heavy. A warm, *blissful* heavy that made my skin sing with satisfaction. He kissed my neck, while bracing his hands on either side of my head.

I realized he'd licked every part of my body and I'd barely touched him. Tension rolled through him as my hands slid down his back, his sides, and when they settled on his abs, he closed his eyes, his jaw tightening.

My fingers trailed the line of hair below his navel, but as they reached the waistband of his briefs, I hesitated. I'd been with a man, but that didn't mean I knew everything about touching one.

"Lower," he gritted.

My heartbeat fluttered with expectation and uncertainty, but I slid my hand down until I cupped his erection through his briefs. His forehead fell to rest on mine and a rumble escaped his chest. He pressed himself further into my palm.

I felt how hot he was through the fabric, how thick, how big and hard and utterly masculine. Any hesitation was pushed away by a rush of longing, and I slipped my fingers beneath his waistband and wrapped my hand around his length.

"Ah fuck," he groaned.

So hot and *smooth*. Holding it in my palm filled my lower stomach with warmth. I could taste the anticipation of how it would feel inside me. A pulse bloomed between my legs. I ran my hand down to the base and then all the way back up.

"I want it," I breathed.

His hand cupped the side of my face.

"Ask me nicely," he rasped, nipping my jaw.

When I squeezed, he hissed and shot me a narrowed gaze. I gave him a slow, gentle tug and whispered in his ear, "*Please*."

His eyes were lazy and dark as he dropped to his back beside me and pulled off his briefs. My face burned as I watched him grab his erection at the base and reach for a condom on the side table.

The action was so primal, so surprisingly *hot*, something burned to life inside of me. Before I knew what I was doing, I straddled his hips. Resting my hands on either side of him, I leaned forward and kissed his throat like I would his mouth.

"Fuck." His hand cupped the back of my head, his fingers lacing through the strands.

He tasted like he smelled, and I couldn't get enough. I was all over him, running my hands over his biceps, pecs, and into his hair. I kissed his throat with tongue, nipped at his earlobe, and sucked on his neck.

"Enough," he growled with frustration, and fisted the hair at my nape to make me stop.

I pulled back with half-lidded eyes. My breasts brushed his chest, sending sizzles of pleasure lower and making me ache for friction. I ground down on his erection. It spread a fire through me that made me drop my head and dig my fingers into the sheets.

"Wait," he gritted, tearing the condom open with his teeth.

I had a fever. A hot and itchy and *empty* one, and it wasn't possible to stop. I rolled my hips against him, using his chest for leverage and rubbing my wetness up and down his length.

Just as he got the condom out, he froze, and then groaned so deeply I could feel it vibrate through his chest. I'd ground down hard enough the head of his erection had slipped inside of me. He was so big it stung. A tremble rolled through me, my exhales heavy and uneven. My fingers curled on his abs as I sank onto him another inch. As the pain faded into a delicious fullness, a throaty sigh escaped me.

His body was pulled taut beneath my hands. The condom wrapper crinkled as it disappeared into a clenched fist.

"No. Condom," he ground out.

It might have been the stupidest, most impulsive thing I'd ever done, but I didn't want to use a condom from his nightstand that he reserved for all his randoms, or, even worse—a regular. I wanted to be different, *needed* to be.

My response was a whimper as I slid further down until half of his length disappeared inside me. We both watched it happen, my breaths coming out erratic. I was so filled it burned. As I held myself there, my thighs ached like I'd run a mile.

He stared at where we were joined with a dark look rivaling madness. And then, with a growl, he tossed me onto my back and thrust all the way inside of me.

I cried out, my back arching off the bed. So full, *too* full. I pushed on his chest to get him to ease out, but he remained so deep I could feel him in my stomach. His body was so heavy as he lay on top of me, one hand braced on the bed and the other cradling my head.

We stayed like that for a moment, his chest panting for air against mine. His ragged breaths fanned my neck while he remained still.

His lips pressed against my ear. "You want to know a secret?"

I shivered at the deep voice, but I didn't answer because I was still trying to figure out how to breathe with him inside me.

"I've never fucked a woman without a condom." He nuzzled my neck. His voice was warm and smooth, but his teeth were clenched. "And I'm afraid you've just created a monster."

He held me by a fistful of hair at my nape and then he fucked me.

Skin against skin. A scrape of teeth. The heavy weight of him. *Unrelenting.* It was so intense I fought to find air to breathe, to find any-thing that wasn't harsh and him. Soon, the intensity softened, my body warming and molding to his. Every thrust began to kindle a spark in-side of me that only the next thrust could sate. My nails dug into his biceps, and a small shudder rolled under his skin.

He talked while he screwed, right against my ear in a deep rasp, and it made me crazy.

"You take it so good," he praised.

"So *fucking* tight."

"So wet for me."

The words sank into my skin and filled every space in my body with warm satisfaction.

Every time his pelvis ground against mine, molten heat spread from my clit outward. A throaty moan escaped my lips with every thrust, as though he pushed each one out of me.

I was nothing but heat and flame and pleasure.

"Fuck, you've got to be quiet," he groaned in my ear. "Or this is going to be over before I'm ready."

I tried to stop, but I couldn't. It was like trying to stop breathing.

He covered my mouth with his palm, while the other hand re-mained fisted in my hair. It was rough and restrictive and so *addictive.*

And I suddenly knew *this* was what had drawn me to Nicolas Russo. What fascinated me. Maybe the *Cosa Nostra* had tainted me from the start, like a poison in the water supply, because I needed this: restraint, domination, to feel him everywhere. I'd known it would be like this, so intense, but it felt so much better than I'd ever envisioned.

The orgasm was immediate and so violent it sent a shudder through me that chattered my teeth. Heat pulsed in my lower stomach before branching out in tingles and dazzles of the best feeling ever.

When I came down, it was to him motionless inside of me, watching me with a gaze dark as night. He pulled his hand from my mouth, and by the teeth marks I realized I'd bitten down on it when I came.

"Who fucks you?" he growled.

I shivered. "You do."

"Who else?"

"Just you," I breathed.

A rumble of satisfaction came from his chest, and he rested his forehead against mine. "I'm going to come inside you and then I'm going to fuck you again." His lips hovered above my own. They were so close that with a slow thrust and a tense breath, they brushed mine so lightly it was like it never happened.

I could almost feel his lips pressed against mine, sliding and licking and biting. Wet and messy and rough. Because that's how Nico would kiss. I wanted to experience it violently enough it was a war between my head and my mouth.

He'd taste like whiskey and bad decisions.

This time, my head won.

He stayed like that, our lips inches apart, as he thrust inside of me, deep and *slow*, and with an intimacy that made me feel like someone had rubbed my skin with sandpaper until I was raw and exposed.

But I couldn't escape it, not with his fist in my hair and his body on mine. Not with his dirty words still resounding in my ears. Not with the warmth that blossomed in my chest at the mere mention of his name.

I'd let him inside of me.

And now I'd never get him out.

CHAPTER
Thirty-Eight

"Love is like a virus. It can happen to anybody at any time."
—Maya Angelou

Elena

HEARTBEATS ARE FICKLE THINGS. BEATING ONE MOMENT AND THEN STOPPING the next. Raging a storm and then lying as still as a tranquil sea. But what I didn't know is that they change. They glow and warm and expand in a chest. They ache and yearn for a reason to *beep*.

My heartbeats had a fondness for the romantic.

They began to skip, to multiply, to fill with a contentment as thick as honey and as warm as the sun. They did it all as my skin grew cold and while I stared at the ceiling and tried to ignore them.

I couldn't fall in love with this man.

I would rather never fall in love at all than to experience it unrequited. I'd seen it enough times to despise the possibility.

I couldn't love a man who treated me like a commodity, or even worse—a pretty bird in a cage, and not like a wife. If there was anything I knew with a certainty about Made Men, it was that they couldn't grasp the concept of fidelity. Those heartbeats tied into a knot, a strangling, uncomfortable ball in the back of my throat.

I smelled like him. He was *all* over me, and I'd asked him nicely for it. Someone needed to save me from myself before I got on my knees and professed my inevitable love to him. Might as well make it right after he finished screwing another.

Bitterness cut through my chest, and I moved to get up and leave but an iron grip wrapped around my wrist.

Slowly, I glanced at the man who lay like a freshly fucked king next to me. I bet his heartbeats were satisfied that he'd finally laid his *easy* fiancée. But as soon as I looked at him, the resentment faded into a different kind of ache. When had he become so handsome it hurt? I fought not to rub at the pang in my chest.

He didn't say a word, just watched me with a lazy stare while inhaling rough breaths. It'd been only moments since we'd had sex again. But in my head, it'd felt like an eternity as the seconds mocked me with the inevitable that he would soon hold another like he had me.

I was ruining a moment I'd wanted badly enough it felt like a need. But now I couldn't stop myself from analyzing everything—the possibilities and outcomes—and it didn't look to be in my favor.

When the eye contact began to burn, I tried to pull my wrist away, but he wouldn't let me go. His expression didn't show a hint of emotion, as though he could hold me here effortlessly. As though he might hold me here forever.

A moment later, his grip slid from my wrist, releasing me. Something dipped in my chest, though I pushed it away before I could analyze it. I got off the bed and, as I took a step toward the door, something dug into the bottom of my foot. I halted and glanced down. The ring sat there, forgotten, like the sweet boy who'd given it to me. My stomach twisted.

Without a thought, I picked it up. A wave of tension brushed my back, evoking a prickling sensation that ran down my spine. The silence was an antagonistic one, the kind that doesn't contain words but says everything.

Nico hated this ring, and I could only ascertain he knew it was connected to a man—or believed it was. Nobody knew about the ring but Adriana, and even then, the only thing I'd told her about the incident was that *he'd* given it to me.

My promise remained with or without the fifty-cent piece of

jewelry, but . . . I hesitated.

I would never be with another man but the one in this room. We both knew it, and that removed any type of advantage I would've had in the Outside world. If a man knew you'd give it up to him and no one else and that you couldn't even *leave* him, what would ever encourage him to be faithful?

He had the upper hand in every aspect of this relationship. Maybe the only thing that would save face was that Nico didn't know the man who'd given this ring to me hadn't meant anything. I imagined believing one's fiancée was in love with another man would cut any boss's ego in half, especially Nico's giant one.

I could tell him everything. Bare my soul and be honest. Be an open person and hope that good would win.

But maybe I'd always been as manipulative as him.

Maybe this was the only way I'd survive him.

I slid the ring onto my finger and walked out of the room.

Nico

I'd never hated a thing in my life.

I resented the Zanettis, who killed my father and uncle in that shooting five years ago, and while I might have shot them in the goddamn heads like they'd deserved, I hadn't hated them.

Like regret, there wasn't room for hate.

Hate changed someone's make-up. It made them reckless. Hate killed its host.

I never let myself hate because I loved to live.

But right now, I could say I hated something. Two things. That goddamn ring and the man who gave it to her.

Hatred fucking burned, like inhaling mace, getting punched in the throat, and being stabbed simultaneously. That was my comparison gathered from trial and error as a Made Man. Add in a dose of poison that eats you from the inside out, and that's hatred.

Fuck.

My chest tightened, each breath a burn in my lungs.

I stood, and before I even knew it was in my hand, I chucked a lamp at the wall. The porcelain shattered with a crash that would wake the entire fucking neighborhood. I took a deep breath and shook my head. She definitely heard that. She always did say I was a psychopath—might as well show her one.

My gaze paused on her clothes still lying on the floor. They sat there, hers, probably smelling like her and shit. I picked them up and dropped them in my top dresser drawer right next to her white bikini top. If she wanted them back she could fucking ask me nicely.

I sent Luca a text and got dressed. A suit as black as my mood. I had to get out of this goddamned house before I did something stupid, like demand she forget every man she'd ever met but me.

Instead of taking one cigarette from my nightstand, I grabbed the whole pack. I was going to smoke every last one of them.

Her door was shut and the light was off as I passed her room. Annoyance flared in me that she hadn't even come out to see the damage. The last time I'd thrown something at the wall was when I was young enough to be kicked in the ribs for it. Maybe she should take responsibility for how crazy she made me.

I opened the garage door and leaned against the worktable, taking a deep drag on a cigarette. I could still smell her on my hands, and every time I brought the smoke to my mouth a memory of fucking her rushed in.

Fuck, she was the best lay I'd ever had. A chill ran down my back from the thought of it. I gritted my teeth and tried to shake the strange feeling off. Nonetheless, my body was alive like she was still touching me—her pink little fingernails digging into my biceps, her hand wrapped around my cock, her smell all over me. So damn *sweet*. I braced my hands on the table and hung my head.

I should have taken Salvatore's other offer when we'd found out Adriana was pregnant—a corner of his territory that would've filled my pockets, and one I'd wanted for a while—because Elena fucked with my head, made me destroy the furniture and smoke more than I should. And I had a bad, *bad* feeling that if this girl used the word *please*, I would give her anything she wanted.

I'd fucked her raw, so fucking *raw*.

I was twenty-nine and had never been stupid enough to fuck without a condom until today. Now I was ruined—with my little fiancée, anyway. I didn't think I'd ever slept with a woman who I hadn't found out my cousins were fucking as well, or even better—Tony. No chance I was trusting the lot of them to be clean, so I'd always wrapped it up. My jaw tightened as I wondered about Elena's sexual history. I wanted to know how many men there'd been, their names, and everything they did to her, so I could do it twice as hard and make her forget they existed.

I wondered if she was on the pill, and in a disturbing way kind of hoped she wasn't. I wanted an irrevocable tie to this woman. I wanted to write my name on her skin, to do all kinds of fucked-up shit so she knew she was mine. Like lock her in my room and hand-feed her. With indifference, I finished my cigarette and contemplated the logistics of that.

Luca's headlights pulled into the drive. He tucked his shirt in and fixed his cuffs as he got out of his car. "I'm gonna take a wild guess. It was the little pink princess that pissed you off and ruined my night."

I shook my head at his stupid nickname for her and lit another cigarette. "Surprising you could even find someone to fuck that ugly face of yours."

A smile pulled on his lips, and he rubbed a hand across his mouth like there might still be something on it.

"Did you have to pay her?" I asked, listening to the city in the background. Sirens, tire noise, the neighbor John's TV playing endless ballgame highlights through an open window. He was an enforcer of mine, and I considered giving him a raise to fix his goddamn air-conditioner. If I wanted to listen to MLB all day I would've turned it on.

Luca walked to the fridge and grabbed a beer. "Might've been better if I had." He cracked the can and took a seat in a lawn chair. "She fucking talked about you the whole time."

"Interesting." Inhaling deeply to get Elena's scent out of my nose, it smelled like the end of summer. Like fresh-cut grass, motor oil, dying heat, and the urban sometimes bitter smell of the city.

A corner of his lips lifted. "Isabel."

"Ah. If you think I know how to shut her up, you're out of luck."

He laughed.

I actually knew of a few ways, but I didn't want to talk about Isabel. Agitation still rolled under my skin, and I stepped out of the garage and leaned against my Mustang in the drive.

The brief thought of Isabel reminded me that she would be here in the morning. She was just my cook and, to be honest, a shitty maid, though she used to be a regular fuck. Well, Mondays and Thursdays when she was here, anyway. She'd been a convenience, but then she fucked Tony and came with unwanted drama. I hadn't touched her in a year and had only run into her a few times.

I considered what I should do about her. Not even a man in the *Cosa Nostra* would parade a mistress or ex-lover in front of his fiancée. And knowing Isabel, she would go out of her way to try and make Elena uncomfortable about our brief past. Would Elena even care? A burn radiated throughout my chest at the thought that she wouldn't.

"Your pink princess is going to meet her tomorrow," Luca said, though it was more a question about how he should handle it.

A movement in the window upstairs caught my attention.

I took a deep drag and met Elena's gaze behind the glass. Soft lamp light lit her reflection. Messy black hair and soft eyes. My heart rate picked up an awkward rhythm.

I'd gotten what I wanted, what I thought I needed to end this obsession with Elena so I could stop fixating on her and get back to my life. But as I looked at her now, a throb ached in my chest, right behind the breastbone. Like her gaze had bruised me with a mere look.

My eyes narrowed on her as I blew out a breath of smoke.

"Let her."

CHAPTER
Thirty-Nine

"Life is really simple, but we insist on making it complicated."
—Confucius

Elena

IRDS CHIRPED. SUNLIGHT STREAMED IN PLEASANT RAYS THROUGH THE window. And it felt like I'd been ridden hard and put up wet. A twinge of soreness ached between my legs, and my skin felt tender, as though Nico's rough hands and scruff had rubbed me raw.

The reminder made me warm everywhere, though I knew it shouldn't. My feelings toward him were flighty and annoying to even myself. I wanted a straight path to follow, with maturity and thoughtfulness, but I couldn't seem to find that with him. He made me hot and then he made me cold. He was soft and then he was intense. He was rude and then he killed a man so he could have me.

I wasn't using my brain when I thought of him, but another organ entirely.

One with a pulse.

I'd fallen asleep to still smelling him on my skin, in my hair, everywhere, and contentment had filled my chest. Though, there was a prickling sense of unease as well—at the crash that had come from his room shortly after I left, and the animosity seeping under the door. The violence was a normal staple in my life, but it was the *cause* of it that worried me.

Maybe Nico was finally realizing I came with baggage I wasn't ready to give up. And I could only imagine he was regretting not getting a virgin wife. He didn't like to share—that much was obvious.

Maybe I wasn't what he thought he wanted.

Maybe he would return me now that he'd gotten me in his bed.

My papà would surely kill him if he tried that, but Nico never did seem afraid of breaking the rules. However, if my father wasn't happy with the match, as I'd heard, maybe he would be glad Nico changed his mind?

My throat tightened. I'd believed that's what I wanted—not to marry Nico—but, now that I thought about it . . . something wrapped around my lungs and squeezed. And it wasn't because it would obliterate my already marred reputation.

With a little pang in my chest, I pulled myself out of bed and padded down the hall. I took a long, hot shower. My arms and legs were sore, and I hadn't even done any of the work last night. I wondered if he still felt me somewhere. I wondered if he thought about me as much as I thought about him.

I hadn't seen him after he left late the night before, and I wasn't sure he'd even come home. If he had, he'd already gone to work. I didn't believe he was here; it was too quiet and neither did it smell like bacon.

I slipped out of the shower, dried off, and wrapped a towel around myself. As I reached for the door handle, it opened, and a body that reeked of cherry blossom bumped into me. It was a collision, my skull hitting hers before I fell back a few steps.

"Ow."

"What the hell?" a feminine voice muttered.

A woman's narrowed gaze centered on me. I rubbed my forehead with a grimace, but then that fruity scent hit my nose again.

Cherry blossom.

My throat closed up.

The shampoo.

I'd known there would be another woman in the picture, but I hadn't thought I'd have to stand face to face with her in a towel.

"Who the hell are you?" she snapped, rubbing her forehead as well.

My gaze swept downward and so did hers. Our eyes took in the other like we were at a public function and realized we wore the same dress. In this case, we happened to be screwing the same man.

She kind of looked like me. Her hair was medium-length and dark brown, but her features were soft and her body shape similar. *Lovely.* Nico had a type, and I'd been added to his group of hookups.

"Do you talk?" she bit out. "Or are you mute?" She put her hands on her hips and ran a condescending gaze down my body. "Would make the most sense for why Ace brought you home."

I blinked.

I'd never had to respond to such a catty statement before. Had never even heard one come out of a woman's mouth that wasn't on TV. If any of my male relatives had heard, they would've lost it. Evil eyes and narrowed gazes? Of course, but only because men were oblivious to that sort of thing.

It was clear to me that Nico didn't share the same values in regard to respecting the women in his life. If he had, he wouldn't have even allowed her to be here. My chest tightened. *And it began.* He was going to parade girls in front of me like I was nothing. Maybe he thought that because I wasn't a virgin I didn't deserve his respect.

My palms grew clammy, my heartbeats icing over. However, something hot and bitter crept through me. *Anger.* He was upset enough about a fifty-cent ring that he threw something at the wall, and I had to share a bathroom with his whore?

My gaze found the other woman's with indifference, and then I responded to the question regarding whether I spoke. "Sometimes." Lifting a shoulder, I said, "Though I choose not to converse with spiteful shrews until after nine a.m." I glanced at the clock on the wall that showed it was five minutes till.

Her mouth dropped open. "Well, you're a real bitch, aren't you?"

"And you're in my way."

Her eyes narrowed, but she stepped to the side so I could get through. "You know," she said a little too saccharine, "I was curious why Luca is downstairs. Must be here to help you with your walk of shame."

"I think I'll stay for a while," I responded as I passed her.

"You'll *stay?*" she repeated, like I was a bit crazy.

"That's what I said." Frustration had infiltrated my heart, burning a hole in my chest as I walked down the hall. Before I knew what I was doing, I stopped in front of Nico's room. "And by the way"—I turned to look at her before opening my fiancé's door—"you're almost out of shampoo. Do you think you can get some more?"

Red crept into her cheeks just before I shut the door behind me.

I stood in Nico's room for a moment, leaning against the door and staring at the wall. My chest constricted. I didn't think I'd ever felt this frustrated. Maybe resentful regarding how my papà chose to handle my past transgressions, but not pure *anger*. This feeling that seared with a bitter, cutting flame. My eyes burned, and I blinked to keep the tears at bay. Nicolas Russo was not going to make me cry.

I'd prepared for this my entire life. Had told myself lies and prayed that when the time came I would *believe* them—that I didn't need love or fidelity.

I put up walls. And he'd somehow knocked them down in a laughable amount of time.

I wanted to turn back the clock and never step into Nico's room last night. A few moments ago, the memory of his hands had been warm, pleasurable impressions. Now, they were stains I couldn't wash away.

From the exaggerated banging and clatter of pans downstairs, it was safe to say *Isabel* and I hadn't hit it off. I'd realized shortly after shutting the door that it was Monday and the cook was supposed to be here.

Isabel comes Mondays and Thursdays, Nico had said. And then something about her cleaning too, though that was either code for "She fucks me too," or she was the worst maid I'd ever seen. My gaze coasted Nico's messy bedroom, taking in the shattered lamp with detachment.

Ever since I'd met him I'd resorted to immature games that put me in awkward situations. Like now, as I stood in a towel in his room to spite his mistress. I banged my head on the door. He made me do stupid things and I hated it.

I crossed the hall and put on my nicest maxi dress. A pretty outfit always made me feel better, though it didn't seem to help today. I did my makeup, all the while hearing Isabel clanging around until a "Jesus Christ, woman. Shut up," came from a disgruntled Luca.

I made my way down the stairs, and relief hit me when I found the kitchen and living room to be empty. I didn't want to be unkind anymore; it was exhausting.

The office door was cracked, and Luca and Isabel's hushed voices came from within as I got the coffee started. I checked my phone that had been charging on the counter. I had a text from my mamma about some wedding details but nothing else. I wanted to speak with Adriana, but I knew she wouldn't have gotten her phone back. I was about to call the landline when the talking in the other room stopped, and now sounded suspiciously like . . . kissing.

A grimace pulled on my lips.

It felt like I was trapped in a Gabriella situation, though this time I was on the opposite side of the scenario: the girlfriend instead of the relative. I didn't like this new angle at all.

A little moan.

I shifted on my feet. Were they seriously going to mess around with the door open? They had to know I was out here; the coffee was brewing and the creak in the stairs had been loud enough to wake the dead.

"Shit," Luca coughed.

Yep, messing around.

I could only assume Isabel was trying to make me as uncomfortable as she could, and Luca was just a man and couldn't turn down sex.

My stomach twisted as I imagined it was Nico in there with Isabel instead. I would have to grow used the possibility, and so I forced myself to believe it was him. I let the ache in my chest unfurl until it would scar.

I pulled up Benito's number and sent him a text.

Me: *Please come pick me up.*

Three dots appeared right away, showing he was typing.

Benito: *You know I can't do that.*

I expected his response, but it felt like all the walls were closing in on me and squeezing my lungs. If I didn't get out soon, I wouldn't be able to breathe.

Me: *Please. I just want to talk to Adriana.*

Benito: *Call the home phone.*

Me: *No, I need to see her.*

Benito: *Dammit, Elena.*

Me: *Ple.. . .*

Benito: *Fuck. The things I do for women.*

Relief filled me, and I sucked in a breath.

Benito: *Is Ace there?*

Me: *No. Just Luca.*

Benito: *Make sure you ask him.*

Me: *Yeah, I know, Benny.*

Benito: *Don't Benny me. Be there soon.*

I took a cup of coffee to my room and waited for him to arrive. When I got a text saying he was waiting out front, I hopped up and headed downstairs, only to find Luca and Isabel still preoccupied. It'd been a good twenty minutes, at least. I hesitated. I couldn't stay here for another second, but the thought of confronting either of them made my stomach dip.

I found a piece of paper and wrote a quick note that Benito had picked me up and I was going home for a couple hours. My hand faltered on the word *home*. I didn't believe I thought of my parents' as home anymore, but today the last place home felt like was *here*.

I left through the front door since Benito waited on the street, but that wasn't only it. I didn't want to use the back door in case Luca would hear. An awareness itched in a corner of my mind that he might not let me leave, and that wasn't an option. My heart beat with uncertainty as I let the screen door shut with a quiet click.

I climbed into the passenger seat.

Benito was sending a text, probably to some unlucky lady. He was a sight for sore eyes, and for some annoying reason tears began to well.

"I gotta tell you about this one, Elena," he said, tossing his phone in the center console. "Blonde, tall . . . and these legs. *Damn.*" He made a circle with his thumb and forefinger in the "perfect" sign and looked over at me. His hand dropped, and his expression darkened. "What did that asshole do?"

"Nothing." I shook my head, wiping my eyes. "I'm just being a stupid girl."

His gaze narrowed. *"Elena."*

I threw myself at him, wrapping my arms around his neck. He smelled like hundred-dollar hair gel and his signature cologne. "I don't know how you get any women with how much cologne you wear. Could smell you from a mile away."

He hugged me back. "Makes them come in droves."

"Thanks for picking me up."

His arms tightened around me. "If he hurts you, you'll tell me."

It wasn't a question, though it felt like one. We both knew there was nothing he could do if it came down to that. Nobody meddled with a man's wife or relationship in the *Cosa Nostra*. It wasn't anyone's business, regardless if he was abusive.

"I'll tell you, but he hasn't." I pulled back and put my seatbelt on.

"So, what is this?" He wiped a tear off my cheek with a thumb. "Period shit? Aunt Flo in town?"

I laughed. "I missed you."

"Missed you too, cuz. Let's go home."

Home.

It didn't feel right when he said it either.

CHAPTER
Forty

"If the Sun and Moon should ever doubt,
they'd immediately go out."
—William Blake

Elena

THE GRANDFATHER CLOCK'S *TICKS* AND *TOCKS* FILLED THE SILENT ROOM.

Mamma took a sip of wine and stared at me.

Nonna sat on the adjacent couch, watching me like she knew I'd had mind-blowing, premarital sex last night.

I flushed.

She smiled like a cat.

"Have some fruit salad, Elena." Mamma set down her wine glass to push a plate across the coffee table. "I just made it last night."

"I'm not hungry, Mamma."

Both of their gazes widened as though I'd confessed I wanted to join a convent. I suddenly regretted not accepting the salad.

My mother placed a hand on her chest. "I knew that Russo was abusing her."

I sighed. "He's not—"

"*Please,*" Nonna scoffed. "It looks consensual enough from where I'm sitting." She observed me like someone would a bride in an off-white gown.

"Nadia," Mamma scolded. "That's not what I meant."

"No, it wouldn't be. You're the biggest prude on this side of the Mississippi."

"He's not abusing me, all right?" I crossed my legs in discomfort. "I'm just not hungry."

Mamma didn't look like she believed me, and my grandmother's expression softened as well.

"You're always hungry," Nonna muttered.

"Am not," I replied like a two-year-old.

Mamma shook her head. "We should've never let this happen." She pushed the plate closer to me. "This is the worst thing your papà has ever done."

I raised a brow. *The worst?*

Nonna harrumphed.

"Nobody cared when he handed Adriana over without a second thought."

"Of course we cared," Mamma said.

"No, you didn't. I distinctly remember you telling me to 'trust my papà.'"

"Adriana would have been fine. You—" she cut herself off.

"Me, what?" I said calmly, though my cheeks heated in frustration. They didn't worry about Adriana because they thought she could handle herself. They didn't think the same of me.

She pursed her lips and nudged the plate. "Why don't you eat the salad?"

"For the third time—I'm not hungry."

"It's the depression," Nonna whispered to my mamma.

I exhaled. "I'm not depressed."

"Then eat the fruit," Mamma suggested.

"Yeah, *cara mia*. You need to eat the fruit. You're too skinny as it is."

"She's not too skinny," my mamma said. "She's just right."

Nonna eyed me with a frown. "She's all boobs and nothing else." Then muttered, "No wonder that Russo's so hell-bent on having her."

I scoffed. "If I *were* depressed that wouldn't be a comment that would help."

They both watched me like I'd just admitted I *was* depressed.

Mamma jumped up and shoved the plate closer. Another inch and it would be in my lap. "You'll feel better after you eat."

My teeth clenched. "For goodness' sake, I'm not going to eat that stupid salad, Mamma."

"We can't help you if you don't help yourself," Nonna mumbled.

I rubbed my temple. "Why don't you think I can take care of myself? I can be just as assertive as Adriana."

"Of course we know that," Mamma said a little too quickly. "But maybe you're not as emotionally . . . stable." She closed her mouth like she realized that was worse than saying I wasn't as assertive.

"Keep digging yourself into a hole, Celia," Nonna muttered, taking a sip of coffee. "You'll be to China in no time."

I blinked. *"Emotionally stable?"*

Mamma played with her jacket zipper like it had suddenly become interesting. "Maybe that was the wrong term."

"Please, Celia, do explain yourself," Nonna urged with a grin. "I'm on pins and needles."

"All I meant to say is that you're softer than your sister . . . more docile, and a man like that Russo would abuse it."

I opened my mouth to deny it, but then realized she might be right. It was suddenly clear to us all that I'd lasted not even a week with Nico before I'd come home without an appetite.

"Simply put," Mamma said, "we don't think the Russo is right for you."

"We?" Nonna's brows pulled together. "Who's we? Don't put words into my mouth."

I laughed, though I wasn't amused in the slightest. "I didn't believe he was right for me from the beginning, but it didn't matter. 'It is done,' as Papà said."

Mamma frowned. "Your papà doesn't act like he wants this marriage. He's been in a mood all weekend."

"Don't sugarcoat it, Celia. He's been a downright cad."

"If you tell your papà you are not happy with the Russo, maybe he will change his mind."

I swallowed. Was I not happy? I wasn't today.

"Even if Salvatore does change his mind," Nonna said, "I'm sure she's already as knocked up as your other daughter."

Mamma grimaced. "Don't be vulgar, Nadia."

"*Oh, Madonna, salvami.* I wonder how you ever had three children. You're as squeamish as a virgin."

A headache bloomed behind my eyes and I stood. "I assure you, Nonna, I'm not pregnant. I've been on the pill for years."

Nonna shot Mamma a look. "No wonder your daughters are little floozies. You're practically encouraging them!"

My mamma muttered, "Better a floozy than senile," as I headed out of the room.

The curtains were closed as though someone was in mourning. A lump showed beneath the tangle of blankets on the bed. Smallish in size, and blaring *Seven Nation Army*. I lifted the comforter and climbed in before pulling it back over my head. We lay on our sides facing each other, with Adriana's iPod playing music between us.

When the song stopped, I pushed pause on her playlist. "What did one sister say to the other?"

She fought an eye roll, but a corner of her mouth lifted. "What?"

"Will you be my Maid of Honor?"

Expectantly, she pursed her lips like it was a hard decision to consider. "Your fiancé put Ryan in the hospital."

He was *her* fiancé not even a week ago, but now that he was mine she was quick to make me accountable for his actions. "I know, or I guess I assumed. I'm sorry, Adriana."

"I thought they were going to kill him." Her voice was shaky with relief.

A piece of my heart dissolved into bits and pieces, leaving an empty ache behind. "But they didn't."

"No." She traced the edges of her iPod. "I know it was because of you. You always know what to do."

A lump formed in the back of my throat. *If only that were the truth.* God, sometimes it felt like I was stranded on a raft at sea. Today was one of those days.

"You really love him, don't you?"

"Yes."

My eyes burned. "What's it like?"

Her gaze met mine, her brows knitting. "What do you mean?"

"To be in love."

"But—" She blinked, glancing at my left hand.

Understanding hit me. *Of course* she would think I was in love. I was a romantic at heart and I hadn't even been able to lie to the world, let alone myself. I wasn't a girl to have casual sex and everyone knew it.

I twisted the ring on my finger, and a bitter laugh escaped. "I didn't even know his name, Adriana—*don't* know his name."

"Then why did you leave?" She frowned. "I thought you'd met him somewhere, fell in love, and went to be with him."

Guilt pierced my chest. I was a terrible sister. I didn't confide in her and I'd lusted after her fiancé. If I died before getting to Confession I was surely going to Hell.

I averted my gaze. "You know that little musical carousel I used to play over and over when we were younger?"

"Yeah, it's pink."

I smiled. "Yeah. Well, Nonno gave it to me for Christmas one year, if you remember. Since then, I'd always wanted to see a carousel in real life. A silly childhood dream, I guess. But it never happened . . . you know how busy Papà is." I cleared my throat. "Anyway, that night I left . . . I guess I couldn't take the expectations. Everything felt like too much. Oscar Perez, and the idea that someone like him would be my future. Having to force a smile. Squeezing myself into this person I didn't think I could be anymore. It started all at once; my lungs closed up and I couldn't breathe. All I believed at that moment was that if I didn't get out of the house, I was going to die. The carousel just sat there on my dresser, taunting me with fanciful dreams. I wanted one to come true, even as trivial as it was. So I snuck out, took the bus—"

Her eyes widened, and I laughed.

"I didn't even stop to think that it was winter and the carnival wouldn't be there. I guessed I imagined the carousel would be dusted with a little snow. Anyway, he was a security guard at a mall nearby and stopped to see why I was standing in an empty parking lot alone. And I don't know . . . it just happened from there. I told him I didn't know what I was doing, didn't have much money or a place to stay, and he took me to his apartment to figure something out."

"He was probably trying to get laid," Adriana muttered.

I laughed. "Maybe. Though, he seemed nice and genuine. He was charming, and I liked him . . . but I never loved him."

Silence settled in the space between us, and a heavy weight had drifted off my shoulders. I hadn't realized how much I'd needed to share that with somebody until now.

"I'll be your Maid of Honor," she said quietly.

"Thank God." I put a hand on my chest in relief. "Otherwise I was going to have to ask Sophia, and can you imagine that speech?"

Her laugh was light before drifting off. "I have a doctor's appointment today."

"Yeah?"

"Yeah."

I smiled. "I can't believe I'm going to be an aunt."

She swallowed. "Elena, I was terrified they were going to kill him if they found out . . ." I knew she was trying to explain the reason she'd drunk so much. "And now I'm even more scared I've hurt the baby."

"It'll be okay." I gave a piece of her hair a tug. "An Abelli is stronger than all that. Can you imagine hurting Tony with a few shots of vodka?"

She smiled. "A *bullet* doesn't hurt Tony. Benito sure likes to whine about it, though."

We laughed with a lightness that had been absent between us for a while. The amusement faded into an easy quiet.

"Love . . ." she started. "I guess it feels like you're falling . . . and he's the only one who could catch you."

I thought about it for a second. "Sounds scary."

She laughed. "No, not scary . . . thrilling."

"For you, maybe. You're not scared of anything."

"You're sure you aren't in love?" she questioned once more, her gaze steady on mine.

"No, I'm really not."

"Uh-oh," she muttered.

Before I could question her, a loud commotion drifted up the stairs. The door slamming, masculine shouts . . .

I sat up, pushing the covers off.

When I recognized one of the angry men's voices to be Nico's, my stomach dropped to my toes. "Oh my god . . ."

My pulse trembled as I jumped out of bed and ran down the hall.

I froze at the top of the stairs.

If someone handcrafted nightmares for individuals, this would be mine. Anger permeated the air so thick it touched my skin. Luca, Lorenzo, and Ricardo stood in the foyer with tense countenances.

Something twisted in my chest as Nico and Benito got in each other's faces and grabbed the other by the collar.

Nico shoved Benito against the wall hard enough a vase fell off the table and shattered. "You crossed a fucking line—"

"Ask me if I give a shit about your goddamn line." My cousin pushed him back a foot.

"Maybe you'll give a shit if I draw the line with your fucking body," Nico growled.

They both had their guns pressed against the other's temples before I could blink.

My heart turned to a block of ice.

The front door flew open and slammed against the wall. Papà, my brother, and Dominic stepped in.

Guns pointed in every direction.

Cazzo.

I think I really screwed up.

CHAPTER
Forty-One

"We are all born mad. Some remain so."
—Samuel Beckett

Elena

"**S**OMEBODY HAD BETTER START EXPLAINING WHAT THE FUCK'S GOING ON right *now!*" Papà snapped. When his gaze flicked to me at the top of the staircase, he paused and then his expression became even stormier. He shook his head, gesturing toward me with his gun. "Go to your room, Elena."

On instinct, my feet began to comply.

"Stay." Nico's voice was a deep timbre of control.

He was the don right now. No soft edges.

I halted, my blood going cold with indecision.

Nico stepped away from Benito and faced my papà. My cousin and father had a gun aimed at his head while he held his by his side. A cold sweat drifted down my back.

Papà and Nico stared at each other, communicating with their eyes. Something only dons could understand.

"You've gone too fucking far," Papà spit. "Elena is not yours until the marriage. And if you've somehow forgotten—that hasn't fucking happened yet."

"Let me enlighten you, Salvatore," Nico growled. "As soon as the contract was signed she was *mine*."

"Fuck the contract and. Fuck. *You*. Ace."

Nico ran a hand across his jaw with sardonic amusement. "You're backing out?"

"That's what I said."

My heart threatened to beat out of my chest.

Nico took a step toward my papà. "You want to know how to start a war with me, Salvatore? *This* would be how to do it."

My eyes widened. *This can't be happening . . .*

Papà's jaw tightened. Tony and Dominic remained silent and unreadable, their attention and guns unmoving from the Russos in the foyer.

"Come here, Elena," Nico demanded.

Papà shot me a narrowed gaze. "You'll go to your fucking room. Now!"

Indecision twisted so violently in my stomach it felt like I might be sick. I didn't know what to do, who to listen to. Why this was happening to me. *I wrote a note . . .* I should have known Nico wouldn't have found that sufficient.

Nico's gaze flicked to me. His eyes were dark around the edges, but the irises were shimmering depths. Awareness ran through me. He said nothing, though he didn't have to. He wanted me to choose him and he was letting me see it. It was the most vulnerable thing I'd ever seen him do, and the fact that he might show me a side of him not many had before sent a throb to my chest.

As my hands grew clammy and my breaths short, I did the thing that had been ingrained in me since I was a child. I listened to my papà and took a step toward my room.

But something stopped me.

If I picked my papà's side, it could mean violence and death. Possibly *war*.

Although, that wasn't only it.

A tug deep in my stomach pulled me in the other direction. A place near my heart grew cold and empty with the small step I'd taken.

As I hesitated, the tension hung over my head like a formidable cloud.

My papà sold me to Oscar Perez.

Nico killed him for me.

I avoided my papà's gaze as I descended the stairs, but his anger was strong enough it burned my skin. I sucked in a shallow breath as Luca reached out and wrapped a heavy arm around my waist as though I might change my mind.

My gaze met Tony's. While he was usually the first one to pull out a gun at the word *war*, he didn't seem to want the same thing as Papà, or he wouldn't have let me by him. Maybe he and Nico were on better terms now that they'd beaten the crap out of each other. Whatever it was, I was grateful.

I'd already been the cause for one man's death.

I couldn't survive another.

Luca walked me like a prisoner to the car, his arm a warm shackle around my waist.

Nico and the others were still inside, and I prayed they were doing the Made Man version of hugging it out, which usually involved violence of some kind, but not *war*.

"Instead of running off next time," Luca said dryly, "I'm betting if you ask him for something he might just give it to you."

"I didn't run off. You were a little *busy*"—my gaze hardened—"so I left a note on the island."

His eyes narrowed. "There was no note."

I blinked. *What?*

He watched my expression before giving his head a shake, muttering, "*Fucking Isabel.*"

I sat cross-legged on my bed, flicking the Zippo open and closed.

If you ask him for something he might just give it to you.

I'd come to the conclusion that Nico made me as crazy as he was. Because *asking* was an easy fix to a problem I wouldn't have hesitated to utilize with anyone else. It was simple: when Nico was in the equation, all rational thoughts were lost.

I flicked the lighter open, and hope ignited with the new flame.

Perhaps I didn't have to see him with other women, to *share a bathroom* with one. The hope was only an ember, barely flickering with light, because the idea that there would be other women at all cut me straight through the chest, leaving a raw and bleeding ache behind.

However, infidelity was a fixed denominator in a Made Man. Like a surfer and a board. A writer and a pen. You couldn't separate the two. And asking would be a fruitless endeavor.

Out of sight, out of mind, as the saying went.

I could live with not knowing.

My grip on the lighter faltered when the quiet purr of an engine drifted to my ears. I walked to the window to see Nico get out of his car and head into the garage. Luca had hung out in there since we'd gotten back close to an hour ago.

When I'd come inside, I found my crumbled note in the trash. *Fucking Isabel* was right. I hadn't gone about anything the right way, but I hadn't left without telling anyone, as Nico must have believed.

Shame became a heavier weight on my shoulders with every minute I waited. I'd been upset, and the choice to leave was rash and not me.

Luca left the garage and rubbed his jaw before getting in his car. I stood there, waiting for Nico to make an appearance, but he didn't. I'd spent the last hour wondering how he would react, what I was going to say to him, and now that he was here, a restlessness inside me demanded I get it over with.

I headed down the stairs and out the back door. The cement was hot against my bare feet as I stood in front of the garage. Nico's hands were braced on the worktable, a glass of whiskey sitting nearby. His shoulders tensed when he realized I was here.

His gaze came to me. It was dark, warm, every emotion in between. A shiver danced across my spine, and before I knew what I was doing I walked toward him. I didn't expect a rough palm to cup my face and brush across my cheek. My heart glowed like a Zippo flame.

He made a quiet noise of satisfaction when I pressed my face into his chest. His hand slid from my cheek to the back of my head, his fingers threading through my hair.

He smelled *so* good. Felt so good. Like comfort, security, and *need,* all in one. There was a name to it, but I didn't know what.

"I'm sorry," I breathed. "I didn't mean for any of that to happen."

He let out a breath in between disbelief and amusement, and I thought he muttered, "So this is the Sweet Abelli."

He'd done something no other Made Man should do and paraded his mistress in front of his fiancée, and somehow, I had ended up apologizing for the outcome.

My nonna and mamma were right.

This man would eat me alive.

But he was so warm, felt so *right*, it was hard to even care.

His fist tightened in my hair, tilting my face to his. His gaze hardened.

"Where's your cell phone?"

I suddenly realized I hadn't taken it with me when I left. I hadn't had one for so long it was hard to remember. "I forgot it."

"Convenient."

I swallowed. "I wrote a note."

"So I heard." His gaze fell to my hand. "Where did you find that?"

I glanced at the lighter, recognizing I'd brought it with me. "On the floor after you got into it with my brother."

"You kept it."

"Yes."

"Why?"

I hesitated, a lie forming on my tongue before I swallowed it down. I felt bad enough about today that I couldn't stand to be untruthful.

"It was yours," I breathed.

It went so quiet I could hear the beats of my heart.

Bu-bum.

Bu-bum.

"You're forgiven," he rasped.

A heavy pressure drifted off my shoulders.

His tone was harsh. "You won't leave this house again without talking to me first, do you understand?"

I nodded.

"Say it."

I forced myself to meet his gaze. "I won't leave the house without talking to you first." My lungs tightened because it wasn't a promise I could keep. Not yet.

"If you want to see your family, I'll take you."

I chewed my bottom lip. "My papà might shoot you."

"Maybe." He seemed unconcerned.

Something twisted in my chest at the thought. Made me feel hollow.

He pressed my back to the workbench, braced his hands on either side of me, and then he leaned in and kissed my throat. I sighed and tilted my head. I hadn't expected it to go like this, but it could be said I never was that great at guessing what Nico would do.

"Can I ask for something?"

"Shoot," he drawled against my neck.

I said it before I could stop myself. "I want Isabel gone."

His lips traced my ear, and seconds passed as I held my breath.

"Done."

My heart ached.

His hand ran up my thigh and around to my ass, pulling my body against his. He kissed a line down my throat.

"Can I ask for one more thing?" I breathed.

I felt a smile on my neck. "You're awfully needy today."

I swallowed. "No women . . . not here, okay?"

He stilled for a moment, and with a sinking sensation in my belly I wondered if I'd taken it too far. If he would say no.

"That's what you want?"

No. I want to be enough for you.

I want you to want only me.

"Yes."

In the next moment of silence, the anticipation of his answer wrapped around my lungs and squeezed.

His face came up to mine. Our gazes met. Lips inches apart.

I wouldn't take a simple ring off when he'd asked, nor would I kiss him. The knowledge settled between us, mixed with the smell of motor oil and summer.

What he didn't know was that soon I would ruin everything to the point he'd never trust me again.

A thumb ran across my lips, down my chin. "Done."

The band around my lungs released, though a tainted feeling remained. Thick as tar and black as night. Like a venomous snake in a tropical paradise.

"So loyal to your family," he said quietly. "Yet you listened to me and not your papà. Why? Preventing a war?"

That's what he expected. I could read it in the way he looked at me with a sort of forced detachment.

I did it because it felt right.

An unfamiliar ache began in my chest. A need for him to know.

I met his gaze, as golden as the glass of whiskey beside me.

"Maybe I wanted to," I whispered.

He watched me for so many seconds it made my pulse race. He closed his eyes and shook his head. "Come on. Let's go inside." He grabbed my hand and tugged me along.

I followed.

He was comfort, security, and *need,* all in one.

It had a name.

Home.

CHAPTER Forty-Two

"A kiss that is never tasted, is forever and ever wasted."
—Billie Holiday

Elena

HE HELD MY HAND AS HE SHUT THE BACK DOOR BEHIND US.

My breaths turned shallow as he pulled me to the couch. He sat, and I stood between his legs, waiting to see what he wanted. I would do it all, anything he told me to. Maybe it was my submissive heart, or maybe it was the romantic one trying to find a way to thrive.

His palms skimmed my legs, pushing my dress up until he found bare thigh. My skin danced with anticipation. His hands fit me so right, were the perfect roughness and the warmest heat. I suddenly didn't know what I would do if I could never feel them again.

He tugged the backs of my knees, pulling me closer until I straddled him.

Chest to chest. Heartbeat to heartbeat. My pink dress to his black dress shirt and tie. We were so different, I realized then. Big and small. Hard and soft. Demanding and docile.

We breathed each other's air for a moment before he leaned in and ran his lips down the length of my throat. "You smell so good," he rasped. His scruff tickled my neck as he trailed downward past my collarbone and then pressed his face into my breasts. "And fuck, these tits."

I sighed, my hands running down his chest. "My nonna said you only want to marry me for my boobs."

"Not true." I felt him smile against my skin. "This too." I yelped at the sharp smack on my ass. He tugged my dress off my shoulders, baring my white strapless bra. My breasts tingled as he palmed and squeezed them through the fabric.

"My boobs and ass, then?" My words ended on a moan as he folded a cup down and ran his tongue across a nipple before sucking. My head lolled, a breathless haze overcoming me.

He cupped me between the legs. "This is also the nicest puss—"

"Nico," I cut him off, every inch of my skin warming.

He chuckled.

I loved the sound of his laugh, the way the warm timbre ghosted down my spine.

I shivered.

He ran a thumb across the goose bumps on my arm. "Cold?"

I shook my head, pulling my bottom lip between my teeth. "Nervous."

He unclipped the back of my bra, his eyes darkening as I straddled him topless with my dress around my waist. "Why?"

My hands slid downward, his abs tightening under my touch, to even lower. I traced his belt buckle with a finger. "I want to do something," I whispered. The insinuation that I wanted to please him, to taste him, was heavy and thick in the air.

His gaze immediately flicked to my face. Nerves danced in my veins as I began to undo his belt. He tensed. I leaned forward, pressing my breasts against his dress shirt and my lips to his neck. God, he smelled so good it made me dizzy. I nuzzled him, trying to soak it all up.

His hand cupped the back of my head, sliding downward to my nape. "Why would that make you nervous?"

I swallowed. "Because I haven't done it before."

I tried to slide backward to my knees in front of the couch, but he suddenly grabbed me by a fistful of hair. His gaze swam with turmoil and disbelief.

"You're lying." His voice was sharp.

I laughed weakly, though in truth his words pierced my chest. "I'm sure you'll find out soon enough that I'm not." I was so nervous it vibrated beneath my skin. My hands were clammy, and I fought not to wipe them on my dress. Like an idiot, I wondered how many blowjobs this man had gotten and from how many experienced women.

I tried to pull away again, but his grip only tightened. He watched me with a tension that radiated from his gaze. I swallowed as awareness settled between us. Keeping his stare, I slipped the ring off and let it fall from my fingers. His fist loosened, and I slid to the floor.

He stretched out, like he was getting comfortable, like a woman on her knees at his feet was a daily routine. *God, this man.* He never made anything easy.

I unbuttoned his pants, and the sound of the zipper sent a seductive echo through the room. He rested his elbow on the armrest and watched me.

I hesitated. I knew I couldn't do this with perfection, and I wished I'd had more practice so I *could*. He certainly knew what he was doing in the oral department, and I was scared I'd be a disappointment.

"You gonna stare at my crotch all day or take it out?"

He looked like a king sitting there, demanding and impatient. Though, I believed he was close to unraveling by a tightness in his shoulders and the tension passing through his eyes.

My hands trembled as I pulled his briefs down and wrapped my fingers around his erection. How was I going to get this thing in my mouth? Even though a part of me was apprehensive, an unexpected tenacity demanded I try. He was so smooth and warm. Hard and thick. He felt so good inside me, and I wanted to thank him for it. I leaned in and rubbed his erection across my cheek.

His thighs spread further, a hand running across his mouth while the other clamped into a fist on the armrest.

My mouth watered as I rubbed my face, my lips, all over him. I drew my tongue out and licked him like an experiment. I did it again, all the way from the base to the top. His stomach tightened, a quiet groan escaping him. His reaction was so hot that a hum of satisfaction traveled up my throat as I gave him little licks everywhere, not missing a spot.

"Quit playing with it," he said harshly.

Jeez, he was moody about his blowjobs.

I shot him a narrowed gaze.

"Suck," he demanded.

In an unhealthy way, his bossy tone sent a warm wave between my legs. I obeyed, running my tongue around the head before sucking it into my mouth.

His head fell back with a "Fuck, that's it."

My breasts rubbed against his thighs, and sparks of pleasure fluttered through me. I sucked him again, taking more in my mouth and gliding up and down.

"Just like that," he hissed, his hand grabbing a fistful of my hair. He moved my head, controlling the rhythm. Up and down, and deeper into my mouth every time. "Look at me," he ordered roughly.

My gaze flicked to him.

"Fuck," he muttered.

When he pushed himself deep enough it hit the back of my throat, I gagged and my eyes watered. With a groan, he pulled me away from him. His breaths came out heavy as he rested his head against the couch and watched me with a half-lidded gaze.

I wiped my mouth with the back of my hand. "What's wrong?"

"Gonna come," was all he said.

My brows pulled together. "That was quick."

I meant it as I wasn't ready to be done, but as soon as I said it I realized it sounded like he was a two-pump chump.

He let out a laugh. "I'm going to fuck you hard for that."

I flushed.

His gaze burned hot and lazy. "Take it all off and come here."

I stood and slipped my dress and thong down my legs. As soon as I straddled him, his mouth latched onto my breast. Fever consumed me, a shot pouring straight in my bloodstream. He touched me, rough and urgent, and it only fed the fire.

My hands buried in his hair as he sucked and nipped on my breasts, on my throat and neck. He squeezed and smacked my ass, grinding me against his erection.

"Stand up," he rasped. He barely got the words out before he was jerking me upward and then pulling me down on his face. I groaned, bracing a thigh on the back of the couch and a hand on his shoulder. He sucked and licked while I rolled my hips against his mouth. My skin burned. Pressure built and built.

"So close," I moaned.

I gripped a fistful of his hair right before the release shot through me, buckling my legs and stealing my breath. I slid to his lap, gasping for air. Before I realized his intentions, he grabbed my hips and slammed inside of me.

I choked as pain spread through me. "Nico, I'm so sore."

His hands gentled on me. "Fuck, baby, I'm sorry." He leaned forward and captured my top lip between his, kissing me with a sweet pull.

We both realized what had happened the second his mouth left mine.

He froze.

My pulse skidded to an awkward stop.

Unease poured into my bloodstream; warm as whiskey neat, yet as cold as ice. He was deep inside of me, so deep it stung, but all I could focus on was how my mouth tingled where he'd kissed me. I licked my lips, and his gaze darkened as he followed the motion. I could taste a hint of myself, but not enough of *him*.

The air stilled. Indecision shook in my hands. My heartbeats danced, warmed, pulsed like they were finally alive.

I couldn't stop myself.

A tremor ran through me as I leaned forward, close enough our breaths intermixed. And then closer until my mouth brushed his. So soft, so him, so *mine*. When he parted his lips, I pressed mine to his and slid my tongue inside. A groan came from deep in his chest, his hands tightening on my hips.

I pulled back, trying to catch my breath. But before I caught it, I leaned in and kissed him again. Lazy and wet, I licked inside his mouth. His hand cupped the back of my head, and he sucked on my tongue. I moaned, my fingers running down his tie. The next kiss was rough, with a scrape of his teeth before easing into a wet slide. My blood drummed in my ears, rushed through my veins, incinerated like fuel and flame.

I was so full of him, and with his mouth on mine I felt overwhelmed. Complete. *Consumed.* And I never wanted to come up for air.

He tried to slow the kiss, but I didn't want to stop. Couldn't.

I pressed my mouth to his, gave his top lip a gentle lick, stole his breath straight from his lungs. He tasted so good. Like me, and warm vanilla whiskey.

He nipped my bottom lip, telling me enough.

"Fuck me or get off."

I faltered at his sudden change of mood. However, I soon realized what this was. He was pissed that I'd never kissed him and now he was going to withhold it from me. My eyes narrowed, though I wasn't that moved. Another man in the *Cosa Nostra* would've never respected my wish not to kiss him, and this one had. Now that I was trying to eat him alive, the proud boss was reminded of it.

I rolled my hips, slow and lazy at first. The soreness was like standing near a fire that was a bit too hot but you'd die without its warmth. I wrapped my arms around his shoulders and pressed my face into his neck.

A shiver rolled through me, pressure and heat sparking as I ground my clit against his pelvis. His hands ran down my back, gripping my ass and pulling me harder against him. I was only rubbing myself against him, not fucking him yet, but he didn't seem to mind.

The sensation of him deep and still inside of me drove me to the edge. An *mmm* sound escaped me as I rose an inch and then slid back down.

"Fuck, those noises." He captured the next one in his mouth. His palms ran to my ribs, spanning my waist. A shudder rolled under his skin as I began to slowly move up and down.

Rough hands held me tightly.

Teeth nipped my jaw.

Lips ran up my neck before pressing to my ear.

"You gonna keep your mouth from me again?"

I shook my head.

"Because it's mine?"

"Yes," I breathed.

He groaned from his throat before grabbing the back of my neck and kissing me hard. Wet and messy. Wild and rough. And then slow, wet glides and licks, like he was trying to taste every inch of my mouth. Warmth spilled into my chest and spread outward.

He let me get used to fucking him before his hands started moving me up and down. Sweet, *hot* pressure began to build. I moaned in his mouth. He kissed me and kissed me until I couldn't breathe anything but him.

When his head lowered and he sucked a nipple into his mouth, the pressure boiled over. A shudder shook me as pleasure burst and finally dissipated. My breath came out heavy and erratic, my forehead resting on his.

His body tensed, and his hands tightened on my waist as he rocked me.

"Ask me to come inside you."

"*Please* come inside me," I sighed against his lips.

He pressed his face against my throat, let out a masculine groan that sent goose bumps down my body, and bit my neck hard enough it would leave a mark.

I sat there with my arms around his shoulders, my breath fanning his throat. His presence soaked through my skin with each inhale. His touch and taste and smell sank so deep they filled the cracks of my heart. He was becoming a drug, an addiction I would have to feed every day. From the recent hit, euphoria filled my veins and relaxed my limbs.

He was an infatuation, a craving, a *need*, and I was sure it was unrequited. But as my fingers ran down his tie and rested on his chest—

Bu-bum.

Bu-bum.

Bu-bum.

His heartbeats raced for me.

CHAPTER
Forty-Three

"We do not remember days, we remember moments."
—Cesare Pavese

Nico

RAN MY HANDS DOWN HER BACK, MARVELING AT THE SOFTNESS. SHE WAS SO small and breakable in my arms—I could snuff the life right out of her with little effort. The thought made something tighten in my throat.

I didn't know what to do with this woman, but I did know I was keeping her. Every time I saw her, my blood burned hotter, searing the word *mine* into my chest. If it were only the greedy Russo in me driving this infatuation, it would've gone away the moment she left my bed. Everyone at the Abelli house today knew that hadn't fucking happened.

I'd come to the conclusion I didn't give a shit if she wanted to be with another: she couldn't. It was that simple. I kept myself from digging into her past because I knew if I found something I didn't like—specifically, a *lover*—I wouldn't be able to handle it with a clear mind. And the thought of earning her hatred sent a hollow ache throughout my chest.

Her breath fanned my neck, and I ran my fingers through her hair. There was so fucking much of it. I'd had to hold it out of her face while she sucked my dick. She hadn't been lying—that was the first time she'd done it. A heady rush consumed me. Maybe she wasn't as experienced as I'd believed.

What else hadn't she done? I wanted it all. Everything. The urge to demand she tell me was on the tip of my tongue, but I forced myself to keep it in. I didn't want to talk—or even *think*—about her sexual history. I had a feeling it would only end up with another broken piece of furniture.

She chose me instead of her papà.

And fuck, if that hadn't filled me with a warm wave of satisfaction.

Her fingernails ran into the hair at my nape, and it sent a chill down my spine. "Nico, are our families going to kill each other at the wedding?"

Amusement rose in me. "Maybe."

She tilted her head, and all of her silky hair slid across my hands. "I don't think my papà likes you."

I laughed. "I don't think many Abellis do."

"I do," she whispered.

Fuck. "Yeah?"

"Yeah."

Warmth flamed to life inside me. "You'll be a Russo soon, so it doesn't count."

She trailed a finger down my neck. "Next weekend."

Tomorrow. But she didn't need to know that yet.

After her papà had threatened to change his mind, I'd decided I wasn't risking waiting. Elena was mine, and tomorrow she'd take my name to prove it.

"I think we should have a couple more functions before then," she said. "Somewhere our families have to interact." She paused. "Like the casino."

I chuckled. "Probably not the best idea, baby."

"Oh," she laughed, and the sound hit me in the chest. "I forgot you're a bunch of cheats."

"*We're*," I corrected.

"We," she whispered, as though she was trying it out on her tongue. I wanted to know how it tasted.

She leaned back, and my dick began to harden from the sight of her tits in my face. I pulled my briefs over my growing erection and restrained from touching her. She was sore, and I felt bad enough about hurting her earlier. Though, I didn't regret it now that her mouth was mine.

She smoothed my tie, running her fingers down my chest and stomach. I could sit here and let this woman touch me all day and I'd never grow bored. She lifted my hand, brushing my knuckles with a thumb. "Am I ever going to see these not busted up?"

I gave them a glance. "Probably not."

She put her palm to mine, measuring the difference. "You hit Luca?"

"Yeah." I'd hit him so hard I was surprised I didn't break more than skin. Fucker had a hard face.

She smiled. "So honest."

"Always."

Her gaze came to mine, a little crease between her brows. Damn, she was too beautiful. It fucking hurt to look at her.

"Really? You'd answer honestly to anything I asked?"

I tucked a piece of hair behind her ear. "I'll be honest, but some things you don't need to know."

Her hand faltered against mine, and I suddenly realized how that came off. She thought I meant women. Jesus, I didn't think I'd fucked another woman since I'd met this girl. Truthfully, I was pretty sure I was obsessed, and I didn't give a single fuck about it anymore. I just wanted to keep feeding it. Fucking her, kissing her, eating her out, over and over, until I was dead. The idea that I couldn't made me feel sick, like I was catching a bad case of the flu or something.

"I'm talking about business, Elena."

She focused on our hands, interlocking her fingers with mine. Resting her head on my shoulder, she quietly said, "I hear you're a bad man."

A smile tugged at my lips. "You believe everything you hear?"

"Just what I see. Why did you kill your cousin?"

My lips pressed against her ear. "He had a gun to your head."

A shiver rolled through her. I'd known she was mine even then.

"Nico?"

"What?"

"Your come is running down my thigh," she whispered.

Fuck. That was the hottest thing I'd ever heard. My dick throbbed.

I found the wetness dripping down her leg. Running a finger upward, I pushed it back inside her. She made that breathy *mmm* noise of hers that drove me crazy. Damn, I was turned on. If she didn't get off me, I was going to fuck her again, and I'd already told myself I wouldn't.

"I have to go to work for a while," I told her. "I have a meeting with your brother."

She tensed. "Please don't kill him."

A noise of sardonic amusement escaped me. I hated how that bastard had her loyalty. I wanted it all. It was irrational, I knew, but I didn't know how to deal with how I felt about this girl. Everything was amplified. Burning hot. And impulsive.

"I'm not going to kill him. Your papà and I decided not to work with each other anymore. Tony will be an intermediary of sorts."

"Oh." She swallowed. "Try not to let him kill you either."

"And if he did?"

She paused, like she hadn't considered it and didn't know. I realized she didn't want to answer the question when she pressed her mouth to my throat and slowly kissed her way up. Her lips skimmed my jawline before settling on mine. Heat erupted in my groin. She deepened the kiss, sliding her tongue into my mouth, and my cock went hard as a rock. *Shit.* I grabbed a fistful of her hair and pulled her back.

Her eyes were dark as night, her mouth swollen and pink.

"And if he did?" I repeated.

She went silent for a moment, pulling her bottom lip between her teeth. "I'm sure when people find out I've lived here there won't be one man who would want me."

Irritation ignited in my chest. Not the answer I was looking for, and not even true. Any man would give up his life savings and left nut for Elena. My eyes narrowed.

"There is no other man for you."

Her lips quirked. "You'd make sure of that even in death?"

"Yes," I told her, though I didn't know what the fuck I was saying.

"If anyone would go to those extremes, it would be you."

My glare intensified, because I didn't believe she meant that as a compliment. "Are you on the pill?"

Her cheeks flushed a pale pink. She sat on my lap with her tits in my face and my come running down her thighs, and still she blushed from a simple question.

"Yeah," she answered, fingering the end of my tie.

"When are you going to stop taking it?"

She blinked, and then she laughed in disbelief. "You're crazy," she announced, before dropping my tie and getting to her feet.

"I asked a question, Elena."

"And I chose not to answer, Nico," she parried as she walked toward the bathroom completely fucking naked.

I internally groaned at the view. "You're not going to stay on it forever."

"No, but I think I'd like to be *married* first before I even consider it."

I rubbed my jaw.

Fine. We'll discuss it tomorrow then.

"Stupid move today, Ace." Tony sat on my office couch with an arm resting on the back.

I flicked a glance toward him. "Did I ask for your opinion?"

He rubbed a hand across his smile. "Just assumed you'd want it, is all."

"You assumed wrong," I said dryly. "If we wrote down all the stupid shit you've done, that book would be thicker than the fucking Bible."

He sank a little further into the couch. "Everything I do is premeditated. Just have a quicker thought process than most."

"I can smell your bullshit from here. Honestly, I don't know how the fuck you're still alive."

He smirked. "You're just upset you can't kill me."

"Never tried to kill you."

"Debatable. But I know you won't now. You like my sister and my sister loves me."

I like his sister? Was that what it was? Sounded mediocre in comparison to what I felt about Elena.

Gianna's words suddenly filled my mind.

Because you'll fall in love with her. And she won't love you back.

Well, Jesus H. Christ. Gianna was right.

Fuck. This was inconvenient.

I tapped my pen on the desk, leaned back, and refused to reply to that ridiculous statement. Tony laughed, and I gritted my teeth.

"Finally, the black-hearted Russo knows what it's like to be whipped."

I gave my head a small shake. "There's a big difference between you and me, Tony. Whipped or not, I'm not a fucking doormat."

Tony's gaze hardened, but he only lifted his feet onto the coffee table.

"Jenny pulls you around by your cock and you let her. Might as well buy her a strap-on."

"You know," he said, "I could live without you saying her fucking name."

"And I could live without your shoes on my coffee table."

He left them there, smoothed his tie, and rested a bandaged hand on his stomach. "I got a hot date tonight."

"I think 'hot' loses its steam after every man in a ten-mile radius has had a piece of it."

His jaw ticked. "I love my sister, Ace, but it's not like you're getting a cherry with your fiancée either."

Annoyance unfurled in my chest, and his gaze flickered with pleasure when he noticed he'd gotten to me.

"If you want to sit around and talk about me fucking your sister, be my guest. Brings back good memories."

He picked a piece of lint off his suit jacket. "If it was up to me, I'd never have let Elena stay with you until the wedding."

"Good thing not much is up to you," I said dryly. "New York would burn under one of your massive tantrums."

"If I lit fire to the city, it would deserve to burn."

I let out a half laugh. "More likely a man tossed your girlfriend some quarters and took her for a ride."

He pulled on his collar, his gaze heated. "She's not a fucking hooker."

"Coulda' fooled me. If I gave her the watch off my wrist, she would've done anything I asked of her."

"Any woman would. You look like a tool walking around with that thirty-five-thousand-dollar watch."

I would've easily agreed with him before I met Elena—the *any woman would* part, not the fucking *tool* comment—but now I couldn't imagine her giving it up for a large sum of money. And it wasn't because she already had plenty of it.

Jesus, we hadn't even gotten to business yet and a headache already bloomed behind my eyes. "Maybe we could get this over with?"

"Sure thing, Ace. But I gotta say something first."

I tossed my pen on the desk. "Can hardly wait to hear it."

"For whatever reason—most likely Stockholm—Elena chose you, and I respect her choice. But if you hurt her, I'll have to kill you."

I laughed. I was pretty sure I'd rather cut off my left arm than ever hurt her, but fuck if I was going to let him know she was my biggest weakness.

My gaze froze to ice. "Since we're getting the threats out of the way—if you ever do anything stupid enough to get another gun pointed at her head, I'll skin you alive. Got it?"

He smirked. "Got it, bro."

Jesus. As of tomorrow, this idiot was my fucking brother-in-law.

The clock said two a.m. when I got home. Tony and I had finished the meeting without trying to kill each other—a success in my book—and then I had some other business to take care of. Annoying business that left a red stain on my shirt.

The trashcans near the garage were full of bags, and a small smile came to my lips when I realized what Elena had thrown away. She was like a fascinating creature in my house, and I'd never know what she would do next.

Luca left after filling me in on Elena's amusing activities today. I knew he was getting tired of having to stay here—and I also needed him back at work—but I wasn't sure who else to trust. Usually, I would have left Lorenzo with this kind of shit—but with Elena? Fuck no. I briefly wondered if eunuchs were still a thing.

Truthfully, I hated the idea of leaving her with another man at all, but her safety was more important to me than that. Also, there was an itch in the back of my head that kept reminding me she'd tried to run only six months ago. Did she leave because her papà was a fucking scrooge, or for another man who possibly still lived? My teeth clenched.

I headed upstairs and decided I needed to do something about the creak in the stairs. It was loud as shit.

I'd been chafing to come home. Just so I could fuck Elena soft and easy, all night long. I wanted to draw it out, soak up her moans, make her sweat and shake beneath me. I was fucking rock hard at the idea.

After going to my room and finding my bed empty, a growl sounded in my throat. I pushed open the spare bedroom door to see her fast asleep. The window was cracked, letting a breeze in that rustled the sheer curtains. The streetlight shone a yellow glow across her face, and my chest ached at the sight.

I dropped to my haunches next to her. She slept on her side, facing me. One smooth thigh was outside of the covers. She had on a tiny t-shirt that had ridden up to right below her tits and a fucking *thong*.

The curve of her bare ass was right there, begging me to bite it. My dick insisted that I be an asshole and wake her up. *Shit.* I rubbed my face and gave my head a shake. I couldn't do it.

Her lips were slightly parted, and her breaths came out even and shallow. Dark eyelashes fanned her cheeks. I stared at her for a moment. How peaceful it must be in that head of hers to have such a sweet expression. I wanted to keep it that way, to make sure she never worried about anything again.

Fuck, I *was* whipped.

If perfection had a face, a body, a voice—this girl would be it.

I skimmed a thumb across her soft cheekbone.

My gaze found her ring and my throat tightened. Gianna's words filled my mouth with a bitter taste.

I would make this girl want me, need me, love me, because fuck if I was going it alone.

CHAPTER
Forty-Four

"We are most alive when we're in love."
—John Updike

Elena

IT SMELLED LIKE FRESH AIR AND EXPECTATION. A WARM BREEZE FLOWED through the cracked window and I realized I left it open all night. That wouldn't be good for Nico's electricity bill, though I was sure he had enough money to power New York City for years.

I got up and closed the window, and then padded toward the bathroom. After I appeared halfway presentable, I headed downstairs. My feet froze at the base of the stairs, but unfortunately, this time it wasn't due to a half-naked Nico.

A quiet "No" escaped my lips.

"Yes," Nico said.

My heartbeats ricocheted like pinballs in my chest.

I glanced from him in his black three-piece suit to the white dress lying over the back of the couch. A cool rush of unease drifted through my body, but there was something else intertwined. A warm kernel of pleasure, of *relief*, expanding like a balloon. I didn't realize that living with this man unmarried had bothered me until now—and it wasn't because of what it would do to my reputation. As much as I loved the freedoms such a liberal world provided for others, my heart bled for the *Cosa Nostra*, for everything romantic, and for the structured walls of tradition. Also, the idea that he would grow bored and decide not to marry me had been a cold whistle of alarm in my blood.

I wanted to be married, to have a husband of my own, but the sunny, white picket fence dream I'd always envisioned would be marred by the shadows of other women. I couldn't share. Not this man. The idea made me feel sick to my stomach, cut my breaths in half, sent an ache radiating through my chest.

"Why did you kill Oscar Perez?" I blurted.

Nico stood with his hands in his pockets as he leaned against the island. His gaze was as calm and deep as the sea. "Because you were mine."

I swallowed the lump in my throat. I didn't think he would lie about the question, but I did believe he'd evade it. I suddenly knew that this throb in my heart would be worse than any physical pain Oscar could have inflicted upon me.

"Maybe you screwed fate." My voice was a whisper as I stared at the white summer dress on the couch.

I didn't look at him, but I didn't have to, to know that my words struck a nerve. The heat of his stare burned my cheek.

"There is no such thing as fate," he snapped. "And even if there were, the last thing anyone would ever do is pair you with Oscar Perez."

"The Fates would pair me with *you*? You're no saint."

"Do you want a saint, Elena?"

No, I want you. But I don't want the heartache you'll bring along.

"Nico, we don't know each other . . . I don't even know your middle name."

"Angelo. Now, go upstairs and get ready. We leave in an hour."

I didn't move. "I've already picked out my dress, Nico . . . it's perfect." I sounded like a frivolous girl, but that's who I was. He should know what he was signing up for. I wondered how he'd gotten a marriage license without me, but realized it was probably the easiest of illegal things he'd done.

"I want my wedding," I said firmly.

"You sure you want two ceremonies with me? Looks like you can hardly stomach the first." His tone seeped with irritation as he pulled out his phone to reply to a text.

"No, I'd prefer one. *Next weekend.* I'm not going anywhere today." I turned around but didn't make it up three stairs before an arm wrapped around my waist and my feet left the floor.

"We're getting married today, Elena. Not tomorrow, not fucking next weekend. *Today.*"

My back was pressed to his front, my toes skimming the floor. This wasn't exactly how I imagined a man would profess his desire to marry me; in fact, it was kind of rude and totalitarian.

I tried to fight my way out of his grip. I did it just so I could see how I couldn't get away.

"Let me go, Nico." *Hold me tighter.*

"You gonna take this dress upstairs and put it on?"

"You want a virgin," I protested. "You chose Adriana over me." I tried to pull his arm off me, but it was like trying to pry steel.

His laugh rumbled down my back. "Is that what you think? That I chose your weird sister over you?"

My teeth gritted as he dropped me to my feet. "She's not weird."

"Your papà told me you were unfit for marriage. I didn't pick between the two of you."

Soaking that in, my chest grew lighter. I turned to face him and met his gaze. It looked like he wanted to fuck me into my place and was barely holding himself back. A shiver coasted through me.

I fingered the hem of my t-shirt. "I want my wedding, Nico."

His rough palm brushed my face. "Then it's yours. But you'll be Elena Russo today, no later."

Pressing my cheek against his hand, I whispered, "Elena Russo."

It tasted like hope and happiness. But as the words faded from existence, the slightest aftertaste of heartbreak remained.

Honking, the shouts of someone arguing with a cab driver, and the bustle of the Bronx's Grand Concourse converged into white noise in my mind. My pulse beat in my throat as we walked toward the Supreme Court Building. As we reached the doors, I turned around. Nico grabbed my clammy hand with a quiet chuckle and pulled me inside. I didn't miss Luca's eye roll. He was our witness, but I thought I'd prefer the homeless man we passed a block over.

We didn't have to wait. A receptionist with a blond chignon walked us to where we needed to be, and by the uneasy, flighty air about her, she knew who we were. I wondered how much Nico had paid the City of New York to get such service on a busy Tuesday afternoon. Or maybe he hadn't needed to fork over a dime. He *was* King of the *Cosa Nostra*.

My rapid heartbeats counted the ceremony from start to finish. I remembered the gurgle of the judge's words, the cold sweat encasing my body, and Nico. His presence and the light scent of his cologne consumed me in familiarity and broke through the thumping mantra of my pulse.

"I do." The two words were spoken by a don, but his gaze burned like warm vanilla whiskey. And then he promised to love, honor, cherish and protect me, forsaking all others and holding onto *only* me. By the way he'd said it, you'd almost believe him.

I repeated the words as I was told to, and then the exchange of rings came. I stared at the fifty-cent ring already on my left hand. It was *much* cheaper than the one Nico had told me was his mamma's on the drive over. The room's awkward silence touched my skin. The judge cleared his throat. Luca looked at his watch. I wore the ring on my middle finger, but it looked like Nico was going to stand here and make a scene until I removed it, so I pulled it off and put it on my right hand. Nico slipped his mamma's on my finger, echoing the judge's words.

He loved his mamma. My heartbeats latched onto the thought, flipping, turning, and burning it into my skin.

I kissed him on the lips. Soft and sweet and heartbreaking.

And then I was Mrs. Nicolas Russo.

Outside, New York sun shined bright, like fiery rays in a cloudless sky.

"You did good," Luca drawled. "Only made the judge think we'd kidnapped you a couple different times."

I stopped in the middle of the sidewalk. The nerves still vibrated in my veins and were slowly replaced with a heady rush of relief. Nico stepped in front of me, and my gaze lifted to his. It felt like I'd been twisted inside out in the past twenty minutes, but now, in the middle of my city with this man next to me, it felt like I'd broken a finish line ribbon.

"Nico, what if the Three Fates were real and I'd been destined for another?"

He slipped his hands into his pockets, his gaze igniting with a spark. "I guess I'd have to find those Fates and burn them to the ground."

I bit my cheek to hold in a smile and gave my head a small shake. "You're crazy."

He let out a laugh, looked at the sky, and muttered almost inaudibly, "Crazy about something."

My entire body froze except my heart. It grew twice its size. I wanted to pretend I hadn't heard it, but I was stuck like a deer in headlights. His heavy gaze met mine, and it grew more intense when he realized that comment didn't get past me. He stared at me, making me squirm with his indifference.

Luca stood nearby, a grimace pulling on his lips as though he was watching a Christmas movie on *Lifetime*.

I swallowed and then announced, "I'm hungry."

Luca let out a noise of amusement. "Plenty of stuff at Ace's if you wouldn't have thrown it all away."

I did do that, and then I made Luca carry all the bags outside. I pulled my bottom lip between my teeth. I wasn't going to sit around and eat *Isabel's* prepared meals. It'd seemed like a rational reaction at the time . . .

Nico's gaze flickered with amusement, though he wasn't surprised. He must have noticed the empty fridge this morning.

As we walked to lunch, my reservations about this marriage disappeared under the glow of the sun, the gentle breeze, and *Crazy about something*. Nevertheless, it didn't take long for a foreboding to creep in with the reminder of one slip of paper in the bottom of my duffel bag.

CHAPTER
Forty-Five

*"If I'm honest I have to tell you I still read fairy-tales
and I like them best of all."*
—Audrey Hepburn

Elena

THE QUIET ON THE WAY HOME COULD BE CHIPPED AT WITH AN ICE PICK. Luca drove himself, so it was only Nico and me, husband and wife, engulfed in a plague of thoughtful silence.

I was desperate to know what he was thinking. Did he regret today? I'd experienced many feelings across the board, but I couldn't say I would take it back. Maybe, at first, marriage was a high like a drug, because even within the turmoil, I felt revived, *unbreakable*. Was this how it felt to be a Russo?

Nico had one hand on the wheel, and the sun glinted off his silver wedding band. I guessed he would carry around a reminder of me on his finger everywhere he went. I hadn't realized *he* would be marrying me as much as I would be him. I might not be able to control him like he could me, but in a way, I *owned* an important piece of Nicolas Russo.

As soon as we got home, Nico headed straight for the minibar. He had a drink at lunch too, and I was beginning to think he needed alcohol to deal with marrying me. *What a confidence boost.* Though, I couldn't exactly talk when I'd acted like I was stuck in a cloud of terror.

To be honest, I was glad I got another wedding because I'd really screwed the first one up.

Bracing a hand on the door, I slipped my heels off. "I've never been married before."

Nico pulled the top off a whiskey decanter. "Me neither."

"Really?" I asked with mock surprise. "I was sure with your reputation you'd have a harem of wives you killed off one by one when you got bored."

He turned around, a smile pulling on his lips. "Nah, I got men to do my dirty work for me."

I nodded like I understood. "Killing wives *is* dirty business." Grabbing a hair tie from the island, I pulled my long strands up and off my neck. "Well, I hope when you get bored of me, you'll give me a head start."

He slipped a hand into his pocket, watching me. His gaze burned like a lit match, just as it had days ago when he'd said: *There's nowhere you could go that I couldn't find you.* A shiver, equal parts hot and cold, ran down my back. It suddenly felt like I was in a twisted fairy-tale where the princess becomes infatuated with the evil king, and she chooses to stay in her tower even though the door is never locked.

I'd been right from the beginning. I'd never survive this man . . . but it was too late now. I would just have to enjoy my time while it lasted.

Goose bumps trailed down my arms as I padded toward him on bare feet. It was too damn cold in this house, and Nico was always as hot as a furnace. He could share some of his warmth.

"You're not bored with me yet, are you?"

He ran a hand across his jaw. "I think you've got a few days, give or take."

Stepping into his space, I gripped the end of his tie. "Only a few days?" I inhaled a deep breath of him. "I guess I better make them last then." Rising to my tiptoes, I tried to kiss him, but he turned his head.

Maybe I would've been dismayed by his reaction not long ago, but I knew him better now. It also helped that he had a hard-on I could feel against my stomach. So I ignored his rejection and pressed my lips to his jawline instead. He'd shaved this morning and the skin was smooth for a change. I kissed a line down his throat, growing dizzy from his taste and smell.

He brought the tumbler to his mouth like I wasn't making out with his neck. "Thought you'd rather jump off the Brooklyn Bridge than go through with it today."

"No." I shook my head, running my tongue up his throat and my palm down to cup his erection. He pushed my hand away. "Maybe the Washington Bridge, though," I added. "It's much closer to the ground."

I rested my hand over his hard-on again, rubbing the entire length of him. He let me, but still held that stupid glass of whiskey. I kissed my way up to the corner of his lips, and he finally turned his head and swallowed my sigh in his mouth. The kiss was wet and rough, maybe a little annoyed. My tongue slid against his, and a flame pulsed to life in my lower belly.

He nipped my bottom lip. "You make me fucking crazy."

"Don't blame me for your psychosis."

"You *are* my psychosis."

"Rude," I breathed against his lips.

He set his glass down, grabbed the back of my neck, and then kissed me deep and slow. He kissed me until my heartbeat throbbed between my legs. A frenzy burned through my blood. I pressed my body to his, raked my blunt nails down his stomach and tugged at his belt buckle. He made a rough sound in his throat, but his lips began to slow against mine. When I realized he was pulling away, I moaned in frustration.

"Nico . . ."

His thumb brushed over my mouth. "Surely a woman who acts like she's at a funeral instead of getting married doesn't want her husband to fuck her."

"She does," I protested.

Sex was sex and marriage was *marriage*.

Why was he always interweaving the two?

Didn't he understand how much I wanted him? The words escaped me before I could stop them.

"I thought about you, you know . . . before we were engaged." My blush was so intense it burned in my chest and made my heart race.

His body stilled for a split second. "Yeah?"

A tight sensation wrapped around my lungs—a mixture of fear, embarrassment, and vulnerability—but I needed him to know I wanted him. The truth was, I *needed* him in a way I couldn't even fathom, but I couldn't let anyone know it was that severe, especially him. Finding the courage somewhere deep inside of me, I rose to my toes and pressed my lips to his ear.

"After that moment in the kitchen at my parents', I was so hot I couldn't even think . . . so I went to my room and lay on my bed. And then I slipped my fingers inside me and pretended they were yours."

Three heartbeats drummed in my ears.

"Fuck me," he groaned, before grabbing my hips, lifting me, and meeting my mouth with his. *Finally.* My legs wrapped around his waist and my hands buried in his hair.

Walking me backward toward the stairs, he kissed me like he was trying to eat me alive. He was such a selfish kisser. Kissing me only when he wanted, biting me, controlling every dip, lick, and press of our lips.

He trailed his mouth down my neck, and I worked on his vest and shirt buttons. I wanted his skin against mine, something I'd only felt once, and something I ached for. I got all of them but the cuffs, which were impossible since his hands were kneading my ass. I tugged the white undershirt out of his pants and ran my hands beneath it. Over the hot skin of his stomach and chest. He hissed through his teeth, and a lungful of air escaped me when he fell on top of me on the bed.

He yanked on my dress, and a rip sounded as the straps came loose. "That was *Chanel*," I breathed against his lips, but all thoughts vanished when he pulled down my bra and sucked on my breasts. His hands gripped low on my ass, and I sighed when his fingers slid beneath my panties, brushing my clit and teasing my entrance.

"Fuck, you're wet," he groaned.

I tensed when his finger inched into the *wrong* hole.

"Nico," I gasped.

Beneath my palms, a tremor rolled through his chest. He slowed, kissed my cheek, and murmured against my lips, "Tell me to stop and I will."

I didn't believe I was an adventurous girl, but I suddenly knew I would do anything to feel this man shudder like that.

His gaze liquefied when I didn't say a word. He watched my face as his finger pushed further inside of me. It was a strange feeling, but I grew hotter than I'd ever been at the way his breathing turned ragged and his body grew tense, as though he struggled with holding himself back.

Two of his fingers slid inside while one still filled my ass. I groaned when he began to move them in and out slowly. The fullness was intense, *delicious*, and close to tipping me over the edge. He kissed my throat, and I shook beneath him as his fingers fucked me agonizingly slow.

I fisted the sheets, dug my heels into the bed, and when I came he swallowed my noises in his mouth. The finesse of the kiss faded. He nipped at my lips and jaw. Sucked on my tongue. Clinked my teeth.

It was messy and dirty. And everything him.

"I'm going to fuck you slowly," he breathed in my ear.

He did as he said.

And in every possible way.

The kitchen. The living room. The shower. The hallway. His bed.

Seven days passed, and I grew very familiar with Nico, sex, and every possible place and position to have it.

I didn't think it was healthy.

I breathed, slept, and consumed everything Nicolas Russo.

The first time I attempted to leave his bed after we were married, he grabbed my wrist and watched me with that lazy stare again. This time, he *would* hold me there forever. Not once had he complained about the ring, and I could only assume he felt better about it now that his was on my finger as well.

I slept in his bed. Sometimes with my face in his chest. Sometimes with his body spooning mine and his arm around me. *Always* with him pressed against me. Always with his hands on me and his smell every-where. I didn't know how or even when it happened, but somehow, he'd found a way to tear down my boundaries and embed himself in every piece of me.

Something touched me deep in the chest.

Something warm and fragile.

Something unraveling like a rope.

He didn't go to work those seven days.

He taught me how to cheat at cards. How to fuck. And how to make an omelet.

His mamma was a good cook, he said. *When she wasn't high,* he was quick to specify.

I soaked up any and all information he shared, no matter how small it was. Soon I would have every piece of the puzzle.

Slowly but surely, I was learning how to cook.

"I'm telling you, Mamma, it's all watery," I sighed into the phone.

"You didn't make the roux right."

"I did it exactly how you told me!"

"My recipes are *buono*, Elena. It is you who's the problem."

After a few of those similar conversations, I learned *Google* was a much better teacher. Nico might be able to make an omelet, but he was just as inept at everything else.

We ate *a lot* of takeout, but he never complained. In fact, he never complained about anything. Not when that itch for his attention began and I bothered him in his office, and not as I sat on his lap when he was on the phone talking business. While that bossy, totalitarian side of him was never going away, I was beginning to learn he was more laidback, more gentle, than I'd ever imagined a man like him could be.

I wished he was awful. Because I would soon deserve it.

He kissed me soft and slow. Ran his fingers through my hair. Let *me* pick the movie, though we never got through one film the entire week. Once his thumb started tracing circles around my belly button,

I was dying for his hand in lower places and he always gave me what I wanted.

His body covered mine, so heavy, so *perfect*.

Skin against skin. The demanding way he tilted my head to kiss me deeper. The roughness of his palm sliding down my throat. His handprints burning me like brands.

It was all a blur. A feeling that coalesced in my chest.

I pressed my face into his neck and breathed him in. His smell was like nicotine, the drug burning through every capillary and spreading through my bloodstream.

The last thread of the rope snapped.

And then it was nothing but me, him, and a long way to the ground.

Thrilling, she'd told me.

She never said it would hurt.

CHAPTER
Forty-Six

"I fell off my pink cloud with a thud."
—Elizabeth Taylor

Elena

THE SUN SHONE A WARM GLOW AGAINST MY SKIN, BUT IT COULDN'T THAW the coldness that had slid into my stomach throughout the night. I'd lain awake for hours, listening to Nico breathe and debating what I would do.

For my conscience, for my sanity, for *him*, doing nothing wasn't an option.

I wished I was a different person, one who could put it past me and forget, just so I didn't have to ruin the small amount of trust Nico had in me and push him into another woman's arms. Just so I didn't have to destroy the contentment that filled me whenever he was near.

He was awake and, by the dip in the mattress, sitting on the side of the bed. His gaze touched my skin, but I didn't open my eyes. What if he saw everything I was thinking?

His thumb brushed my cheekbone. "You gonna laze the whole day away?"

I nodded.

"Been craving your famous runny soup, though."

"Don't be an asshole," I murmured.

He chuckled.

"I told you I couldn't cook, and you still chose to marry me," I complained.

"You also said you spend a lot of money and you haven't."

"Just wait until I go shopping."

He laughed, and then I gasped when he ripped the covers off me. My eyes flew open. "Nico, it's cold!"

I was naked. If I wasn't naked in the past week, I was only wearing a t-shirt and panties. Best days ever.

His body came down on mine. I slid my arms beneath his white t-shirt to steal some of his warmth. I was sure this man could survive a night in the Arctic without a coat by the amount of heat he put off.

I loved how big he was and how I always felt small and safe with him. The truth was, I loved everything about him and there was no going back. It was full speed ahead, like a train that couldn't stop for the girl standing with wide eyes on the tracks.

Bliss hummed beneath my skin as he lay on top of me. He ran a rough palm across my cheek and cupped the nape of my neck. His lips brushed mine. "You're so fucking beautiful."

The rasp of his voice wrapped around my heart and squeezed. Seared it with warmth and the acidic bite of guilt. I used to hate that word, beautiful. How dirty it sounded no matter which language it was spoken in. However, the deep, sincere way it rolled off his lips was how my romantic heart had always imagined it to be said.

He kissed me, and I melted beneath him, running my hands over the smooth muscles of his back.

His lips trailed down my neck. "You know what you mean to me, don't you?"

My heartbeats slowed to nothing, while my conscience spun so fast everything blurred.

Why?

Why was he doing this to me?

So many feelings, from happiness to anger at my situation, roared to the surface and vibrated beneath my skin. Tears burned the backs of my eyes. I was so tense there wasn't a chance he didn't notice, but he only kissed my throat as though he'd anticipated this reaction.

An ache cut through my chest.

His forehead rested on mine. Inhaling a breath from between my lips, he kissed me softly. And then he was on his feet, saying he'd be in the garage, before walking out of the room and leaving me cold in his wake.

I'd lain in his bed for two minutes after he left, listening to the tick of a distant clock and letting the cold seep through my skin until a numb-ness spread.

If I didn't do it now I never would.

Not if he kept saying things like that to me.

Especially not if he said them as though he'd never been more sure about anything.

With trembling hands, I slipped on a pair of jeans, running shoes, and a jacket while watching through the spare room window. Nico had grease up to his elbows as he walked to his worktable. He hadn't been in his garage once in the past seven days, but last night he'd said he needed to finish rebuilding the valve train, or something like it. That sounded like a project. Hours, maybe, with Nico busy, without Luca watching me like a hawk. I knew it was the best shot I had.

Digging through my duffel bag, I found the note I'd copied and a letter I wrote months ago and slipped them in my back pocket. My heartbeat matched the patter of my steps as I trod downstairs. I grabbed some cash from the counter and then stopped to eye my cell phone nearby. A strong desire demanded I take it; I told him I would always keep it on me. I also promised not to leave the house without telling him. It felt like I was going to be sick by not listening, but I knew he'd have GPS on my phone.

Leaving out the front, I shut the screen door quietly.

I headed down the steps but froze as my gaze clashed with a man's, who stood on the porch of the house to the left of us, smoking a cigarette. The neighbor who always had baseball filtering through his open windows. He had the *Cosa Nostra* in his eyes.

My stomach swam with unease.

He let out a breath of smoke and watched me.

If I didn't make this look normal I was going to be stopped before I made it to the sidewalk. I gave him the shy Sweet Abelli smile, as though I'd been caught doing the walk of shame. I didn't think Nico had announced our marriage yet, but it was all over if he had.

After a second, the man gave me a small nod.

The tiniest amount of relief spread through me, but I didn't trust him yet. He worked for my husband, after all. As I headed down the street in the most normal pace I could muster, his gaze touched my spine with every step. The hair on the back of my neck rose.

Once I was past sight of the house, I speed-walked around the corner to the bus stop. Only two Asian girls and one black man with his headphones in waited. According to my app, the bus was scheduled to be here now, on the dot.

Three minutes passed.

I shifted. *Come on.*

Two more minutes.

A cold sweat drifted down my spine.

A small part of me believed Nico might have helped me with this if I asked him—but there was also a larger possibility he wouldn't. And in that case, I would lose the opportunity for good.

I could never forget who my husband was, that if it was his female relative found with a man, Nico would've been the one to shoot *him* in the head.

I could taste the respite when the bus pulled up to the curb with a screeching grind. I climbed on and sat far in the back.

Slipping the ring off my finger, I turned the piece of jewelry in my hands. The relief I believed I would feel was now mixed with regret as I watched home fade from view. But I had to do this, to remove the weight pressing on my shoulders, to right a wrong in the only way I could. I put the ring in my pocket and prayed Nico would understand. He had to.

I stood in front of Francesco's double green doors. The window was already replaced and most likely now bulletproof. The Closed sign hung in the window and the bread rack sat empty, but when I tried the doorknob it was unlocked.

My eyes adjusted to the dim room. Goose bumps ran up my arms as the memory of rapid gunshots filled my mind. The restaurant was immaculate, however. Nothing to hint at the shooting that had taken place. The clank of pots and pans came from the kitchen and I heard my uncle's voice amongst the commotion.

As I took a step toward my destination, a girl with a swinging blond ponytail came out of the back room, carrying a tub of new glasses. "Elena. Hi!"

I internally cringed. Her voice was loud enough to be heard in Korea. "Hi, Sarah. Is my uncle around?"

"Yes! He's in the kitchen. I'll go get him!"

"No, that's okay," I blurted. "I'll go surprise him."

"Oh, perfect! Mum's the word!" She locked her lips and threw away the key. Setting the tub on the bar, she smiled at me like we shared a big secret before disappearing into the back room. Sarah had worked here for a few years. Zio liked to say she was *sole che cammina.* Walking sunshine. It was the best way to describe her.

No matter the whole display of locking her lips, I didn't believe she was going to keep quiet long. The secret would burst from her like pure sunlight. Heading into the hallway near the bathroom and private dining rooms, I stopped before a wooden door.

Please be unlocked. Please be unlocked.

The door pushed open and I exhaled, taking the stairs two at a time. The apartment was half the size of the restaurant below and always a bit too warm with how heavily the sun streamed in. I found my way into Zio's office and sat at his desk.

A drop of sweat ran a lazy path down my back.

Tapping a few keys, I woke the computer up. When the screen asked for the password, I said a quick prayer that Zio hadn't changed it in the past six years.

Dulce. His late wife.

The rainbow spinning wheel went round and round, and as the computer opened to the home screen, another heavy breath rushed past my lips.

When Adriana and I were younger and Mamma and Papà had dinners to attend, they'd drop us off here. Most kids watched Disney movies and ate fruit snacks at the babysitter's. I sat on Zio's lap at his desk while he cooked books and let me have tiny sips of scotch.

I'd watched him transfer money a hundred different times, but I didn't remember there being so many programs as there was now.

Please, Memory, don't fail me now.

Five minutes later, I found what I was looking for just as my nerve endings threatened to jump out of my skin.

I typed in the information from Nico's personal bank account and then mine.

Entered a seven-digit number.

And pressed Transfer.

On my way out of the bank, my shoulder collided with another's. "Oh, I'm sorry," I said, giving the man a glance. My stomach dropped like an anchor to my toes.

Sebastian.

"My, my, what do we have here?" Intrigue glinted in his dark eyes as he ran a hand down his navy blue tie.

My heart beat in my throat. This was probably the worst thing that could have happened—running into one of my husband's newest business partners—but I didn't come this far to stop now.

"You know you sound like a cliché villain, don't you?" I responded, continuing down the sidewalk and into the bustle of the city.

Sebastian caught up to me, his Ferragamos in sync with my sneakers. "Oh, Elena. I *am* the villain." A dark undertone slipped into his light Colombian accent. His gaze coasted the area. "Why do I have a feeling you're out here all alone?"

I ignored his question. "Have you gotten laid yet?"

A soft laugh escaped him. He ran a thumb across his bottom lip, his gold watch glinting in the sun. "*Sí.* I found the most accommodating ladies."

"Ladies, huh? Not prostitutes?"

"*Ay,* Elena." He pressed a hand to his chest. "You wound me. Give me twenty minutes and I could charm you out of those . . ." His eyes drifted down. ". . . Jeans."

"And you're starting by stalking me?"

"No. I'm stalking you because I'm beginning to believe you really are alone, and if I didn't, my new business partner would try to shoot me."

I raised a brow. "Try?"

"I'm hard to kill." He winked.

We stopped at a stoplight and Sebastian rolled his shoulders in the smooth lines of his gray suit as the corner filled with people.

"How do you speak such good English?" I asked. If he was going to be invasive by following me around, so was I.

He slipped his hands into his pockets. "My mother's Australian. I went to school in Sydney." That made sense. No wonder Oscar was so fair. His brother received the goldenness of a Colombian, however.

I scrunched my nose. "They have a lot of snakes and spiders there."

"They do. But I think you have bigger problems here," he said, grimacing as a taxi driver screamed at a man on a bike to get out of the way.

The light turned green and Sebastian continued to follow me all the way to the bus station. I stopped at the kiosk to get my ticket, but my fingers faltered on the screen when Sebastian coolly said, "Two."

"No," I breathed. "Thank you for offering though."

"If that's how you want it, Elena. I was planning to give Ace a call anyway." He reached for his pocket, but before he could get his phone out I turned and grabbed his hand. A smirk pulled on his lips. "See what I mean? I've hardly begun charming you and you're already dying to touch me."

I swallowed. "Don't call him."

Darkness flashed through his eyes. "Why not, Elena?"

"Just . . . you can't."

"Are you running?"

"No," I insisted. "I swear it. But there's something I need to do."

"With thousands of dollars in your pocket?" he asked with a sardonic tone.

I only nodded.

"And a thoroughly pissed don on your trail?"

Another nod.

He gave his head a shake, tightening his jaw. "What the hell," he muttered. "This city was beginning to bore me anyway." His hand dropped from his pocket and his dark gaze met mine. "Two. Tickets. Elena."

With no other choice in the matter, two tickets it was.

CHAPTER Forty-Seven

*"I have killed no men, that, in the first place
didn't deserve killing."*
—Mickey Cohen

Nico

THE FAN WHIRLED AS SWEAT DRIPPED DOWN MY BACK UNDER THE HEAT OF the sun. I wiped my neck and tossed the rag on the worktable. Tension coiled beneath my skin, and I gave in and grabbed a pack of smokes from a drawer and lit one. I inhaled until my lungs burned and nicotine spread through my veins in one relaxing rush.

In all honesty, I didn't feel like working on my car right now. I felt like fucking my wife, or even staring at her. Whatever I could get. But I came out here for a reason. Inside, she was everywhere. The sound of her voice. Her soap in my shower and her clothes in my room. Her hair ties and little wedding notes on every surface. The soft scrape of her nails on the back of my neck whenever she sat on my lap.

Fuck, I was in so deep I didn't know the way up.

I needed a few hours to think, or maybe just to stew in spite over never getting that fifty-cent ring off her finger. I wanted her. Her genuine smiles. Her loyalty. Every fucking piece of her. I'd been testing the waters earlier, but as tense as she got I realized she was nowhere near where I was. Not by a long shot.

I gave my head a small shake.

The worst had happened. I loved the fucking woman. And now my biggest weakness walked outside my body, with soft brown eyes and long black hair. There were a lot of men who would love to hit me in my weak spot; the reason I had never wanted the vulnerability. But what I didn't expect was this calmness to come with it, this surety that I would fucking die before I let them.

My cell phone rang on the table, and I picked it up without looking to see who it was. "Yeah?"

"Hello, this is Judy from AMC Gold. Am I speaking to Nicolas Russo?"

"You are."

"I just need you to verify your birth date before I can proceed."

Jesus, the lady fucking called me. I rubbed a thumb across a brow and rattled off the information.

"Great, thank you. There's been some suspicious activity reported on your account, and I'm calling to make sure you've authorized it."

I leaned against the table and blew out a breath of smoke. "What kind of suspicious activity?" Hell, everything I did was suspicious.

"A transfer from your savings account today, on August sixteenth, at eleven-forty-two a.m."

I stilled. "The amount?"

"Two million dollars even, sir."

I ran my tongue across my teeth, a sardonic breath escaping me. "This transaction already went through?"

She hesitated. "Yes, sir. There was a note on your account not to flag transactions, but we appreciate your business here at AMC Gold and wanted to inform you in case it in fact wasn't authorized. You have sixty days to dispute the charge—"

"It was authorized." It goddamn wasn't. But I didn't deal with thieves through the normal channels.

"Oh, thank goodness," she said, before awkwardly clearing her throat. She apparently knew who I was. "That's great to hear. I'll go ahead and note it on the account. Have a great day, sir."

I ended the call, my gaze coasting to the spare room window.

Sunlight glared on the glass, but as I stood there looking at it, some-thing abnormally cold settled in my stomach. I took one last drag and then put the cigarette out on the wooden table.

Heading to the house, I opened the back door to see a silent kitch-en and living room. A breath of cool air hit my skin, but inside my bloodstream heated as though held over a burner. The house was still, nothing but the air-conditioning and my boots against the hardwood sounded as I walked into the kitchen.

Her phone sat on the counter and I grabbed it as I walked past.

As I made my way up the stairs, that god awful squeak cut through the air and somehow settled under my skin with a grating texture. I rolled my shoulders to push the odd sensation away.

With an unnatural calmness, I searched every room. Mine—*ours*. The spare rooms. The bathrooms.

All empty.

Something tightened in my throat and pierced me in the fucking chest.

She ran. She fucking stole from me and ran. To be with another man? He was the deadest goddamn man to ever exist.

Her clothes were here as well as her bag, but maybe she hadn't needed them. Maybe they would've slowed her down.

I inhaled deeply and made my way down the steps while making a call. The ringing sounded faraway, blurring with the drumming of blood in my ears.

"Allister." Christian's cold tone crept through the line.

"Find my wife," I rasped. "She has a bank account downtown. She's either been there or will be soon." I gritted my teeth before add-ing, "And then most likely the bus station."

Two quiet moments passed.

"Give me an hour."

He hung up, and I slipped my phone into my pocket. I still held hers in my other hand, and before I knew it, it was flying across the room and hitting the wall.

"Fuck!"

I swept all the decanters off the bar before pushing the entire thing over. Glass shattered and skidded across the hardwood. The strong smell of liquor hit my nose as the liquid spread to my boots. Bitterness bit into my chest. I ran my hands through my hair and let a dangerous calm settle over me.

Crazy, she called me.

She had no idea how goddamn crazy I could be.

I'd give Christian an hour before I started tearing this city apart piece by piece.

The flames flickered and crackled in the fire pit. I sat on the edge of my seat, my elbows on my knees and a steady burn radiating in my chest. I heard the back door slam shut but didn't look up. I didn't even remember what I'd texted Luca earlier, but he'd gone inside without a word when he got here a few minutes ago.

"A little warm for a fire," he commented, sitting in a lawn chair across from me.

I didn't respond, just watched the blaze eat the pink fabric alive.

"Burning her clothes already?"

Using the poker, I pushed the Yankees shirt further into the flames.

"Look, Ace, I know you're pissed right now—" He paused when I shot him a dark look. "But she left all her pink clothes here—"

"Shut up, Luca," I snapped. I didn't want to hear his stupid theories about why she left. I didn't fucking care. No, that wasn't true—I cared so much it pissed me the fuck off.

He put his hands up but opened his mouth again. "Just don't see a girl like her leaving her family behind, is all."

"She's done it before."

He shook his head. "She wasn't running. She didn't even leave the city."

I let out a bitter laugh when I realized it made more sense that she would stay for her family than she ever would for me.

"You're not thinking with your head, Ace. Fuck, walk in your house."

Been there. That's why I was sitting out here.

My narrowed gaze found his. "Why are you sticking up for her?"

"I'm not. She's making me wear a fucking pink tie to your wedding." He grimaced. "Once her papà finds out you lost her, she knows it'll get violent. She's not dumb. I'm just putting the facts together and it doesn't add up."

It made perfect sense to me. That stupid ring. How tense she'd gotten this morning. She loved some other man and had left everything behind to be with him. My throat tightened, a hollow fucking feeling unfurling in my chest.

"Two million, Luca. Explain that."

He was silent.

I gazed into the flames. I didn't know what I would do when I found her, but Luca was right. My head wasn't on straight concerning her. She'd always be my wife, but I didn't need to be in this deep, especially when she wasn't.

My phone rang, and I picked it up.

Christian rattled off an address, and my heart rate spiked.

"Just a warning, Ace. She's not alone."

His words hit me like a punch to the chest, and my grip tightened on the phone.

"Got it."

CHAPTER
Forty-Eight

"I think you have to pay for love with bitter tears."
—Édith Piaf

Elena

"Y OU KNOW,"—SEBASTIAN SCRATCHED HIS JAW—"I DON'T KNOW MUCH about New York City, but my guess is this neighborhood isn't one of the best."

He sat beside me on a green bench that was sticky with spilled soda and other things I didn't want to think about. If there ever was a neon sign flashing "steal from me" it was him, in his crisp gray suit and gold watch and cufflinks that sparkled in the sun. I'd dressed the way I had for a reason, but it was pointless now with him stuck to my side. I wasn't that concerned for my safety, however. He might look preppy and ostentatious, but the darkness of his profession reflected in his eyes whenever the light hit them just right.

He sat back against the bench. "So, what do we do now? Just wait?"

"Yes."

Across the trash-littered street sat a row of rundown townhouses. Barred lower windows, chipping paint, and sagging chain-link fences. My focus was on the gray one far enough away we were fairly hidden by a few trees, but close enough I could still make out the front door.

It had taken thirty minutes to find the right house, the entirety being filled with thoughts from seven months ago. I wished I could say my memory of *him* was poignant and unforgettable, but in truth, he was just a shadow in my mind, the only thread holding *him* together, guilt.

A small park sat off to our right, and Sebastian watched as a group of boys pretended to shoot each other with finger guns.

"Maybe they could come work for you and my husband," I said.

He laughed. "I'll give them a few years." Resting his arm behind me, he said, "You do know he's going to try to kill me, don't you?"

"Why did you insist on coming if you believed that?" I shook my head in disbelief, but a cold sweat drifted through me. "I won't tell him you were involved."

He let out a breath of amusement, his gaze following a cop car that drove past us suspiciously slow. "Oh, Elena, he already knows."

The hair on the back of my neck rose.

Movement caught in my periphery, and I fought not to shift to the edge of the bench. I didn't want to bring more attention to myself when I already had a Colombian drug lord sitting next to me.

"Looks like we got a bite," Sebastian said.

She appeared to be in her fifties, with graying blond hair swept into a bun at the nape of her neck and a haggard expression that only hard work could create. Walking toward us from the other side of the street, she wore blue scrubs, but I knew she wasn't in the medical field. She washed laundry at a local nursing home from four a.m. to noon, and then worked at a gas station until midnight.

She was blonde, like *him*, but that was the only similarity I could see. Though, to be truthful, I'd mostly forgotten what he looked like. My fingernails dug into my palms as she walked up her porch steps while rooting for her keys in her purse. She halted and glanced at her feet. I held my breath as she bent down and picked up the green money bag.

I remembered only pieces of that weekend. The whirring sound in my ears as my uncle shot *him* in the head and the warm spray of blood against my face had filtered into the other memories and blurred them in red. But I did remember how much *he* worked: three jobs and longer hours than I had ever imagined was possible. Most of the time, I was alone in his friend's apartment, who'd gone to jail for petty theft, while *he* went to work to support his mother and a younger sister still in high school.

He wanted his sister to go to college, not to live the same life as him, working hours and hours and never making enough. For families out here, it was like a merry-go-round that could never be stopped. What I did remember was blood, lifeless eyes, and how passionately he spoke about his family. He would have done anything for them, and I couldn't sit by and do nothing when I had the means to help.

She unzipped the money bag. Her purse dropped to the porch as a hand flew to cover her mouth. There was fifty-thousand dollars cash in that bag. It was all I could get from the bank on such short notice, and even then, probably just because of my last name. It was still legally Abelli, and I wondered what they would have done for me if it were Russo. The rest of the money was via a cashier's check, and I was going out on a limb hoping she would cash it quickly. Nico could shut down my bank account fast, as well as get the transfer reversed if he claimed fraud, though that might take longer.

First, she pulled out the ring, and I rubbed my bare finger before she put it back in the bag. Next was the note I'd written. My throat felt thick as she unfolded it. After a moment, her shoulders shook with sobs and she slid downward to sit on the steps. A tear ran down my cheek and I wiped it away. I didn't deserve to grieve with her; it had all been my fault.

I'd known *his* name for months now. There was no getting past it when I had to research his death so I could find out his mother's information. But we had a deal: he wouldn't tell me his name until I told him mine. And as he wasn't alive to ever hear mine, I'd pretend to never know his.

A few minutes later, she stood, wiped her cheeks, and went inside.

Some pressure drifted away like a bird on my shoulder. I couldn't give her son back, but I could ease both hers and her daughter's futures. Stop the merry-go-round so they could get off before it spun again for the rest of their neighborhood.

Sebastian brushed a piece of lint off his suit. "That's it? I expected something more . . . climatic."

I gave my head a shake, but I couldn't respond because my breath caught in my chest and my veins turned to ice.

"Never mind. Here it comes," he said with a sigh.

Nico's car came to a stop in the middle of the street. He got out, slammed his door, and strode toward us with a blank mask. He was the don now, but something all Nico flickered in his eyes. Volatile depths that made my chest clench.

Sebastian got to his feet. "Glad to see you finally show up."

I cringed at his words, but before I could even blink, Nico reached Sebastian, pulled his gun out of the back of his waistband, and back-handed him with it so hard he fell back two steps.

Sebastian froze with his head cocked to the side. "You know," he said, wiping the blood off his lip with the back of his hand. "I'm taking this a little personally."

Calmly and without a word, Nico pointed his gun at Sebastian's head. My heart froze over, and I jumped to my feet and stood in front of him. "Nico, stop!"

"Get in the car," he said, keeping his gaze on Sebastian.

"No," I breathed. "This had nothing to do with him."

His burning eyes finally met mine. "Did you let him in my club?"

I blinked. "What?"

"Did you let him into my goddamn club!"

I took a step back and bumped into Sebastian. I'd never heard Nico so angry, and my heart tried to flee from my chest.

"N-no," I stuttered. "Why would I do that?" Awareness settled over me. He thought I was having an affair with Sebastian? "It's nothing like that at all, I swear. Please, let me explain," I begged. One glance toward the kids at the park showed they were all staring at us, wide-eyed.

Sebastian pushed me out of his way and stepped toward Nico until the barrel of his gun pressed against his forehead. All his playfulness disappeared; nothing but darkness leaked into his gaze. "She wouldn't need any of your money to run away with me, Russo. Nor to sit in some shitty ass neighborhood for an hour."

Luca's car pulled up behind Nico's, and I said a quick prayer that he would talk some sense into Nico. My husband and Sebastian stared at each other. My blood drummed louder in my ears until it was all I could hear.

"Nico—"

His gaze coasted to me. It was cold enough to freeze me to my spot. "Get. In. The. Car."

"Please don't kill him."

His jaw ticked. "If I have to say it again, he's dead."

With nausea churning in my stomach, I walked toward his car. As I put my back toward them, a shiver ran down my spine, every nerve anticipating a gunshot to cut through the air.

A few cars idled in the street, not being able to get past Nico's Audi taking up both lanes. I climbed in and shut the door, closeting myself in the scent of leather and him. They exchanged more words. Words that appeared to be calm and reasonable. Just as relief crept in, Nico backhanded him with his gun again. Annoyance flared in Sebastian's eyes as he spit out a mouthful of blood. Luca grabbed Sebastian's arm and pushed him toward his car.

Nico walked across the street. He still wore jeans and a grease-stained white t-shirt. I wished he hadn't. I could deal with the don in a black suit, but this Nico intimidated me. He had so much more to take away.

He got in and shut the door. Thick tension rolled off him, sucking all the air out of the small space. His fist tightened and released before he put the car in drive and headed down the street. The atmosphere was hostile; one tiny spark and it would explode. It took five minutes to gain the courage to say anything.

"Nico—"

"Don't say another fucking word to me right now, Elena," he snapped.

Something grabbed my heart and ripped it into two pieces.

After what I had done, I didn't have it in me to defy him. Nothing but tire noise, the outside sounds of the city, and my painful heartbeats filled the car. All I wanted was to go home, press my face into his chest, and apologize. To promise I would never keep anything from him ever again.

My papà kept his bank information locked in a safe not even Tony had the code to, and then Nico's had been lying there on the counter. It was too tempting, maybe my only chance. Men like him were all supposed to be the same. Stealing from Nico should've been like stealing from my papà, but it didn't feel that way. It felt like the worst sort of betrayal.

We weren't going home. I didn't dare say a word, but as the awareness settled in of where we headed, a hollow ache in my chest grew emptier every mile.

He parked, and I got out of the car and followed him. I stood side-by-side with him in the elevator, but he'd yet to even look at me. A *ping* sounded, and the doors opened to the penthouse apartment. Every shallow breath hurt.

A dark-haired man in a suit stood in the small hallway. I vaguely recognized him, but couldn't put a name to the face. He gave my husband a small nod.

Nico unlocked the door and flicked on the lights. Numbly, I stepped inside behind him.

He stood by the open door, his gaze focused above my head. "James will be outside. He has a phone you can use if you need anything." His voice was cold and distant.

I wanted to say something, anything, so he would look at me. "I want my own phone."

His volatile eyes finally came to me. I ached for him to touch me, for the roughness of his hands on my face, his deep voice in my ear.

"You had a phone. You chose not to use it."

"I will now," was all I could think to say.

His jaw tightened. "I'll have one brought to you then."

He'll have one brought to me.

He was done with me then? He hadn't even let me explain. Maybe he didn't care. I stole from him, and that, he couldn't forgive. My eyes burned, and I blinked to keep the tears at bay. "Thank you."

His bitter laugh was quiet. A small shake of his head.

"Luca will bring your bag by soon," he said, turning to leave.

"Nico."

He stopped with his back to me, his shoulders tensing.

"I'm sorry," I breathed.

A few seconds passed, and when I thought he might respond, he walked out and shut the door behind him.

I stared blankly until the numbness turned into despair that scratched at my chest, stole my breath, and bubbled up my throat in sobs.

CHAPTER
Forty-Nine

"So the lover must struggle for words."
—T.S. Eliot

Elena

MY HEARTBEATS SHATTERED ONE BY ONE, SENDING A RAW ACHE THROUGH my chest.

My vision blurred behind tears and the shimmer of the sun on the marble floors. Once the crying began, it flowed like I'd just opened a dam that had been closed off for years. I stood in the middle of a beautiful apartment and felt nothing but cold and empty. The emptiness expanded until it threatened to eat me alive.

How fitting my belief had been that Nico was an addiction, because this felt like the worst sort of withdrawal. I was beginning to realize it was more than that—it was love, and this was heartbreak.

I went to the master bathroom, turned on the shower, climbed in, and cried some more. My mind spun with desperate thoughts of how to fix this, but they all ended on a hopeless note when I thought of his coldness today.

Nausea rolled in my stomach.

I'd tried not to fall in love with him, and I'd fallen so hard I was physically sick at his rejection. I could have laughed if I'd had any energy leftover from crying.

I got out of the shower, wrapped myself in a towel, and walked into the bedroom. My bag lay next to the door, and my heart clenched at the sight. A weak sense of vulnerability coasted through me at the thought of Luca hearing me cry. Any other day it would have been humiliating, but as a numbness settled in, the thought drifted away.

Instead of wearing something of mine, I found one of Nico's plain t-shirts in the dresser and slipped it on. He could be done with me, but I wasn't ready yet. I missed him already, with a physical sense of loss that ached.

It was still midday when I climbed into bed. It felt too large without Nico. I'd been sleeping with him for a week and now there was a big void on the mattress where he should be.

I wondered if he would let some other woman sleep in his bed. My chest tightened and burned at the thought. I hated any woman who got to touch him, to hear his voice in her ear and have his full attention. I hated her so much and she wasn't even real yet.

If anything, I now understood why women stuck by the men in this world, no matter what they did or said. *Love.* Why couldn't it work both ways?

I lay there and watched the sun drift behind the horizon until I finally fell asleep.

Red and yellow lights blurred through the floor-to-ceiling windows and into the dark room. I blinked at the alarm clock that read one a.m. and then rolled onto my back. Fear hit me in the chest, but it was quickly replaced with a relief so strong I felt breathless.

He sat on the side of the bed with his back toward me, his elbows on his knees, and his gaze out the window.

From his mere presence, my heart began to sew itself back together. I knew the stitches would tear once he walked away from me again.

"Start at the beginning," he rasped.

Every cell in my body filled with desperation, *longing*, and hope.

I sat up. "Of today, or—?"

"Last winter, when you ran."

Inhaling a shaky breath, I began to tell him about how and why I left. Everything from Oscar to the carousel to *him*. How I met him, how I had to watch my uncle kill him, and, wanting to get everything out in the open, that I slept with him.

His shoulders tensed. "You realize you gave him something that belongs to me, don't you?"

I opened my mouth and closed it. How very Nico-like to claim ownership of my body before he'd even met me.

"How many?" he asked.

"How many what?"

"Men," he growled.

I wanted to say, "You first," for the sake of pointing out a double standard, but truthfully there wasn't a tiny part of me that wanted to know how many women he'd been with. I pulled at a loose thread on the comforter.

"Two," I whispered. "You and him. I haven't even kissed another man. I swear it."

A stillness settled over the room as I listened to my hopeful heartbeats and he stared straight ahead. He still wore the same clothes from earlier and I wondered what he'd done today, who he was with, and if he'd thought of me at all.

"Tell me why you were with Sebastian," he said.

"I ran into him at the bank. I told him not to follow me but . . . he's persistent."

"He's a fucking idiot," was what Nico muttered.

Is. Present tense, meaning he was currently alive. Relief filled me.

I could see the lightest reflection of him in the window, smeared with yellow city lights. He glanced at his hands, asking, "Did you love him?" His tone was indifferent, but a hint of something raw bled through.

I knew he was no longer speaking of Sebastian.

"No," I said. "I hardly even knew him."

He let out a dry breath, running a hand through his hair and down the back of his neck before giving his head a shake. "Your sister seems to be under a different impression."

I closed my eyes when I remembered our last conversation and her "Uh-oh." After sawing my bottom lip between my teeth for a moment, I said, "Adriana assumed, nothing more."

Sirens echoed up the walls of the building as silence swept back in. A heavy tension lay beneath.

"The ring?" he asked.

"I wore it because I felt guilty, not because I loved him."

"Wore?"

"I gave it to his mother today." I added softly, "I'll get a job and pay you back."

"You think this is about the fucking money?"

Isn't it? I remained silent.

His gaze found mine in the reflection of the glass. "Do you know how many men would want to hurt you to hurt me?"

I wasn't sure how to fix what I'd done, what to say to make him forgive me. All of it sounded so hollow in my head, a part of me believing I didn't even deserve his forgiveness. I glanced at my fingers as they pulled at the thread.

"I'm sorry."

"Fuck, Elena, it's not that easy." He shook his head in disgust, and my stomach twisted.

He hated me.

I loved him, and he hated me.

The backs of my eyes burned, and a tear ran down my cheek. "If you're so disgusted by me then why are you here?"

It was quiet, and then a shift in the air told me he was going to stand. Something pitched in my chest, and my visceral reaction was to lean forward and grab his arm. He couldn't leave. The thought sent the stitches in my heart ripping apart one by one.

He tensed but didn't get up. I inched my way closer until I sat behind him on my knees. My skin sang under the weight of his presence and warmth. Sliding a hand from his arm to his waist, I kissed the back of his neck. "Please don't go," I whispered.

A chill rolled through his body.

"There was never another man since we met." I pressed my forehead to his neck. "No one but you."

He grabbed my hand on his waist and pulled me around him and off the bed. Our gazes clashed like a shot to my chest. It was so intense I kneeled between his legs so I didn't burn under the closeness of his stare.

His thumb ran down my lips. "Why keep your mouth from me then?"

I averted my gaze, not being able to say this as I looked him in the eyes. "Men like you break a woman's heart . . . I didn't want to love you."

His deep voice filled my ears. "Did it work?"

My heartbeat drummed.

"No," I breathed.

A quiet noise crawled up his throat, a mixture of satisfaction and anger. He brushed a palm across my cheek and my head lulled to the side as warmth fired in every synapse.

"Look at me."

My gaze flicked to his that burned dark and hot.

"You fucking lied to my face."

I nodded, remembering my promise not to leave without talking to him.

"You didn't take your phone."

I nodded again.

His palm ran down to my throat. "You stole from me."

I swallowed under his hand.

His grip tightened, and he pulled me to my feet. We were eye-to-eye now, and a shiver coasted through me. His lips brushed mine. "I felt fucking crazy wondering where you were," he bit out.

I nodded again.

"You don't know," he growled. "I can't stay away from you for more than a fucking day and you can run off without a second thought."

I shook my head, but his grip slid to my chin and stopped me.

"You. Don't. Know."

He pressed his lips to mine, softly, confusing my senses with how volatile his mood was. He deepened the kiss and I melted like butter, my heart glowing and mending itself back together. I moaned when his tongue slid into my mouth, my hands resting on each side of his face.

His palms skimmed up the backs of my thighs and stilled when they met my bare ass cheeks. He slowed the kiss, pulling back to look at me in his shirt.

His gaze sparked. "Take it off."

My skin burned as I grabbed the hem of his shirt and pulled it over my head. I stood there, naked and breathless. He lifted my breast to his mouth and sucked on the nipple. I yelped when he bit down.

"Fuck, I'm still so pissed at you, baby."

"But you won't leave me here?"

"No," he rasped. "I can't fuck you way over here." He cupped me between the legs, sliding two fingers inside of me.

Relief and a spike of heat ran through my veins.

He kissed me, and this time it was laced with every ounce of his anger. Deep and rough and consuming. Reality faded away to nothing but him—his heat, scent, and my eager heart feeling whole again with every touch of his hands.

The kiss burned into madness. A breathless, greedy sort of madness. His hand fisted in my hair, his lips and teeth trailing down my neck. I ran my arms around his shoulders, pressing my body against his. He stood, lifted me, and dropped me on the bed. His heavy weight settled on top of me and I released a sigh.

With his mouth on mine, he lifted my thigh and pressed his erection between my legs. Sparks fluttered through me before dissolving and eliciting a need for more. I tugged at his shirt and he pulled back to take it off. He nipped at my breasts and stomach as his mouth drifted downward. Something in my subconscious tickled.

"Wait," I breathed, blinking to clear the lust-filled haze in my mind. Nico's hands tightened on my legs as he kissed the inside of my thigh and then the other, and before he could get to where he was heading and I lost all train of thought, I blurted, "Platonic."

He tensed but stopped, his gaze hot with lust and frustration.

I swallowed. "I don't want to do this if there are going to be other women, Nico. I can't."

He watched me for two tense seconds.

"You're enough for me."

My heart grew. I suddenly realized that even if I'd heard those words from him at the beginning, I wouldn't have believed them. However, now an unexplainable feeling told me his words rang true.

He pressed his face between my legs and I burned with bliss.

I kissed him for hours, fucked him until I was sore and there was a reminder of him inside me. He was still mad at me. I felt it with each nip of his teeth, each smack on my ass, and everything I'd had to promise to get my orgasm: Not to endanger myself by leaving the house alone. To take my phone everywhere, or else he'd glue it to my hand. To not fucking steal from him. And to always wear his t-shirts around the house and nothing else.

It wasn't an unreasonable list, I had to admit, though I did believe the last one was selfishly motivated. I promised him everything because of four words.

You're enough for me.

The metronome in my chest pulsed to a different rhythm. One of sleepless nights, rough hands and white t-shirts.

I lay my head on his chest and listened to his heartbeat, how strong it was, how in sync it was with mine.

Regardless of what I was born into, I'd always thought of myself as a moral and honest person. Maybe my roots were too deep, or maybe love gave a woman a reason to let her dark colors shine, because I suddenly knew I would lie, cheat, and steal for this man.

I would burn the world for him.

He was King of the *Cosa Nostra*.

And he was all mine.

CHAPTER Fifty

"If you are not too long, I will wait here for you all my life."
—Oscar Wilde

Nico

I BLINKED AGAINST THE SUNLIGHT STREAMING THROUGH THE WINDOWS LIKE Heaven was descending upon us and realized why I'd always hated staying at the penthouse. No fucking curtains.

Reaching toward the other side of the bed and feeling nothing but sheets, something jack-knifed in my chest. The clanking of pots and pans from the kitchen sent an instant rush of relief through me. I ran a hand down my face. *Jesus.* I'd wanted a wife and I got a damn heart-attack waiting to happen.

After leaving her here yesterday, I'd gone to my club with every intention of shooting Sebastian Perez in the head, regardless if he touched Elena or not. He was in possession of my wife and he hadn't contacted me. I'd been out of my mind while he sat his ass on a park bench beside her and chatted the hour away. I didn't know what stopped me from sending his body back to Colombia in a box—well, I guess I did. Sebastian was a smooth-talker and I admired how well he could dig his way out of shit.

He'd kept her safe while she went on some mission in fucking East Tremont. If I would've stopped her before she could go through with her plan, that ring would still be on her finger, I'd still believe she was in love with another man, and she'd still be harboring secrets until she felt her conscience was clean.

I got up, took a piss, and slipped on a pair of boxer briefs before going to see what my thieving wife was doing.

The news played quietly in the living room while she stood in front of the stove, wearing one of my t-shirts that stopped at the bottom of her ass. Her messy black hair trailed down her back, and, for fuck's sake, my chest grew all warm at the sight. I walked up behind her and slid a palm beneath the hem of her shirt.

She yelped, throwing a hand on her chest. "Oh my god, Nico! You scared me."

Good. Maybe she felt an ounce of what I did yesterday.

I rubbed her bare ass cheek before pulling her against me and looking over her shoulder. "What are you doing?"

"Trying to make you breakfast."

I eyed the burnt eggs in the pan. "Not going so well, huh?"

"No," she sighed.

I chuckled. "You're a bad cook, baby." She got distracted too easily, by anything and everything: the TV, reading, eating cereal, painting her nails. She had the attention span of a kid. "If you want it done right you have to stand by the stove until it's finished."

"I did this time, I swear," she insisted. "But then Mamma called your cell phone, so I answered, and she was going on and on about being 'worried sick' because my phone wasn't working. I told her it must have died or something."

Yeah, didn't really care to share that it was currently lying in pieces on my living room floor. In fact, we were staying here until Luca had someone go clean the mess up so Elena wouldn't know I'd lost my goddamn mind and destroyed the house. And because she reminded me she'd made me act like a lunatic again, I slapped her ass hard.

"Ow!" she exclaimed. "What was that for?"

"Stealing from me. Lying to me. Pick one."

She went still, her guilt-ridden thoughts swirling in the air around us. I sighed, turned her around, and pressed her face into my chest. She wrapped her arms around me, and satisfaction hummed in my throat.

Maybe I shouldn't have trusted a thing she'd told me last night, but I did. I'd thought she was difficult to read before, but that might be because I found it hard to focus on her face. Now, I could see her thoughts leak into her soft brown eyes and hear them in her voice. She had a long way to go to be a Russo, but hell, I'd walk with her the whole way.

Elena

A sharp sting on my butt cheek caused me to spin around, narrow my eyes, and rub the sore spot.

Nico glared at me with a towel in hand that he'd just used as a whip. He only wore a pair of black boxer briefs, and his hair was still wet from our shower.

"Explain what's happening tonight again."

I rolled my eyes like I was put out, but in reality, I had to bite my cheek to hold in a smile as I turned to walk into the bedroom. "Male strippers. You know, men who dance while taking their clothes off."

Nico and I had spent another night at the penthouse, though I would rather go home. I stayed entertained by smothering myself with him day and night, so I guessed it didn't matter where we were, as long as he was near.

I'd gotten a call from my mamma at eight a.m. and Nico had handed me his phone and fell back asleep while I chatted about my bachelorette party tonight—hence him snapping my ass with a towel.

I headed to my bag that sat on the dresser and dug through it for some clothes before he could welt my bare skin again.

He walked up behind me. "There's not a chance some man's putting his hands all over you, Elena."

I turned, my lips pulling into a frown. "Do strippers touch?"

"It's called a fucking lap dance, baby," he growled.

"Oh," I said nonchalantly and turned back around. "Good to know."

"Good to know, why?"

"I'll have to shave."

That comment got me tossed on the bed, and I was laughing before I hit the mattress.

"Who the hell thought it was okay for you to have strippers at your party?" he said, exasperated.

"God, you're crazy. I was just messing with you! We're going to a burlesque show." I sighed, leaning back on my arms. "You're no fun to play with."

He stood at the end of the bed with narrowed eyes. "Am I supposed to find other men touching you funny?"

Something vulnerable climbed up my throat. "You're full of double standards, Nico. I know you're going to a strip club tonight, and I know how happy everyone will be to chip in for all *your* lap dances." I knew there was no way to keep this man out of a strip club—I was sure he owned one or several—but the idea of some woman with her hands on him made me feel sick.

"How do you know where I'm going? I haven't even heard about it."

"Benito told my mamma."

"Benito." He grimaced. "How would that asshole know?"

How could he not like my cousin? Everyone liked Benito.

"What else would you do, Nico?" A strip club was the tamest thing possible for a Made Man's bachelor party. One of my older cousins had gotten married last year and there were hookers rented out for the night. I only knew that because Benito texted me to ask how to know a woman wanted him if she'd already been paid to sleep with him.

"I'd rather call the whole thing off. I don't like dropping you off at your parents'."

"Why?"

"I don't trust your papà."

"He's your father-in-law now, Nico. You'll have to learn how to get along."

He let out a breath of amusement, running his hand through his hair. "I seem to be getting a whole lot of baggage with you, woman."

I frowned.

His heavy gaze burned mine. "Nobody touches you, Elena, no matter what you do tonight. Do you understand me?"

"Nobody touches *you*," I shot back.

We stared at each other for a moment, the realization of how deep we were both in sweeping into the room. Amusing, as we were married, but also thrilling in its possessiveness and need. He was *mine*, and nobody else could have him.

"Sounds like we've got a deal," he drawled, before yanking me closer by the ankle and climbing on top of me. Happiness filled my chest like a balloon, and I wondered if you could love someone so much you'd burst.

♠

Nico's car had been idling in front of my parents' place for a solid two minutes now, while he sat in the driver's seat, tense and silent. I reached for my door handle, but he pressed the lock button before I could open it.

"Nico, we can't sit in here forever," I sighed.

His gaze met mine. "Screw the parties. Let's go home. I'll fuck you nice and slow all night long."

Amusement bubbled up my throat. "You have a romantic way with words."

He ran a hand across his mouth. "Who did you say was taking you?"

"Dominic, and the two men you're secretly putting outside the club."

A small smile pulled on his lips. "You're nosy."

"You talk loudly on the phone."

"You got money?"

"Yes."

"Your cell phone?"

"Yes," I said, "though I don't know why I needed a new one."

He lifted a shoulder. Maybe it had been easier to buy a new one than to go home and get mine. We hadn't been back to the house today, having stayed at the penthouse until now. I still had to find something to wear tonight, though most of my clothes were here at my parents', anyway.

Benito came out to stand on the porch and Nico's eyes narrowed on him. "You gonna break the news that we're married?"

"Yes, I'll make sure everyone knows I'm legally bound to Nicolas Russo."

His amused gaze came my way. "Never thought my wife would have such a smart mouth."

"Is it disappointing?"

His hand slid around the back of my neck and pulled my face to his. "There could be worse things." He kissed me deep and slow. "You gonna have a fun time tonight?"

"Maybe," I whispered against his lips. "But I'll be missing you more."

"Damn," he drawled. "You're sweet when you aren't stealing from me."

I flushed. "Are you going to let me get a job and pay you back?"

He laughed. "Do you know how much you stole? It would take you twenty years at best."

"Well . . . I'm not going anywhere, am I?"

His gaze burned. "No. I think I'll keep you."

"Nico . . ." I swallowed. "I really am sorry about the money—"

"Don't be. I'm impressed," he said, amusement coating his voice. "There might be a little Russo in you yet."

I knocked softly on the doorframe and cleared my throat. "Hi, Papà."

He glanced up from the paperwork on his desk with an unreadable expression. "I hear you've gotten married."

Everyone on the block must have heard it with how loud Mamma had screeched when she saw my ring. It wasn't an ecstatic screech either—more like a horrified acquiescence.

I shifted in the doorway. "Yes."

"He didn't ask me if he could push the wedding up," Papà grunted.

"You didn't ask me before selling me to Oscar Perez." My heart raced once the heated words passed my lips. I didn't believe I'd ever have the courage to talk back to my father, no matter what he said or did.

His jaw ticked, but he only shuffled through some papers. "I didn't sell you. You know how this life works, Elena. If you lived on the Outside and got to make all your own decisions, you'd never last. They'd chew a girl like you up and spit you out. I was trying to protect you."

My father's vision for my happiness and well-being were so skewed I knew we'd never agree on a thing, so as asinine as I believed his beliefs were, I dropped it.

"I don't want there to be issues between you and my husband."

He scoffed.

"Why do you dislike him?" I sighed.

"He's a hothead and a cheat."

I opened my mouth to disagree but then closed it. It *was* a little hard to dispute.

"He sees something he wants, and he takes it—just like his papà. I fucking knew I shouldn't have let him see you until he married your sister."

"Why did you tell him I was unfit for marriage?"

"Because he doesn't deserve you!" Papà slammed a hand on his desk. "Oscar understood how you are. He would've made you a good husband."

I laughed with bitterness. "*How I am*? Do you think I'm made of glass, Papà? You don't even know who I am because you haven't spent one day getting to know me since I turned ten."

He gave his head a shake.

My throat felt tight. "Firstly, you've been misinformed about the kind of person Oscar was. Look into him a little deeper and think for a moment that you almost sold me to him. And secondly, regardless of your reservations about Nico—I've known him for a short amount of time and yet he knows me better than anyone else. He's my husband, Papà . . . and he's come to mean something to me, whether you like it or not." I swallowed. "If you care about me at all, you'll be civil with him." After a moment of silence, I turned to leave but then paused at his voice.

"Even though you can't see it sometimes, I love you, Elena, and I want the best for you. You'll come to me if he's ever bad to you."

I nodded, though I knew it would never come to that.

For the first time in my life, I felt free to be me. To curse if I wanted, to keep my smiles for who deserved them, to be bad at something, to fall in love.

Nico didn't treat me like glass. He shattered the reflection of an empty life staring back at me.

He taught me how to soar.

CHAPTER Fifty-One

"A woman should be pink and cuddly for a man."
—Jayne Mansfield

Elena

"SOPHIA ANISE!" MAMMA SCOLDED, AS A HALF-DRESSED MALE DANCER humped a woman on stage who turned toward the audience, put a hand toward her mouth, and gasped. "I thought this was a family show?"

Sophia laughed, tossing her hair over her shoulder. "Elena is getting married! Who wants to see a family show?"

Mamma had put Sophia in charge of choosing the club and performance, and she had expected something PG?

"I love it!" Gianna exclaimed. "It's been so long since I've been to a burlesque show."

When we arrived, it was to find Gianna standing outside the club, chatting with the bouncer like she'd known him all her life. Turned out she'd met him three minutes prior. Poor guy probably thought he was getting laid tonight, when really Gianna was bubbly to everyone—well, besides the FBI agent anyway.

Our table was full, but it felt empty without Adriana and Nonna. My sister had severe morning sickness. Nonna said she was "sick as a dog" and that she had it coming to her for getting knocked up out of wedlock. She also said she had to stay home and make sure Adriana was okay, but really, I thought it was just an excuse so she could maintain her eight p.m. bedtime.

The lights sparkled, my cheeks were warm, and my chest felt light, as if it were full of happiness about to escape. I stood and announced, "I need to use the restroom."

"Well, go then," Mamma said. "You don't have to tell the whole room."

I laughed.

Mamma rolled her eyes. *"Mamma mia."*

Dominic's gaze narrowed on me from where he stood leaning against the wall with his arms crossed. He looked sharp in his suit and as broody as usual.

"I'll go with you!" Gianna got to her feet. She wore ballet-pink velvet pumps I couldn't help but envy.

"No, no, no!" Sophia said. "You can't break the seal already! The night just started!"

"What do you know about 'breaking the seal,' Miss Nineteen-Year-Old?" Mamma muttered as Gianna and I walked toward the bathroom.

"That's a myth, you know. Breaking the seal." Gianna linked her arm with mine. "Apparently it's all in our heads."

"I wouldn't know either way," I admitted. "I'm not a big drinker."

"Really? I guess you and Ace are perfect for each other then, aren't you?"

My brows pulled together. "But Nico's always drinking."

"Yes," she laughed, nudging my shoulder with hers. "But never excessively. The last time I saw him drunk was six years ago, and I'm positive it was only more incentive for sobriety."

"Why?"

"Er, well . . ." She sighed. "Maybe that's something Ace should tell you."

"You slept with my husband, didn't you?" In my inebriated state, the invasive question slipped from my lips.

An awkward laugh escaped her. "Well, it's out in the open, isn't

364 | DANIELLE LORI

it? It was one time, and we were both so drunk neither of us even remembers it."

Maybe it was because I was a few drinks in, or maybe it was because I had already assumed it to be true, but I wasn't that upset. I knew Nico was far from a virgin, and I wasn't sure I wanted one of those anyway. He wouldn't be the same man he was now.

We did our business in the bathroom and then stood side-by-side at the sink washing our hands.

"So, you're married, huh?" I asked.

She rolled her eyes with a sigh. "Don't remind me."

"I'm sorry to hear it isn't a marriage of love."

She leaned toward the mirror, applying a fresh coat of cherry-red lipstick. "Don't be. It was my choice."

"Really?"

"Yup," popped from her lips as she pressed them together to spread the lipstick evenly. "I married Antonio when I was twenty. He died three years later. After I got into a little trouble with the law, Nico gave me a choice to go home to Chicago or marry again."

She held out her lipstick to me and I had a refusal on my tongue, but . . . why the hell not? Elena Abelli never wore anything so bold, but I was Elena Russo now. I took it from her and began applying a liberal coat.

"So, you chose to marry?"

"Yes." She grabbed my left hand to look at my ring in the light. "That was a no-brainer."

Apparently, her home life wasn't that great.

"You're going to think I'm horrible, but I chose the oldest candidate available for obvious reasons."

"I don't think you're horrible at all." It was the truth. I wouldn't have the courage to marry a man three times my age. I couldn't even imagine the wedding night without my skin crawling. "Nico won't make you marry again?" I asked.

Her eyes narrowed, and she dropped my hand. "No."

Well, well, there was some passion beneath the bubbly persona.

I handed her the lipstick and pressed my lips together while

observing my new look in the mirror.

My eyes had a haze over them, the alcohol seeping through my bloodstream and lightening my tongue. "He promised me fidelity," I announced, the words rolling off drunken lips. I had no idea why I'd shared it, but there was something liberating about opening up to another woman in a bathroom.

This was what girls did, and it was the first time I was a part of it.

Her dark eyes filled with sympathy. "You poor thing, you. Looks like you're stuck with him for good. Ace might be a cheat at heart, but he always does exactly what he says he's going to do."

"How old is your cousin again?" Gianna's voice was loud enough it echoed across the street.

Dominic flicked a glance to us, and I honest to God giggled. "He's too young for you. You're like . . . ten years older than him."

Gianna frowned, leaning against the brick wall for balance. "He's eighteen? He doesn't look eighteen."

"No, twenty." I zigzagged over to her, and when I managed to bump into her shoulder, I stayed there.

"He's hot."

Dominic stood at the curb, pretending to be texting and not listening to our conversation.

"Eh, he's okay," I said.

His lips tipped up.

Benito had picked up Mamma and the others a couple minutes ago, but Dominic stayed to wait for my husband to get me. Nico had texted me three times tonight and I managed to reply each and every time. I deserved a medal. *Are you having fun?* Yes. *Are you ready to go?* No. *How drunk are you?* Somuch.

A couple of minutes later, when I noticed Nico get out of his car on the street, my drunk heartbeat skipped with satisfaction. Though I stayed exactly where I stood—or *leaned*—because these three-inch heels didn't pair well with more than three drinks. And I'd lost count since that number.

Nico's eyes narrowed slightly when he saw Gianna and me, leaning against the wall and each other as if we offered a little better support than just the brick.

He stopped in front of us with his hands in his pockets. "You're drunk as shit."

I nodded slowly.

Amusement ghosted through his eyes as he ran a thumb across his bottom lip. "Can you walk?"

I nodded again but didn't move. If I did I thought Gianna might fall over.

His gaze coasted to her, before he turned and spoke to Dominic for a moment. My cousin slipped his phone in his pocket and gave Nico eye contact. What did I need to do to get that kind of attention from him? I stared at my husband while he talked to Dominic. He was so handsome something touched me in the chest.

"Come on." Nico grabbed my hand. "Let's go home."

"But Gianna—"

"Dominic's taking care of her."

"Oh . . . I drank *so* much tonight."

Nico laughed. "Yeah?"

"But I loved it," I blurted. "I had so much fun."

Nico opened my door and I dropped into my seat. He lowered to his haunches beside me and buckled me up. "You've been hanging out with Gianna?"

"Yes!"

His eyes narrowed. "No drugs, Elena."

"Yes, sir," I laughed.

"I'm serious."

Something sober settled in me when I remembered his mamma. "No drugs," I said.

"Promise me."

"I promise, Ace."

His lips tipped up. "Ace, huh?"

I nodded lazily. "I'm trying it out." And from that moment on, I called him *Ace* whenever I was drunk, *Nicolas* when I was mad, and *Nico* all the times in between.

He ran a thumb across my cheek. "Are you going to puke in my car?"

I wrinkled my nose. "Why would I puke? I feel great."

He made an amused noise. "Fuck, this will be fun." He shut my door and I watched him through the windshield as he walked around the car. He looked like a don tonight, and I was dying to take him home and rip off his clothes to humanize him a bit.

My head rolled against the headrest to look at him once he was in the driver's seat. "How are you so handsome?"

He chuckled. "God's gift, I guess." He gripped my cheek and pressed a deep kiss on my lips that made me melt into my seat.

I fell asleep somewhere between the club and home, but I made it all the way to the toilet to puke.

CHAPTER
Fifty-Two

"Love is a strange dark magic."
—Atticus

Elena

SUNLIGHT SHONE THROUGH THE HIGH WINDOWS OF THE CHURCH'S BRIDAL suite, lighting dust particles in the air like tiny flickers of gold. Nausea swirled in my belly, and I pressed a hand to my stomach and tried to breathe through it.

I swayed as Mamma tugged at my laces. "You've got to suck in, Elena. I've barely begun tightening it up."

Che palle. It felt like she was squeezing the life out of me.

"For goodness' sake, Celia, she can't suck in her boobs," Nonna commented from her seat in the corner. She had a *Vanity Fair* magazine in one hand and a cup of coffee in the other.

"It's her backside I'm having trouble with. The laces are gonna be gaping at the seams if I can't cinch them in any tighter."

And they wonder how I could ever be depressed . . .

With another jerk on my laces, I breathed, "Oh, God," and covered my mouth as nausea traveled up my throat.

"Quick, Adriana! The waste bin!" Nonna exclaimed.

My sister hopped from her chair, and I met her halfway across the room before throwing up my breakfast of coffee and toast in the small trashcan.

"*Che schifo.*" Mamma grimaced.

Adriana rubbed my back. She wore a pink off-the-shoulder brides-maid's dress and her hair and makeup were done. My cousins were still in the room across the hall finishing with theirs.

"Welcome to the club," she muttered. "I puked three times this morning."

I already knew because I'd heard her through the bathroom door. I'd stayed at my parents' last night for formality's sake. Nico wasn't happy about it, but I only got one wedding and I wanted to keep the tradition of being separated the night before, regardless that we were already married. I'd kissed him in his car for ten minutes when he dropped me off. It was only one night apart, but something tugged deep in my chest as I walked away from him.

I'd always imagined love as a concept—a genuine smile, a couple holding hands, a life partner. Now, I knew it was more dimensional; a maddening, possessive, and overwhelming presence that bloomed in your chest, with the power to make you feel so alive or shatter you to pieces.

Nonna fanned her face with the magazine. "Another daugh-ter of yours, Celia, who got what was coming to her. You girls think you can go out and fornicate with the world and there won't be any repercussions."

Adriana rolled her eyes and sat down, her engagement ring spar-kling in the light. She was marrying her gardener; she'd told me last night. Her ring was almost bigger than mine and I knew Ryan couldn't have afforded it. Most likely my papà bought it and gave Ryan a certain amount of time to propose. Whether Ryan liked it or not, he was now in this world for good.

I grabbed my glass of water from the table and pressed it against my cheek. "I'm not pregnant, Nonna. I'm just nervous."

"Why?" She frowned. "You're already married."

Maybe so, but this was my *wedding*. The day I'd secretly dreamed about since I was five with wide-eyed wonder.

"I just want everything to be perfect."

"It will be," Mamma assured. "But take that glass from your face. You're ruining your makeup." She slapped my hand and with a jerk of alarm, the glass fell from my fingers and shattered on the floor.

"Mamma," I scolded, my heartbeat racing. "You could have soaked my dress!"

She covered her mouth and then laughed. Nonna chuckled from her spot in the corner. Adriana's eyes widened but amusement poured from her lips.

"Really?" I said. "Am I the only adult in here?"

They laughed harder.

I held in my smile because I wasn't going to encourage them.

Heading to the sink, I brushed my teeth for the third time and then paced around the room, feeling caged. It was so warm in here. Heat crawled beneath my skin, and with the five-foot train pinned up, my dress felt like it weighed twenty pounds.

"Gosh, it's hot," I complained. "Mamma, take this dress off. I gotta go outside and get some air."

"No!" Mamma shouted.

Nonna's gaze narrowed at her, and my senses were immediately on alert. I eyed the both of them. "What's wrong?"

"Nothing, *cara mia*." Nonna waved a hand. "But you can't go out. Your hair and makeup's all done. We don't want your husband to see."

"He won't care—"

"You've already gone and ruined your engagement by rolling around in the hay with him how many times and then eloping, for goodness' sake. Now listen to me—you don't want to jinx your marriage."

I wasn't a superstitious person, but I didn't want to argue with them about it. Besides, the room dimmed as clouds began to overcast the sky. "It's going to rain, isn't it?" I sighed. "That would be my luck."

"Oh no, *cara mia*, rain is good luck on a wedding day. It symbolizes fertility." Nonna paused, pursed her lips, and then glanced back at her magazine, muttering, "But I suppose we already know there's no issue with that."

I shook my head, amusement rising in me. I wasn't pregnant and wasn't planning to be soon. I was only twenty-one—I wanted a couple years to walk around naked, have sex on the couch, and smother myself in my husband. But I couldn't say the idea of a mini Nico and me didn't make my heart fill with warmth. I at least had to learn how to cook first, though that endeavor was looking a little grim.

Nerves vibrated beneath my skin and I dropped into a chair. I rested my head on the back but then lifted it when Mamma shouted that I was ruining my hair.

The door burst open. Sophia stepped inside, holding two bottles of champagne, and squealed, "Let's get this party started!"

A smile pulled on my lips.

Indeed.

A cold whisper brushed my back as my steps grew in sync with the soft piano notes. My clammy hands gripped my bouquet in front of me, and three-hundred pairs of eyes touched my skin, though for a moment there was only one I was aware of.

A few rays of sun shone through the stained glass windows and stopped before his feet.

Whiskey and flame. Sleepless nights. Tattooed skin, white t-shirts, and rough hands. Love and lust and happiness. He was everything.

The violins of *Canon in D* drifted through the church and a shiver erupted at the base of my spine. I couldn't breathe as he watched me walk toward him. He could convey so much with one look, with an intensity powerful enough I'd freeze in my spot or warm enough to make my heart beat just for him.

His mamma might not have been a good parent, but without her he wouldn't exist, and without Nico—and the way he was looking at me—well, that wasn't a world I wanted to be in.

My heartbeats jumped and dived in my chest, and I broke free of his gaze so I could catch my breath. My eyes landed on Mamma, who was sobbing—in sorrow or happiness, I didn't know which—to Papà, who gave me a small nod. Maybe things would be all right, after all, because if my father made me choose between him and my husband for good, I wouldn't have to even think it through.

Pure bliss flowed in my veins. The only thing keeping me from dissolving into happiness was this heavy dress weighing me down.

My eyes burned when Benito caught my gaze, his thumb and fore-finger forming the "perfect" sign. Tony shot me a wink, and Jenny, who stood next to him in a flashy red dress, mouthed, "Ohmygod."

This time I repeated the priest's words with conviction.

This time I burned under the timbre of Nico's voice.

This time I kissed my husband on the lips like I meant it.

The guests whooped and hollered, and Nico chuckled at my enthusiasm.

"You're all mine," I breathed against his lips.

A rumble of satisfaction traveled up his throat and he pressed an-other kiss to my mouth. He slipped his hand in mine and walked me down the aisle. As soon as we made it into the entrance hall, I blurted, "It was perfect."

Nico laughed quietly, turned to face me, and brushed a thumb across my cheek. "You're perfect."

I flushed and blinked at him. "You like my dress?"

His hand ran to the back of my neck and he kissed me deeply. "You're beautiful, baby."

I swallowed the lump in my throat. To keep my blush from setting fire to my cheeks, I yanked his tie from his vest. "I like it. Pink suits you."

"Yeah?" he drawled. "And where's your pink?"

A flirty smile pulled on my lips. "Wouldn't you like to know?"

He fixed his tie and looked at me with an inquisitive stare. "I'll find out sooner or later. More sooner than you'd like if you don't share."

I rolled my eyes but lifted the hem of my dress to show him my light pink heels. There might have been more pink, but that was all he was seeing right now.

He smiled, rubbing a thumb across his bottom lip. The commo-tion from the rest of the wedding party spilled into the room, and Nico grabbed my hand and pulled me to the front door.

"What are you doing, Nico? We can't leave yet."

"We're not going anywhere, just outside."

I blinked. "Why?"

"Need a cigarette."

My brows pulled together. "You want to smoke right now?"

"That's what I said, wife." He held the door open for me, but I paused before it as a rumble rolled across the dimming sky.

"Nico, it's going to rain. My dress—"

"I'll buy you another."

I hesitated, but as his gaze pinned mine with insistence, my reservations melted away. The man was just too handsome. I told myself not to marry a handsome man, and what did I do? It was all my fault if I got rained on.

I headed outside, lifting my skirts and watching my feet as I carefully made my way down the steps. As my train dragged across the pavement and through all kinds of dirt and grime, I was chastising myself for not knowing how to tell this man no a little better.

My gaze lifted, and my heart stopped.

When my pulse started back up, it drummed in my ears and stole my breath.

Amongst cracked pavement, the fading sound of sirens, and the taste of urban air, the yellow lights of a carousel blinked bright beneath the overcast sky. It sat static, alone and beautiful.

I walked closer, the train of my dress forgotten. My eyes burned, and a tear slipped down my cheek. Nico's familiar presence brushed my back.

The first drops of rain fell from the sky and they chimed like music off the golden carousel.

His deep voice slipped into my thoughts. "Do you like it?"

Do I like it?

Slowly, I turned to look at him. Confusion passed through his eyes when he saw my expression. "What's wrong?" He brushed the tear from my cheek.

The rain was warm and light, and I blinked it off my eyelashes.

"I love you," I breathed.

His gaze burned around the edges, as the mantra of my pulse filled the space between us.

Love me too. Love me forever.

He stepped forward until his tux brushed my dress, slid his hand to my nape, and pressed his words to my ear. "And I love you, Elena Russo."

Nico might have been a bad man, but where he lacked in morals, he more than made up for as a husband.

He loved me forever.

The End

Acknowledgments

The Sweetest Oblivion took six months to complete, with ups and downs and sudden periods of "This is great!" to "This is a giant heap of garbage." However, now that it's over, I already miss writing it.

I want to thank my friends and family for their continued support, and their thoughtfulness to always ask me if I'm still writing "those porn books." Forever and always.

To my husband. Thank you for being my rock, my inspiration, and always answering my strange questions without a blink.

To my beta readers. Tawni, you deserve your own sentence because you're amazing, girl. Emilia, Kristin, Samantha, Elizabeth, August and a countless number of others—thank you! This book wouldn't be what it is without each one of your suggestions. You're my village.

To my editor, Bryony. Your attention to detail has made this novel so much better. And my proofreaders who helped make every sentence shine: Juli Burgett, Khalima Bolden, and Jessica Bucher.

To Sarah at Okay Creations for the amazing cover. And Stacey Ryan Blake for the beautiful formatting.

To the bloggers and reviewers who helped spread the word about this book. I appreciate every one of your emails, reviews, and comments. I write because I love it, but you guys make it that much more enjoyable.

Last but not least, a book is not a book without a reader, so thank you for making The Sweetest Oblivion tangible. It means the world.

Love,
Danielle xo

I was a simple farm girl living in the magical land, Alyria, where men ruled and women only existed.

Call me sheltered. Call me naive. I was probably both. I never expected to be the key to Alyria's destruction.

The journey I was on wasn't only one to save me. But one where I had a lot of learning to do. With men. With magic. And with myself.

But I wasn't alone. I had an escort. One I wasn't so sure about. But one I couldn't afford to lose and one I wasn't so sure I could even leave.

I had many hopes. But the most important one was that my name wouldn't become my fate.

A Girl in Black and White (Alyria #2)

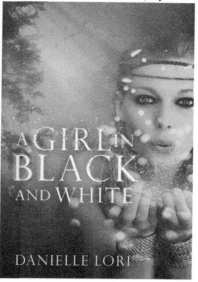

My once upon a time didn't end with happily ever after—but with blood-stained hands and cold blue eyes. The story of my life had been laid beneath my feet since childhood, but until death, I'd never known that road was paved with stones called lies.

In this city of sun and heat, cloaked in dark, both inside and out, I became somebody other than Farm Girl. There was no assassin behind my back. No, my shackles were just as tight but came in a different form.

Like Death's icy fingers running down my spine, the ones that had gripped me for months, my past haunted my present in the guise of nostalgia. My old chains still left marks on my skin, their owner's gaze following behind. But he didn't know I lived. He didn't know I was so close, that I heard his name spoken every day. That I still hated him. Until my hate started tasting suspiciously different.

One mistake and everything I'd created unraveled. A liar. Corruptor. He stood in front of me now. The air was heavy with expectation, tense with the possibilities of how this would unfold, of what he would do. But there was always two sides to every story, and maybe in this version, the corruptor wasn't him, but me.

Connect with Me

Sign up for my newsletter to receive information on upcoming releases and sales.
authordaniellelori.com

Like my author page on Facebook.
www.facebook.com/authordaniellelori

Follow me on Instagram for pictures of my dinner.
www.instagram.com/authordaniellelori

Follow me on Amazon.

And don't forget Twitter.
twitter.com/DanielleLori2

authordaniellelori@gmail.com

Printed in Great Britain
by Amazon

19708129R00222